TOTAL SURRENDER

BEST SENSUAL NOVEL OF THE YEAR
ROMANTIC TIMES MAGAZINE

"Cheryl Holt is something else again. I was totally blown away by *Total Surrender*, a tale both erotic and poignant. Sensational characters, and a very compelling read that readers couldn't put down unless you're dead! It's also the dynamite sequel to last year's *Love Lessons* . . . don't miss this author. She's a sparkling diamond."

—Readertoreader.com

"Cheryl Holt scores big with *Total Surrender*. Following in the erotic path set by Robin Schone, Lisa Kleypas, and Catherine Coulter, she taps into secret fantasies tied closely to a romantic love story."

—*ROMANTIC TIMES BOOK CLUB*

"A lush tale of romance, sexuality, and the fragility of the human spirit. Carefully crafted characters, engaging dialogue, and sinfully erotic narrative create a story that is at once compelling and disturbing . . . For a story that is sizzling hot and a hero any woman would want to save."

—*ROMANCE REVIEWS TODAY*

"A deliciously erotic romance . . . the story line grips the audience from the start until the final nude setting, as the lead characters are a dynamic couple battling for *Total Surrender*. The suspense element adds tension, but the tale belongs to Sarah and Michael. Cheryl Holt turns up the heat with this enticing historical romance."

—*WRITERSPACE*

MORE . . .

"A very good erotic novel . . . if you like a racy read, you'll enjoy this one!"

—*OLD BOOK BARN GAZETTE*

"Cheryl Holt is very good at what she does."

—*STATESMAN JOURNAL* (Salem, OR)

LOVE LESSONS

"With her well-defined characters, even pacing, and heated love scenes, Holt makes an easy entry into the world of erotic romance . . . readers will enjoy *Love Lessons*."

—*ROMANTIC TIMES*

"A very sensual novel in the manner of Susan Johnson . . . Holt does an excellent job of raising one's temperature."

—*OLD BOOK BARN GAZETTE*

"A very sensual book . . . I would recommend it to those of you who like Thea Devine or the later books of Susan Johnson."

—Romancereviewstoday.com

"Hot, hot, hot! The love scenes sizzle in this very sensual romance between two people from different worlds . . . readers enjoying an erotic romance will not be disappointed."

—Writers Club Romance on AOL

St. Martin's Paperbacks Titles by
CHERYL HOLT

SECRET FANTASY

TOO WICKED TO WED

TOO TEMPTING TO TOUCH

TOO HOT TO HANDLE

FURTHER THAN PASSION

MORE THAN SEDUCTION

DEEPER THAN DESIRE

COMPLETE ABANDON

ABSOLUTE PLEASURE

TOTAL SURRENDER

LOVE LESSONS

DEEPER THAN DESIRE

Cheryl Holt

St. Martin's Paperbacks

This is a work of fiction. All of the characters, organizations and events portrayed in this novel are either products of the author's imagination or are used fictitiously.

DEEPER THAN DESIRE

ISBN: 0-312-94825-5
EAN: 978-0-312-94825-2

Printed in the United States of America

St. Martin's Paperbacks edition / March 2004

St. Martin's Paperbacks are published by St. Martin's Press, 175 Fifth Avenue, New York, NY 10010.

10 9 8 7 6 5 4

CHAPTER ONE

Salisbury, England, 1813

Lady Olivia Hopkins reached to the library shelf above her head and yanked on the heavy book she was determined to read. It came loose with a whoosh of air, as though it hadn't been moved from its spot in many a year. The weighty tome fell toward her, and she barely caught it before it crashed to the floor with a loud thud.

Cradling it to her chest, she lugged it to a nearby table and laid it down. The cover was deep red, the title—*A Feast for the Senses*—printed in ornate golden lettering that hinted at antiquity. Carefully, she opened it, the binding creaking with age, and her nose was assailed with the smells of dust and mold.

She seated herself in a comfortable chair and turned to the first page, but she was shocked by what she saw. She blanched, her brows rose.

"Dear me," she murmured to the empty room. She peeked about, half expecting one of Lord Salisbury's servants, or her stepmother, Margaret, to leap from behind the velvet draperies and scold her for her nocturnal curiosity.

For the prior hour, she had been studying the works of the Italian masters, and she'd anticipated more of the same, but this was no educational reference, no boring volume of scholarly merit she could carry to her bedchamber as a cure for insomnia.

Before her, dozens of mermaids were strewn across an oceanic scene and lounging on a rocky shoreline.

Disturbingly, they looked like herself—slender, with blue eyes and blond hair. They were serene, beaming with contentment, their flaxen locks flowing into an azure sea, their scaled, flippered legs dangling in the frothy water.

Previously, she'd observed paintings of mermaids, but the illustrations were discreet, the bodily arrangement hiding any sights the viewer ought not see.

In contrast, these were . . . were . . . She couldn't describe what they were.

The mythical creatures were arrayed to startle. Their postures were provoking, their upper torsos exposed, their anatomical curves precisely delineated. The anonymous artist had a particular fascination with the female breast, for each pair was lovingly and meticulously drafted for maximum effect. He was intrigued, captivated by the risqué, and eager to convey his bewitchment to others. Which he did. Quite successfully.

There were large breasts, small breasts, rounded, high, flat, pointy, and voluptuous breasts. Every size, shape, and contour was exhibited. The centers were portrayed in varying hues of peach and rose, an erect nipple conspicuous in the middle of each.

In her twenty-three years of living, she'd never beheld a woman's breasts, and though she endeavored to recall, she wasn't certain she'd ever seen her own, when she definitely should have. She was an accomplished artist herself, but in all actuality, she knew very little about the human form. Aesthetic investigation should have spurred her to master the intimate aspects, but it wasn't as if she— the prim, proper daughter of a deceased earl—could hire a model to pose in the buff, and she was hardly an individual who would stand in front of the mirror and gaze at herself in the altogether, so she hadn't realized that the breast could be so magnetic, so alluring.

She couldn't quit staring.

While she wanted to be disgusted or upset, she wasn't, and she really and truly intended to stop surveying the naughty portraiture, but she was too mesmerized. Sternly, she ordered herself to close the cover, but she couldn't obey the command.

She traced a finger across the fantastical lumps of flesh, and the maneuver had a peculiar and dramatic impact on her physique. Her breasts swelled and ached, and her nipples poked against the fabric of her nightgown, causing her to notice and assess them in an entirely new fashion.

Distractedly, she cupped one of the mounds, testing its plump mass and girth. By accident, her thumb flicked across the rigid tip, and the gesture set off a slew of exotic, almost hurtful sensations. Feeling as though she'd been burned, she dropped her hand and glanced away. Her cheeks flamed with embarrassment.

How could an object as innocuous as a book have such rousing force? Why would something as simple as a painting wield such power? Why did she allow a reaction to occur?

Yearning for a respite from the stimulation, she turned the page.

The next picture was worse—or better, depending on one's perspective—and much more disquieting than the first. A lone mermaid was stretched out on a boulder, the sea churning around her, her finned legs suspended in the water. She too was fully displayed, her pouting, curvaceous breasts visible.

A man was with her. A very handsome, very mortal man, with dark hair and eyes. He appeared to be a sailor, with a loose, flowing shirt and pants. They were ripped at the knee, as though he'd been in a shipwreck and had been tossed up by the waves. He was sprawled behind the mermaid, and she was in his arms, her bottom snuggled between his muscled thighs.

His hands clasped her breasts, his fingers squeezing her nipples. In obvious bliss, her face was tilted toward the stormy sky.

The spectacle stirred an unusual and primal excitement in Olivia. She hadn't known that a man would do such a thing to a woman, that a woman might enjoy it. Instinctively, she comprehended that this was the sort of exploit a couple would engage in in the marital bed, where an episode transpired that was so obscure and so puzzling that a virgin—such as herself—dare not ask others about it, dare not ruminate or speak of it aloud.

The information was frightening, and had her so disconcerted that she couldn't reflect upon it, so she browsed, rapidly scrutinizing the paintings.

Hundreds of legendary animals were drawn, and they were mostly female. Nymphs frolicked in a waterfall, elves danced before a fire, fairies scattered their magic powder. They were ravishing, beguiling, making her want to linger and examine, to dream and fantasize. Frequently, the mysterious man rollicked in the midst of the merriment, the fictitious ladies adoring him and the blatant maleness he brought to their feminine enterprises.

They were touching him, with their hands and their mouths, but the specific deeds were shielded, the nature of the conduct too astonishing to divulge.

If she wed the Earl of Salisbury, Edward Paxton, was this the type of activity he would require? Should she ultimately become his bride, what else was there to discern? Upon what other bizarre, private behaviors might he insist?

Did men and women perform such antics? Did the earl? If he decided to marry her, would he demand such debauchery? She could never be sufficiently relaxed with him to where she could strip off her clothes and romp around. What if it was obligatory? What if he solicited such dissipation on a regular basis?

Could she go through with a marriage to him? How could she not?

Without warning, a shadow crept across the page, and she frowned, in her confused state, unable to grasp what it portended.

"What an interesting choice for nightly reading," a male voice intoned from right next to her. "And one of my personal favorites."

She froze.

A man had sneaked in without her noticing! Her hair was down and brushed out, and she was clad in a flimsy nightgown and robe. Her feet were bare, not so much as a slipper covering them.

Everyone was abed. If she'd assumed differently, she'd never have come downstairs.

Who had joined her? If it was the earl, she would perish from mortification! If it wasn't the earl, it had to be someone with whom he was well acquainted. No one else would be roaming the halls so late.

How could she explain what she was doing, sitting by herself and obsessing over lewd drawings?

Gad! What if she'd wrecked her chance with the earl before the visit had even begun? Margaret would be driven to commit murder.

Terrified over what she'd wrought, she glanced up, and she flinched with shock and surprise.

For a bracing, mad instant, she was sure he was the knave in the book, having vaulted to life from the pages.

But no. Her imagination was merely agitated to a frenzy. He had many comparable features, but he wasn't the same fellow.

He was beautiful, if a man could be described as *beautiful,* with black hair and blue eyes that glimmered in the dim light. His hair was neatly trimmed in the front, but the back was long and tied with a queue. He had high cheekbones, and a mouth ringed with dimples, as if he were carefree and prone to smiling, and he exuded masculine aromas like fresh air, tobacco, and horses.

A few years older than herself, he was tall, with broad shoulders, a thin waist, and lanky legs. As she was seated, he loomed over her, but she sensed no menace or intimidation. A disreputable cad could have taken advantage of her situation, but she didn't perceive a hazard. While he appeared to be the sort who was capable of mischief, it wouldn't be achieved at her expense; she was convinced of it.

She tried to deduce who he might be, but inference was difficult. He was attired as a laborer, in tan shirt and brown trousers, but the clothes were tailored and made of costly material, which verified he wasn't a servant. He didn't have the demeanor of a guest, either, and the earl had no relatives visiting.

If he wasn't an employee, a guest, or kin, who was he? And how could she garner his promise that he'd never tell a soul what he'd seen her doing?

She was going to have a devil of a time worming her way out of the debacle, and she decided to seize the offensive.

"I beg your pardon?" she said. "Were you speaking to me?"

Casually, she closed the book, pretending that he'd witnessed nothing untoward. Exuding bravado, she glowered at him as if she were in the habit of confronting unknown men in the middle of the night, while scarcely dressed and perusing indecent art.

"I'd forgotten this book was here," he replied. "I

haven't picked it up since I was a lad just out of short pants. As you might surmise, I found it quite enlightening."

He chuckled at the memory, a low, beguiling rumble that reverberated through her, rattling her.

"That's not exactly information I'd share with others," she retorted, as though she hadn't just debased herself by greedily analyzing the drawings, too.

"Do you enjoy erotica?"

Erotica . . .

She blinked, then blinked again. She hadn't heard the term before. It sizzled through the room, like a novel flavor she'd never tasted, and she liked the sound of it. It connoted romance, intrigue, mystery—extreme wickedness!—and it conjured up notions of a bohemian life of gaiety and excitement.

What kind of scoundrel strutted up to a woman to whom he'd never been introduced and uttered such a scandalous, delicious word?

"I've no idea what you're talking about," she alleged.

"Erotica," he repeated. He moved until he was behind her chair, blocking her in, and ruining any prospect she might have had to jump up and dash out. "I prefer the French style, but the Italian isn't bad."

He leaned forward, placing a palm on the table on either side of her, so that she was trapped. She'd never been so near to an unfamiliar man before. Hers was a sterile world, where contact was forbidden and avoided, so incidental and sporadic that she occasionally felt as if she were living in a bubble.

She didn't know what to do. Though she knew she should leap up, shove him away, and stomp out, she didn't want to give him the impression that she was apprehensive or unsophisticated, even though she was. And she couldn't leave until she'd smoothed over the awkward encounter.

She *had* to marry the Earl of Salisbury. There was no alternative. They were in dire financial straits, with no options remaining, but she'd never wanted to wed. Her doting father had pampered her, letting her pursue her art by declining every proposal she'd received, a mistake about which Margaret never ceased to harangue.

If Olivia's father had affianced her—Margaret liked to sharply contend—as any normal, sane parent should have done, Olivia would currently be joined with a wealthy, aristocratic husband who could support her family.

Absurdly, she suffered a ripple of irritation at both her father and brother for having had the gall to die, and thus abandoning a houseful of women who'd been alarmed to determine that they were on the verge of fiscal ruin.

Olivia had to work a swift miracle, by expeditiously snagging a husband, even though she had no dowry remaining. Their contrived solution rested with the widowed Lord Salisbury.

Margaret had events plotted out: Olivia would charm the earl, he would be smitten and offer for her, and she would accept. Then, Margaret would advise him of Olivia's plundered dowry, certain that he was too much of a gentleman to recant after an overture had been tendered.

The stratagem bothered Olivia, and ordinarily, she would have stood firm against chicanery, but she was as frantic as Margaret. Not for herself, but for her niece, Helen. Helen was three, and the lone—though illicit—offspring sired by her brother before his death. The girl's mother, a kitchen maid, had died in childbirth, so Helen had no one but Olivia to watch over her, and she definitely needed watching.

Though she was angelically pretty, she didn't talk or interact as a healthy tot would. She was mute and distant. Margaret denounced her as a lunatic, the insanity a symptom of her illegitimacy, so she was concealed in the nursery, with few people aware of her existence.

Helen was Olivia's only kin, her only tie to what had once been a powerful and renowned British lineage, her only connection to the brother and father whom she'd loved.

Safe at home in London, Helen was another secret that would have to be revealed after wedding plans were in progress. After all, with Olivia flaunting herself as a bridal aspirant with an irreproachable ancestry, it wouldn't do to alert her suitor that dementia ran in the family!

At all costs, Olivia would protect Helen, even if it meant she had to marry a mature, reserved stranger, and she couldn't risk that the impertinent rascal with whom she was presently sequestered might spread stories about her midnight wanderings.

He reached for the book, flipped it open, and it fell to an illustration of an Arabian sheik, surrounded by his harem. A concubine straddled his lap, her bosom thrust toward him, and he suckled at her breast as a babe would its mother.

Olivia blushed from the roots of her hair to the tips of her toes.

"Really, sir . . ." she sputtered, unable to find sufficient vocabulary to characterize her outrage. "You presume too much."

"He looks just like me, wouldn't you say?" He was in her peripheral vision, his cheek all but pressed to her own. She could smell the soap with which he bathed, the starch in which his shirt was laundered, could see a nick where he'd cut himself shaving.

"He doesn't look like you at all," she remarked. "He's handsome."

The insult was a lie. He was the most elegant, attractive

man she'd ever met, and his proximity had her thoroughly flustered.

The vain rogue laughed. "Ah, *chérie,* I think you like me."

"Don't flatter yourself." She glared straight ahead, refusing to shift the smallest inch, or she'd be gazing into his mesmerizing blue eyes.

"Do you like the pictures of the women? Or the men? Which arouses you more?"

The disturbing inquiry baffled her. She could deliver no scathing rejoinder, and she dawdled, paralyzed and dumbstruck, as he touched the page and stroked the concubine's breast, his thumb circling round and round the nipple. It produced a peculiar effect, as if he were caressing Olivia's *own* breast, and her nipples wrenched in response.

Were a woman's breasts so sensitive? She was twenty-three. How could she not have known what now seemed to be so vital? Did men regularly fondle women's bodily parts? Was this a typical behavior?

The fevered queries raced by, and she suffered a feeling of unreality, as if she'd been thrust into a foreign country where she didn't comprehend the language or the rules by which to conduct herself.

His motions on the courtesan's nipple became more seductive, more tantalizing, and her embarrassment spiraled. She slapped his hand away, rammed the chair backward, and stood. As she'd suspected, he was a gentleman, and he stepped away, granting her space in which to collect herself, though scant composure could be located.

From the moment he'd entered the room, the meeting had disintegrated. Likely, he deemed her to be a harlot, or worse—though she was too inexperienced to know if there *was* something worse than a harlot. Numerous horrid scenarios careened through her mind, the main one being that she might sustain the calamity of bumping into him the next day while in the earl's company.

The recipe for disaster was fomenting and about to boil out of the pot.

She had to provide him with a viable explanation for her presence, then she had to depart with some amount of aplomb.

"You've mistaken my intent," she declared. "I had selected this book because I'd supposed it contained re-creations of Rembrandt's paintings. I was stunned by its genuine content. Stunned, I tell you!"

He smirked. "Yes, I watched how *stunned* you were after you'd studied it for ten or fifteen minutes."

"I did not!" Wild horses could drag her to her death, and she wouldn't admit to doing any such a thing. "I was aghast—simply aghast!—and I was just about to put it away when you barged in."

Shrewdly, he scrutinized her, recognizing her prevarication. After a lengthy pause, he gallantly replied, "Have it your way, milady. But in case you're curious, Edward has an extensive assortment of erotica. I'd be more than happy to show you the rest of it."

"The earl has more?" She gulped, dozens of turbulent considerations swamping her. The first was that Edward could only be the Earl of Salisbury, her potential betrothed, which meant this villain knew the nobleman well enough to refer to him by his given name.

The second was that the man she might wed hoarded a collection of the risqué. Why would he? What did it forebode?

The implications terrified her, and as she peered down the extensive shelves of the earl's library, her stomach churned. Through the flicker of her candle, she estimated that there were hundreds of books, perhaps thousands, neatly grouped in rows from floor to ceiling.

What secrets were hidden in the dusty multitude? How many were licentious? What kind of person owned such lurid albums? What did that say about his morals and preferences?

The various titles appeared so innocent, so benign, but then so had the tome she'd retrieved. It had been deceptively placed with the others, and she'd assumed it would be in the same vein, a boring, uninspired series of replications that would hastily have her nodding off.

Well, she'd never get to sleep now. Not after this discovery!

"I'm not *curious* in the slightest," she fibbed. "You needn't indicate any more. In fact, I don't need any reading material. I'm off to my bed. If you'll excuse me . . ."

She started toward the door, but unfortunately, the path to freedom was past the wretch who was wedged between the table and the wall. She couldn't walk by without brushing up against him; her conundrum amused him, and he didn't budge.

As if daring her, he tried—with the force of his attention—to compel her to peek at him, but she wouldn't.

Scowling, she advanced, determined to plow through, and just as she would have slipped by, he clasped her wrist. The gesture wasn't threatening, but unexpected, intimate. She halted.

Their sides were merged. Arms, hips, thighs, feet, they were forged fast, and she fit perfectly. His fingers, where he clutched her wrist, were warm, electrifying. They singed through to the bone.

"I won't tell him you were here," he vowed in a whisper, his lips by her ear, his sweet breath rustling her hair.

"Swear it!" she pleaded.

She spun toward him. He was so near, and his eyes— luminous, enigmatic—gleamed at her with splendid intensity. She could lose herself in those eyes, could be

swallowed up into them, and there was something lus-
ciously magnificent about having them focused on her.

"I swear it," he said.

"Thank you."

He confirmed her courtesy with an indifferent shrug.
"You're prettier than the others he's invited."

The statement induced another swirl of confused
rumination. It was common knowledge that the earl had
interviewed several candidates in his search for a bride,
so she wasn't surprised that others had visited. But she
was surprised that her companion was adequately conversant with them to feel he could comment.

And he thought she was pretty. *Prettier* than the others.

The compliment settled deep inside, and her foolish
heart skipped a beat. Though she knew she was fetching, no man had ever told her so. Especially not a man
who looked like him, like a prince, or an angel fallen
from heaven.

"Who are you?" she asked.

"Does it matter?"

"Yes." She waited, but maddeningly, he furnished no
answer. "I have to go."

She tugged her wrist from his grasp, and he released
her. Almost at a run, she sped to the door. When she
would have hurried into the hall, he spoke.

"I'll be here tomorrow evening. Come again. At midnight."

She didn't turn around. "I never would."

"I can't see you in the day. Just here."

"No . . . no . . ." She rushed out, wondering why she
was thrilled by the suggestion, why her spirits soared,
her emotions reeled. She bolted toward the stairs, glad
to have escaped, but his chuckle followed her, echoing
down the corridor with his certainty that she wouldn't
be able to resist.

CHAPTER TWO

Phillip Paxton sipped on a glass of brandy and tipped back in his chair, balancing on the two hind legs.

It was just before the hour of one, and his eyes were glued to the door of the library. As if he could conjure up the petite blond beauty through sheer force of will, he stared into the dark corridor, but soon he would have to admit that she wasn't coming.

He'd been so sure that she would! But then, it wasn't the first time he'd been wrong about a female, and it wouldn't be the last.

He was situated behind the table where he'd stumbled upon her the previous night. The book of naughty pictures lay open to his favorite drawing, that of a pixie flitting through the grass, her fairy wings drifting behind. She was attired in a dress of gossamer fabric that was so diaphanous it revealed most of her feminine form, hinting at detail and making him want more.

As with all the illustrations in the book, it was designed to titillate and arouse, and it certainly did, though he didn't care as much for the artificial stimulation as another man might. He preferred the genuine article to nude portraits. Still, you couldn't blame a chap for looking.

Poor Lady Olivia! She'd gotten an eyeful. She'd been aghast, but also fascinated, and he was tickled by her pluck and had enjoyed teasing her. Though an innocent, she was no swooning girl. She'd been blatantly interested, her inquisitiveness so apparent that her faltering denial of any curiosity had been comical.

An insomniac himself, he'd intruded into the manor, planning to grab a volume on horse breeding Edward had purchased during his latest bride-seeking jaunt to London. With honest purpose, he'd sneaked in, but upon espying her, his innocuous excursion had been dramatically altered.

He'd been pleasantly surprised to find her up and about, and he'd been intrigued by her choice of reading material. He'd tarried in the shadows, watching her, and he'd had a jolly adventure counting how often her brows had risen—twenty-eight!—as she'd flipped from one lewd page to the next.

Instantly, he'd realized who she was—Olivia Hopkins, special guest and spousal candidate of the exalted Earl of Salisbury—just as he'd known that he wasn't supposed to be within a hundred yards of the house while she was in residence. In fact, Edward would have his head if he ever learned of Phillip's accidental encounter with the comely noblewoman, and he couldn't begin to guess what Edward might do should he discover that Phillip had solicited a second rendezvous.

But where Lady Olivia was concerned, he couldn't behave himself.

It was Edward's fault, really, that Phillip was dawdling in his library, sipping his expensive liquor, and hoping that the potential fiancée would arrive. Edward had demanded that Phillip stay out of sight while the quartet of Hopkins women were visiting, which, of course, made him want to be as visible as possible.

A pox on them all! As if members of the nobility had never before heard of illegitimate children!

Phillip was used to being Edward's dirty little secret.

As a youth, Edward had dabbled with Phillip's mother, an attractive housemaid. With the sort of abandon that only a wealthy, spoiled aristocrat could manage, he'd sired two children on her—Phillip and his sister, Anne—but when he'd married a woman of his own social class, they'd been hustled off the estate, so as not to dishonor his new wife.

Phillip's mother had acquiesced to their displacement, though she'd refused an annual stipend from the Paxton coffers. They had settled on a small farm on the other side of Bath, where his mother had worked as a nurse-maid and companion to an elderly widow. They hadn't starved, but their life hadn't been easy, either.

Though he'd sporadically quizzed her, she never talked about his father, and Phillip suspected that the foolish woman had loved Edward, that she'd been crushed over their banishment.

What had his father thought of his mother? When they'd been sent away, had Edward been relieved? Sad-dened? Upset? Had he tried to annul the eviction insti-tuted by Phillip's grandfather?

Phillip didn't know and wouldn't inquire. He and Edward had a strained relationship, and it didn't lend itself to confessions.

Phillip's sister, Anne, had never returned to Salisbury, had never seen Edward again, but Phillip had. At his request when he was fourteen, his mother had demeaned herself by writing to Edward to ask if Phillip could have a job. With an unanticipated eagerness, Edward had replied affirmatively, and Phillip had been hired on in the stables under the old stablemaster.

As the only son of the lord, he'd occupied an odd posi-tion. Everyone knew who he was and paid him extensive deference, but no one mentioned his paternity. Fre-quently, he'd gazed at the mansion, pondering Edward's cruel, bitter wife who'd hated that he was on the premises and gainfully employed. He'd gloated that his mother had birthed Edward two children while his highborn, patrician wife had birthed him none.

It seemed so frivolous now. Edward's wife was dead, his father a lonely widower. After her demise, Edward had struggled to make amends for some of the damage she'd wrought. He was forever thinking of tasks they could do together, such as hunting or fishing, that might repair their bond, but it was too arduous for Phillip to pretend they were close.

Yet Phillip was enthralled by Edward, and continued to embrace his attempts at a greater familiarity. He'd even accepted Edward's offer to buy him a commission in the army, with Edward being positive that soldiering was exactly what Phillip should do. Like a lad in need of parental approval, he'd trotted off to war, when all he'd wanted was to remain at Salisbury and tend the horses.

Because he'd followed Edward's advice—advice that Phillip had judged to be asinine—he'd ended up enduring the trials of the Peninsular War and the horrors of the battle of Salamanca. He'd been wounded for his efforts, but luckily, he'd made it home. Edward had been so bloody thankful, so pleased with Phillip's valor, that it had been difficult to be angry.

Phillip had reestablished himself at the estate, had resumed his post as stablemaster, and though his father had suggested he move into the main house, he'd opted for a cottage behind one of the barns.

They'd been making halting progress toward becoming friends, until Edward had blundered into the embarrassing statement that Phillip should be hidden away from the four women of the Hopkins party. Edward acted as though Countess Margaret, along with her daughter Penelope, stepdaughter Olivia, and cousin Winnie Stewart, would have a collective fit of the vapors if Phillip's existence was admitted.

Edward's insulting remarks had rekindled Phillip's animosity. He'd been hurt and resentful, but he was aware of his father's station, and the hypocritical moral tenets that ruled high society. Ultimately, he'd agreed, and he'd meant to avoid Olivia Hopkins.

In a peculiar fashion, he loved his father and wished him content. If a new bride was so important, Phillip didn't want to ruin Edward's chances, but after he'd run into Lady Olivia, his good intentions had flown out the window.

Immature as it sounded, there was nothing he'd like more than to instigate some mischief by sabotaging his father's plans. Phillip was a proud man, and Edward had pricked his vanity.

While it was inappropriate for him to toy with Lady Olivia, or to engage her in a brief flirtation, he couldn't help himself. He'd oft been told he was a bastard, the epithet having naught to do with his birth status and everything to do with his character. He could be irksome, overbearing, intolerable; in truth, very much like Edward, and he could skew his father's matrimonial prospects with nary a flicker of his conscience.

He glanced at the clock as it struck one. When he'd tossed out the invitation for her to meet with him, he couldn't have predicted if she'd dare, so he'd given her plenty of time to muster her courage. But she hadn't, so he'd have to provoke another rendezvous.

What man in his right mind could pass up the opportunity for an assignation or two? Not himself, certainly. He'd never been a gentleman, and he wasn't about to change his tendencies at the ripe old age of twenty-seven, but his machinations with the lady would have to wait for another day. In the morning, he had an abundance of chores on his plate, and he needed sleep.

Downing his libation, he replaced the book on the shelf, blew out his candle, and started toward the door when furtive footsteps echoed in the hall. He paused.

The treads grew nearer, and he smiled. Lady Olivia was slinking in, obviously hoping to ensure that he was absent. After all, it was a full hour past midnight, and she likely presumed he was gone, or that he hadn't been serious and had never arrived.

He smirked with satisfaction. However the episode played out, whatever the impetus that had brought her to him, the tryst would be a grand lark. Hurrying to a window, he slithered behind the drape, shielding himself from view.

She halted outside the door, peeking around the frame, holding her candle to survey the room and guarantee it was empty. Then, she crept in, her path taking her by the spot where he was lurking in the curtains.

To his immense disappointment, she had on more clothes than she'd been wearing before, but they were in a casual disarray that he found charming. She'd felt the need to dress before descending, but it wasn't as if she could ask her maid for assistance, so she'd done the best she could by herself. Her gown was partially buttoned down the back, her hair messily braided into a thick, lengthy strand.

Since she had no petticoat on underneath, her skirt dragged and she had to lift the hem when she walked, providing him with the information that she was barefooted.

He was most delighted to note that she hadn't been able to don her corset. Her breasts were unencumbered, and they shifted enticingly. Her pulse rate was elevated from her dangerous trek down the stairs, and that, along with the cool temperature, had raised her nipples. He could detect the alluring nubs through the bodice of her gown.

What a fetching piece of baggage! Why had no man snatched her up before now? Why was she still single at twenty-three, and sniffing after stuffy, tedious Edward?

She was carrying a leather satchel, and she centered it and her candle on the table, then she marched to the bookshelf and yanked down the erotic book, opening to the page with all those slippery, sexy mermaids. For a few minutes, she examined it, then she reached in her satchel, pulled out blank papers and pencil, and . . . and . . . began to draw?

He couldn't believe what he was witnessing! He narrowed his focus, wanting to be sure that his eyes weren't deceiving him, but his initial impression had been correct: She was dissecting the various nudes, then sketching her own version!

Was she practicing?

How odd! How thrilling!

For a protracted period, he spied on her, until she had many samples strewn across the table. Then, he strolled from behind the drape.

"Good evening, Lady Olivia." He moved toward her, blocking her in so that she couldn't escape unless he was inclined to let her. "How nice to see you again."

At the sound of his voice, she leapt to her feet, shocked by his sudden appearance. As with their previous encounter, she'd been absorbed by her task and hadn't been alerted to his presence.

Much like a skittish colt, she was nervous and fidgety, frightened by his presence, then she straightened, seeming to administer a mental shake. Her pert nose stuck up in the air, she confronted him.

"You!"

"You're late," he mentioned. "I'd given up on you."

"Must you continue to sneak up on me?" She was simmering with ire.

"It's already a habit, I'm afraid."

"Didn't anyone ever tell you that it's simply proper manners to announce yourself?"

"I've never cared much for courtesy or etiquette." He chuckled. "I've heard it said that I'm an unconscionable boor."

"You won't catch me arguing the point."

She was more intrepid than any individual he'd ever met. Though she was surrounded by dozens of ribald illustrations she'd created with her own hand, she was gathering them up and cramming them into her satchel, determined to keep him from perceiving what was in plain sight.

As if he'd fail to note those pages and pages of breasts! What kind of woman skulked out of her bed in the middle of the night to sketch nudes?

"How did you know my name?" she demanded, as she hid the last picture in her portfolio.

"Everyone is aware of who you are."

"And why I'm visiting?"

"Yes."

"Who are you?" she snapped. "You've accosted me here twice, and I'm growing weary of it."

"*I* have accosted you?"

"Without a doubt!"

"Phillip," he replied, eager, for some reason, to reveal it. "My name is Phillip." But he didn't add the surname of Paxton, and luckily, she didn't ask for it.

"What is your position at the estate?" She questioned him with the sort of conceit that only the pampered daughter of an aristocrat could display. He'd begun to think they'd all been born with that snotty tone imbedded in their tongues.

"I work in the stables." He'd vastly distorted a situation where he was the boss, in charge of the lads, and exercising free rein over the administration and breeding of the animals.

"I don't believe you," she proclaimed.

He frowned. "Why wouldn't you?"

"No stablehand would be so bold as to prowl around the manor as you've done."

"Maybe I'm braver than others you've known."

"Or perhaps more foolish."

"Perhaps," he allowed, grinning. "I see you've retrieved your favorite book." Taunting her, he brushed his fingers over it, caressing the colorful drawing. "Would you like to look at it with me?"

"No!"

"Then why have you come again? Was it just to be with me?"

She scoffed. "Aren't you an arrogant peacock!"

He approached, and she stood her ground. She was wary, speculating as to his purpose, but she refused to be intimidated, nor did she flee as any sane woman would, and he had to admire her mettle.

The consequences, should they be discovered, were so precarious and so nasty, that he couldn't fathom why she'd dawdle and risk so much. If they were caught, he had naught to lose, but she could forfeit everything. Her very future, the caliber of the rest of her life, was at stake, so she was either very courageous or very imprudent, and since she seemed to be very bright, he couldn't decide what to make of her.

He wasn't worth the peril she faced.

Sidling in, he let the toes of his boots slip under her

dress, the billowy fabric of her skirt tangling around his legs. The air between them came alive, their proximity generating an energy that sparked and sizzled.

He was immensely experienced with women. His handsome appearance, coupled with his father's being an earl, and himself a bastard, was a combination that most couldn't resist, so many an elegant beauty had graced his bed.

The exhilaration Lady Olivia evoked was a sign that they possessed a natural desire for one another, the type that only a few fortunate couples ever managed. If they recklessly became lovers, they would have a bond others never attained.

The notion terrified him. He didn't want to suffer an attraction to her. He merely wanted to torment and plague her until she cried off with Edward. He had no more lofty or low designs on her than that.

Stepping away from her, he let the agitated atmosphere calm. He was determined to keep their interaction frivolous, to participate in flirtatious repartee and nothing more.

He mimicked a credible pout. "Are you positive you haven't been pining away?"

"You are the most vain creature I've ever met."

"Vanity is one of my most stellar qualities."

"You're right about that."

Oh, and wasn't she sassy? Alluring and adorable, and from their pithy banter, he liked her much more than was wise.

She reached for her satchel, ready to tuck it under her arm and waltz out, but he snatched it away before she could get a firm grip. Panicked, she lunged for it, but he held it out of her grasp.

"Give it to me!"

As she fought to recover it, they had a brief wrestling match, with her flailing and clawing at him. Before he could subdue her, she landed a kick to his shin, and a punch in the ribs that was severe enough to make him wince. Using his superior build, he pushed her to the wall, his torso flattened to hers all the way down.

He could feel her breasts, the flatness of her stomach, the curve of her thighs, and his body's response was predictable. His phallus swelled and grew hard as stone. She was too unschooled to understand his physical volatility, and cad that he was, he leaned in, reveling in the forbidden contact.

Their breathing was labored, their tempers elevated, and she was glaring up at him, her sapphire eyes accusing, reproaching, denouncing, and he could deduce every emotion hidden in their depths. Fury. Apprehension. Dread. Mistrust. But also her increasing appreciation of himself as a man, and of herself as a woman. Of the intimacy their stance engendered, the excitement their adjacency induced.

Her brow furrowed in confusion, her bewilderment plain. She could sense the anatomical thrill and tumult just as he could, and while *he* knew it meant they were compatible in a corporeal way, she had no background that would help her to interpret the stimulation, or that would prepare her for how to deal with it.

Her lush, ruby lips were slightly parted, moist, and only inches away, and he was so very tempted to close the gap between them, to press his lips to her own. Suddenly, he was frantic to learn what it would be like to kiss her, and the power of his craving was so potent that it scared him. There was an ancient, primal beast lurking within, coveting her at any cost.

With stupendous strength, he pulled himself from the brink of his unruly hunger, forcing himself to focus on their surroundings, to remember who he was and who *she* was, and he grappled to reassert the levity with which he wanted their assignations to progress.

Tucking her at his side, he pinned her arms so that she couldn't deliver any blows. Then he placed her satchel on the table and, fumbling into it, extracted her sketches.

"Don't, please," she begged, but he was too much of an ass to heed her request. He spread them out, critically evaluating them. When she realized he wouldn't desist, she slumped into him, seeming to deflate, as though her bones had melted, and he was propping her up, balancing her on his hip.

"You're very talented," he said after an extensive review.

"Thank you," she mumbled.

"You like to draw, don't you?"

"Not really."

She was lying. Her ability to capture nuance was clear and unmistakable, and he couldn't comprehend why she'd deny her expertise. Tenaciously, he repeated, "You like to draw, don't you?"

"I suppose I do."

Embarrassed, she shrugged him off, and he released her as he raised the issue that had vexed him ever since she'd entered the room. "Why the fascination with nudes?"

"I know next to nothing about the human body. It's not as if I can have anyone pose naked."

"No, you can't."

"When I chanced upon this book, I thought it might be a simple method to . . . to . . ." She couldn't finish the sentence.

"To what?"

"To practice. I'm not permitted to draw, you see, and so I have limited opportunity."

It was the strangest edict he'd ever heard. "Who said you shouldn't draw?"

"My stepmother, Margaret." He tensed, recalling the fussy, pompous older woman he'd witnessed from across the yard, and she hurried on. "It's a long story," she claimed, "but she doesn't think Edward—that is, Lord Salisbury—would approve of my interest, and it's so very important that he like me."

This last was mouthed so quietly that it barely registered. He bent forward, striving to catch the utterance, just as she peered up and impaled him with her steady gaze.

"Swear to me that you won't tell him."

As if he could! Not with her beseeching him as though the fate of the entire universe depended on his silence.

"No, I never would."

"How can I believe you?"

"I give you my word."

She pondered him, delving and prying into the secret sections of his black heart where his pettiness and resentment fermented, and he endeavored to shield his true self from her keen assessment. While usually he didn't care about others' opinions, he wanted her to picture him as a better man, more kind and noble than he was.

Returning her stare, he tried to let her ascertain only the good and none of the bad. He yearned to have her perceive him as remarkable and heroic, loyal and reliable, someone she would consider a friend.

Scooping up her papers, he stuffed them into the satchel, secured the flap, then extended it to her. "Here," he said. "I never saw them."

Despondent and forlorn, she clutched the packet to her chest. She was desperate for Edward to fancy her, which indicated that she was in some sort of trouble, and in dire need of the protection that marriage would bring her.

He couldn't bear it that she was distraught, that she'd

been afflicted by adversity, and he found himself stupidly disposed to assist her in any way he could. With the exception of his mother and sister, he'd never been a pantywaist for a woman in distress, but had it been five hundred years earlier, he imagined he'd be wearing the shining armor of a knight.

Apprehensively, she regarded the door, eager to rush out and be away, but he didn't want her to go. He wanted to chat and babble, to query her as to why she'd traveled to Salisbury, about what problem was harrying her, and he endured a silly vision of himself, down on bended knee, imploring her to stay.

With no effort, she was transforming him into a gelding!

She inhaled, having made the weighty decision that he just might be trustworthy. How he hoped he wouldn't disappoint!

"Might I ask you a question?"

"Anything."

"How long have you known Lord Salisbury?"

"All my life," he was able to truthfully state.

"Would you deem your acquaintance to be close?"

"Well . . . yes." A complete explanation was much too complex, and he wasn't convinced he could supply the correct answer if he had a week to devise it.

"You mentioned that he has a collection of this . . . this . . . erotica."

"He does, but it's not all his. The men in the Paxton family have a fondness for it and have purchased various rare volumes over many centuries."

"I'm not very conversant with such things, and I was wondering . . . that is . . . if you . . . well . . ."

He was tickled by her reticence, and seized the informality of the moment to use her given name. "You can say it, Olivia. Go ahead. It's all right."

Bolstered by his coaxing, she blurted out, "Why would a man own such a book?"

A flippant retort was his habitual style, but she was so serious and so solemn that he couldn't make light of her earnest inquiry. It was too sincere. Yet at the same juncture, he didn't want to shock or startle her.

Cautiously, he clarified, "Men enjoy looking at nude women. It arouses them, in a manly way."

"To what purpose?"

He actually blushed. The past few years, he'd spent so much time around soldiers and whores that he'd forgotten there were still naïve souls in the world. "For the types of behaviors that couples revel in in the marital bed."

"They disrobe?"

"Aye."

"The husband would *want* his wife unclothed?"

"He would."

"So that her breasts and her . . ."

They were both stunned by her voicing of *breasts* in his presence. It produced an immediate, monumental shift in their relationship.

"Above all else, a man delights in observing and touching a naked woman. It's a male curse, the beast in us."

"If I marry Lord Salisbury, will he expect me to . . .?" Her cheeks flushed crimson, and just when he would have responded, she held up her hand, stopping him. "Never mind. I really, really don't want to know."

Frazzled, she circled around him, needing to be away.

"Livvie . . ." He shortened her name, liking how it sounded and finding it suited her far better than Olivia. "Tarry with me. We'll talk about this and—"

"No. I must go."

It was already evident that he couldn't refuse her anything. Not even a mere plea that she be allowed to depart unimpeded. How did she do that? Why did he let her? What phenomenon was luring him into her orbit, and why did he not wish to fight it?

"Then come tomorrow night."

"I can't!" she said.

"Do it for me."

She shook her head and ran out, and long after her footsteps had faded, he stared at the spot where she'd been. He'd be waiting for her the next night, and if she didn't show up, he couldn't predict what he might do. But he *would* see her again. Of that much, he was certain.

CHAPTER THREE

Olivia sat at a table by the window in her room, gazing across the rear gardens of the estate. The July sun was shining, the sky blue, the grass green. She was supposed to be outside in the balmy weather, doing her best to socialize with and impress Lord Salisbury, but she couldn't force herself downstairs.

She had managed to pen a letter to her niece, Helen, but that was all she'd accomplished. Her thoughts were in such disarray that she couldn't concentrate beyond a simple task.

Her sketching pad lay before her, and she scowled at what her hand had inadvertently created. Naked women! Dozens and dozens of them. Frontal views, profiles, backs, and sides. Whenever her pencil met the page, she'd start out innocently, then her legitimate endeavor would turn lewd.

In an obsessive fashion, she'd fixated on the erotica in the library. No other topic could wedge itself into her mind. Her musings were filled with wanton themes, the scenes from the book clear and precise and disturbing her in an unexplainable, titillating way.

The women she'd depicted had their breasts prominently displayed, and in the past forty-eight hours, she'd drawn so many bosoms that she was becoming a veritable master at depicting shape and size.

Upon witnessing how many there were, she groaned

and pushed the drawings away. What was happening to her?

In each illustration, she'd posed a man in the middle, and she'd surrounded him with adoring, worshipful females. Disgracefully, he looked like that bounder Phillip, who was more handsome than any man she'd ever encountered, than any man had a right to be. She couldn't keep from struggling over the details that made him so magnificent.

Disgustingly, she'd also fussed over the women, trying to produce the appropriate expressions of adulation, when it had occurred to her that all those nymphs and fairies resembled herself.

Glancing down, she couldn't deny what she hadn't wanted to recognize: She'd sketched herself over and over, bared, vulnerable, impish, and blatantly flaunted for Phillip's male approval.

What did this mean?

She shivered, but not from the cold. If she was to wed Edward, he would count on her disrobing, on her parading in a naked condition.

She couldn't exhibit such flagrant behavior for the older aristocrat. From the interactions they'd enjoyed so far, she'd describe him as reserved, polite, and much too stoic to be overcome by a passion that would cause them to undress and romp. Should she be required to strip for him, she'd expire from mortification.

But I could do it with Phillip . . .

The audacious thought popped up out of nowhere, and was so twisted and so unconventional that she couldn't fathom from where it might have sprung. Was there a bawdy side to her disposition of which she was unaware? Had she secretly been pining away for physical intimacy?

Phillip wanted her to meet with him that very night,

and though she'd been cosseted throughout her life, she grasped that he'd invited her with nefarious intent. There was nothing pure or harmless about his solicitation. He was a man, and she was a woman, and he wanted to engage in some of the licentious tomfoolery that was delineated in the erotic book.

What scared her out of her wits was that she wouldn't object to dallying. Once prior, she'd been kissed, directly on the lips, during her first season. It had been a total disappointment, a wet, sloppy affair that she hadn't wanted to repeat. She'd been left to question why women fixated on such an unpleasant event, but something about Phillip told her that kissing *him* would be a new and extraordinary experience.

Why shouldn't she have an adventure, a bit of fun and frolic? Especially if she was about to become betrothed to safe, sane Edward? She was attracted to Phillip like a moth to the flame. He made her reckless, ready to throw caution to the wind, to attempt any negligent feat without regard to the consequences.

He'd called her Livvie, the beloved nickname that only her deceased father had used. The sentiment was endearing, delightful, and if she was brave enough she might be able to—

A sharp rapping on the door had her tumbling back to reality, her introspections tripping over themselves as she strove to bury them in the remote recesses of her mind.

"Olivia!" Margaret hissed from out in the corridor. "Are you in there?"

She jumped to her feet. She couldn't allow Margaret to find out that she'd been drawing, particularly given the subject matter! Like a crazy woman, she stuffed her supplies into her satchel and shoved it under the bed.

"Just a minute, Margaret." She forced calm into her

voice. There was charcoal residue on her fingertips, and she hurried to the washbasin and doused away the evidence.

Olivia's mother had died when she was a baby, and her father had wed Margaret when Olivia had been ten, so Margaret was the only mother Olivia had ever had, but they'd never gotten on. Margaret could be difficult, fussy and cantankerous, harping about everything. She was too imposing, too tyrannical, and Olivia's placid temperament grated on her more acerbic one. They'd stumbled through the years together, no small feat with Penelope in the house.

Penelope was Olivia's sixteen-year-old stepsister, Margaret's sole child from her first marriage. Margaret believed Penny could do no wrong, which had resulted in Penny having had little discipline and being horridly spoiled, so much so that they'd had significant debate as to whether Penny should accompany them to Salisbury. Even though she thrived on causing trouble, Margaret had insisted she come along.

The two females created constant stress, yet they were family, the only one Olivia had.

She went to the door, and the moment she spun the knob, Margaret hustled in, closing it behind her. With a firm grip on Olivia's wrist, she whisked them across the room so that no servant could lurk in the hall and eavesdrop.

"Where have you been?" Margaret barked, but softly so that no one could hear them. "The earl has been waiting for you for over an hour."

"I'm sorry, Margaret." Out of habit, her instinct was to soothe Margaret's ruffled feathers. It was the fundamental rhythm of a relationship that had been established when Olivia was just a wee lass. Margaret was perpetually in a dither over what she judged as some lapse or error, while Olivia tried to keep things on an even keel. "I completely lost track of the time."

"Are you mad? How could you act so irresponsibly when we have so much at stake?"

At fifty-two, Margaret was twice widowed, a prideful countess who had not aged well. Her hair, which was regularly pulled into a taut chignon, was gray and dull, her tall, thin figure so gaunt that she appeared to have been afflicted with a vile disease. The creases on her face indicated that she wasn't prone to smiling, and her blue eyes were icy with disdain and hauteur.

"I apologize again," Olivia murmured, knowing it was best to avoid an argument.

"As well you should," Margaret fumed. "Winnie has been keeping him occupied, but she can only do so much."

"Oh, dear."

Thank goodness Winnie had been available to entertain him! Winnie was Margaret's thirty-five-year-old cousin, a confirmed spinster who had lived with them for years. She was friendly and charming, but as Margaret had snidely implied, she was a commoner and therefore possessed none of the traits that Edward was searching for in a bride.

He held one of the most ancient titles in the realm, his fortune was vast and secure, and according to Margaret's gossip sources, impeccable lineage mattered to him above all else.

"He's noticed your absence," Margaret accused, "and he probably suspects you're still abed! Is that the perception you want him to have?"

"No, no," Olivia fretted.

"Our fates are riding on you," Margaret reminded her. "If you have no concern for Penny and myself, at least have the decency to consider Helen. What will happen to her if we're tossed into the streets? How will you care for her?"

Olivia hung her head, ashamed that she'd been dawdling in her room, doodling and swooning over the enigmatic Phillip, while fantasizing over potentialities that could never be.

How could she have been so selfish?

From her encounters with Lord Salisbury, it was obvious that he wasn't enamored of her, that she hadn't made much of an impression, so she would have to struggle to win his approval. Now, he likely deemed her a laggard or a slugabed, when neither portrayal fit her in the slightest.

"I'll go down immediately." And she scurried out before Margaret could hurl another remark.

Winnie Stewart leaned against the balustrade of the verandah and stared across the rolling lawns of the estate. There were horses grazing in a pasture, a colt kicking up its heels and chasing after its mother, and she smiled at the sight. It was so bucolic and peaceful, like a fairy tale.

How she loved the country! How she hated knowing that she'd have to return to the city in a few weeks. She wished she could tarry in this enchanting location forevermore. There was nothing for her in London, and with their finances in such disarray, her situation was even more precarious.

Margaret had explained their plight ad nauseum, and the necessity for journeying to Salisbury so that Olivia could investigate the possibility of a marriage.

But what if the match wasn't brought to fruition?

From the dirty looks Margaret occasionally flashed, Winnie wondered if she shouldn't be seeking employment, though at age thirty-five, she couldn't guess what she could do to earn a salary. She hadn't worked a day in her life, had no idea how one found a job. Plus, she had no skills or aptitude.

If only she could remain where she was! Perhaps she could convince Lord Salisbury that she was indispensable in some capacity. Maybe she could dredge up one of his decrepit old aunties who needed a companion!

Ruefully, she grinned. To what a pathetic state she'd descended! As a child, she'd supposed she'd follow the course of other women, that she would marry, have a home of her own, and a gaggle of children to keep her busy. How sad that none of it had occurred. With each passing year, it was more clear that she was destined to subsist through the benevolence of others, an amiable spinster with no one and nothing to call her own.

She couldn't recollect when she'd last taken a trip outside London, and she wasn't sure why Margaret had let her come this time. When the Hopkins family had been financially solvent, the earl active and healthy, they'd often traveled to their ancestral seat, but Winnie rarely went with them. Though Margaret had never said so directly, Winnie had been made to feel that she'd be overstepping her bounds by tagging along.

Haven't we done enough for you? Margaret's eyes would seem to inquire. *Must you impose further?*

It was so dreadfully humiliating to be the poor relative, and she strove to never be a burden or a bother, to never be seen as wanting more, or hoping that her lot would improve. When she'd been invited to move in with the wealthy Hopkinses, the opportunity had been a godsend, a boon she hadn't taken for granted, and she never said or did anything that might give someone cause to believe otherwise.

Some thirteen years earlier, she'd been in a dismal quandary, and Margaret—with strong urging from

Olivia's father—had helped her through it, then the earl had insisted she stay on. With her parents deceased and no other kin to speak of, save Margaret, she hadn't had many choices. She'd embraced his offer and had never left.

A wave of melancholy swamped her, and she tamped it down. More and more, she was despondent and glum, and praying she could leap out of the rut into which fate and circumstance had landed her.

How was it that she—who had perpetually been a vibrant, energetic, and unflagging individual—had descended to this disappointing juncture? How had she come to be thirty-five and so alone? Why had she ended up settling for so little?

For an instant, she unlocked the door to reminiscence, to Gerald, the lord's son who had swept over her like a gale, who had tantalized her with a taste of elegance and passion, but who'd also broken her heart, shattered her world, and left her with the tiny baby girl she'd birthed and Margaret had put up for adoption.

Rebecca . . .

The forbidden name whispered through her head, but she shuttered it away, declining to wallow in the desolate trough where her grief deposited her. She would not be maudlin on such a glorious morning!

Behind her, a door opened, and she presumed it was a maid carrying more food for the buffet that had been laid out. A feast awaited—should anyone show up to eat it. Or it might be Margaret, having completed her search for Olivia.

No doubt, she'd want to complain about Olivia, and Winnie hoped not. She wasn't in the mood for Margaret's petulance or criticisms. Margaret found fault with everyone, most notably Olivia, when Winnie considered Olivia to be very fine. Winnie abhorred her untenable role of confidante, specifically when she'd like nothing more than to give Margaret a brisk shaking and tell her to shut up.

She glanced over her shoulder, and much to her surprise, there was the earl, Edward Paxton. When she'd initially arrived, she'd been presented to him, but since then, she'd elected her customary route of being accommodating and inconspicuous, and she'd kept to herself, even taking her meals in her room, so she hadn't seen him again.

After the scramble of introductions, she'd had a fleeting recollection of a pleasant, dark-haired gentleman, but not much else, so she was astonished that she hadn't noticed how handsome he was.

At six feet tall, he was wide at the shoulders, thin at the waist, with long, lanky legs. He was in commendable physical condition, probably through fencing or some other activity, and though his hair was peppered with gray, he didn't appear to be anywhere near forty-five.

He was striking, the sort who grew more distinguished with age, who turned heads when he entered a room. Raised in affluence and privilege, he'd effortlessly donned the mantle that birth and title had provided. He was satisfied, comfortable with who and what he was.

He was peering across the verandah, evaluating her as though he couldn't recall who she was or why she was on his patio. His gaze was astute, keen, and pathetically, she wondered what he saw when he looked at her.

While she wished he would perceive her as vibrant, interesting, and fetching, she was sure he beheld her as she truly was: a stodgy, short, rather plump woman who was past her prime, whose once-bright brunette hair was sporting a few strands of gray, too.

He was advancing on her, and she watched his lengthy strides. He moved with a lithe grace, much like the enormous African cats she'd seen once in London.

As he neared, she suffered the strangest sensation, that her destiny was approaching, that her future had finally unfolded, and a ripple of gladness surged through her. Her pulse was pounding, her ears ringing, and she shook off the peculiar impression.

With her increasing age, her sentiments often gushed out of control. She jumped to outlandish conclusions, wept over the most minor developments, raged over the smallest injustices. Now, she was fantasizing in an almost hallucinatory fashion!

Spinsterhood was driving her mad!

She dropped into a curtsy. "Lord Salisbury."

Like a benevolent king, he took her hand, lifting her to her feet.

"We don't stand on ceremony here in the country." His voice was low, charming, gallant, and it swept over her, causing butterflies to rumble through her stomach.

"Thank you." She stared at his chest, afraid to look at him. She was so nervous that she was positive he would detect her confusion and yearning.

He was studying her; she could sense his appreciative regard. After a protracted pause, he admitted, "I'm embarrassed to say that we were introduced the other day, but for the life of me, I can't remember your name."

"Winifred Stewart," she said. "My friends call me Winnie."

"Winnie . . ." He rolled the word on his tongue. "How unusual. It suits you."

The compliment gave her the courage to meet his gaze, but she hadn't been prepared for how dazzling he would be up close.

He was smiling at her, his brown eyes sparkling with masculine curiosity.

Her heart literally skipped a beat.

"I would be honored if you would call me Winnie."

"If *you* will call me Edward."

"I will."

He hadn't released her hand, and like a pair of enamored half-wits, they gawked. She felt a powerful connection to him, their bodies seeming to tilt toward one another, and Winnie sustained an insane impulse to lean into him, to snuggle herself against his chest, comprehending that she would fit perfectly.

He felt their potent link, and he scowled, trying to deduce the reason. Stepping away, he freed her hand, severing their attachment as though she'd suddenly gotten too hot to handle.

At a loss, he grappled to reassert the smooth, urbane façade that had temporarily vanished. He cleared his throat and straightened his cravat, so disconcerted that she would have been sorry for him had she not been appalled and frightened by her own reaction.

"Would you care to join me at the table?" he asked, nimbly covering over the awkwardness.

She couldn't think of anything more dangerous, or more enticing, than to sit down and converse with him through a leisurely meal. She endeavored to find an excuse so that she might cordially refuse, when Olivia emerged through the French doors.

Attired in a stylish blue daydress that accented her winsome features, she was pretty and fresh, graphically and painfully reminding Winnie of the divisions between them, of the fact that Edward wanted to wed a sweet, innocent, biddable girl. A nobleman's daughter. All that Winnie was not and never would be.

What was she doing, loitering where anyone could see, and mooning over him like an infatuated ninny? Chagrined, she pulled herself together, masking further response, a knack she'd acquired through years of practice.

"I really can't, Lord Salisbury." Rudely, she used his title, and he frowned that she'd so quickly decided *not* to refer to him as Edward. "But thank you for the invitation."

Before he could reply, she stumbled over to Olivia, made a few inane, prattling comments—that she later wouldn't be able to recall—then she rushed into the manor, running till she located an empty salon.

In abject misery, she balanced herself against the wall, needing the support to stay upright.

She was sexually attracted to Lord Salisbury! Olivia's potential husband!

When she'd been dawdling on the verandah, she'd been scared to classify what she'd felt.

But it was blatant, heady sexual desire. She was no simpering miss, no naïve child, so she was well aware of what had sizzled between them. Disgustingly, she'd enjoyed every second of the encounter, and if they'd had the privacy and the time, she'd have gaily acceded in pushing the rendezvous to another level.

Women such as herself had names, and she knew them all: hussy, slattern, trollop. She'd assumed that she'd ventured beyond this stage, that her degraded constitution was an aberration, a delirium of youth and immaturity, but apparently not.

Better than anyone, she understood how easy, how perilous, it was to succumb to the pleasures of the flesh. The results could be deadly. For years, she'd labored to restrain her base nature, fighting the insistent urges, and living so soberly and so sedately that she might as well have taken vows and become a nun.

Yet Edward Paxton had but smiled at her, and she was ready to fling her principles and virtue to the four winds. She felt as if the lid had been torn off a Pandora's box where she'd hidden her sordid traits, and she was terrified that she'd never be able to put it back on.

Previously, she'd proven that she couldn't trust herself, that given the slightest provocation, she could and would commit any licentious act. Hadn't she learned any lessons from the past?

With a groan of dismay, she peeked into the hallway. There were no servants about, so she sneaked out and made for the stairs and the safety of her room.

Because she'd been feeling blue and housebound, she'd let the beautiful weather lure her outside, but it wouldn't happen again. She mustn't cross paths with the earl, mustn't say or do anything that might encourage him. Her degraded spirit, and lack of morality, couldn't be allowed to taint Olivia's chances.

She owed it to the family; she owed it to herself, and she would not relent.

CHAPTER FOUR

Margaret sipped her morning chocolate, mentally arranging her day. She'd been up since dawn, and she was dressed, her hair done, but she hadn't exited her room, for she didn't want others to know how early she'd risen. It wasn't fashionable, so people would have found the conduct odd, and if there was one thing she insisted upon, it was exemplary behavior.

As the daughter of a baron, who had wed and buried two earls, she had an image to maintain.

Sleep didn't come easily anymore. Too many worries plagued her, and as usual, this most recent debacle had fallen squarely on her shoulders. It was up to her to save them all, and the unwanted burden made her furious. Just once, couldn't others have carried the load? She'd had two exalted husbands, neither of whom had been worth the price of the suits in which they'd been interred, and what did she have to show for it?

Not two pennies to rub together!

They'd both been scalawags, prone to overindulgence in strong drink, gambling, and strumpets. She'd put up with their shenanigans, and where had it left her? With no assets, and a mound of debt she couldn't hope to pay off in ten lifetimes! That's where!

If Olivia didn't come up to scratch in their quest to snag Lord Salisbury, Margaret couldn't predict what she might do. She wasn't about to let poverty degrade her as it had Winnie, yet Olivia had less ambition than anyone she'd ever met, and she had no knack for flirtation or wooing.

Why couldn't she buckle down and apply herself to the task?

Well, if Olivia couldn't figure out how to beguile Edward, maybe Penelope could, though the prospect was remote. At sixteen, Penny was too young to assume the onus of being a wife, or to execute the duties of countess. Besides, Margaret didn't aim to settle for a lowly earl as her son-in-law.

She had much grander aspirations for her daughter.

With Penny's parentage and looks, coupled with a sufficient amount of plotting and positioning, she could be a duchess, or a princess.

Who knew where the road might take them? Queen, perhaps?

There was no end to the benefits of an advantageous marriage, and Margaret was willing to do whatever was necessary to catapult Penny into the maximum union, but first things first. And that meant having their finances stabilized, their immediate futures assured, so that she could focus her energies on their subsequent destinies.

At all costs, and before their visit was over, Olivia had to be engaged to the earl. No other conclusion was acceptable.

Olivia had no clue as to how far their circumstances could plummet, and therefore she had no conception of the drastic decisions that frequently had to be made to guarantee one's security and that of one's family.

Margaret could make those decisions without batting an eye. She'd done it with that horrid baby Winnie had birthed all those years ago, and she'd just done it again with Helen. Back in London, if matters had evolved according to plan, Helen had vanished without a trace.

When Olivia married Salisbury, there would be no

insane niece to cloud the nuptials, no discovery later on that might lead the earl to feel he'd been duped as to the purity of the Hopkinses' blood.

If Helen's existence was detected, what kinds of stories might circulate? What if Penny garnered a royal fiancé, and then news was disseminated that she had a crazed relative stashed away at home? Even though Penny and Helen weren't blood kin, no one would wait to hear how distant their consanguinity before the betrothal was terminated, and Margaret wasn't about to risk having Helen's lunacy reflect badly on Penny.

A knock sounded, and Penelope pranced in before Margaret could bid her enter. Penelope was aware of how much it irked Margaret when she demonstrated such shoddy manners, and a sharp rebuke was on the tip of her tongue, but Margaret tamped it down.

Penelope was in the worst stages of adolescence. She flourished on mischief, and when given a command or scolding, she ignored every word. If someone made a suggestion as to how she should comport herself, she did the opposite of what was advised.

Very likely, she'd intruded just to get a reaction from her mother.

Margaret knew Penny's game, and she wasn't about to play it. Not when there were bigger fish to fry.

Margaret's greatest fear was that Penny would behave inappropriately around the manor, that she might draw attention to herself in a way that would be detrimental to Olivia. While customarily, Margaret couldn't care less about Olivia, in this situation, deportment was paramount.

Penny was spirited and vivacious, and others didn't always comprehend how to interpret her conduct.

Margaret felt as though she were walking a tightrope,

which only served to increase her agonizing over their collective fates. She'd explained their quandary to Penny, and how imperative their trip to Salisbury, but Margaret couldn't say too much more. The least comment would have Penny scampering off in the wrong direction.

Penny had invariably been stubborn, but currently, she thrived on being contrary, and this sojourn was so important that Margaret couldn't indulge her typical peevishness. So far, Penny had done naught but complain about how boring the estate was, and how she was desperate for some excitement. She'd been pleading to return to London in all haste.

"Good morning, Margaret," Penny said as she flounced in.

"Penelope." At the disrespectful form of address, Margaret nodded and silently gnashed her teeth. The discourteous salutation rankled, so Penny regularly used it instead of the boorish *mother*.

"Why are you hiding in here? It's ten-thirty."

"I was just coming down." Margaret was irritated by Penny's sniping. If she had been anyone else's daughter, Margaret would have taken a switch to her.

"There's no need to hurry. The earl has eaten and departed."

"You had breakfast with Lord Salisbury?" Afraid that Penny might offend or antagonize him, Margaret didn't want any cozy parlaying between them.

"Yes."

"Was Olivia with you?"

"No. I haven't seen her."

Margaret's blood boiled. Olivia had strict instructions to be stationed in the dining parlor before eight each morning so that she could greet the earl whenever he chose to show himself.

Between Penny and Olivia, and their unbefitting attitudes, Margaret wondered if she would survive the next few weeks. Doubtless, she'd end up bald from tearing out her hair.

She rose and marched to the door, when it occurred to her that Penny had donned her riding outfit.

"Where do you think you're going?" she questioned, though she already had her answer.

"Riding," Penny replied defiantly.

"No you're not."

"The earl said I could."

"You shouldn't have put him in such a position, because you know I won't allow it."

Penny's hazel eyes flashed with ire. She shook her head, and her lush auburn tresses swished across her back. In an earlier century, a priest might have decried it as a witch's mane, and Margaret often speculated as to whether the ancient priests' admonitions about red hair weren't true, that it was indicative of an unrestrained character.

As a juvenile rebellion, Penny liked to wear it down, but Margaret had forbidden her to leave her bedchamber with it hanging free.

Her locks were fiery and arresting, and with the blossoming of her figure, she'd recognized the power she wielded with that hair. Men gazed at her, followed her, and wheedled for introductions, and she was thrilled by the control it gave her.

Though Margaret had warned her about the perils of coquetry, she wouldn't listen, and Margaret couldn't make her appreciate the dangers she tempted by flaunting herself. Unfortunately, she'd inherited her father's penchant for base amusement, as well as his demand for instantaneous gratification. Whatever she wanted, she wanted it at once, and at times, Margaret despaired for her.

She'd developed a fancy for a lower sort of boy, the kind of rough, crude fellow who drove a delivery wagon or poured beer in a tavern, and Margaret had to constantly guard her to keep her from doing something reckless.

Disgustingly, she had a fondness for stablehands and, on one astounding afternoon, Margaret had caught her kissing a hired man. She'd had him whipped, then fired, and had imprisoned Penny in her bedchamber for a week, with just bread and water to sustain her.

When she'd been released, Margaret had barred her from sniffing around the horses.

"You can't tell me what to do," Penny declared.

"Watch me." Margaret shot her a malevolent glare. "Go straight to your room and ring for a maid to pin up your hair. Don't come out until you've had it fixed in a suitable style."

"Witch . . ." Penny muttered.

Margaret slapped her as hard as she could. Though Penny's cheek snapped to the side, the recalcitrant child exhibited no other evidence that the blow had affected her. Slyly, she smiled, making Margaret uneasy, and she wondered if Penny had intended to instigate the discord, if she'd deliberately goaded Margaret into expressing strong emotion.

She didn't understand her daughter and never had. If she hadn't seen Penny slip from her body, she'd disavow the girl as being hers. Perhaps the old wives' tales about changelings had some basis in fact!

"Get out of my sight," Margaret seethed.

Penny strutted out, laughing as she sauntered down the hall.

Penny strolled the corridor, peeking in doors to ascertain who was in their rooms and who wasn't. She liked to know where people were. Over the years, she'd stumbled upon many interesting baubles in the chambers of others, so she was extra observant when walking about.

At Olivia's, she halted, surprised to find her present. Olivia thrived on arising at the crack of dawn, because she had so many inane projects to slave away on throughout the day.

Though Olivia could be reserved and stern, Penny liked her well enough. She never tattled, no matter what Penny did. When they were younger, Olivia would refuse to spill the beans, even when Penny had acted outrageously and Olivia was punished for it.

Penny admired her for that; she also judged her to be incredibly stupid. Who would take discipline for another? Especially when Margaret could be so viscious at dishing it out!

"Hello, Penny," Olivia welcomed as she did a final check in the mirror.

"You're off to a late start."

"I didn't sleep very well. I guess I'm nervous." She blushed and changed the subject. "You're looking very fashionable. Are you going riding?"

No one was aware of the incident in the Hopkinses' stable, or of Margaret's edict prohibiting Penny from approaching any building vaguely resembling a barn. Margaret had been too mortified to discuss Penny's amorous adventure—even with her sainted cousin Winnie.

"I might."

"It's been a while," Olivia pointed out. "Are you sure you're up to it?"

"I don't really care if I ride or not, but one of the men who works in the stable—I suspect he's the stablemaster—is the most handsome chap. He has blue eyes to die for, and I want an excuse to talk with him." She wiggled her brows, then ambled over and flopped down on the bed. "Hopefully, he'll agree to chaperone me for a tour around the property."

Olivia gawked, then she strode to her dresser and pretended to search for an item in the drawers. "Should you be loitering and chatting with such a person?"

Penny laughed. The women in her life were such stuffed shirts! "Honestly, Olivia, it's not as though I'm asking him to make mad, passionate love to me."

"Penny!" Olivia scolded, whipping around.

Olivia was so straitlaced; it was entertaining to shock her. "What about Lord Salisbury? Has he kissed you yet?"

"Penny!" she repeated. "I scarcely know the man. *And* he's a gentleman. Why would you imagine he had?"

"Aren't you the least bit curious?" She rose up on an elbow. "If I were being forced to wed, I'd want to learn if he was a good kisser. What if you delay until after the ceremony, and you discover he's terrible at it?"

"Where do you get these ideas of yours?" She rolled her eyes. "Besides, I'm not being *forced* to marry anyone."

"It seems like it to me." She paused, and cunningly inquired, "*Have* you ever been kissed?"

Olivia's quick rejoinder was prim. "I won't answer such a—"

"I have," she interrupted.

"I don't believe you." Cutting off the conversation that Penny was eager to have, Olivia proceeded to the wardrobe and retrieved her walking hat and wrap, and she shut the cabinet with a sharp click. "In the future, if you confide such an outlandish tale, I will inform Margaret of what you claim to be doing in your spare time."

An idle threat. "You don't have to be such a prude. Not around me," she asserted. "Do you want to know what will transpire on your wedding night? A scullery maid told me all about it."

"You're lying again, and I wish you'd stop it." She tromped to the door and opened it. "Let's go down, shall we? I'd like to see if there's any breakfast remaining."

"No, thank you. I ate with the earl ages ago." Penny accompanied her into the hall. "He waited for you for over an hour."

"Oh, no!" Olivia groaned, panicked by the news.

"When he left, he was quite perturbed." Which couldn't have been further from the truth. The earl had been pleasant and cordial, had eaten a speedy meal, then had dashed out, explaining that he was off for his habitual morning ride. He hadn't mentioned Olivia, but it was fun to set her worrying. She was the type who'd fret all day.

"Your mother will have my head!" Off she went, mumbling to herself.

Penny tarried until she'd disappeared around the corner, dawdled another minute to be sure she hadn't forgotten anything, then she reentered Olivia's room and spun the key in the lock.

She enjoyed rummaging through Olivia's belongings. Her stepsister had such pretty jewelry and clothes. Sporadically, Penny pilfered from her, and Olivia never missed what Penny stole, or if she did, she blamed it on crazy Helen and, therefore, didn't fuss over the loss.

Penny liked to keep track of Olivia, to be apprised of what was occupying her, and what she was thinking. She read her diary and correspondence, and of course, it was always humorous to snoop at her sketches. Olivia assumed she was so clever, hiding the art she was forbidden to create, skulking up into the attic to paint whenever Margaret was out of the house.

As of yet, Penny hadn't considered blathering to Margaret that Olivia was drawing—despite Margaret's orders to the contrary—but she hadn't put off the notion altogether. There might come a moment when it would be lucrative to divulge the news, but it hadn't arrived.

She riffled through Olivia's dresser, examining her undergarments, then her jewelry box, though any actual valuables had been sold and substituted with fakes.

After a painstaking inspection, she lay down on the bed, staring up at the canopy, listening as a servant tried the knob, then moved on. She relished being on the other side of the door, knowing that she was inside when she wasn't supposed to be.

Flipping onto her stomach, she pressed her body into the mattress, and her breasts rubbed across the covers. She pushed with her hips, mimicking the thrusting motion that the stable lads had shown her when she'd still been able to sneak off.

On a particularly naughty afternoon, she'd permitted the best-looking boy, Jeremy, to lower the bodice of her dress and peer at her breasts. They'd been full and round, her nipples sticking out. He'd been excited, enthralled, and she'd liked how it had felt to have him so awestruck. She hadn't let him touch her, but she'd promised she would on the next visit, then there hadn't been a *next*.

She rotated onto her back, so that she could fondle her breasts. The boys had done the same, through the fabric of her gown, and she'd been thrilled by their groping and pawing. But now that Margaret was continually hovering about, she couldn't slip away, and she regretted that she hadn't let Jeremy do more during that conclusive, torrid rendezvous.

He'd wanted to kiss and suck on them, but she'd said no, and oh, how she rued that she had. She closed her eyes and envisioned that it was Jeremy's coarse, work-hewn fingers manipulating her, and the stimulation had her wet and tingling down below.

Thoroughly aroused, she returned to her stomach, and burrowed her nose into the pillows. While stretching her arms, she banged them against a solid object, and she recognized its shape. Olivia's portfolio! She pulled it out and lifted the flap, surprised by the number of pictures.

As she tugged them out and arranged them in a neat pile, astonishment gripped her. She'd expected the usual array of boring sketches—of Helen, of Winnie, of the town house, of a street vendor—but this was something else entirely, so unanticipated and sensational that she scarcely knew what to make of it.

"Nudes!" she murmured. "How absolutely grand!"

Olivia had drawn herself over and over, her bust bared, her breasts naked and depicted from every angle. With her, in the center of every page, was Lord Salisbury's stablemaster!

In the week they'd been at the estate, Penny had caught several glimpses of him. Once, he'd had his shirt off, his hairy chest and muscled shoulders visible from the secluded walkway where she'd spied on him. He was the most gorgeous creature she'd ever witnessed. Plainly, Olivia thought so, too.

In every scene, he was simpering toward her exposed bosom, and in the last one in the stack, she was on his lap, and he was caressing her with his large hands. She was in ecstasy, his stroke electrifying and exhilarating her.

Penny looked and looked, so wound up that she could hardly breathe.

Why had Olivia done this? What did it portend? Was she having an affair with the stablemaster? She was too much of a stick-in-the-mud to commit so wicked an exploit. How had she had the opportunity or the inclination?

"Oh, God!" She squealed, teetering over and clutching the pictures to her chest, while she chortled with delight.

This was too delicious to be true!

Olivia and the stablemaster!

What a luscious secret to possess! How could she use the information to the greatest advantage?

Carefully, she replaced the illustrations in the portfolio, and buried them under the pillows, adjusting the bedcovers so that there was no hint that they'd been ruffled. With a hasty glance around, she made certain there was no sign she'd been snooping.

Then she crept into the hall. Finding it empty, she tiptoed out and shut the door.

Jane stood in the matron's office, the deadly quiet of the orphanage resonating behind her. The children were working, so no chattering was allowed, and any burst of merriment was instantly muffled, the offender paddled for insubordination.

The tiny girl beside her had obviously come from a rich family. She'd already been stripped, her hair raggedly chopped off, and she was attired in a standard gray pinafore, but her other apparel was on a nearby chair. Her pink dress, the matching bloomers sticking out beneath, was stitched to perfection. Her coat was crafted of the finest wool.

The garments would be sold, and it was such a pity that the dear things would be forever lost to her.

She was only three or four, but the most beautiful child Jane had ever seen. With her white-blond hair, her big blue eyes, rosy cheeks and lips, she looked like an expensive doll.

What tragedy had befallen her? How could such an immaculate child end up in the same situation as Jane?

The clock struck three and she winced, praying Mrs. Graves would finish with the admittance papers so that Jane could get the girl settled and be rid of her. Jane had been interrupted with various tasks all afternoon, and she was an hour behind at her stitching. She didn't dare lag further.

Whereas previously an anonymous benefactor had paid her room and board, the subsistence had suddenly stopped, and Mrs. Graves never ceased to remind her that she now had to earn her keep or go. The burden was intense, the threat genuine, and the possibility terrifying that she could be thrown out into the slums of London.

Jane hadn't been told much about who she was or from where she'd come, but she knew for sure that she was twelve years old. The concept of fending for herself was too gruesome to consider. Occasionally, there were children who were brought in off the streets, so she'd heard the stories of what it was like on the outside, and she'd do whatever was required to prevent herself from being evicted.

There was also the danger that Mrs. Graves might take her to the special "house" she'd mentioned. After Jane's funds had been cut off, Mrs. Graves had raised it as an option, stating that many girls chose it as an alternative to homelessness. Though she claimed it was a nice, warm residence, where rich gentlemen visited and gave gifts to the inhabitants, one of the older boys had subsequently advised Jane that she should never agree, that it was an evil spot, so she'd declined the offer.

Jane didn't trust Mrs. Graves, and any suggestion the

dour older woman conveyed wasn't for Jane's benefit, but because Mrs. Graves would make a profit.

"What shall we call her?" Mrs. Graves broke the silence and tossed her papers aside.

"Why don't we just ask her her name?" Jane broached.

"She's daft as a loon. Can't talk." Mrs. Graves ventured, "How about Martha?"

When Mrs. Pendleton had been alive, she'd taught Jane to read, so even though the documents were upside down, she could see that the girl was Helen Hopkins. Under Mrs. Pendleton, the children had kept their names, or been provided with names if they were babies, but Mrs. Graves didn't regard them as individuals and couldn't distinguish one from the other.

They were all either Mary or Martha, even if they were mature enough to remember their original identities. *Helen* would never be uttered in the dreary place.

"Martha it is," Mrs. Graves chirped, as though they'd discussed it, and Jane had concurred. "Take her upstairs, show her her bed, then see what kind of work you can get her to do."

"She doesn't have any support, then?"

"No."

Mrs. Graves didn't elaborate, and Jane could barely dissuade herself from voicing the dozens of questions she had.

How could such a girl be disposed of with no stipend? Was there no one to fret about where she'd gone?

Maybe her wealthy relatives were ashamed of her abnormality, and they had wanted to hide her from the world. But didn't they comprehend what the orphanage was like? Hadn't they checked?

What would become of her?

That she could be sent here—dumped here, really,

with only the precious clothes on her back—was the saddest tale Jane had ever heard, and as she stared down at the impassive, serene child, a wave of protectiveness swept over her.

Jane rarely bonded with any of the orphans, for it was too depressing when they left or died. But for some reason, Helen was different. Nothing bad would happen to her while Jane was around.

Jane held out her hand, and Mrs. Graves didn't notice when Helen reached out and grabbed for it.

"Daft, indeed!" Jane grumbled indignantly, as they strolled out. The child might be mute, but she was smart as a whip. Whoever had labeled her as stupid had no idea what they were saying.

As they passed the front door, Mr. Sawyer entered to begin his evening shift. He was the new attendant Mrs. Graves had hired. Jane avoided him and started up the stairs.

When they were at the landing, she paused, peeping down to where he was removing his hat and coat. She turned Helen so that the child could clearly view him.

"Don't ever speak to that man," she whispered. "And don't *ever* go off alone with him."

Helen made no comment, but she scrutinized Sawyer, and Jane could tell that the warning had registered. As if they were magically bound together, she felt she could discern the girl's thoughts.

"You understand me, don't you?" Jane mused, as though Helen had communicated aloud. "Well, I don't care about the others. I'll always call you Helen."

Helen flashed a brilliant smile that lit up the dim corridor. Jane said nothing and continued to climb.

CHAPTER FIVE

Olivia tiptoed down the darkened hallway, convinced she'd lost her mind.

She'd spent the entire day doing what was required of her and keeping herself occupied.

From the moment she'd risen—grouchy and exhausted from another night of restless sleep—she'd told herself that she would not think about Phillip, would not consider the indiscreet discussions they'd had, or his request that she join him in the library.

She was very good at focusing herself, and for lengthy periods, she'd managed to forget about him, until Penny had coaxed her out for an afternoon stroll. They'd sat on a bench, sheltered from the manor by a thick hedge, when she'd noticed that she could observe the rear of the stables.

Phillip had been there, covered with dust and sweat. As she'd spied on him, he'd yanked off his shirt. It had been the first time she'd beheld a man's chest, so she had no examples with which to compare it, but she was positive his was an excellent specimen.

His shoulders were broad, his arms muscled and strong, his waist thin. Tanned and hale, he'd glistened in the bright sunlight, and the vision jostled her innards, making her crave and yearn for things she didn't under-stand.

There was a coating of hair across the top that had narrowed to where it disappeared into his trousers, and her hands had itched and tingled as she'd wondered what it would feel like to run her fingers through it.

Would it be scratchy? Or soft and velvety?

She hadn't known that men had hair on their chests. She, who deemed herself a proficient artist! Avidly, she'd analyzed him, scouring for every detail she could glean in the short interval she'd had to watch.

He'd been loitering next to a water trough, and he'd dipped his soiled shirt and used it as a cool cloth to smooth over his heated skin. Then he'd immersed his head, after which he stood shaking it as the water cascaded down his front.

At the sight, her heart had begun beating so hard that she'd been afraid Penny, who had been perched beside her, might have heard it. Luckily, Penny hadn't perceived anything to be amiss, hadn't seen the mostly naked Phillip strutting in the yard. But, as though she'd sensed turmoil, she'd kept her gaze glued on Olivia.

"What's the matter?" she'd asked. "You seem distraught."

Olivia had leapt to her feet and hurried her stepsister inside, ushering her into the music salon, where they'd performed faltering duets on the pianoforte until Olivia had calmed sufficiently to go upstairs and dress for supper.

She'd forced herself through the rituals of the evening, had dawdled through the interminable repast, had politely conversed with the earl—even though it was increasingly apparent that they had nothing in common—had dealt cards and chatted until it had grown late enough that she could plead fatigue and go to bed.

But once she was sequestered in her room, she could concentrate on naught but Phillip.

Though it was risky and wrong, though it went against all she believed and had ever been taught, though it could wreck any slim prospect she had of securing her family's finances, she had to be with him again.

Like a thief, she crept to the library, frantic and crazed and praying that he was expecting her.

She stopped outside, took several deep breaths, trying to steady her nerves, then she peeked around the corner.

He was there!

Her relief was so great that her knees were wobbly, and as she crossed the threshold, she suffered the strangest impression: it was as if she were leaving her old life behind. If she progressed, the person she'd been for twenty-three years would cease to exist. With a staggering certainty, she felt he was her destiny, that she'd been waiting for their paths to collide, and that after this rendezvous, she would never be the same.

The sentiments were so powerful, and so vivid, that she couldn't disregard them. They induced a wave of gladness and exhilaration, and whatever transpired, now or after, she would never regret what she was about to do.

He was slouched on a sofa, a single candle flickering on the table next to him. Shadows played across his face, making him look dangerous. Cradling a libation, he hoisted it and sipped, and as he drank it down, he didn't take his eyes off her.

For an eternity, they stared at one another, then he motioned with his glass.

"Shut the door, Livvie. And lock it."

The notion of barring the door, of being secluded with him, was so improper, and so thrilling, that she shivered even though she wasn't cold.

She hesitated, and he scrutinized her, speculating over what she would do, if she would have the courage to proceed. As she vacillated, he smirked, sure she'd never comply, that she was a weakling or a coward, and she hated that he would presume her to be so irresolute.

Never timid, she wasn't about to allow any ambivalence to ruin the glorious encounter. She found the key and did as he bid her.

"Come here," he ordered.

His voice was low and quiet. He was changed from how he'd been previously. Before, he'd laughed and spoofed, his demeanor merry, but now he was in a very different mood. Something distressing must have happened.

Though he appeared to be relaxed, he wasn't at ease. He was restive, impatient, like a predator about to pounce on its prey.

A wiser woman might have declined to approach him under such conditions, so she was pondering her sanity, but he was reeling her in like a fish on a hook, and she couldn't halt her advance.

He seemed angry, acrimonious, ready to lash out at the world, and as she was the only one there, she worried that his ire might fall on her. But she discounted the idea.

He would never hurt her. She knew it as completely as she knew the sun would rise on the morrow.

She kept walking until they were toe to toe. He didn't stand, as courtesy and civility demanded. With their proximity, she could detect the odor of alcohol hovering about him. He'd had too much to drink, and she was nettled by the discovery.

For years, Margaret had railed about the mischief caused by men and their liquor, but Olivia had had scant experience with the situation. Her father and brother were the sole men with whom she was familiar, and she couldn't remember either of them overimbibing.

What would an excessive amount do to Phillip's temperament? Would he be more aggressive? More hostile? More imperious? More amorous? Or would it have no effect?

Insolently, he perused her, his torrid attention lingering—on her lips, her bosom, her legs—and the strength of his inspection was so extreme that she felt as if he could peer through her clothes to the naked skin beneath the fabric.

She was tempted to squirm and fidget, to shudder in maidenly affront and clasp her arms across her torso, but she didn't. While she blushed, her cheeks glowing crimson, she showed no other reaction. Although she couldn't decide why, it was obvious that he was hoping to rattle her, or chase her away. But that confused her. If he wanted her gone, why had he invited her in the first place?

She was no shrinking violet, and never had been, and she wasn't about to slink away. Surprising him, she sidled nearer, just when he'd assumed he'd offended her to the extent that she would stomp out in a huff.

"If you're trying to frighten me," she said, "it won't work."

He raised a brow, neither denying nor admitting that he'd been endeavoring to alarm her. "Would you like to draw some erotica?"

The leather-bound volume *A Feast for the Senses* lay on the table, filled with romping pixies, fairies, and the Arabian sheik who could be his twin.

"Not tonight."

"Then why are you here?"

A more sophisticated female might have flirted around the answer, might have teased or vamped, but she'd never been one to circumvent an issue. "To see you. I couldn't stay away."

"If you're caught with me, you'll never be able to marry your precious Edward."

"Suddenly, it's a chance I'm willing to take."

"Why?"

Would he think she was mad if she confessed what she'd been contemplating all day? Or if she alluded to the perceptions that had swept over her when she'd entered the library? She couldn't account for them to herself, so she couldn't explain them to him.

"I had to come."

It was the best she could do, the lone justification she could provide without sounding like a lunatic.

"Sit with me."

He held out his hand, and she took it, lacing her fingers with his, but he applied no pressure to pull her down. If she was to join him, it would have to be of her own accord.

Almost as if it were actually there, she could envision a line painted between them. It was the line between right and wrong, morality and vice, virtue and wantonness. If she crawled onto the cushion next to him, she'd be stepping over the line to the side of iniquity, and she could never get back.

Appallingly, she didn't care. Not about Edward, or Margaret, or Helen, or the family, or the vow she'd made to rescue them. Only Phillip mattered.

Despite all, she *had* to be with him. There was no other choice, and she was prepared to commit any imprudent act, so long as they could be together.

It occurred to her that this was the reason girls were chaperoned, that they were protected and sheltered. Others understood, as she had not, that for every woman, there was a man like Phillip who could rout all discretion.

In the stark light of morning, she would locate plenty of excuses to chastise herself, to rue and lament, but not now. Not when they were isolated, and he was watching her as if he could set her afire with the intensity of his gaze. She'd never felt so magnificent.

"You're upset," she mentioned.

"What makes you say so?"

"I can tell."

He shrugged. "I was fighting with my father. It was nothing."

The frank admission had him visibly disconcerted, and a thousand questions flitted by: Who was he? Who were his people? Had he always resided at the estate? What was his position in the stables? How had he earned it?

She was eager to discern his favorite color, his favorite food. Did he love to read? Could he strum the lute or dabble at the pianoforte? Did he like to dance? To sing? What garnered him joy and pleasure?

Knowing her, perhaps?

"What were you fighting about?" she brashly probed. With anyone else, she'd never have dared inquire.

"My life; his women."

His father's *women*? It was such a curt, strange reply that she wasn't certain where to go next. "Does your father live at Salisbury?"

He chuckled. "Yes."

"And your . . . mother?"

"Died ages ago."

"I'm sorry."

He shrugged again, then he altered the configuration of their hands, so that he could stroke his thumb across her palm.

"I don't want to talk about my parents."

"What would you like to talk about?"

Tired of waiting for her to make a decision, he tugged on her wrist, and the slight tension spurred her to do what she couldn't accomplish on her own. She clambered onto the sofa, just to her knees, her skirt trailing behind and dangling over the edge.

He gripped her waist and tipped her forward so that she would fall against him. The intimate contact was coming too soon, too fast, and she braced herself on her arm to prevent it.

"Have you ever dallied with a man before?"

"No."

"There are things I yearn to do with you," he proclaimed. "I want to touch you and kiss you. Will you let me?"

A vivid picture from the erotic book flashed into her mind—of the stranded sailor with the mermaid snuggled between his legs so that he could fondle her breasts.

Was that what he proposed? Was he inclined to that sort of outrageousness? Did he want to view her in the nude? Maybe massage her private parts?

The notion was so beyond her ability to process, and had been dropped so speedily and so early in the conversation, that she was paralyzed. She couldn't move or speak, but apparently, no reply was required.

He leaned toward her, and she yelped with astonishment as she thought he was going to kiss her, but he didn't. Instead, he dipped down and nuzzled at her nape.

His chin rasped her, and her stomach tickled as she realized it was rough from his whiskers, that he needed to shave. A man's face could feel rugged? What a fascinating fact to mull over!

She tried to calm herself, to focus on what he was doing. Bizarrely, he was tasting her, as if absorbing her very essence.

He bit her! His teeth latched on to the most tender area of her shoulder, and he nipped. She jerked away, glaring at him and rubbing the spot. Though it throbbed, it didn't ache.

"Why did you do that?" she snapped.

"I like the way you smell," he asserted, which wasn't really a clarification.

He studied her, and there seemed to be a confidence

he wanted to share, a secret he wanted to divulge, but he said nothing.

"What do you want from me?" she finally asked, when she couldn't bear the silence.

His response was to drape her across his lap. Her hip was pressed to his groin, her bottom burrowed onto his thighs.

Her breasts were flattened to his chest, her nipples growing hard and erect, and poking into him like shards of glass. Whenever he shifted the tiniest amount, they abraded in a fashion that was exciting and sublime.

"You shouldn't be here." He forced her breasts closer. "Where you're concerned, I haven't a single honorable intention."

"I don't care."

"You should."

He reached for the erotic book and balanced the spine on his palm. The pages fell open to one of the lewd scenes, but she didn't glance down, terrified of what she might see, of what he might say.

"Look!" he commanded. "Look at it."

Her eyes darted to the side, then widened. It was an illustration she didn't recall from her prior review. A satyr—half man, half animal—had snared a woodland nymph. He was clutching her back to his front and restraining her against her will.

The female was frantic, fearful, while the satyr was arrogant, undaunted, satisfied with his pursuit.

"Do you have any idea what he's doing to her?"

"No, no . . ."

"He's mating with her; rutting with her from behind."

"I don't know what that means."

"He's raping her." With a flick of his wrist, he slammed the book shut and tossed it on the floor. "That's what I want to do to you. I want you—even if you don't agree. I want to hold you down and pilfer all that I can never have. What if I did, you reckless girl?"

"I told you: I'm not afraid of you. You'd never hurt me."

He tightened his grip, making it explicit that she couldn't escape unless he allowed her to. "What if you're mistaken? What if I proceeded? Right here. Right now. How could you stop me?"

"I wouldn't want you to stop."

"Well, I wouldn't, either, you little fool. So where does that leave us?"

For another agonized moment, they stared each other down, lovers in a fierce quarrel, when she wasn't even sure about what they were arguing. Then, he narrowed the distance between them, his mouth capturing hers in a torrid kiss.

For a brief, idiotic instant, she resisted, but she promptly recovered and relented. She'd trekked to the library, praying that something of this magnitude would occur, and now that it had, she didn't want him to think she wasn't receptive.

His lips were warm, his breath sweet, and he tasted of the brandy he'd been drinking. Though he was tense, and seemed to be angry, he was cradling her gently, prudently, as if she were made of fine porcelain and should be handled delicately.

Her hands rose to slip around his neck, her fingers going to the queue that bound his hair so that she could explore the lush, dark locks. Shiny and luxurious, it descended past his shoulders, and she reveled in the palpable delight of sifting through the strands. The simple gesture was decadent, thrilling.

His own hands were never stationary. They were everywhere—her shoulders, arms, back, thighs—running up and down, stroking in languid circles.

A zealous pupil, she followed his lead, wanting and needing to caress him as he was caressing her. Tentative, then bolder, she investigated, letting her palms rove over muscle and bone.

Their lips parted, and he kissed across her cheek, her brow.

"I've been longing to do this since I first laid eyes on you," he claimed.

"You couldn't have."

"There's something about you, something that I . . ." He couldn't complete the sentence. Did he not wish to tell her what it was? Did he not know? Was he incapable of describing his feelings?

She hoped his sentiments matched her own, that he was grappling with an impression of unreality, as if they'd leapt through a magical window to a place where no one had ever gone before, that they had found the perfect opportunity to wallow in felicity and bliss.

She wanted him bothered and perplexed, just as she was, herself.

"I saw you today," she blurted. "From out in the garden. You were behind the stables, rinsing in the trough."

"You minx! You were spying on me through the hedges!"

"Yes," she admitted.

"Were you shocked?"

"I'd never seen a man without his shirt before," she confessed. "But I wasn't shocked!"

He chuckled and fumbled with the buttons of his shirt, undoing it to the waistband of his trousers, then he yanked the lapels aside. The curly matting of hair tempted and amazed her.

"Touch me," he directed. "Touch me all over."

Nervous and puzzled, she sat motionless, so he clasped her hands and rested them—palms down—on the center of his chest, guiding her until she joined in, then he left her to her own devices.

With great relish, she learned his shape and build. Throughout, he watched her, his discomfiture increasing.

Inhaling, she exulted in his smell, his heat, as she pressed her ear over where his racing heart pounded. It was the most extraordinary, most enchanting sound she'd ever heard, and she could have lain there all night, listening to the steady tempo.

He was kissing her once more, her forehead, her cheek, her nose, moving downward to her mouth. Ardor flared anew, his tongue flicking out to trace across her bottom lip.

"Open for me," he coaxed. Asking. Asking again.

Eagerly, she submitted, and the sensations were so exhilarating, so mesmerizing, that she could only hang on, as if clinging to a raft in a violent storm.

She was swept away, by emotion, by stimulation. She hadn't realized that the human anatomy could experience such tumult, that the mind could be so overwhelmed. An invading army could have rushed into the room, and she wouldn't have noticed, would have had no power to desist.

Without her being aware, they'd changed positions. She was prone on the sofa, and he was on top of her, his torso pushing her down, his weight crushing her, yet he didn't feel heavy. He felt gloriously welcome.

His hips flexed into hers in a magnetic rhythm, one that she intuitively recognized and needed to emulate. Of their own accord, her legs spread, the fabric of her skirt bunched up, providing him with a buffer against which he could thrust. There was an unusual ridge in his trousers; she didn't know what it was or why it was there, but she accepted its presence and battled to be nearer to it.

Again and again, he drove into her, becoming more intense, more demanding. He began petting her breasts through the material of her gown. As she was wearing only a thin chemise under it, it seemed as if he were fondling her bare skin.

Molding and sculpting the two mounds, he trifled and played. The action aroused her nipples, and they were peaked into taut buds. Pinching them, he squeezed in a way that made her writhe and moan, and she was rising on a tide of unfamiliar desire, seeking a goal that was just beyond her. She was desperate to attain it, and she labored toward it.

Somehow, he'd unbuttoned her dress, and the chilly air washed across her nipples. In some far-off section of her brain, she understood that she shouldn't permit the liberty, that she should grab for her bodice and conceal herself, but her arms were inert. She couldn't hinder him, nor did she want to.

He abandoned her mouth, and kissed down her neck, her chest, and before she knew what he was about, he'd wrapped his lips around her nipple and was sucking at it.

The maneuver evoked such agitation that the core of her body started to weep. She felt as if she were dying, as if her heart might quit beating.

It couldn't be healthy to undergo such torment!

He nipped at the rigid nub, licking, laving, and torturing it, till it was inflamed and raw. Just when she could tolerate no more, he shifted to the other, giving it the same fierce attention.

With each titillation, she perished a little more. She wanted to order him to halt; she wanted him to continue on forever.

He pulled away so that he could scrutinize her exposed breasts, and the cessation of contact allowed her a pause to wrestle with her equilibrium, to reassert some smidgen of control.

She'd never dreamed that she could behave so wickedly. The encounter was depraved and dangerous. While in the throes of passion, she'd neither noted nor heeded the dissolution, but the delay was excruciating because it offered her a chance to reflect.

"So pretty, Livvie," he murmured, "and all mine. I can't let anyone else have you. Not after this."

He laughed, and there was a hidden meaning to his words that she didn't like or comprehend. He was arrogant and possessive in a manner he hadn't been previously.

Seizing her hands, he pinned them over her head, and she wanted them free, her bosom covered, but he wouldn't oblige. She commenced tussling with him, her hips thrashing and squirming, but he enjoyed the enhanced commotion.

They had vaulted to a higher level, and she had landed herself in a perilous situation. Whatever destination he planned was exactly where she shouldn't go.

Decades of lectures, about men and their nefarious aims, were cascading through her. She had to arrest their forward progress, had to slow him down, but the physical acts he was committing against her person were so stupendous that she couldn't reason clearly.

He was inching up her dress, the hem already past her knees. She was about to be nudely displayed, but it was unfolding too fast, and she couldn't brazen it out.

She struggled in earnest, slapping at his shoulders, and scuffling with her legs, trying to loosen her skirt from where it was tangled beneath him.

"Phillip, please." Her voice was breathy, weak, and nothing like her customary, confident self. "Phillip!" she repeated more forcefully.

Frowning, he hesitated. Bewildered, reeling, he peered

down at her as though he couldn't quite identify her or grasp why they were sequestered in the isolated room.

"What is it?" he queried. "What's wrong?"

"I . . . I need a moment." To her mortification, tears flooded her eyes. She was confounded, and worried that she might collapse into a weeping ball of misery. She swallowed. "You're scaring me."

Glaring at her, he studied her features, then he slid off so she had the space to escape. She wedged out from under him and took several steps away.

Showing him her back, she floundered to arrange herself so that her modesty was restored. Behind her, she could feel his regard, hot and potent, but he didn't approach, and she was relieved.

"I thought I could do this," she explained, gazing at the far wall, "but I was mistaken."

"What were you expecting?" he bitterly retorted. "Flowers and candy? Bad poetry and vacuous compliments?"

"I don't know," she answered truthfully. "I've never done anything like this before."

"Obviously."

His tone made it apparent that she had no skill at love games, and she was humiliated that he would comment upon her dearth of ability.

"I shouldn't have come," she said, more to herself than to him.

"Foolish girl."

"I'm sorry."

"Go to your room, *Lady* Olivia."

His use of her title cut like a sharp blade, and she winced. She heard him stand, and she spun to face him.

As she'd straightened her attire, so had he. His shirt was buttoned and tucked, his trousers adjusted. He looked cool and detached, evincing no hint of what they'd been doing, and they pondered each other across an expanse as vast as an ocean.

He was a stranger, and his indifference flustered her, and stupidly, she begged, "You won't tell anyone, will you?"

"Oh, for pity's sake," he barked. "Just leave. And don't return. I won't be here waiting for you." He strolled to the rear of the salon, tossing a final, demeaning glance at her over his shoulder. "I don't need the complication you'd bring to my life. I've plenty without adding you."

With that, he crawled out a large window and evaporated in an instant, vanishing so quickly that it seemed as if he'd never been there at all. She blinked and blinked, trying to draw him into focus, but he was well and truly gone, and the sole clue he'd been there was the ribbon she'd removed from his hair.

It dangled on the sofa cushion, and she picked it up and wove it through her fingers.

An immense silence descended, and it occurred to her that their tryst might be the only exciting, exotic thing that would ever happen to her. The notion was so depressing that she couldn't bear to contemplate it, and she felt more lonely and more discouraged than she'd been in a very, very long time.

She whirled away and sneaked to her bedchamber.

CHAPTER SIX

Edward Paxton walked through the stable and out the rear door. The sun was bright, blinding after having strolled through the darkened barn, and he blinked to clear his vision.

Phillip was across the yard, leaning against a fence and laughing with several of the men who helped him care for the horses. Edward paused, as he always did, and watched, delighted and pleased, but also unsettled.

He could never get used to the notion that Phillip was his son. He could go for hours, for days, without recollecting, so he was thrown off guard whenever they were abruptly brought together. Even now, when he'd sought out Phillip, the reality was discomfiting.

Phillip was distrusting and hostile, and Edward was confused and abashed, so they couldn't establish a rhythm to their relationship.

Were they friends? He didn't think so, but he wanted to be. He would hate to spend the remainder of his life unable to leap beyond the strained status of employer and employee. It was dismal to consider that too much had happened—or not happened—over the years, and they would never progress beyond where they were entrenched.

Looking at the past through wiser eyes, it was embarrassing to evoke that period three decades earlier when he'd been so enamored of Phillip's mother. She'd been comely, spirited, and alluring, while he'd been spoiled, selfish, and with too much leisure time and not many ways to occupy it.

Juvenile and foolish, he hadn't found anything wrong with his affair. His randiness had prevailed, and neither morals nor integrity could dissuade him from his course.

When his father had learned of their liaison, he'd ranted and raved, had warned of impending doom, and how Edward's irresponsible conduct would inflict catastrophe on all concerned. But he'd been obsessed with the woman and couldn't desist.

In his immaturity, Edward hadn't comprehended how dire the consequences could be. He'd been scant more than a child, himself, and she'd been his first love, so he'd indulged in their fervent amour.

While he'd known that children could result from what he was doing, they had been a nebulous concept. After Phillip and his sister, Anne, had been born, Edward's lust for their mother had waned, and shamefully, he'd never felt much of a connection to them, had never viewed them as a part of himself to whom he owed loyalty and commitment.

Though it was mortifying to admit it, when his betrothal had approached, and his father had suggested moving the children and their mother off the estate, Edward had been relieved to be shed of them.

But of late, the tragedy of that era weighed heavily upon him. Maybe advancing age was making him maudlin, but he couldn't stop ruminating on his mistakes, on the paths he might have chosen.

Many a depressing morning, he stared at himself in the mirror, trying to locate remnants of that heartless boy. Had he really been that cruel? That frivolous? That ruthless? How could he have imagined the children to be a burden? How had he convinced himself that they hadn't needed him?

They'd been toddlers, barely two and three, when they'd gone, and Edward could distinctly remember that afternoon. Coward that he'd been, he'd hidden in his room, following the proceedings by peeking out the window until their carriage had disappeared down the road. The children had been prettily dressed, so well behaved, their mother stoic and brave as they traveled off to an uncertain future.

He still flushed with guilt when he recollected his father's biting words, advising him that Phillip's mother would not accept a stipend from the Paxton family. That she'd claimed she would work, and work hard to support them. That they could *get on* just fine without Edward's dubious charity. And apparently they had.

He'd never again communicated with Anne, though he knew she was a spinster, residing in a house in the country outside Bath.

With Phillip, he'd been granted the chance to repair some of the damage he'd wrought, though too much water had flowed under the bridge, and he'd never had much success. When Phillip had shown up at the estate, fourteen and brimming with mischief and energy, Edward had been stunned. Phillip had been so handsome, so smart and clever, a boy of which any father could have been proud.

Unfortunately, while Edward had been thrilled by Phillip's arrival, his wife hadn't been. She'd been aware of Edward's bastard children, having confronted him early in their marriage over rumors that were circulating. When he'd notified her of Phillip's request to return, she'd begged him not to allow it.

By then, they'd been married for a comfortable interval, had abandoned any prospect of having children of their own, and she'd felt threatened by Phillip's very existence. She'd vented her enmity, regularly exhibiting malice toward him in public that Edward hadn't halted. He hadn't known how.

How did a man force his wife to be civil to his illegitimate child?

His chagrin over her treatment of Phillip had never abated, and it was simply another way he'd failed his only son.

Phillip glanced up and noticed him, and he was held motionless and spellbound, impaled by Phillip's brilliant blue eyes that were an exact copy of his mother's, and whenever Edward noted them, he suffered the oddest sensation of melancholy.

Those exhilarating days of ardor and lust were so vivid in his memory. Every aspect had seemed so vital and essential. There had been no average emotions. He'd been giddily happy, animated, and overjoyed. In comparison to the rapscallion he'd once been, he was now an unmitigated bore, a stick-in-the-mud, a curmudgeon. He carried on as if he were closer to eighty-five than forty-five.

When had he become so staid and tedious?

Previously, he'd lived life to the fullest, had made each minute count, while currently, he thrived on routine and habit. Excitement and change were to be avoided at all costs, and he wryly speculated as to whether he should have the servants dredge up a wheeled chair. They could park him in the corner, with a blanket over his lap, like someone's ailing grandfather!

Phillip uttered a snide comment—Edward couldn't hear it—but from the reaction of his associates, the remark hadn't been complimentary. Brows raised, the men snickered then departed.

In a defensive posture, Phillip stood, legs braced, hands on his hips, as though he were prepared for a fight.

Edward sighed. How had they descended to this pitiful juncture? Would he ever be able to fix things between them? Would Phillip ever look up, see him, and be *glad*?

He could only hope.

"What now?" Phillip queried as he neared.

Edward was baffled by Phillip's irritation and animosity. "Whatever do you mean?"

"You never come down here unless I've upset you."

Was that how Phillip perceived their talks? How terrible! "You know that's not true."

"Isn't it?" Phillip assessed him, no visible sign of lingering affection in evidence. "Well, let's have it."

"Actually, I wanted to discuss the horses," Edward lied.

In light of Phillip's hostility, he put off the reason for his visit, inquiring instead about a mare and her breeding schedule, a carriage horse that was lame, a colt that wasn't growing at an adequate rate.

Phillip loved the animals, wouldn't leave the stables if he didn't have to eat and sleep, so it was an easy method to draw him out. Though Phillip was suspicious, he warmed to the task and answered every question until Edward could think of no more and ran out of excuses to delay.

"By the way . . ." He endeavored to sound casual, but something in his tone wrecked any camaraderie they'd just achieved.

"Yes?" Phillip snapped.

"I need to ask you to be more circumspect. You were washing in the trough the other afternoon. I guess you'd removed your shirt, and . . ."

Phillip tensed. Menace and temper rolled off him in waves. "What about it?"

"One of my guests saw you, and she was a tad disturbed."

"Which *lady*?" he acidly demanded. "Your precious Olivia?"

"No, no," he interjected. "The younger one, with the auburn hair. Lady Penelope. She's a sheltered, naïve—"

Phillip scoffed. "I wouldn't bet the estate on it."

Edward was disconcerted by the statement. Phillip was frequently privy to information that Edward, himself, couldn't have gleaned. Was he implying that Lady Penelope wasn't virtuous? How would he have garnered such a scandalous tidbit? And how to tactfully quiz him about it? Edward had no idea.

"Be that as it may," he fumbled, "we need to be mindful of our comportment when she's out and about."

"Let me give you a little hint about *Lady* Penelope." Phillip shifted, as if to relay a dreadful secret that Edward didn't want divulged. "I doubt that *my* chest was the first she's stumbled upon. You'll never get me to believe it was much of a shock for her."

"What are you saying?"

"Several times already, I've had to chase her out of the stables. She's developed a *fondness* for some of the lads—if you get my drift."

"Lady Penelope?"

"She's a born troublemaker, and she has the morals of an alley cat. So *you* had best be careful, or you'll find yourself with a ring on your finger and wed to the wrong girl." He stomped away and muttered, "It would serve you bloody right."

"Phillip!"

Phillip whipped around, ablaze with a level of ire and fury that, considering the innocuous tenor of their conversation, made no sense. "Isn't it embarrassing to picture yourself with a bride who's young enough to be your granddaughter? Or do you merely have a passion for adolescents?"

"Of all the outrageous, inappropriate—"

Before he could finish voicing his affront, Phillip

marched off, and though Edward shouted after him, he didn't slow. He kept on till he'd rounded the barn, and Edward dawdled in the grass like a petty supplicant.

Nobody spoke to Edward as Phillip occasionally did, and he couldn't decide what to do about it. He peeked around to ensure that none of the servants had witnessed the horrid scene.

Phillip wasn't a tot who could be paddled, and he was too valuable a horseman to be fired. Too bad flogging wasn't an option!

Tormented, dejected, he strode away and went to the garden, meandering down an isolated path. Wearily, he plopped down on a secluded bench, his head in his hands, as he contemplated his miserable lot.

He was a widower, with no heir, no legitimate offspring, and his only family was two children he'd cast off like so much rubbish when they were babies. One was a beautiful, industrious daughter he hadn't laid eyes upon since she was three, and the other, a dashing, extraordinary son who despised him.

What a contemptible fellow he'd turned out to be! Phillip was correct: how pathetic that he'd been reduced to sniffing after girls for a potential wife.

Was the entire estate tittering about his nuptial investigations? Were his retainers gossiping and laughing at him behind his back?

Yes, he was desperate for an heir, and yes, he was bound and determined to wed a female with an exemplary pedigree, but Olivia and Penelope—as well as the other maidens he'd interviewed—were so immature. And so exhausting. He had nothing in common with any of them. They knew nothing of the rigors of life, its bliss or sorrows.

When he'd initially married, he and his wife had been the same age, and they'd grown older together. They'd been compatible, had had matching hobbies, likes and dislikes, and he was beginning to suspect that it wasn't possible to attain harmony with women who were so much younger than him. The years were an insurmountable barrier.

What a quandary!

If only Margaret's cousin, Winnie Stewart, were of the nobility. How easy his choice would be!

He recalled the day she'd been loitering on the verandah, admiring the grounds. With her brunette hair glimmering in the sun, her tidy gown outlining her glorious figure, he'd deemed her the most fabulous creature he'd ever observed. She'd stirred him in a primal fashion, and he'd found himself wishing he could act upon it, but she hadn't stayed around long enough for him to explore its intensity. Like a frightened goose, she'd fled, and he hadn't seen her since, and to his consternation, he searched for her everywhere.

Out of frustration, he'd once mentioned her to Margaret, pretending a polite curiosity, and when Margaret had claimed that Winnie did not care to socialize, he hadn't dared broach the topic again lest his interest be erroneously construed.

After his vile behavior toward Phillip's mother, he'd sworn to himself that he'd control his base impulses, so he didn't dabble with the women of the lower classes. He didn't tumble the maids, or frolic with the neighborhood widows. Nor did he acknowledge the come-hither smirks of the loose hussies of the *ton* when he went to London. He never partook of whores, or prowled around at brothels as many other chaps were wont to do.

He was so lonely!

Yet he couldn't make the jump to a sexual relationship. Not out of any loyalty to his deceased wife, but because he wanted more than stealthy, hurried couplings that required sneaking in and out of back doors, hiding his horse, and keeping his trousers close in case he needed to execute a hasty exit.

There was never a shortage of available paramours, but he didn't trust any of their motives. While he was repeatedly offered the use of their lush bodies, they all wanted boons from him in exchange. His title. His money. His patronage.

It was hell being an earl, and he envied Phillip, who could meet up with a pretty girl and philander without having to fret about whether the world would end if he did.

Footsteps echoed down the walkway. Whoever was approaching wouldn't be able to see him till they'd rounded the curve in the hedge, and he glanced up, praying it wasn't Olivia or Penelope, or worse yet, Margaret. A more dour, disagreeable individual he'd never encountered.

To his utter and complete delight, it was Winnie, sauntering along by herself. She was lost in thought, her lovely face shaded by a parasol balanced on her shoulder.

At the same instant, their gazes locked, and she started in astonishment. Clearly, he was the last person she'd expected. She wasn't happy at discovering him. In fact, she appeared terrified.

While he'd accepted Margaret's insistence that Winnie preferred her privacy, he still had the impression that she'd been avoiding him. Why? Had he said or done something uncouth of which he was unaware?

"I didn't know anyone was out here," she contended. "Pardon me for bothering you." She whirled and hastened away.

"Winnie!"

She halted, hung her head, her shoulders stiff with tension. "Don't ask me to tarry."

"I want you to. Just for a bit."

"Edward—"

"Please!"

She vacillated forever, and he watched her, realizing that a severe struggle was being waged within. Finally, she spun toward him, her anguish palpable.

"What is it, Winnie? Have I offended you?"

"*You?* Offend *me?* How could you think it?"

He held out his hand, utilizing the full force of his station to coax her into taking it, and she couldn't refuse. She wavered, then reached out, as though it were the most difficult task she'd ever been required to perform.

Linking their fingers, like juvenile sweethearts, he urged her onto the seat next to him. He was assailed by her heat, by her smell. Her skin had an intriguing aroma, like a mixture of flowers and tart apples. It teased and tantalized his male sensibilities, making him want to lean in, to sniff and taste her.

Generally, he was the consummate gentleman, a restrained, courteous chap who minded his manners in the presence of a lady. However, with Winnie Stewart, there was nothing genteel about his feelings. He suffered a primitive, almost savage, attraction to her that had him wild to engage in any wicked behavior she would allow, and even some she wouldn't.

While he'd been infatuated with many women, he'd never experienced a connection that was remotely similar. He wanted things from her he couldn't begin to name, first and foremost being the chance to take her to his bed, to have her naked, her creamy, smooth flesh crushed to his own.

The erotic notion was so out of character that he had to ponder whether she hadn't bewitched him. Or, more likely, the celibacy he'd practiced since his wife's death had driven him over the edge!

He was perched much nearer than propriety permitted, touching her all the way down, her skirt tangled around his legs and feet. The contact thrilled him, made him pulsate with vim and vigor.

Amazingly, his trousers were tight! He was becoming aroused merely from her proximity, while she was too distraught to look at him. Like a shy girl, she stared off to the side, so he shifted into her line of sight. Her eyes were hazel, winged by dark brows, her cheeks rosy from her stroll in the fresh country air.

She was so fetching, so alluring, and by doing nothing at all, she tempted him beyond measure.

He had a perception of recognition, as though he'd always known her, and he inquired, "Have we met before you came to Salisbury?"

"No." Her mouth quirked in a half-smile.

"Are you sure? Perhaps in London or—"

"I'm positive. I'd have remembered."

"Yes, so would I."

"Are you all right?" she queried, out of the blue. "You seem troubled."

So . . . she felt it, too, their bizarre bond. He was doleful over his quarrel with Phillip, and it wasn't surprising that she would notice his distress.

As his response, he posed, "Do you ever wish you could alter the past?"

"Yes, all the time."

"I'd like to invent a machine that would enable me to travel back and erase all my mistakes."

"That would be grand, wouldn't it?"

She nodded, and there was a sadness about her, an ingrained sorrow and solemnity that hinted at prior tragedy, at great adversity and misery that had been routed, and he wondered what had happened to her. What misfortune had she weathered? What hideous event had left its subtle mark?

Without pausing to reflect, he narrowed the distance between them, and kissed her. The move was so forward and so presumptuous that he thoroughly shocked her—as well as himself.

For the briefest second, they clung together, so ardent that they might have been the last two people on earth. Then, as abruptly as it had started, the embrace ended. She wrenched away and leapt to her feet, her cheeks flaming, her fingers pressed to her lips.

His primary reaction was to apologize, but he wasn't sorry. Instead, he asked, "Would you walk with me some night? In the moonlight? I'd like to see it shining on your hair."

"No, I never could."

"Why?" he questioned stupidly. As if he needed her to tell him it was an idiotic request!

Acutely afflicted, she falteringly explained, "You may—or may not—marry Olivia. But if you decide *not* to, the reason can never be because of me. The Hopkins family took me in when I had nowhere else to go. They've been kind to me."

"I understand."

"You shouldn't beg me to sit again. Or to linger." She strode farther and farther away. "I'll want to say yes, but it's not a good idea. For anyone."

"You're correct, of course."

She departed, vanishing behind the shrubbery, and he listened to the brush of her slippers until they faded away.

Their affinity could only lead to disaster and regret, for it would be the height of disrespect and cruelty to dally with Winnie when he was pursuing Olivia for possible matrimony. Yet he couldn't keep himself from fantasizing over how marvelous it would be to have her as his own, or from yearning to make it a reality.

With a heavy heart, he stood and returned to the house. Alone.

CHAPTER SEVEN

Olivia sat in the garden, on the bench Penny had shown her, where she could peek through the hedges to spy on Phillip.

Margaret was visiting one of Edward's neighbors, so Olivia had come outside with her portfolio, and was pretending to draw the yard. If anyone chanced by, she had various mediocre illustrations that would prove her interest in art was a ladylike hobby and nothing she pursued with any enthusiasm.

In reality, she was drafting copies of Phillip from memory, while eager to catch a glimpse of him.

It had been three days since she'd seen him. Or more precisely, three nights. After their terrible row in the library, she'd sneaked down often, hoping he would be waiting for her, that she might apologize or discuss what had transpired, but as he'd vowed, he hadn't deigned to join her.

She was desperate to know his opinion of their tryst. For her own part, she was confused, perplexed, and restless. The ways he'd touched her had stirred her body in a fashion she didn't understand. She couldn't eat, couldn't sleep, and she was never comfortable.

Her nipples had taken on a life of their own. They were constantly erect and rubbing her chemise. Her breathing was elevated, making her corset intolerable because she couldn't fully inhale. Her loins chafed and itched for a manipulation she didn't comprehend, so she was forever shifting about on chairs, yearning to alleviate the torment.

Was he suffering misery that was remotely similar?

Oh, how could he have forsaken her so easily? She'd felt such a sense of connection with him, and it made her worry over her obligations to Lord Salisbury. Was she loose? Fickle? How could she be so enamored of Phillip when she was trying to entice Edward into marriage? What did her behavior say about her character and morals?

She'd liked what Phillip had done to her, had liked it so much that she was wild to do it over and over, as soon as a rendezvous could be arranged. Her greatest regret was that she'd panicked and had begged him to stop.

If she hadn't, they could have continued. Phillip would have unveiled the mysteries of what happened between men and women. Most certainly, he would have assuaged the corporeal distress that was driving her mad.

There had to have been an end point to their conduct, a goal or destination they were attempting to attain, and if they'd kept on, she wouldn't be languishing so dreadfully.

Through the bushes, movement captured her attention, and she slid down the bench so she could have a better perspective. Phillip! Finally! Surrounded by several men from the stables. He was leaned against the corral fence, an arm tossed across the top board. His head was tipped back, the sun on his face, and he was so handsome she could barely look at him.

A charcoal pencil was clutched in her hand, and she'd planned to sketch him, but she was frozen, unable to do anything but stare and admire. She'd had the fabulous rogue all to herself, had explored and caressed and fondled, had kissed him as if there were no tomorrow, and she was ready to do it again, if she could finagle another appointment.

But how? How to persuade him to spend time with her? It wasn't as if she could stroll over and ask him to chat. Their stations were so disparate that there was no excuse she could give as to how she'd met him. He'd declared that he wouldn't parley in the library, so what was she to do?

Morose and depressed, she observed as he tensed. The men with whom he'd been joking scattered, and another man came into view.

It was the earl! Talking to Phillip.

Seen together, they were two peas in a pod. The same height, the same broad shoulders and striking features. The only genuine contrasts were their ages, and the fact that Phillip's eyes were blue, while Edward's were brown.

Phillip was Edward's illegitimate son! There was no question. No other could have sired him. How could she not have noticed?

She was furious. He'd never told her, and that seemed like a betrayal.

She'd thought they were friends! That they'd established a bond that went beyond rank and class. Couldn't he have trusted her? Was he afraid she'd have swooned? Did he assume she'd been so sheltered that she'd never heard of bastard children?

The men exchanged harsh words—Phillip was notably aggravated—then he stomped away. Edward appeared lost and bewildered, and he lingered, then he too walked on.

For many minutes, she glared at the spot where they'd been, then she slammed her papers into her portfolio, tied the string, and in a huff, marched to the house.

How dare he ignore her! How dare he act as if she were invisible! How dare he carry on, unaffected by what had passed between them.

She rushed up the stairs to her room, and rang for a maid, who aided her in donning her riding outfit.

If Phillip wouldn't come to her, she would go to him.

Ordinarily, she wouldn't have fussed with her hair or attire, but she was resolved to be as fetching as possible during the pending confrontation, so she strutted and twirled before the mirror until every aspect was perfect. Then she waltzed downstairs and outside, her heart beating frantically.

Could she pull it off?

She flounced into the stable, and a boy greeted her, his awe apparent.

"I would speak with the stablemaster," she haughtily intoned.

The lad scurried off, and he returned with Phillip. When Phillip saw her, he shielded any reaction.

So he *worked* in the stable, did he? The lying bounder! She was so irate she could have chewed nails in half! "*You* are the stablemaster?"

"Aye." Caught in a lie, he flushed. "May I help you, milady?"

"I should like to ride. I haven't been in a long while, so I'll require you to attend me."

At her arrogant attitude, he bristled, but he replied politely. "I have a very experienced groomsman who will be more than happy to—"

"No. It shall be you."

"I'm very busy."

"Really?" she queried. "Too busy to accompany *me*? I'm the earl's *special* guest, and I implore your personal assistance. Do you refuse to provide it?"

A muscle ticked in his cheek. There were a thousand scathing retorts he was burning to hurl, a hundred ways he'd like to bring her down a peg, but the stableboy was dawdling next to him, so he couldn't unleash his wrath.

He bowed, acknowledging defeat. "At your service, *milady*."

The boy escorted her to the mounting block where she waited. Shortly, Phillip emerged, leading two horses. Aloof and efficient, he lifted her up, but the instant she was seated, he jumped away.

Without glancing at him, she spurred her horse forward, and she knew he'd follow. He couldn't let her traipse off unchaperoned. Soon, a second pair of hooves trailed along behind. Rage at her autocratic manner billowed off him in waves and, she had to confess, she was a tad shocked herself. She never flung her position or status at others, and the sole rationale she could devise for exhibiting such snobbery was that he mattered to her, and she was determined to be with him.

She hated having him watch her. While he was an equestrian expert, *she* was a novice. It had been years since she'd ridden, and she hoped she hadn't forgotten how, that she wouldn't embarrass herself by losing her balance and falling on her rear. What a jolly laugh he'd have at her expense!

The mare had a smooth gait, so she adapted and did her best to feign skill. Without delay, they were away from the yard, alone, and on a quiet lane, shaded by trees. She glowered over her shoulder and accused, "You haven't come to the library."

"I told you I wouldn't."

"I didn't believe you."

He shrugged, as if he couldn't care less. Considering how thrilled she'd been at meeting him, and how their secret assignations had absorbed her every waking moment, his detachment infuriated her.

"You're his son, aren't you?" she blurted, wanting to jolt a response out of him.

"Whose?" he casually inquired.

"Lord Salisbury's."

He shrugged again.

"At least have the decency to admit it to me!" she shouted.

"Yes, I am Lord Salisbury's son. Phillip Paxton. Is that what you're dying to learn?"

She tugged on the reins, her horse whirling toward him, and she sidled over until they were side by side, the animals facing opposite directions, her knees and legs squashed against his.

Phillip scrutinized her; he was nervous and disconcerted, as though—given her condition—he couldn't predict what she might do.

Good! Let him stew!

"Why couldn't you confide in me?" she demanded. "Was I simply a bit of fluff you found amusing to tease and to—"

He reached across the space separating them and laid his hand atop hers, the gesture stopping her petulant tirade. "He insisted that you not know. That I hide myself."

His rejoinder was the last one she'd anticipated, and it sucked the force from her anger. "Why?"

"Because he didn't want your exalted presence to be sullied by mine."

"But that's . . . that's . . ."

She was about to say *cruel* and *stupid* and *uncalled for,* except that Edward's conduct was not only normal but expected from a nobleman who was entertaining a bridal candidate. He wouldn't want his potential wife's initial opinion of his integrity to be based on the news that he sired illicit children on inappropriate women.

"Idiotic?" he finished for her.

"Yes."

"Typical is more likely," he scoffed. "He's always concealed me from your kind. I'm used to it."

He made the assertion flippantly, but she discerned

that this was an old wound, festering as though it had just been inflicted.

"Who was your mother?"

"A housemaid. Who would you suppose?"

"Did he love her?"

"*Love* her? You're jesting. He was eighteen, the lord's son, and he could do whatever he pleased—to whomever he pleased. She was young and foolish and presumed his promises held some value."

"I see," she mused.

"No you don't. You don't *see* anything." He tightened his grip on the reins. "I don't have the patience for your nonsense. Let's get back."

His coldness and nonchalance baffled her, and she yearned to break through the wall of indifference he'd built, but she wasn't sure how.

"I don't want to leave. I want to talk with you."

"Well, milady, *I* don't want to talk with you. Don't seek me out. I have a job, and I'd like to keep it."

He was antagonistic, callous, and his demeanor offered no hint of the impertinent, intriguing man with whom she'd trifled, and a terrible suspicion dawned on her.

"Why did you philander with me in the library? Was it merely to retaliate against your father because he'd warned you away from me?"

"Of course," he contended. "Why else would I have done it?"

"Of course," she repeated somberly.

How pathetic she was! How daft and obtuse. She was so unschooled that she'd irrationally succumbed to his flirtations, reading into them all sorts of affection that didn't exist.

She'd never been more humiliated, and she was desperate to flee to the manor so she could lock herself into her room till her shame waned. Though in light of her level of mortification, she might be sequestered through-out eternity!

"I apologize for accosting you, Mr. Paxton. It shan't happen again."

She'd intended to ride on, with her head high and her pride intact, but chagrin brought on a flood of tears, so that she couldn't detect the road, and she prayed the horse could make its way home by itself.

He noted her dolor, and before she could urge the mare away, he murmured a command that had the animal halting in its tracks.

"I didn't mean what I said," he claimed.

"Yes you did."

"I'm sorry."

"Just let me go."

"The night we met, I stumbled upon you by accident."

"Have mercy, Mr. Paxton! I've no need of an explanation."

"I was angry at my father, so I thought it would be amusing to pester you. But after—the next time and the next—I came because of you. It didn't have anything to do with my father."

She was torn, pining to believe him but not certain she could. Where he was concerned, she was out of her element, and so greedy to assume his fondness was sincere that she would likely ascribe credence to any remark he chose to utter.

He pulled her off her horse and onto his own. She was on his lap, in his arms.

"I want you, Livvie," he declared, "as a husband wants his wife. With every breath I take, I long for you to be mine. But to what end?"

"I don't know," she wailed.

"Where can this lead us?"

"I have no answers."

"Do you have any idea of the catastrophe that will result if we're discovered?"

"Yes."

"But I could never marry you, as circumstances would warrant. I have no property, scarcely any salary. Only the clothes on my back are my own. I have nothing. I could give you nothing. Do you understand?"

It was so hopeless! They were crazed to persist, but his mouth was on hers, and he was kissing her with a wild abandon that made her ignore her family's dire plight, her marriage to Edward, Helen's welfare.

When he touched her, she became someone else, someone she didn't recognize, who was equipped to forsake all propriety, all virtue and respectability. She would gladly submit to any reckless deed if he was the one who asked it of her.

What had befallen her? Why couldn't she control this bizarre spiral?

His hands were on the front of her dress, and he caressed her breasts through the fabric. With an incorrigible, rash hunger, she needed this licentious fondling, and she groaned with delight.

"God, you're so passionate," he maintained. "So eager."

"For you, Phillip," she pledged. "Only for you."

They kissed for an eternity, there on the isolated lane, the sun shimmering through the trees, the birds squawking from the branches. The ardor gradually faded, and their lips parted.

Phillip stared, cataloguing her features. "So . . . we're to keep on?"

"There's no alternative, is there?"

"No, I don't imagine there is," he said, resigned. "Visit me tonight."

"In the library?"

"No. At my cottage behind one of the barns. I'll show you where it is when we approach the manor. Can you?"

"I'll find a way."

He released her, positioning her on her own saddle. During the fervid embrace, her hair and gown had been mussed, and he straightened them until she was in a satisfactory condition.

They'd have to arrive in the yard as the strangers others envisioned them to be, and she hated having to pretend no knowledge or partiality.

She traced a finger across his cheek, his lips, imprinting the memory.

"Don't ever shun me or send me away," she implored. "I can't bear it."

"I won't," he promised, but as he made the vow, she knew he would never be able to keep it.

What did the future portend? How could this debacle have a favorable conclusion? Had she no common sense remaining?

Apparently not, for she was ready to risk any hazard simply to be with him.

Discouraged, frightened, weary, she nudged her horse away and started toward the house. At a proper, allowable distance, he tracked after her—the perfect groom.

They rode on—the noblewoman and earl's daughter, the working man and employee—the vastness of an immense universe separating them.

Penelope peered up and down the pretentious supper table, assessing Lord Salisbury's guests. He'd invited many people: the neighboring gentry, the vicar and his wife, the local squire. The stodgy group was supposed to impress, but Penny found them to be boorish and dreary.

A predictable country soiree, it had commenced with

the tedious drinking of spirits in the parlor, followed by the monotonous repast in the enormous dining room, then the chatting and socializing.

It wasn't as formal and stuffy as the parties Margaret hosted in London, but still, Penny was bored to tears. Even the prospect that there might be dancing later had failed to elevate her spirits.

As usual, Margaret was watching her like a hawk, prepared to pounce for the least indiscretion. She couldn't walk in the garden without feeling like a felon. She'd tried to flirt with some of the lads at the stables, but the stablemaster had made short shrift of any attempts at fraternization.

The sole diversion to be had was her regular jaunts to Olivia's bedchamber, where she sneaked peeks at her portfolio. What a scandalous thrill that daily ritual had turned out to be!

Olivia expended an excessive amount of energy drawing her lover in various stages of dishabille.

How had Olivia initiated the brazen affair? It was a question that vexed Penny. Her stepsister was too sedate and dignified to remove her clothes and fornicate with a man, and Penny had no doubt that was what was occurring. Olivia couldn't have dreamed up the wicked scenes. They were too lifelike.

Where did they convene for their assignations?

She'd striven to catch them together but hadn't had any luck. The lone occasion she'd coaxed Olivia out to the yard, so that she could gauge her reaction to the half-naked, burly fellow, Olivia had hardly evinced any response, and Penny had been so disappointed.

What she wouldn't give to spy on them while they were in the throes of passion!

Across the table, one of the earl's neighbors, who'd been introduced as Freddy Blaine, was furtively appraising her. He was the son of a lowly baronet, and she'd overheard her mother muttering that he was a ne'er-do-well and a miscreant, so Penny's curiosity had been piqued.

Anyone Margaret didn't like, Penny tended to like very much; in addition, there was the merriment to be had by goading Margaret into a dither.

Though he endeavored to hide it, he was inspecting her with an obvious, nefarious intent. Whenever he could get away with it, his gaze dropped to her cleavage and lingered, so as she felt it, she thrust her bosom up and out.

Hah! Let the old reprobate see what he was missing!

She guessed his age to be near to the earl's, and with his wavy brown hair and hazel eyes, he was handsome, in a crude sort of way. He was tall and thin, not gone to fat and gout as so many of the older men had done, and the gleam in his regard was exciting.

After viewing Olivia's pictures of the stablemaster, she was curious about dallying with a grown man. While boys appealed to her, their awkward fumbling in dark corners had left much to be desired, and she conjectured as to how a more mature chap would differ. Would it be more fun?

She glanced around. No one was paying her any attention, especially her mother, who had harangued the vicar's wife into a stupor, so she latched onto Mr. Blaine's stare. For a moment, they connected, and in a flash, a world of understanding passed between them. He lifted a brow and quirked his head, accepting her forwardness as a proposition.

The interminable feast finally ended, and she was forced to endure several hours of inane mingling. While there was card playing, nobody was sufficiently enterprising to rearrange the couches so there could be dancing. The only benefit of the horrid evening was that Margaret was engaged in conversation, so Penny could pilfer from the brandy decanter without others noticing.

While Margaret permitted her to have watered-down wine with her meals, Penny preferred the stronger spirits that Margaret had strictly forbidden her to sample. She liked how liquor made her tingle and prickle, how she felt powerful and invincible, and by the time the guests began to depart, she was giddy, though she masked any exuberance.

Freddy Blaine had sought to get close all night, but there had always been so blasted many people flitting about that they hadn't had a second to palaver privately. As he went to make his farewell to the earl, he sauntered by where Penny was loitering next to the sideboard.

"Meet me in the gazebo," she whispered. "In fifteen minutes."

Heart pounding, she dawdled until another couple had exited, then she pleaded her own fatigue and obtained Margaret's permission to retire. In her bedchamber, she tarried just long enough to fetch a cloak, then she tiptoed down the servants' staircase. In a thrice, she was stealing across the rear lawn.

The gazebo loomed, white and eerie in the moonlight, and the air was so still that she wondered if he was truly inside. Then a horse snorted from behind the decorative building, and with a look over her shoulder, she climbed the steps.

He was sitting in the shadows, lounging on a cushioned bench, one ankle crossed over the other.

"Well, well," he chided, "if it isn't the earl's wee daughter." Suddenly unsure, she hesitated, and he patted his leg. "Come here, you impertinent wench."

"I can't stay. I—"

"Now!" he hissed, intimidating her with the harsh edict, and without argument, she did as he bid.

Seizing her wrist, he jerked her down, her bottom perched on his thigh, her breasts crushed to his chest.

Her prior forays into coquetry had been leveled on boys, so she had no experience in dealing with an adult male. He knew what he wanted, and it dawned on her that she might have been a tad more adventurous than was wise. She braced against his shoulder, trying to push herself off him, but he wouldn't let her go.

Where her hip was wedged into the vee between his thighs, his manly rod was erect, and he didn't strive to conceal it. She knew what it meant for him to be so cocked—the housemaids were incredibly indiscreet with their chatter—and butterflies swarmed through her stomach.

"What do you want of me, little girl?"

"Nothing."

"Liar," he scolded. "This is your party, and I'm here at your request."

"Well, I've changed my mind," she pouted. "I don't like you. You're entirely too arrogant."

He chuckled. "You were plenty flagrant with your *appetites* at supper. Don't let shyness overtake you this late in the game."

"You flatter yourself if you thought I was interested in you."

Bold as brass, he cupped one of her breasts. "You're awfully proud of this pair," he taunted. "Are they real? Or do you use padding to disguise the fact that you're a child?"

"I'm not a child!" she huffed, and she was furious.

Who was he to scorn her? To harass and insult? The gall! She started to resist, wanting to return to the manor, when he slipped his hand under the bodice of her dress and tugged the fabric down so that her breasts were exposed, her nipples puckering.

"Aye, they're *real* enough," he derided. "Not much to speak of, though."

"Bastard!" she seethed. She tried to slap him, but she had no leverage with which to land an effective blow.

He countered immediately, with scarcely any effort, pinning her arms behind her back. The maneuver further revealed her breasts, providing him with an even better glimpse of what she no longer wished to show him. He gripped one of her nipples and squeezed until it hurt.

"Let me go!" She kicked with her feet and wrestled with her hips, yet she didn't actually want to get away. She was stimulated by how he was holding her captive, how she couldn't escape.

"You like it rough, do you?" He was hauling up her skirt. "Well, so do I."

In a coarse fashion, he bent over and sucked at her nipple, while his fingers slithered into her womanly sheath. She was wet, ready, and the location of his hand was so naughty and so wrong that it seemed to burn her.

Abruptly, he withdrew, and bluntly inquired, "Is this a narrow, virgin's puss?"

She was determined to put him in his place, to have him deem her to be older than she really was. "Hardly," she boasted. "I've had dozens of lovers."

"I'll bet you have, you slattern."

No one had ever been so rude to her! "Don't call me names."

"If the shoe fits . . ." He stood and began to unfasten his trousers.

"What are you doing?" she asked nervously.

"I aim to find out if that mouth of yours is good for anything besides spewing sass." The last button fell free, and his phallus was hovering behind the loosened placard. "Get down on your knees."

She was aware of what he wanted—her coterie of admiring boys had often joked about it—and she was paralyzed between apprehension and willingness. He clutched her shoulder, her mouth in front of his crotch.

"Suck me off," he decreed. "I would have a French kiss."

"No!"

He retrieved his John Thomas from his pants. It was her first chance to see one, and she was only inches away. The dastardly thing was mesmerizing, hideous, all red and covered with thick, pulsating veins. She was fascinated, terrified.

He stroked the crown against her lips. "Open up, my pretty harlot."

She wouldn't, keeping her lips compressed, and he grasped her neck, battling to compel her to take him inside. They scuffled, but he grew weary and tossed her away. Banging to the floor with a loud thump, she struggled to her knees, then her feet, straightening her gown, shielding her breasts from his torrid gaze.

Disgusted, he loomed over her.

The presumptuous swine! How dare he think poorly of her!

"You're a pathetic cock tease," he sneered as he stuffed his privy parts into his pants. "Strutting your ass all over, and cramming your tits in a bloke's face whenever he turns around. Lucky for you that I refuse to copulate with children."

"I'm not a child!" she angrily repeated.

"How old are you? Twelve? Thirteen?"

"How old are *you*?" she snapped.

"Forty-three. I'm a full-grown man, and I know how to act like one."

"I'm twenty-two," she fibbed, desperate to sound more sophisticated than she was.

"Right!" he scoffed. "Well, don't come sniffing round me again unless you're prepared to follow through. Next time, I won't be so accommodating of your maidenly hysterics."

"Ooh, you . . . you . . ." She couldn't conceive of a derogatory word to describe him.

"Begone," he muttered. "I'm sick of your juvenile ways."

He shoved her toward the stairs, and like a frightened nitwit, she ran off into the night.

CHAPTER EIGHT

Phillip stood next to the door of his cottage, watching for movement on the length of lawn that separated the manor from his humble domicile. Off in the distance, thunder rumbled with the approach of a summer storm, and the air smelled verdant and moist.

Olivia was coming to him. Any second, she'd be flitting through the hedges in a wild dash to his cottage, but what did he intend when she arrived?

Would he have sexual intercourse with her? Was he bent on ruining her? Could he cuckold his father so horridly?

The obvious answer was no, he couldn't. In the beginning, he'd considered an affair, but the reality was that, deep down, he loved Edward and couldn't hurt him. So if he didn't contemplate fornicating with her, what was his goal? Why had he urged her to visit?

It was a query that vexed him. Though he'd fumed and ruminated, he had no explanation for his behavior. He *had* to see her again, *had* to seize this rare opportunity to be with her, and he couldn't predict a future beyond that limited, selfish focus, even though what he was doing was wrong.

Across the way, he saw her. Though she'd tossed a cloak over her golden hair, he could tell from her smooth gait that it was she. Any passerby would suspect her to be a housemaid, sneaking out for a rendezvous.

There was a pounding in his ears, and he didn't know

if it was the impending thunder or the frantic beating of his heart.

The expanse of grass seemed impossibly long, and her trek transpired with an eerie slowness of motion that had him mulling why he'd suggested she make the dangerous journey. Each step was fraught with peril.

The library had been a precarious location, and they'd courted disaster in the times they'd met there.

He'd deemed his home to be a better alternative, and he had to admit that he was vain enough to want her in his own house, in his own bed, to imagine her there after she'd gone. Or perhaps it was more complicated. Perhaps he couldn't stand to woo her under his father's roof.

Finally, finally, she was across and, ere she could utter a word, he swept her into his arms and over the threshold, closed and barred the door.

For several moments, she tarried—hushed and still—peering out from beneath the hood of the cloak. Her blue eyes were round, luminous, and tension rippled off her. He reached up and pulled down the hood.

"I'm glad you came," he said, shattering the silence.

"So am I."

Her voice was tremulous, her anxiety palpable, and he hugged her, stroking his fingers up and down her back.

"Don't be afraid," he whispered.

"I'm not."

Untying her wrap, he slipped it off her shoulders, hanging it on a hook by the door, and the garment looked incongruous next to his functional coats and hats.

He took her hands in his, clutching them and running his thumbs over the centers of her palms. Like a smitten dolt, he could have dawdled all night, gawking at her.

"This was a bad idea," she ventured.

"I know."

"We're crazy."

"Without a doubt."

In tacit recognition of their mutual insanity, they smiled, but neither was willing to call a halt or recant. Phillip felt as if they'd been bound with a rope that was dragging them toward an unseen destiny. They couldn't hinder or reverse the tugging toward this inevitability; they could only hold on.

He kissed her, a soft brushing of his lips to hers. The contact was fleeting, tempered, the sort a boy might bestow on his sweetheart. As their lips parted, she was staring up at him, her candor and genuineness visible, and his conscience had him squirming.

She was so fine, so much more than he'd ever pictured for himself, and he was so unworthy of her, but he couldn't stop what he was doing. He *had* to have her and damn the consequences.

"Come." He led her to the bedchamber at the rear of the cottage. As they went, she glanced around, assessing his possessions, and he couldn't help but wonder as to her opinion.

What would she make of the person they depicted him to be?

His lodgings were a bachelor's abode, with simple furnishings, plain rugs and curtains, stark mahogany against white walls. There was no feminine touch evident, no knitted throws or crocheted pillows, no needlepoint samplers or colorful figurines on the mantel. It was tidy, due to the efforts of a maid Edward sent on a regular basis.

Books were stacked on a shelf along the wall—titles on animal husbandry with a few scattered novels cast into the mix—a chess set on a table, a desk littered with account ledgers where he recorded the expenditures of the stables for his father.

They were modest chattels that indicated an unpretentious, uncomplicated existence, and though previously, he'd felt content with his assets, compared to hers, his status appeared paltry and insignificant.

Would she scorn him for his lack of wealth?

As they crossed into his room, she espied his bed and hesitated, then followed, which he considered to be very brave. This had to be the first occasion she'd ever been in a man's bedchamber. He proceeded straight to the bed and lay down, bringing her with him so that the awkwardness would be over before she could reflect upon it.

She stretched out, her skirt floating down to tangle over his legs, but, unable to dispel her nervousness, she braced herself on an arm, hovering above him. Her hair was down, secured by a loose cord of green ribbon. He jerked it away, and her locks cascaded over her shoulder in a luxurious blond wave. She looked wanton and seductive, goading his masculine sensibilities to a new height.

Though he couldn't resolve what he wanted to do with her, he was afire, his restraint tethered by a slender thread. He needed to slow down, to ponder his path lest he overwhelm her with his burgeoning ardor.

Rolling to his side, he shifted her so that they were facing one another, his eyes searching hers.

"Are you going to marry my father, Livvie?"

"I thought I could but . . ." The comment faded, her distress and bafflement apparent.

"Why would you? The two of you are a strange pair." She was troubled by his inquiry, and he soothed, "You can confide in me. It will be all right."

After an arduous vacillation, she said, "You must swear that you'll never repeat this to another soul."

"I promise."

"My father died last year."

"I'm aware of that."

"Since then, we've been informed that the estate is bankrupt."

"So you must wed him."

"Yes."

"Have you apprised Edward of your financial quandary?"

"No"—she gripped his arm—"and you vowed not to tell. I have no dowry remaining, and if he learned the truth . . ."

Did she presume it was a keepable secret? That his solicitors wouldn't investigate? "When are you planning to break the news to him?"

"My stepmother is convinced that if he proposes, he'll be too much of a gentleman to renege when he's advised of our plight. You're well acquainted with him. Are we foolish to hope?"

"Edward can be very generous," he acknowledged. With his vast fortune, and benevolent nature, he was the type who might assist them. "Is the situation really that dire?"

"There are five females in my family. We have no revenue or resources, and my niece, Helen, is—" She stopped.

"Is what?" he prodded.

"Is ill," she claimed. "Their fates are riding on me, and the pressure is enormous. What if I can't win Edward's favor? What if I can't save them?"

Dispirited by her admissions, he snuggled her to him. What folly had he instituted by pursuing her? While he'd fathomed that any association was infeasible, he hadn't realized the full extent of the circumstances that were motivating her. They could never wed, and even though he grasped this fact, it was difficult to accept.

Idiotically, he wished that *he* had the capacity to aid her, that it could be himself, instead of his father, who was rich enough to effect a rescue. For once, he was desperate to act as champion and savior.

They couldn't aspire to intimacy. She had to be free of his shadow so that she could fraternize with Edward unencumbered, so that she wouldn't be tempted or swayed into doing what she oughtn't.

He would protect her from herself. As an adult, conversant with the perils of desire, he knew—as she could not—how it could lead her astray. She needed to focus on Edward, and not be sidetracked by their flirtation into thinking that Phillip was the superior choice.

But still, even as he chastised and reproached himself, he couldn't let her leave. If nothing else, he could introduce her to the rites of passion, so that—on her wedding night—she would have some idea of what would occur. Without venturing too far, he could confer the experience she lacked, could alleviate many maidenly fears.

Draping her across his front, he clasped her buttocks, pulling her loins into his, and kissed her, a leisurely, methodical exploration.

"I want to make love to you." To himself, he added, *Just this once. Then never again.*

"I'm not sure what that means."

"We'll start out as we did in the library." He was unbuttoning her dress. "Only we'll continue."

"To where?"

"I'll show you."

"There's an end?"

"Oh, yes. There's definitely an end."

"I'm so glad to hear it!"

He chuckled, elated that she'd been aroused and out of sorts. In her elevated condition, what he was about to do would be so much more satisfying.

The bodice of her dress was slackened, and it slithered away. Her breasts were bare, the two delicious mounds revealed, and the delightful, elongated tips dangled over his eager mouth.

"I adore it when you don't wear your corset." He nestled down to garner a better vantage point, and he played, nipping at and nursing on her.

"Ooh . . ." she murmured, "I've been dying for you to do that."

"Have you?"

"Yes, you cad. You'd left me in a desperate condition. I've been cursing you all week."

He pinched and squeezed. "Poor baby."

"I've been so miserable! I kept feeling as if I were going to burst."

"We can't have that, can we?"

He sucked at her nipple, taking it far inside, taunting and biting it until it was raw and distended, then he moved to the other, laving it with the same fierce attention. Of their own accord, her hips flexed, and he matched her languid tempo, but he was too aroused by her. His lust was increasing, and he grappled to constrain himself. He needed to bridle his hunger, to make the experience last as long as he was able.

Easing her onto her back, he inched her skirt up her legs, his torment multiplying. She arched and purred, acquiescing as he petted her calves, her knees, but as he reached her thighs, she tensed.

"Relax," he coaxed, gentling her as one might a skittish colt.

"This doesn't feel . . . you shouldn't be . . ."

"When we're together like this, everything is allowed."

"It's too personal, too . . . too . . ."

He slid up till he was rubbing her belly. "Too what?"

"Phillip!" she squealed.

"Everything is allowed," he repeated.

To stifle her protests, and to keep her distracted, he abandoned her bosom, blazing a trail up her chest until he was kissing her once more. As she eased into the kiss, he flattened the heel of his hand on her mons. The silky hairs of her privates prickled his skin.

"What are you doing to me?" she panted. "And why?"

"There's pleasure to be found here. Let me give it to you."

"Pleasure? How? Where?"

"I'm going to touch you, as no one else has." With no further warning, he slipped two fingers inside her. She was wet, her womanly juices flowing. Her sheath was tight, virginal, and her inner muscles clenched around him.

"Oh, God . . ." she breathed. "What's happening to me?"

"This is how a man caresses a woman, how a husband caresses his wife."

"It can't be!"

"It is, Livvie. Trust me."

Commencing slowly, he stroked inside her, back and forth, back and forth, letting her acclimate to the glide of his hand, the illicit intrusion. Initially, she was rigid, strained, shocked by the strange and unexpected trespass, but gradually, she relented and accepted his ministrations.

He intensified the massage, delving more deeply, penetrating as far as he could, then pulling out, mimicking the thrust of a phallus, giving her the stimulation she craved.

She was spiraling higher, her sensual nature taking wing, her erotic instincts conveying her to where she'd never gone before. From her trepidation, it was obvious she'd never journeyed down this prurient path, and he pushed her faster, faster.

She writhed, frantic, her hips working furiously. Though her mind was at odds over what she wanted, and how she should behave, her torso knew what it needed. She was at the precipice and ready to jump over the edge.

"Please," she begged, "I don't like it. I can't bear any more."

"We're almost finished."

"Phillip!" she wailed.

"Now, love. Do it for me."

He dipped to her breast, suckled her, while he flicked his thumb, dabbing at her sexual center. With great relish, she soared to the heavens, and she cried out, thrilling him with how completely she fell to pieces.

Kissing her soundly, he swallowed her joy, reveling in the moment, ecstatic that he'd imparted her first orgasm.

As the turbulence diminished, her agitation abated, and she calmed. He softened his kiss, tasting and savoring her essence. Heedful that she might be embarrassed by her raucous display, he extracted his hand, and lowered her skirt.

Eventually, she exhaled a huge breath of air. "What was that?"

"The French call it the *petite mort.*"

" 'The little death,' " she translated. "I can see why."

"It kills you a bit, every time."

"It can happen more than once?"

The innocent question charmed him. "Over and over."

"I'll die in your arms."

He laughed. "I doubt it."

She frowned, her pretty brow furrowing. "How could I be twenty-three years old and not know about this?"

"It's a secret of the marital bed."

"Aah . . ." she mused, contemplating, then she halted. "Wait a minute. Have you ever been married?"

"No."

"Then how do *you* know about it?"

He blushed. While he was no flagrant fornicator like some of the aristocrats' sons with whom he'd soldiered, he'd never been a monk.

"Well I . . . I . . ." he stammered.

He couldn't clarify whereby he'd gleaned his information.

"Oh, I get it," she chided. "You're a scoundrel and a rake, the type about which my stepmother has always admonished."

As she was arrayed on his bed, with her breasts naked and her dress rucked up, he couldn't deny it.

"Perhaps," he allowed.

"No wonder we virgins are counseled about you knaves. If we were apprised of the forthcoming wickedness, we'd never delay to our wedding nights."

"That is a major concern."

She chortled and extended her arms over her head. Her breasts were still uncovered, and she was at ease with him, in no hurry to shield herself now that the ardor had waned, yet he was in a serious state. His appetite hadn't been slaked, and it was difficult to pretend he was in the mood to chat. What he truly wanted to do was ravage her, and it took every ounce of his willpower to check himself.

"Why haven't you married?" she queried out of the blue.

"I never met anyone who tickled my fancy."

"Would you?" She rotated to her side, assessing him. "If you found the right girl, I mean."

"Of course."

"Would you marry *me* if you could?"

He smiled. She was so sassy, so rumpled and disheveled. What man wouldn't grab her if he had the chance? "In a heartbeat, Lady O."

She smiled, too, then snuggled herself into the crook of his neck where she confessed, "I wish you could."

"So do I." The admission surprised him. The notion of wedding her was so far-fetched that he couldn't believe they were discussing it.

What was to be gained by such irrational speculation?

She was an untried maid, and he needed to tread carefully with her. Passion could befuddle and overwhelm. She'd just had an orgasm, and she was already confusing carnality with affection. He needed to ensure that her imprudent emotions didn't take her where she could never go.

They were silent, treasuring the quiet companionship, when she drew back to look him. "Tell me more about it."

"About what?"

"The wedding night and what transpires. Suddenly, I realize that I am ignorant of many important facts that could soon rule my life."

"I'm not the person who should advise you."

"Why not?"

"Well, it *is* your husband's privilege and duty," he stupidly proclaimed.

She glanced down at her bared bosom. "It's a tad late to worry about that, don't you think?"

Giggling, she spun away, laughing full and long, and he joined in her mirth.

Their situation was ludicrous. She was destined to wed his father, or another nobleman like him. Phillip had no place with her, and never would. She had burdens and obligations that weighed her down, that he could never assume for her.

He had no business instructing her in the art of loving or anything else, but he'd just had his mouth on her breast and his hand inside her feminine sheath. They were far beyond polite discourse or drawing room etiquette.

What conduct was appropriate from this point onward?

"Explain the rest," she implored. "I would have you relieve me of my naïveté."

And maybe her virginity, if they weren't cautious.

Before she'd arrived, he'd pondered whether he intended to proceed to deflowerment, and he now conceived that the brazen act would never be attempted. He couldn't ruin her for the beneficial marriage she was desperate to make. He liked her too much to undermine her prospects, and he wouldn't permit himself to cross that decisive line.

But without doing any irreversible damage, he could verbally educate her as to what was coming.

"Do you remember in the library," he began, "when you were quizzing me about the erotica?"

"Aye."

"You asked me if your husband would expect you to disrobe."

"And you said yes."

"He will require much more than your removing your clothes."

"What more is there?" She was solemn, the jocularity having faded.

"A man and woman do things to each other, to physically titillate."

"And their deeds involve nudity?"

"Usually."

"It's enjoyable?"

"Very."

"I was skeptical before"—she flashed a naughty grin—"but your current performance has forced me to conclude that you could be correct. I never thought I'd admit that stripping myself could be . . . so . . . so stimulating."

"Your reaction will be ever more vehement, as you grow more comfortable with your partner."

"How could it possibly become more intense?"

"Repetition. Familiarity. They decrease your restraint and wreak havoc on your control."

"Hmm . . ." She reflected. "I like the sound of that. And as to the man . . . what does the woman give to him?"

As they talked, she was toying with his shirt, the buttons being unfastened one by one, until the front was open, and she was stroking his chest. The seductive massage, coupled with his unsated desire, made it hard to concentrate on what she was saying.

"The male is built differently from the female."

"How?"

"In his private parts." He guided her hand to his crotch, letting her investigate the bulge in his pants. "A man has a sort of rod or staff between his legs, where a woman has none."

"What's this rod called?"

"It has many names: a phallus, a cock, a penis."

"For what is it used?"

"For mating. And for pleasure." She was exploring, manipulating the fabric in an effort to estimate size and shape.

"How does one go about mating? I've always been curious."

"The man thrusts the rod inside the woman's body—"

"Inside? You're joking. Where?"

"Here." He cupped her. "Then he flexes his hips in a brisk rhythm, and the motion produces a friction that causes a white cream to erupt from the tip. The cream is his seed, and when it's spewed into the womb, they can create a babe."

She gawked at him. "That is the strangest tale I've ever heard."

"It seems implausible—until you experience it for yourself."

"Can a man be *satisfied* without actually mating?"

"Oh, yes."

She was more bold in her examination. "How is it accomplished?"

"Well"—she grazed her thumb directly on the tip, and his discipline nearly snapped—"a woman can rub the man's phallus with her hands, or take it into her mouth."

"Her mouth!" She inspected his pants. "Very intriguing."

With each detail he divulged, she was more inquisitive, and she clambered up on her knees, straddling his thighs to better peruse his loins. "How do you walk about with this protrusion in the way?"

"Normally"—he chuckled—"it's flaccid."

"It's not flaccid now."

"No, it's not. I'm aroused."

"You are?"

"Very much so."

"You want me." She was amazed. Exhilarated.

"Yes."

"When a woman trifles with a man's phallus, does he feel what I did a few minutes ago?"

"It's very similar."

"Will you show me how to do it for you?"

Sweat pooled on his brow. She was loosening his trousers! He'd never been much of a gentleman, but in this instance, he'd planned to do his best, and he was determined to stop her—he really and truly was—but somewhere between his brain and his tongue, the command to desist was lost. He was struck dumb, and all he could do was observe the subtle glide of her slender, crafty fingers.

"Livvie," he ground out, "you shouldn't do this."

"Why? You did it to me. It was magnificent."

"But you don't understand how it ends." She dipped her fingers under the placard, and bare skin impacted with bare skin. Her fist encircled him. "Oh, Jesus . . ."

She paused. "I want to look at you. May I?"

No, no, no, his brain shouted, but he merely glared at her. He was frazzled, strained beyond his limit. If she journeyed a step further down this road, he couldn't be responsible for what he might do.

"Livvie," he barked, "a man can become too eager, to where he can't curb his behavior. You're playing with fire."

"But you would never hurt me."

"Not deliberately."

She smiled, not believing his admonition, and with a flick of her wrist, she had him exposed to the cool evening air. Mesmerized and enthralled, she visually analyzed every inch. Under her torrid scrutiny, his cock came alive. It was savage, throbbing, distending even more, and stretching out toward her.

"It's huge," she remarked, unperturbed. "Are they all so large?"

"I'm big. Bigger than most."

They engaged in a staring contest, and he didn't know if he was daring her to progress or daring her not to. If she touched him again, he'd explode. If she didn't, the same result would occur.

Without warning, she leaned down, gripped him and . . . took him into her mouth! The deed was so unanticipated, so shocking and so outrageous, that he almost spilled himself.

Wildly, he grabbed for her and tossed her aside, then he jumped out of the bed as though it had snakes in it. His breathing labored, his pulse pounding, he stomped across the small room, facing away from her, a hand balanced on the wall.

His knees were weak, his composure shattered. How had he plummeted to this bizarre juncture? With her practically begging to be compromised, and himself fighting to keep her chaste. He'd never suffered through such a ridiculous, incongruous moment in his entire life.

"Phillip," she hailed from behind him, "what is it? What did I do wrong?"

"Oh, Livvie," he groaned, calming, and stuffing his privates into his pants. "It wasn't *wrong*."

"But you said women put their mouths on you. Wasn't I supposed to?" She was climbing off the bed and crossing to him, and she rested her palm on his shoulder. "I only wanted to make you happy."

He wrapped an arm around her, nestling her to him, and he kept her there as he collected himself. When he could speak without sounding like a fool, he kissed the top of her head.

"You must return to the manor."

"Don't be angry."

"I'm not. I just need some time to think."

"About what?"

"About us"—he gestured between them, indicating what he couldn't put into words—"and where this attraction is leading. I want you more than I've ever wanted anything, but I can't do this to you. Or to my father."

"But I've decided I can't marry him. Not after being here with you."

"Don't say it." He pressed a finger to her lips, silencing her. "Especially now, after our passions have so recently flared. You need to reflect, too."

"No I don't," she insisted. "After I've lain with you, I could never do the same with him."

"But Livvie, even if you cried off with Edward, *we* could never marry. There are too many people depending on you. You can't forsake them for the likes of me."

"What if I did?" she suddenly, recklessly broached. "What if, for once, I considered myself, and what *I* want and need?"

Though he recognized that she was spewing nonsense, his idiotic heart leapt at the marvelous possibility, and he tamped down his asinine exuberance. "That's not who you are. You could never abandon those you love."

They'd never discussed this facet of her personality, but he knew it with an unwavering certainty. Though she might fret over the onus placed upon her, in the end, she would do her duty.

"Let's get you back to the house." He led her out to the main room. She followed and dawdled as he retrieved her cloak, as he settled it over her shoulders, and adjusted the hood. He brushed a kiss across her lips, and she crushed him in a fierce hug.

"I'll come to you tomorrow night."

Tell her no! his mind screamed, but what emerged was, "All right. I'll be waiting."

He peeked outside to ensure it was safe, then, without a farewell, she slid away and was swallowed up by the shadows. Loitering, he listened and watched, until he saw her sneak in the servants' entrance, and he sank against the stoop.

What was he doing? What was he hoping to achieve? How could this have a good end?

Disturbed, distraught, more sexually frustrated than he'd ever been, he went inside and shut the door.

CHAPTER NINE

Winnie stood in the middle of the dark garden, her hair down and blowing in the wind, her robe and night rail flattened to her torso. Lightning rent the black sky, and the crack of thunder that followed was too close and rattled through her bones.

Like a pagan goddess of old, she curled her toes into the grass and lifted her arms to the heavens, reaching out in supplication for a solace she couldn't name.

The weather was warm and sultry with the prospect of imminent rain, and the approaching storm sizzled through her, leaving her wanton and rash. Her restlessness had compelled her to escape the stifling confines of her bedchamber, but it was impossible to flee from the dissatisfaction that was slowly eating her alive.

She couldn't run far enough or fast enough.

The trip to Salisbury, her encountering the earl, had stirred the soul of a woman she'd believed buried, and for some reason, her meeting Edward Paxton had effected a resurrection.

For almost two decades, she'd convinced herself that she was content, that her serene, tedious existence in the Hopkinses' home was all she needed, all she deserved.

She'd committed many sins—chiefly against the daughter she'd abandoned to adoption—and she'd persuaded herself that she didn't merit more than the cards fate had dealt her.

As a girl, she'd been beautiful, vain, confident of

whatever course she'd embarked upon. She'd had such a zest for life, and had seized every moment, but her arrogant enthusiasm and romantic heart had steered her to heedlessness and delinquency.

She'd paid for her transgressions by smothering the facet of her personality that had gloried in hedonic conduct. When she'd moved in with the Hopkinses, she'd sworn to Margaret that she would never shame the family, would never perpetrate any act that might raise a brow or cause a tongue to wag.

She drifted on the fringe. Always pleasant, always good-humored, never quarrelsome or cross, she spent every waking minute ensuring that she wasn't a burden, that she offended no one, bothered no one, disturbed no one.

Smiling, amenable, and tractable, she didn't want to furnish the impression that she wasn't grateful, because she was. Grateful and indebted and beholden to others for every stitch of clothing she wore, every bite of food she put in her mouth.

Years had passed in which she'd never offered an opinion, had never participated in an important discussion, or mentioned when she'd been maltreated or slighted by the people on whom she depended for her very survival. She'd masked her emotions for so long that she didn't know how to *feel* anymore. She was invisible, had so thoroughly concealed her passionate, animated self that she'd grown indistinct, a shapeless, vague, blurred creature that had no substance.

Another clap of thunder rumbled, and huge drops began to fall. They pummeled her, and she twirled in circles, her face upturned, letting them cool her heated skin. The rain soaked though her robe, then her nightgown, so that the material hugged her form, outlining her erect nipples, her curvaceous buttocks and thighs.

She wished she had the temerity to strip it all off, to strut in the buff, while the gale lambasted her. The fabric was too restrictive, and she couldn't bear it. She felt trapped, weighed down, her lungs not large enough to retain the air she needed.

Perhaps it was the turbulence in the atmosphere, for she was wild and impulsive, incautious, and inclined to engage in any careless act that might soothe the demons rampaging inside her.

The tempest battered her, and she started to shiver. Goose bumps prickled as another lightning bolt struck close by, and she sprinted to the house, rushing to the verandah and sneaking in the rear door.

Disregarding the dripping tracks she left behind, she tiptoed up the stairs. Bursts of lightning cast eerie shadows on the walls. She arrived at the landing where she should have proceeded down the hall to her room, but something—a force, a compulsion—halted her, and she glanced around.

At the end of the other corridor, Edward tarried at the threshold to his suite. Clad in a pair of trousers, his chest and feet bare, he was imperiously balanced on the doorjamb. His gaze was fierce, discerning, missing no detail of her body that was delineated by her flimsy, wet apparel.

Uttering not a word, he extended his hand. An invitation. A command.

Do it! a voice in her head cajoled. *You want it. You want him. Go!*

Despite her pretenses, she was naught but a trollop. Before she could stop herself, she was running down the hall as though it were afire. A hazardous gauntlet, it took forever to get to him, and with each step, she was overcome by the uncanny perception that she was racing to her destiny.

He dragged her into the room, shut and locked the door, then fell on her like a starved animal. She met his tempestuous kiss, wrapping her arms around his neck, her legs around his waist.

His tongue in her mouth, his fingers on her bosom, he was not polite, he showed no deference to her womanly state. Rough, painful, his actions were the deeds of a desperate man who'd been goaded beyond his limits.

This raucous, crude handling was just what she needed, just what her untended, neglected anatomy had been coveting.

Dipping down, he nipped at her enlarged nipple, and she squirmed and moaned. "Yes, yes," she begged, "touch me all over."

Gripping her buttocks, he spun her around, the swiftness making her dizzy. He carried her to his massive bed, and laid her down, his brown eyes intent and savage, but still he didn't speak. Kneeling before her, he massaged up and down in a deliberate path, grazing her bust, her stomach, her mound, then up to repeat the torment.

He tugged off her robe, then wrestled with her nightgown, but it was too damp and plastered to her skin. Frustrated, unable to tolerate any delay, he grabbed the bodice and ripped the garment down the center, to her feet. The two pieces fluttered away, and she was naked.

Shimmering with excitement, he looked like a conquering soldier, about to ravage her against her will. There would be no stopping him, and the ravenous ferocity of his lust was thrilling. She was eager to supply any decadency he demanded.

Three of his unrelenting fingers slipped into her. It had been ages since a man had fondled her there, and the intrusion hurt, but she didn't care. Billowing with pleasure, she arched her hips, but he pressed her down, refusing to let her flex, to find any relief.

"Don't ever say no to me again," he decreed, and he bent down, not to her breasts as she'd expected, but to her mound. Parting her with his tongue, he thrust inside in a concise parry, then he sucked at her clitoris. His fingers remained in her sheath, stroking . . . stroking . . . in a brutal rhythm.

Her orgasm commenced, the tension in her loins erupting, and the exultant bliss swept her away. She was so titillated that she couldn't hide her response, but she was unconcerned if he thought her lewd or dissolute.

The gratification was extreme, unlike anything else she'd known, and she flew across the universe, soaring to the pinnacle then back to earth, and as she reassembled, and became cognizant of her surroundings, he was unbuttoning his pants.

After loosening them, he jerked them down to his flanks, revealing his phallus, the cushion of masculine hair, the two sacs dangling below. He was huge, imposing, the tip moist and oozing his erotic juice. She spread her thighs, and he chuckled at her impatience.

"My little hellion," he said, "permit me to give you more of what you so obviously crave."

He traced the blunt crown across her, then clutched her hips and plunged inside. He hadn't hesitated to ascertain whether she was a virgin, hadn't paused to wonder—praise be, he'd not asked her!—but had progressed, and she was so glad. Had he dawdled another second, she might have exploded.

The moment he entered her, another orgasm inundated her, washing over her with more severity than the first. He pushed into her hard, hard, conferring his full length and girth as desire whisked her away.

She couldn't be quiescent through the tumult, and she called out, so he silenced her with a kiss, his tongue invading her mouth and matching the tempo of his hips.

The tang of her sex was on his lips, and the salty piquancy was an aphrodisiac that inflamed and spurred her to new heights of ecstasy.

As she spiraled down, he was braced over her, a feral, primitive aura glowing about him.

"Welcome to my bed, Miss Stewart." He affected a regal mien. "It would seem that you've ended up just where you belong."

"Aye, milord," she agreed, "it seems I have."

"With your evident partiality for licentiousness, I may never let you go."

"I'm to be your sexual slave?"

"A marvelous notion," he mused. "I'll take it under advisement."

He increased the pace, each penetration banging her into the headboard, and she had to grasp at the bedding to stabilize herself.

More of her sanity had returned, and with it, her better sense. She couldn't believe she'd done this, that she was here, nude, and with her legs secured behind him. Yet she wasn't sorry or chagrined.

The escapade felt right, as if she'd found her way home after being lost for years.

Straining toward fulfillment, his pulse hammering at his ribs, sweat pooling on his brow, he was but a few insertions from spilling himself against her womb. She couldn't let him commit such an improvident act—it was too dangerous for both of them—but she wanted to bestow a release that was as magnificent as hers had been.

Seizing control, she rolled them so that he was on the bottom, and she was perched on top. His rod was a steady, untamed presence between her legs, pounding, pounding into her.

"My goodness, Winnie," he pondered, "what's happening to us?"

"I don't know, Edward."

"If I perished this very instant, my whole life would have been worth it."

"Well, cease your morbid reflection," she laughed. "I'm not about to allow you to expire. At least not until I've dabbled with this delicious cock of yours."

With her carnal remark, she'd rendered him speechless, and she slid off, blazing a trail down his chest, to his navel, to the bristly hair on his lower abdomen.

Nuzzling through it, she laved and rooted, and he shifted uncomfortably, anxious for what she was promising.

It had been so very, very long since she had romped so indecently. Her entire being cried out with joy at unleashing her scandalous character. She leaned down and licked him, licked him again.

"Winnie," he cautioned, "I'm so aroused. If you take me in your mouth, I don't think I can restrain myself."

"I don't want you to restrain yourself," she insisted. Her pleading eyes linked with his. "Let me do this for you."

She didn't wait for his reply, knowing that as she proceeded, he would be in no condition to complain. She flickered over the crown, then opened wide and let him thrust. He tasted sublime, all heat and salt and male, and there was a musky flavor to him that seemed to have been created for her and her alone.

"Oh, God," he groaned, and he applied himself with a renewed stamina, then he froze, his torso stiff. He lunged. Once. Twice. Thrice. Then he spewed himself into her throat. She accepted all he had to give and more, reveling in every brazen, crude aspect of the wicked maneuver.

She kept him there, buried deep, until he exhaled. The urgency dissipated, his weight dropped into the mattress, his erection began to wane. Only then did she kiss up his stomach, his chest, needing to be snug in his arms.

No doubt, there were a thousand questions cascading through his mind: What type of spinster was she? Why wasn't she a virgin? What was the cause of her disgraceful level of morality? How could she tumble into his bed, with no comments being exchanged to lure her there?

She prayed that he was too much of a gentleman to pose any of them. She had few answers, and she imagined that, come the morn, she'd suffer shame and regret, but for now, she was elated, and perhaps a tad smug over the fact that she had reduced him to such a drastic situation.

Though she'd tried to deny this side of herself, her efforts had been in vain. While she was here with him, she wouldn't disavow what they'd just shared, wouldn't attempt to explain or rationalize it. She'd wanted the boisterous coupling, and she also wanted what would transpire now that it was over. The quiet companionship, the suggestive teasing, the serene contentment, was even more special to her.

As she wasn't ready to hear whatever he might say, she initiated a kiss so that he wouldn't speak. He joined in, his tongue toying with hers. When their lips separated, he declared, "I adore having the tang of my sex in your mouth."

Blushing, she was unsure of how to respond, and he saved her by scooting off the bed, walking to a table by the window and retrieving a glass of wine he'd been drinking. He brought it to her, rested a hip on the mattress and held it while she took several lengthy draughts.

"The storm woke me," he divulged, "and I saw you outside." He ruffled her hair. It was mussed and wet. "Are you cold?"

"No." She shook her head, but he covered her with a blanket anyway, then he stood and removed his trousers, and she perused every detail as he tugged them down.

Slim and tall, handsome and fit, he was a fine specimen. He was slightly cocked, as though their frenzied frolicking hadn't allayed his lust, and he wasn't shy about prancing naked in front of her.

He pulled at the blanket and climbed under it, snuggling next to her and stretching out so that they were tangled together. She quivered with pleasure at the taut play of his muscles, the scratch of his coarse bodily hair on her smooth skin, and she cuddled him nearer, her hand on his buttocks, guiding their loins into closer contact.

"If you keep that up"—he flashed a salacious grin—"we won't have much of a chance to chat."

"So who said I want to *chat*?"

"Wildcat." For a protracted interval, he studied her, assessing her features as though trying to guess what made her tick, and he indelicately mentioned, "You're not a virgin."

"No, I'm not."

"Lucky for you." He chuckled, making the awkwardness of his statement easier to bear. "You bring out the beast in me, Miss Stewart. If you'd possessed a modicum of chastity, I'd likely have rent you in half."

"You couldn't have, milord. I'm hale and hearty."

"Edward," he chided. "Remember?"

"Yes, I remember," though she didn't want to use his given name, didn't want any excuses to further the emotional intimacy that was blooming at an alarming rate.

Nestling into the pillows, he slipped an arm around her shoulders. "How do you account for our attraction? I'm randy as an adolescent boy."

She reached down and stroked his phallus, and it leapt

to attention. "There's not much of the lad in you. If asked, I would be forced to describe you as a vigorous, manly fellow."

"Stop that, you minx." Merrily, he slapped her hand away. "I must catch my breath. I'm forty-five, for God's sake. You can't expect me to fornicate like a rabbit."

She laughed, and relocated her naughty fingers to his bottom, which was an excellent spot to linger. "Considering your decrepit circumstance, I'll grant you a respite, but you shan't be permitted to dawdle too long."

"Yes, Your Majesty." He stole a quick kiss, then grew serious. "Tell me about the chap to whom you gifted your virginity. Is he still a part of your life?"

Evidently, he couldn't abide the thought of her being with another, and he was determined to have her confide that she had no beau.

What an hilarious notion! That she—dull, dreary Winnie Stewart—could have a clandestine swain! The only way her existence could be more tedious was if she died!

"No." She blushed again. "It was many, many years ago."

"Did you love him?"

"Yes, I did. Madly and passionately. I was very young and foolish."

"But he never married you?"

"He couldn't."

The allusion to her old flame—the lord's son, Gerald, for whom she'd surrendered everything—disturbed her, and she was inundated with tears that she couldn't conceal.

How mortifying to have him witness her dolor!

"I don't want to talk about that time."

"I shouldn't have been so frank," he maintained. "I'm sorry."

"Don't be. It's an old wound, but it has the power to hurt me more than it should."

"I can see that."

Some of her tears had overflowed, and he used the blanket to wipe them away, then he cradled her face and kissed each of her eyelids.

The gesture was so precious and so poignant that it was all she could do to keep from bursting into a prolonged bout of weeping.

She needed to inject some levity, to change the subject to a less traumatic topic. Reasserting her composure, she smiled. "And how about you? Have you ever been in love?"

He reflected on her inquiry. "I believed I was, once, when I was a youth, but no. I never have been."

"Not even with your wife?"

"We were very good friends."

It was a dismal admission. Men of his station married for many reasons, none of which ever involved affection, but how bleak for him that he'd never experienced the satisfaction love could render!

"If you marry Olivia," she broached, "do you suppose you'll develop strong feelings for her?"

He scoffed. "I can't guess how. She and I have nothing in common."

"How sad for you both."

Though her relationship with Gerald had broken her heart, and wrecked her life, she wouldn't have traded that period for anything. She'd known rapture and bliss to an extent few ever encountered. It had been the sole time she'd felt truly alive.

"Do you regret not having had children?"

"Very much. I was eager to have a few jolly urchins running around this drafty mansion." He lay on his back and pressed her cheek to his chest. "May I confess a secret? But you must swear that you won't inform Olivia or Margaret."

"Of course, Edward."

"I have two children."

"Really?" Stunned by the news, she rose up on an elbow so that she could look at him.

"I've shocked you."

"No," she lied. "I'd just never heard any rumors." And she couldn't fathom that Margaret hadn't unearthed the tidings. The woman liked to wax on over how she'd discovered every aspect to be gleaned.

"It happened before I was married. They're adults now."

"Who was their mother?"

"A girl who was employed as a housemaid. She was so vivacious, and we were crazy for each other." He frowned, as if unable to credit the past. "She's been dead for many a year."

"Are they here at the estate?"

"My son is. He's my stablemaster. His name is Phillip."

"Will you introduce him to me?"

He seemed surprised that she would be interested. "I would like that."

"And the other child is a daughter?"

"Yes. Anne."

"Where is she?"

"She lives near Bath. She's quite a modern, independent woman, or so I'm told."

"You're not certain?"

"I haven't seen her since she was three." It was his turn to blush. "I behaved very badly toward them. They left the estate shortly before I wed, and they fended for themselves, without my assistance. I don't presume Anne likes me very much—if she thinks of me at all. I've never sought her out."

She couldn't conceive of having a daughter, but having no connection with her. Her decision to relinquish Rebecca was a constant thorn that pricked at her, and if she knew where the girl was, she would venture any hazard, overcome any obstacle, to be with her.

"What is preventing you?"

"I'm a coward. I have no other excuse."

"If I were you, I would mount my horse tomorrow, and I wouldn't stop until I was in her yard and down on my knees, apologizing for all the damage I'd done."

"You would, wouldn't you?" He grinned. "I wish I had your mettle."

"I wish *I* had your children."

Their conversation pained her, for it goaded her maternal and womanly instincts to guide and counsel, to soothe and advise, making her yearn to be his wife.

The longing was so potent, it was almost a tangible object between them. It spurred her to want to be dear to him. For all his wealth and rank, his fame and notoriety, he was lonely and so was she, and with their exceptional camaraderie, and their sizzling physical affinity, they were infinitely compatible.

She could love him so easily, and the idea terrified her.

The most ludicrous flight of fancy came over her; she imagined them together, rapt and content, in their golden years. The vision was so vivid, and so distinct, that it was frightening. It had her anxious to determine if she could bring that cheery future to fruition, which made it the most pathetic example of sentimental whimsy she'd ever contemplated.

Once prior, she had frivolously cavorted, and she'd deluded herself into assuming that the impossible could occur. From the outset, she'd understood that Gerald could never marry her, but she'd forged onward, her zeal and fantasies nullifying her discretion.

Her irrational ambitions had destroyed any number of lives, and she'd thought that she'd acquired a smidgen of wisdom from her idiocy, but apparently she hadn't, for she was lying in Edward's arms and conjuring up all manner of outrageous, impractical scenarios.

Would she never learn from her mistakes?

Not only had she philandered with Edward, but she'd flaunted her licentious nature, leaving him with no doubts as to her character. She'd cuckolded Olivia, had perhaps jeopardized Olivia's chances to make the match. After all, why would Edward marry into a family one of whose members was so loose?

And if he did choose Olivia, where would Winnie go? What would she do?

She couldn't remain at Salisbury, as she'd hoped. She would never be able to face Olivia or Margaret. She'd be too embarrassed to join them at the supper table or for holiday festivities. Always, always, always, the memories of this incident would cloud her interactions with them.

Would her lustful tendencies forever rule her? She could no longer blame her inclinations on youth or naïveté, so what pretext could she use to justify what she'd done?

She sighed. It was so difficult to chastise herself when she treasured every second of what was transpiring.

First thing in the morning, she scolded. The personal reproachment could begin at dawn. For now, she would flirt and trifle, would cuddle and pretend that he was hers. Daybreak would arrive soon enough.

"Are you sufficiently rested, you old roué?"

He barked out a laugh.

"Yes, you bawdy wench." His gaze was alight with mirth. "I'll show you what we aging libertines can accomplish, when we set our minds to it."

Covering her, he spread her thighs so that his newly

aroused member could find its way, and with scant effort, he slid into her. She raised her legs and locked her feet behind.

Placing her hands on either side of her head, he linked their fingers, then he started to move. It was breathtaking, sweet, exquisite, the most tender union of heart and soul that two people could ever have achieved.

Their ardor spiraled at the same rate, though on this occasion—with their initial passion sated—the pace was gradual, leisurely, allowing them to enjoy each step of the climb to gratification. But as Edward's corporeal tension mounted, her fear crested.

During their earlier sexual interlude, she'd pleasured him with her mouth, but she couldn't risk his finishing between her legs.

"Edward, promise me something."

"My dearest Winnie, you may have whatever is within my ability to bestow."

"Don't spill yourself in me. I would have your vow before we go any further."

He halted his deliberate thrusting, peering at her with fondness and another emotion—love, she wondered?—shining in his eyes. "I won't. I swear it to you."

His hips resumed their methodical work, and when her orgasm overwhelmed her, he withdrew and emptied himself on her stomach. The smells of sweat and sex permeated the air, and he held her till their skin cooled, then he slipped away and went into the next room. When he emerged, he was carrying a water pitcher and a bowl. He set them on a dresser, dipped a cloth and came to her, wiping away the stain of his seed.

Once more, he nestled with her, dragging the blankets over them both. She was spooned with him, his front curled around her so that she was encompassed by his warmth.

He yawned, and behind her ear, she could sense him smiling.

"I'm happy," he murmured.

"I'm glad."

"Stay with me."

"For as long as I'm able."

His respirations slowed, and he slept. She lay very still, cherishing the moment, memorizing each and every detail so that she would never forget.

What about tomorrow?

Try as she might to shove the question aside, it wouldn't go away.

Where he was concerned, she had no willpower, and she'd be burning to consort with him whenever she had the opportunity. Theirs was an irrevocable, unavoidable attraction, and she'd betrayed Olivia this terrible, remarkable time, but she couldn't do so again.

He'd made no mention of any tryst beyond this one, nor would she have expected him to, but she couldn't bear to think of running into him while she was strolling the grounds or loitering on the verandah.

She had to travel on to London, as abruptly and quietly as a trip could be arranged. As she had no money with which to pay for the journey, she would have to confer with Margaret, which meant devising a subterfuge that would encourage her cousin to send her home.

She didn't know what prevarication she would utilize, but she had the balance of the evening to reflect upon it.

Carefully, she crept off the bed and donned her robe. Her torn negligee was on the floor, and Satan himself must have been perched on her shoulder, for she wadded it up and tucked it next to him, partly hidden by the pillows, but with enough sticking out so that he would notice it as soon as he awoke.

"A souvenir, my darling man," she whispered with a last, yearning look. "Thank you for what you gave me this night."

She tiptoed to the door, peeked out, and sneaked away.

CHAPTER TEN

Freddy Blaine sat at his desk and browsed through the stack of bills that had been delivered from London.

He hadn't realized he'd spent so much during his visit to the city. He recalled purchasing a few sets of clothes, had bought a new horse, but the rest of it . . .

Well.

Cash disappeared so fast, and he had a deuce of a time holding on to it. While he didn't feel he had extravagant tastes, it was so difficult to get by on the meager allowance granted by his oldest brother, Henry. Not that he could complain. In light of his sibling's penny-pinching ways, it was a miracle he received any stipend at all, so he was in no position to gripe or protest.

If Henry were to have an inkling that Freddy wasn't grateful, he was petty enough to cut off funding, so Freddy trod a fine line. He had to be fawning and obsequious to the whiny miser, feigning affection and goodwill, while privately he seethed and plotted.

Image mattered above all else, so he liked to be viewed as a gentleman of substance. He couldn't have others looking down on him, gossiping, or thumbing their noses over his penury.

How he hated poverty!

It was the devil being the sixth son of a baronet. The ancestral estate was small and insignificant, and his irresponsible father had sired twelve children, nine of whom were boys. The three girls had succeeded in marrying, while one brother had taken his vows and another was serving in the army. The other seven, but especially Freddy, insisted on support from the property, for they weren't about to degrade themselves by engaging in pitiable, vulgar labor.

Freddy had his standards, and they were very high. Lamentably, they were also very expensive. Why, his brandy bill alone would bankrupt a less prosperous chap.

He sighed. What was he to do?

He couldn't persist much longer. He was adept at shuffling his liabilities, at hiding his debts, and delaying monies owed, but some of the shopkeepers were tired of waiting for payment and were threatening legal action.

It was a miserable state of affairs when a commoner would dare menace an important person such as himself. To what was the world coming?

If any of the avaricious grubbers proceeded, he'd have to to go begging to Henry, and further entreaty wasn't an option.

After Freddy's last imbroglio, Henry had declared that it was the final bailout, and Freddy was positive Henry had meant it. He still shuddered whenever he recollected the slamming shut of the jailhouse door in that wretched little town where he'd been philandering.

Freddy had a penchant for young girls, and given his inability to repress his base appetites, there had been numerous incidents over the years. After the worst of the lot—when he'd flirted with a duke's ten-year-old daughter—Henry had banished him to the country, buying the property where he now resided, and telling him that he wasn't fit for polite company, and thus couldn't live among his peers.

No one knew of the repeated ignominies. Henry had been accursedly competent in ensuring that cash was spread around to buy the silence of those who'd been wronged, so Freddy maintained an acceptable existence. He was welcome to hobnob with the gentry, was a regular guest at the Salisbury estate and others, was asked to hunt and dine and socialize.

When he could arrange it, he snuck to town, going against Henry's explicit instructions that he not return, but a fellow had to update his wardrobe and fraternize with friends. And, of course, there were his bodily needs to consider.

He really had taken Henry's warnings to heart—that if he continued, there would come a turpitude from which not even the king could rescue him—so he'd checked his rampant cravings as much as he was able. After all, a bloke couldn't amuse himself in these rural hamlets where he was so easily recognized, so he deemed his forays into London to be preventive sexual medicine. He went about his dastardly business in relative anonymity, liberally slaking his desire, which kept it at a manageable level. Then, when he was back at home, he could carry on with his monotonous, staid pursuits.

What he required was a wife with a fortune. A large infusion of capital would provide independence from his brother's purse strings. He'd settle his arrearages, and would have enough left over to frolic and gambol as he chose. There'd be no need to count every bloody farthing.

Sadly, he didn't have any attributes that would attract an heiress. He wasn't going to inherit a title, he had no assets—all of his realty being owned by Henry. If he had the slightest benefit to offer a rich woman, he'd have snagged one ages ago, but wealthy females had never beaten a path to his door.

Factor in his age—forty-three—and his bad habits—strong drink, gambling, and perversion—and he wasn't much of a catch.

What lady with any sense would have him?

Grumbling with disgust at himself, at the sorry condition to which he'd descended, he shoved the papers aside and stomped to the rear of the house and out into the yard. Off in the distance, he could make out a chimney at Salisbury Manor.

What he wouldn't give to be in Edward's shoes! A secure title, loads of money in the bank, and every affluent maiden in the realm vying for his hand.

Some men had all the blasted luck, while some had none!

A vision flashed, of the incautious strumpet Penelope, with whom he'd trifled in Edward's gazebo. What was her game?

Although she'd contended that she was twenty-three, he'd place her closer to sixteen. Throughout the supper he'd weathered at Edward's, she'd flaunted herself at him. She'd been subtle about it, so others hadn't noticed her coquetry, and by the time she'd suggested a tryst, he'd hadn't been surprised.

She behaved like a harlot, yet when he'd attempted to have sex with her, she'd cried off like a frightened virgin. He'd contemplated rape, an act that he'd have regarded as justified after her cock-teasing, but she was a wildcat who'd have fought him, and since he'd over-imbibed, he hadn't been in the mood to scramble merely to accomplish the deed.

She'd been saved by his inebriation, but if he disported with her again, he couldn't guarantee that she'd be so fortuitous. Once challenged, he rarely backed down, and he'd be more than happy to confer what she deserved.

Another, more interesting, thought occurred to him: What sort of dowry did she have? Both her father and stepfather had been earls, imperious, pompous asses whom Freddy hadn't been able to abide. Upon their

deaths, they had to have bequeathed a substantial amount
to assure an advantageous betrothal.

"I wonder," he mused aloud.

How adequately had Lady Penelope's fathers endowed
her? What if she had a *pair* of dowries? A portion from
each earl! Wouldn't that be the ticket!

She was a tad older than he liked, but she was fetching enough to stimulate his aberrant preferences. With
her sass and attitude, he'd never weary of trying to tame
her, or bend her to his will.

The very idea aroused him, his cock stirring in his
pants.

It would be simple to force marriage onto Lady Penelope. As she had the morals of a slattern, it would take
scant effort to lure her into a compromising situation.
Judging from their previous rendezvous, he didn't think
she had much experience—which thrilled him. He was
an expert at coaxing children to do what they oughtn't,
so he wouldn't have to expend much energy in leading
her astray.

A few more furtive glances, a few more whispered
words, another trip or two to the gazebo, and she would
be ruined and desperate.

When they were discovered, there'd have to be a swift
wedding to avoid any hint of scandal. With no delay,
he'd be in control of all her lovely money, and his problems would be solved.

Just reflecting on how he'd toss it in Henry's face, on
how marvelous it would be to escape his brother's pious
influence, made his pulse race.

What a grand scheme! Why hadn't he concocted it
sooner?

He strutted inside and ordered his horse saddled,
while he rushed upstairs and changed into one of his
new jackets. Within minutes, he was trotting toward

Salisbury. If he contrived an auspicious entrance, he could finagle another invitation to supper.

Surely, Edward could use another man at the table while entertaining that gaggle of females.

Laughing, and more optimistic than he had been in a long while, he spurred his horse down the lane.

Margaret loitered on the verandah, enjoying the sunshine, and perusing the post that had been forwarded from London. There was the expected pile of bills, the private letters from acquaintances, and another frantic note from their housekeeper, informing her that Helen still hadn't been found.

After the servant's initial agitated missive had been delivered, Margaret had soothed her by having Mr. Lassiter drop by the town house. A most competent individual, he'd supplied the woman with several vague reports, about false searches that had never been implemented, but the nosy retainer didn't need to know the pesky details.

There were those who'd be shocked by what she'd set in motion, but there were just as many who would have done the same, given the circumstances, and she refused to suffer any guilt.

Over Margaret's strenuous objection, the family had agreed to keep and minister to the lowly creature, when it was obvious that the mother had had tainted blood. Since both parents were deceased, Margaret was left to tackle the consequences of her stepson's negligence.

Margaret wasn't about to allow the mistake of a dead, stupid, juvenile man to interfere with Penny's future— or her own—nor was she about to use any more of their minimal coin to foster the tiny imbecile. Margaret had already devoted much more toil and travail on the child than was warranted.

Olivia would be glad someday. She would! Margaret didn't doubt it. Once she was wed and raising her own children, she'd be relieved that fate had removed the burden from her slender shoulders.

Winnie came out the door, and Margaret slipped the letter to the bottom of the stack, concealing it. If Winnie and Olivia had the least suspicion that something was amiss, they'd insist on scurrying to town, and Margaret wasn't about to tolerate a premature halt to the Salisbury visit. They were scheduled to remain as the earl's guests for two more weeks and that is what they would do. After their affairs were resolved to Margaret's satisfaction, there would be sufficient occasion to wail and moan about Helen.

Winnie approached, and Margaret studied her. She looked altered. There was a sparkle and verve about her that had been absent for an eternity, and the modification made her stand out, made her distinct and blatant in a fashion Margaret didn't like.

Winnie had always been much too pretty. Thankfully, while she'd resided with Margaret, she'd been careful to mute her appearance. She utilized no enhancing facial paints, kept her hair covered, wore prudish, nondescript gowns, and Margaret had been grateful for her modesty.

With her licentiousness proven, and her countenance the type that could tempt any man, Margaret had constantly fretted that the male servants or perhaps—God forbid!—her own husband or stepson might fall victim to Winnie's notorious charms, but her worries had been for naught.

Indeed, Winnie comported herself with the utmost decorum, faithfully endeavoring to be inconspicuous, so what had happened to produce such a vivid transformation?

She recalled a peculiar comment Penny had made,

about having observed Winnie and the earl together in the garden. Margaret had paid it no heed, deeming it to have been merely another example of Penny's penchant for mischief.

Winnie and the earl couldn't be . . .

The thought was so preposterous that she couldn't let it spiral to a conclusion. Since their arrival, Winnie hadn't spoken half a dozen sentences to Edward. She spent every second moping in her bedchamber. There couldn't have been an opportunity for her to . . .

"Good afternoon, Margaret." She was cordial as she pulled up a chair and seated herself.

"Winnie."

"It's so beautiful here, isn't it?" Sighing, she stared across the lawns, her hazel eyes taking in the manicured grounds, the horses grazing off in the distance.

"Olivia could hardly do better than to garner all this for herself."

"Have you received any clue as to the earl's opinion? Is he smitten?"

Margaret scoffed. "His personal feelings have nothing to do with his decision."

"It would be nice for Olivia, though, wouldn't it? If she could make a love match?"

"What folderol!" Margaret waved her hand as though to swipe away the absurd sentiment. Why did the young persist with their romantic nonsense? Winnie was old enough, and experienced enough, to realize the fallacy of ivory towers.

Olivia would wed for accepted, practical considerations.

"Where have you been all day?" Margaret interjected, deftly changing the subject.

"In my room."

"What brings you outside?"

"I wanted to speak with you."

Margaret waited forever for her to begin, and the protracted vacillation grated. "Well . . .?"

"I'd like to return to London."

"You're joking."

"No, and I was wondering if we could manage it."

"You want to leave early? Before our holiday has ended?"

"If it wouldn't be too much trouble."

She wanted to go? Winnie hadn't traveled in ages, because Margaret never let her, and she'd only acquiesced this time so that Winnie would be absent when Helen vanished. The blasted woman was having a fabulous vacation, had just gushed over the splendor of the property. What was wrong with her?

"It would be a great deal of *trouble*," Margaret complained. "We came in the earl's carriage. We'll journey home the same way. If you departed, you'd have to take the public coach. How could you contemplate such foolishness? What's come over you?"

"I guess I'm homesick. And I have to admit that I'm terribly bored. There's so little to do, and I miss the activity that's available in the city." She smiled, her usual pleasant, amiable smile.

Margaret assessed her. Every word she'd uttered was an out-and-out lie. Winnie cherished this sort of idyllic adventure, and it was one of the reasons Margaret had rarely let her go with them to the familial estate. Lest she forget the charity her presence incurred, Winnie needed to be reminded of her place.

"What an ungracious request," Margaret snapped. "Not only would you insult the earl with your egression, but your poor manners would reflect badly on Olivia. And you would impose on me to finance your totally unnecessary and uncalled-for trip." Visibly irate, she shook her head. "For shame, Winnie! For shame!"

"I apologize, Margaret," Winnie declared. "I didn't mean to upset you, but would it really be so expensive? I'd imagine the fare to be but a few pounds."

"You would, would you?" Margaret asked. "What if it is a *few* pounds? You couldn't trot off alone, so we'd have to send a maid with you. We'd need to purchase her fare, as well. Do you think money grows on trees?"

"I know it doesn't."

"You've never had to pay your own way"—Margaret scored a direct hit with the caustic admonishment; Winnie blanched—"so you have limited understanding of how much things cost and how difficult it is to make ends meet, but I would regard such an excursion to be completely frivolous."

"I see . . ."

Nervous and on edge, Winnie peered down at her hands, and for a moment, it seemed she might argue, or spew facts that shouldn't be divulged.

"I suggest"—Margaret hurried on before Winnie could emit a remark that shouldn't be voiced aloud— "that you stroll the garden and ponder why you should be thankful for this brief respite Lord Salisbury has granted us. Should he not choose Olivia, and we retreat to London with our palms out like a pack of beggars, there'll be plenty of time for your selfish bewailing." She fixed her attention on her letters. "Be off, before you say something idiotic that will make me lose my temper."

Winnie dawdled, as if determined to brazen it out, but Margaret had dismissed her, so she didn't dare. She stood and left, seizing upon Margaret's advice that she walk in the garden to compose herself.

She meandered down one of the pathways, and

Margaret scrutinized her retreating figure until she disappeared behind the shrubbery. Then she relaxed in her chair and mulled over the strange conversation.

There were undercurrents to it that Margaret didn't comprehend and couldn't quite define, yet she felt them as plainly as if they were bumping up against her.

Winnie never instigated a confrontation. Why had she now? A dire issue was eating at her. What if she was trifling with the earl? Was it possible?

Margaret would have to keep her eyes and ears open. If Winnie was stupid enough to philander with Edward, which in effect would ruin Olivia's chances to marry him, Margaret had scads of ammunition to hold Winnie at bay.

Winnie had many humiliating secrets, and Margaret knew every one of them. She would have no qualms about imparting Winnie's sordid history to Edward. For a man who focused on bloodlines to the exclusion of all else, Winnie's sins would be unforgivable.

In the interim, she'd check out the particulars as to the public conveyance that carried passengers to London from the area's coaching inn. Should she require Winnie's precipitous exit from the estate, the information would come in handy.

Margaret's gaze roamed past the yard and out to the winding drive that connected the manor to the main road. Olivia had been riding again, an afternoon diversion she'd unexpectedly and regularly embraced, and she was finishing up another jaunt. A groom was behind her, appropriately spaced, apathetic, and proficient in his duties.

There was nothing out of the ordinary about the scenario, and Margaret might not have given it a second thought had she not happened to notice Olivia glance around. While she couldn't observe Olivia's expression, her view of the groom was most distinct. He winked at Olivia, the corner of his mouth quirking up in a half-smile as if they'd shared a private jest.

He was handsome, in a dark, dangerous way that many women liked, and Margaret could appreciate why a female of Olivia's restricted background might be fascinated by such a fellow. Working men had a certain allure to which even her own Penelope wasn't immune.

Olivia wouldn't behave improperly, or engage in recklessness, but she was dabbling in pursuits that didn't involve the earl, so Margaret was furious. She didn't know where Edward was, and in his stead, Olivia's attractive chaperon was a temptation that could distract her from her obligations.

Up until now, Margaret had been content to let the relationship blossom of its own accord, but with each subsequent day, Olivia was less inclined to garner Edward's favor. Her rides were a marked example of how she'd rather do anything but fraternize with the earl. Her recalcitrance, coupled with Winnie's abnormal conduct, had Margaret speculating as to whether she should orchestrate a conclusion.

There were many methods by which she could ensure that Olivia was wed to Edward. Perhaps she should start deliberating as to how a union could be brought about.

She shuffled her papers into a neat pile, and she proceeded to her room and her customary nap. In those minutes before she drifted off, she did her best calculating. Hopefully, when she awoke, she'd have numerous valuable ideas at the ready.

Olivia strode toward the house but, in order to reach her destination, she took a circuitous route through the vast gardens. She'd caught a glimpse of Margaret on the verandah and desperately wanted to avoid her step-mother.

Margaret would want to hash out the details of the pending evening—what jewelry and dress Olivia should wear to supper, what she should do with her hair—when Olivia couldn't bear to discuss any of it.

She'd taken to riding each afternoon, which was an acceptable activity, and it gave her the perfect excuse to dally with Phillip. But the trips were too short, and passed much too rapidly, and after her thrilling hour lollygagging with him, she couldn't abide Margaret's blathering over Edward and the potential nuptials.

What was she to do?

It was more and more apparent that she couldn't follow through on her promise to entice Edward Paxton. While Margaret was counting on her, and they had no other options, she couldn't save them in the fashion Margaret demanded.

If she became Edward's wife, there would be a long string of wretched Sunday dinners, neighborhood gatherings and socials, and she'd preside over all of them, knowing that his son was out in the stable, watching from afar.

Whenever she went into the yard, or needed to use a carriage, she might run into Phillip, and she could envision no greater torture than to be in proximity to him but unable to act upon their nearness. She couldn't go through life as Edward's spouse, pretending that Phillip didn't exist.

As opposed to most girls, she'd never ruminated about being a bride, had never dreamed about her wedding, or fantasized as to what her husband would be like. When Margaret had explained their plight, Olivia had stoically agreed that a hasty wedding was the sole alternative, but she hadn't given the actual concept of *marriage* much consideration.

Since meeting Phillip, she'd brooded over the mysterious arrangement. She now knew something of ardor and physical desire. There was a unique side to matrimony of which she'd been unaware, and she couldn't disregard it.

There was a bawdy, lustful aspect to her character that she'd never noted before. She was entranced, excited and bewitched, by the exploits he'd shown her, but she could only perform the naughty antics with someone for whom she harbored deep feelings.

Which ruled out a typical aristocratic match.

As she had to have the income a husband would supply, she couldn't marry Phillip, but she couldn't marry Edward, either. She couldn't fornicate with a man she didn't love. Not even if he possessed all the wealth in the world. Not even if her dear family was about to perish.

She simply couldn't do it.

How had she stumbled into the middle of such a debacle? Why had she allowed herself to become entangled with Phillip? Previously, everything had seemed so easy, her future had been set in stone, her mind made up, yet she'd taken one look at him and had cast caution to the wind.

By flirting with him, she was courting disaster. If she went to Margaret and confessed her sentiments, she couldn't predict how Margaret might respond. The woman could be vicious, and she might resort to threats or vengeance that would force Olivia to accede in her scheming.

Conversely, if she approached Edward and admitted her reluctance, he would accept her decision, then send them home straightaway. She'd never be with Phillip again, and that notion made leaving too painful to contemplate. They would have to separate, but she couldn't reflect upon that moment, and she couldn't do anything that would hasten the dreadful day.

She could only carry on, feigning a budding affection for Edward, placating Margaret with half-truths and evasions, while making sure she didn't gape at herself too closely in the mirror. An absolute coward, she couldn't stand to see the woman who stared back at her.

What folly! What naïveté and lack of sophistication! She'd believed herself to be so smart, so experienced. How had she gotten herself into this mess?

As she strolled along, the thick hedges shielded her from view. She rounded the corner, and much to her surprise, almost bumped into Winnie.

"Winnie, hello." She smiled, though no reciprocal gesture was forthcoming. "What are you doing out here all by yourself?"

"I might ask you the same question."

She laughed at Winnie's pointing out the obvious. "I'm hiding."

After a lengthy hesitation, Winnie acknowledged, "So am I."

Olivia inspected her. She couldn't recall ever witnessing Winnie distraught. Winnie was constantly serene, tranquil, and obliging. In a domicile where Olivia was surrounded by Helen's awkwardness, and Margaret's and Penny's vitriol and carping, Winnie was an exemplary companion, a breath of fresh air. She never complained or fussed, was amenable to any idea or plan, was cheery and optimistic—however vile the circumstances. Yet of a sudden, she was extremely tormented.

Plainly, she'd been anxiously pacing in the secluded spot, and the realization was so bizarre that Olivia was shocked and worried.

What could have transpired that would have thrown Winnie into such a mood?

"Are you all right?"

"Yes." She turned away and gazed toward the manor, studying it as though she could peer through the walls. "Why wouldn't I be?"

"You seem very upset."

She continued to assess the mansion, and the silence became unpalatable. Olivia took a step toward her, then halted, baffled by Winnie's distress and uncertain of what comfort to offer.

Winnie spun to face her. "You'd forgive me, wouldn't you, Olivia?" she queried. "If I did something terrible to you?"

"Well, of course I would."

"I'd never intentionally hurt you."

"I know that." She gripped Winnie's hands in her own. "What is it, Winnie? What has put you in such a state?"

Tears flooded Winnie's eyes and cascaded down her cheeks. Winnie had lived with them for twelve years, and Olivia had never seen her cry before.

"I want to go home," she said.

"Why? What's happened? Has someone insulted or offended you?"

"No, no."

"Then what is it?"

"I'm so tired of having to rely on others. Just once, I wish I could make my own decisions."

Evidently, the matter of her departure was vital. "Have you spoken to Margaret?"

"Yes, but she insists we can't afford it."

"Maybe the earl would—"

"No!" she interjected. "I would never impose on him."

"Please tell me how I could help you."

"There's nothing you can do," she claimed. "You

have no more money than I with which to purchase a ticket."

"No, I don't, but if I had a single penny, I'd give it to you."

"You've always been so kind to me, when I've done so little to deserve it."

"Winnie! My goodness!"

"Oh, don't mind me." She tried to shrug away her misery. "I've been so desperately unhappy. It's tumbling out. I can't control it."

How long had Winnie been disconsolate? Was it due to a recent incident or had it been fermenting? From how agitated she was, her desolation appeared to have been mounting, and something had brought it to a head.

Her tears flowed, and as Olivia hugged an arm around her shoulder, it occurred to her that, while they were very cordial, she hardly knew Winnie. Their relationship skimmed along on the surface, filled with frivolous conversations about the day, and the weather, and the latest dress styles, but what did she really *know* about her?

Apparently, not much. How could this person of whom she was so fond be suffering without Olivia having the slightest clue that she was afflicted or any hint as to the cause?

The discovery made her feel petty and small. Was she so detached from those around her? Did she shut herself off and shun intimacy? Of was it Winnie? Had Winnie built walls to keep them divided?

Olivia had been so absorbed by her own dilemma that she'd been ignoring others. She was at Salisbury to assist her family, yet one of its members was in total anguish, and Olivia had been oblivious to her plight. If she hadn't chosen to walk through the garden, she still wouldn't be cognizant of Winnie's agony.

How heedless! How cruel! Then and there, she vowed to herself that she would be a better friend.

"Let's get you back to the house," she suggested.

"No, I don't want to go inside." Her vehemence made her seem almost afraid.

"Hush, now," Olivia soothed. "You need to calm yourself. We'll order a scented cloth for your eyes. Perhaps a draught so you can relax."

Olivia had a kerchief stuffed in the cuff of her jacket, and she tugged it out and dabbed at Winnie's tearstained cheeks. "Pull yourself together—just till we're in your room. You don't want anyone to stumble upon you in this condition."

"Especially Lord Salisbury. Don't let him see me."

It was a strange remark. Olivia wasn't aware that Winnie had spent enough time with Edward for his opinion to signify. "I won't." Quietly, she explained, "We'll take the servants' stairs. I know the way. Can you make it?"

"Yes."

Holding hands, they started off.

Chapter Eleven

Phillip stared across the dark yard as Olivia, once again, risked all to sneak to his cottage. He'd pleaded with her not to come, had ordered her to desist with her craziness, but without much energy in his admonitions.

Her previous sojourn, when he'd introduced her to passion, had been his undoing. He'd managed to circumscribe his behavior so that he hadn't pilfered her virginity, but he wasn't certain that he could act so gallantly a second time.

He wanted her. Without restriction or restraint. Without regard to the consequences. His need spiked beyond what he knew or understood about himself. She was the most unattainable female, like an angel in heaven who, for a fleeting moment, had deigned to grace his pitiful life, but she could never be his. This fact was an absolute truth, yet his mind refused to heed its reality.

What was to be done?

Though she hadn't visited since that prior, significant night, she tortured him daily by showing up at the stables, obligating him to accompany her as she rode down the sun-drenched lanes of the estate. Like a besotted boy, he escorted her, following behind as her groom.

The humiliation of trailing after her should have convinced him of the recklessness of his course, for there was no better way to accentuate their differences. Where she was concerned, not even his pride mattered. He didn't care that he had to tag along as the faithful employee. He didn't care that wealth and status divided them. He'd grown to anticipate their forays, until his yearning to be with her superseded all else, particularly his ability to do his job.

Throughout his unending mornings, he'd pine away, anxious for afternoon and the sound of her slippers as she entered the barn. Until the instant that he saw her pretty face, he could concentrate on no other topic.

He couldn't focus, couldn't pay attention to his assistants. Often, they had to repeat themselves over and over before they could garner a response to any question. To him, the only subject of import was Olivia.

For endless hours, he speculated as to where she was, what she was doing. Like a homeless pauper, he would gaze at the manor, perusing the windows, the verandah, eager to catch a glimpse of her as she went about her day.

He was frantic to discover what she was wearing, what she'd had for breakfast, how she was occupying herself and if—by the slightest chance—she might be thinking of him, too.

Their regular rides were producing a dangerous bond that was steady and true, and try as he might, he couldn't discount how much he liked her. The tidbits she'd revealed about herself fueled his ruminations. He was frightened for her, her dire straits worried him, and he aspired to remedy her dilemma.

She'd confessed all: her financial plight, the cantankerous association with Margaret and Penelope, the melancholia she'd suffered after the deaths of her father and brother. She'd even told him about her niece, Helen, the illegitimate daughter of her brother, and how the girl's mental difficulties were creating dissension among the adult women.

Duress was driving her to Edward, and Phillip's frustration was greater than ever. How he wished he had the fortune to aid her! In a heartbeat, he would sweep her off her feet and cure her problems.

The saddest realization was that her vision of the future was so similar to his own. She wasn't chasing after the grand estate Edward offered, or the opportunity to be a countess. She'd be content with a cozy house, where she could read and paint, where she could mother Helen and, perhaps someday, her own children.

When he shut his eyes, he could see the two of them, blissfully wed, residing in a snug rural locale, where he could train and sell horses, while she puttered and fussed in their comfortable abode.

The dreams were so authentic, and so wrenching, that he couldn't bear to contemplate them.

His inadequate options had him so distraught that he'd considered approaching his father, to demand either a financial settlement, or a piece of property and some of the animals as a starter herd. In his reveries, he'd use the business to support Olivia—though how such a modest venture could sustain a group of five females and the children he and Olivia would have, or how they could all cohabit in any sort of harmony, was a mystery, and emphasized the preposterousness of his fantasies.

Yet even though he knew it was absurd to hope, he couldn't put aside the notion that he should try. He'd never begged Edward for a penny. His enormous arrogance wouldn't have allowed it. Everything he'd received had been earned through diligent effort, and his willingness to demean himself highlighted how befuddled he was.

What would he say to Edward if they did talk? *I'm having a clandestine affair with the woman you're courting? I'd like you to endow me with a fortune so that I can marry her in your place?*

The ludicrousness washed over him, and he shook

his head. There were no answers. There was no viable conclusion.

He peered around at the small dwelling where he'd lived for years, at the stables across the way. This was *home*. When he'd been lying in that dusty foreign field in Spain, his blood oozing into the dirt, he'd prayed that he'd survive long enough to return to this special spot, and he eventually had.

He'd recovered his health, had resumed his employment. But would the situation endure? Though Olivia was insisting she couldn't wed Edward, what if she did? What if she decided she had no alternative?

If she married Edward, Phillip couldn't remain at Salisbury. He couldn't spend his life gawking at the manor, and imagining her in his father's arms, in his father's bed. He'd have to leave, but where would he go? What would he do?

He glanced around, at the familiar grounds, at his cherished house, and he pondered whether these were the last few days he'd be surrounded by the chattels to which he was so attached. By falling in love with her, had he wagered not only his heart, but his security, too?

In love . . .

The words echoed past. Was that what he'd done? Had he fallen in love?

"Oh, God," he moaned, unable to fathom the depth of his idiocy, but he had no occasion to reflect.

She was there and reaching out to him, and he hustled her into the cottage and closed the door.

She'd worn her cloak, and he dipped under the hood, capturing her mouth in a torrid kiss. He'd never been one to do anything halfway, and if this was to be the end of the world as he knew it, he intended to go out in a blaze of glory.

When their amour was over—terminated badly, he had no doubt!—he would neither rue what had transpired, nor regret what might have been. He would revel in every delicious assignation he could arrange, until ill luck or circumstances forced a halt.

His hands were everywhere, on her shoulders, her back, her bottom. Gripping her buttocks, he lifted her, whirling her around and carrying her to his bed. He laid her down, still swathed in the cloak, and joined her, stretching out, pushing her into the mattress. He was inflamed by the contact, ardent and ready for whatever he might attempt, and for once, he anticipated that he would *attempt* quite a lot.

"I want you naked." Yanking at her wrap, he untied the hood and tugged it off.

"I missed you, too," she said, laughing.

"If I don't have your clothes removed in the next ten seconds, I can't predict what I might do."

"By all means, then. Help yourself."

Beyond delay, he was desperate to nibble on her breasts, to lick her womanly core. He unbuttoned her dress, and jerked it down. Her nipples were pert, erect, and he bent over and sucked on one of them as he continued on, exposing her abdomen, her mons.

Finally, she was unclad, except for her shoes, and he wrenched them off, tossing them on the floor where they landed with a muffled thump.

Kneeling between her legs, he assessed her body, and she withstood his scrutiny well. Only the blush on her cheeks indicated that this was a new experience for her. She was perfectly formed, wide at the shoulders, thin at the waist, wide again at the hips. Her breasts were full and round, her thighs curvaceous and smooth.

The sight of her, nude, and awaiting his pleasure, thrilled and incited him.

Elevating her feet, he massaged his thumbs into her arches, as he spread her legs, baring her center. She didn't like this novel exhibition, didn't care for the awkwardness of being on display, and she tried to press her legs together, but he couldn't be dissuaded.

"Don't deny me, Livvie. Let me do this."

"It's too strange. It embarrasses me."

"Well, it arouses me. I want to see all of you." He stroked up her ankles, her calves. "Do you remember the book you were studying when we first met?"

"How could I forget? *A Feast for the Senses.*"

"You asked me why it was painted, and I told you because men like to look at nude women. I'm no different." Rubbing his crotch, he strove to ease some of the building pressure. He was so hard for her that he felt he might explode in his trousers like a callow boy of thirteen.

She noticed where his hand had traveled. "Will you disrobe tonight?"

"I believe I will."

"Do it. While *I* watch."

He vacillated. While he was determined to forge ahead in their sexual relationship, he wasn't sure he was cad enough to steal her virginity. He might yearn to do it, and he could arouse her sufficiently so that she would implore him to, but he hadn't resolved to go through with it. However, once his garments were off, he wasn't positive he could keep from taking that ultimate step.

There are many enjoyable things you can do short of her surrendering her virtue.

The voice seemed to emanate from a site just beyond the bed, and it was so clear, and so sly, at urging him to do what he oughtn't, that he wondered if the devil himself wasn't sitting across the room.

Well, he'd always been a sinner, so if Lucifer was spurring him on, the old fiend was going to be very happy.

As she analyzed his every move, he unfastened his shirt, and hauled the hem out of his trousers. When it was free, he pulled it off and discarded it.

"Your pants, if you please," she requested.

He had no qualms about stripping for her. During their previous carnal foray, she'd touched and fondled him, had even sampled his phallus—an act that had had his balls aching for days—so there would be no maidenly shock with which to contend, although he did worry about her viewing the scar on his thigh that had been inflicted by an enemy saber. It was ugly, and he didn't like to chatter about it, or how it had been acquired.

He slid from the bed, plucked the trousers over his feet, and quickly dispensed with his shoes and stockings so that he was standing proud and naked before her.

She examined him, her keen appraisal making him undulate with tension, his cock swell to an even larger size, as she perused every inch of his torso.

Bracing his hands on his hips, he gave her an eyeful, elated that she was interested, excited that she wasn't timid or afraid.

"You don't mind my curiosity, do you?" she inquired.

"Not a whit."

"It's the artist in me. I need to verify what's hidden beneath all that fabric."

"At your service, Lady O."

"Turn to the side," she instructed, and he did, as she evaluated him again. "Now all the way, so that I can see your back and bum."

Complying, he could feel her gaze sweeping over him, could hear her climbing off the bed. She came up behind him, and put her fingers on his shoulders, tracing the bones, on down his spine, across the nip of his waist, the curve of his ass.

She grabbed his buttocks, gauging its shape, its weight, then she dropped to her knees. "What's this?"

"A scar." Obviously! It ran from groin to kneecap.

"From what?"

"I was wounded in the army. In Spain."

"Honestly?"

"Yes."

"A soldier!" She beamed. "My very own war hero!"

"Not really." He blushed. He'd done naught but try to save his bloody hide, which he'd never considered very heroic at all.

She trailed a finger over it. "Does it hurt?"

"When it rains," which was a lie. It throbbed most of the time—a constant and unrelenting reminder of that horrid escapade—and on occasion, he still limped.

Astounding him, she leaned forward and kissed it. Few people had ever extended kindness or sympathy to him, and he was exceedingly affected by her concern. Tears clouded his vision, and he was glad he was staring away from her.

"Will you tell me about it?"

He had to swallow twice before he could reply. "Perhaps."

She let it go at that, intuiting that it wasn't a subject upon which he could elucidate, and he was so relieved.

"Would you let me draw you someday?" she queried, lightening the tenor of the conversation.

Why not? What an amazing lark it would be! "Certainly."

"In the nude?"

The *nude?* "If it would tickle your fancy."

"It would." She chuckled. "It *definitely* would."

She was inspecting him impersonally, as one might a statue, or a remarkable piece of horseflesh, but nonetheless, he was inordinately titillated. The caressing, combined with her inquisitive oohs and aahs, kindled an unquenchable fire, and it took every ounce of his fortitude to keep from spinning around and taking her, then and there, across the edge of the mattress.

Loitering at his feet, she journeyed up until she was behind him, her naked front flattened to his back, and she wrapped her arms around him.

"You're beautiful," she murmured, kissing him between his shoulder blades.

Overwhelmed, he couldn't speak, and he dawdled there with her, in the quiet. He directed her hand to his cock, and circled it around, so that he could flex into it, and he'd planned to languidly dally, but after a few thrusts, he was at the brink and unable to persist.

Whirling, he swooped her up, laying her on the bed once more, and covering her with his long, lean body. As they connected, he hissed out a breath.

"Oh, Jesus, Livvie."

Of their own accord, her legs widened, and he was ideally situated, his cock slithering into place with no guidance. If he but dared, he could rid her of her maidenhood and put the matter to rest once and for all, but for some crazed reason, he didn't progress.

"Are we to . . ." Cautiously, she posed the question, unsure of the terminology.

"I don't think so," he said. "I'm just going to hold you."

"But I want to learn what it's like."

"I know you do, but if I deflower you, you can't ever change what we've done."

"I won't ever wish to."

"You say that," he counseled, "but you can't divine what the future might bring. If I were to proceed"—he nudged two fingers inside her—"there is a thin fragment of skin here, blocking access to your womb, and I would tear through it. It would pain you, and you'd bleed."

"What would it signify?"

"The blood and pain are the indicators to your husband that you've come to your marital bed as a virgin. If I breach it, it won't grow back. We can't repair the damage."

"Oh, I hate this!" she wailed as he began stroking her. "I don't want the possibility of a marriage—that I can't abide—to keep us apart. What am I to do?"

Her confusion matched his own, but he had no answers. Not for her, or for himself.

"I don't want to listen to you prattling on about your marriage," he snapped. "Or your choices." They were too disturbing, because he could never be one of them. There was just the here and now, the two of them alone, and he intended for it to be a magical episode, where the outside world did not intrude. "I care for you too much, so I can't give you valid advice. I'm biased as to the outcome."

"But if you can't help me, to whom can I turn?"

"I don't know," he claimed. "All I can offer is to make the most of the time we have. So that after you leave, we won't regret a single minute."

Glumly, she nodded. "I suppose that's the wisest course."

He nodded, too, then started kissing her again, wanting to halt further discussion. The topic left him so anguished! It was much simpler to make love to her. He could pretend that their association was merely physical, that it had no emotional depth.

Blazing a trail down her neck, he nibbled across her bosom, to her breasts. She was familiar with this licentiousness, and she acquiesced, arching up, and tendering more of herself for his ardent enjoyment. Down below, her hips responded in a slow rhythm, and he nipped down her stomach, to her core. Rooting through her womanly hair, he sniffed and licked her abdomen. She acceded to all, until he lowered himself further, until he delved into her with his tongue.

"Phillip?" She was apprehensive, and she tried to shield herself from his probing, but he was wedged in, and she couldn't push him away.

Separating the folds, he exposed her, revealing her slick haven, and he jabbed at her, as he pinned her down, as his fingers tormented her nipples.

"You taste so fine."

"I don't like this."

"You will."

"No, I—" She struggled to sit up.

"Lie down. Don't fight it."

"Please don't!" she implored. "This is . . . is . . ."

"Indecent? Naughty? Wicked?"

"Yes."

"Precisely why it thrills me."

He went to her clitoris, dabbing at it with quick bursts, and she ceased complaining. Her body was rigid, straining against him, grappling with the torrent of passion.

"Let go, Livvie," he commanded, and he sucked at the aroused nub, as he pinched her nipples. She gave a soft cry, then hurled over the precipice.

He rode the wave with her as she flew to the crest and spiraled down. As she relaxed, he was kissing up her torso, his mouth ensnaring hers.

She was desirable, seductive, her sensuality so at odds with the prim, proper façade of an earl's daughter.

What a lucky man he was to have unveiled this aspect of her personality. How magnificent that he was the only one who knew it to exist.

"How do you do that to me?" she asked.

"You find your pleasure easily. It doesn't have much to do with me."

"Liar," she chided, smiling. "It has everything to do with you."

"Mayhaps, a little." He was preening. They were so sexually compatible. It was a small task to deliver her to orgasm.

"What do you call that? What you just did?"

"A French kiss."

"First the *petite mort,* now the French kiss." She was laughing. "What is it about those French?"

"They know how to indulge themselves."

"They certainly do." She stretched like a contented cat. "I like what you do to me so much. Does that make me a harlot?"

"No, it makes you a lusty, bawdy wench"—he wiggled his brows—"but I like you that way."

While he didn't mind engaging in coital banter, his unassuaged cock was so hard, it was throbbing. There couldn't be many more occasions where he provided her with gratification but attained none of his own. He'd soared past constraint, and if he wasn't soon sated, he might rupture.

She must have recognized his tension, because she clasped his hips and urged him closer. On his end, the move was dangerous. The tip of his cock was brushing against her. She was slick, open, and with a bit of pressure, he could glide into her.

The temptation was extreme, the proximity staggering, and he slid off her and onto his back, nestling her to his side.

"Touch me," he ordered her. "As I showed you before."

She clutched him in her fist, tamely manipulating him, but he needed more stimulation. He enveloped her hand in his, tightening her grip so that she ran her fingers over the end with each stroke.

An avid, eager pupil, she complied with his coaching, but she wanted more, too, and she scrambled up onto her knees and straddled him. With her blond hair flowing over her shoulders, her ruby lips moist and swollen from his kisses, her sassy breasts taunting him to recklessness, she looked like a pagan goddess, a Valkyrie.

He drew her down so that she was directly on him, her center a sleek crevasse where he could flex. The titillation was hazardous as he was, once again, located where he should not be.

"If we were truly lovers," she said, "you'd enter me, wouldn't you?"

"Yes."

"It would hurt?"

"Only the first time."

"Do it!" she decreed.

"No."

"I want you to."

"You assume you do."

"Ooh . . ." she pouted, "you frustrate me beyond my limits."

He laughed aloud. If anyone was frustrated, it was clearly himself! "Take me in your mouth."

"A marvelous idea." She scooted down, abandoning her perilous perch.

Like a skilled wanton, she trifled and teased, going at him as if she regularly luxuriated in the risqué maneuver. She grazed and kissed, laving him over and over, until his sexual juice was oozing, his balls two solid stones, his anatomy stiff with insatiable need, then she slipped her crimson lips over the crown.

Considering how new she was at libidinous games, it was wrong and crude of him to use her so badly, but he *had* to be inside her, even if it was for only a brief moment.

Rotating them, he draped a leg over her. Focusing solely on the impropriety—on her, her mouth, and the driving force of his cock—he was able to fleetingly endure, to relish and revel in the vulgar indiscretion, but he couldn't keep on for long. His craving for release was too strong, and he had to finish.

He pulled away, and she reached out for him, wanting to lure him back, but he slapped at her hand, and dragged her into his arms, his erection squeezed to the silky skin of her stomach.

"I've got to come."

"What should I do?"

"Hold me."

"I will."

Crushing her to his chest, he began the race to fulfillment. There would be no stopping, no demurral, and with a groan of indescribable pleasure, his passion surged, and his semen spewed from his phallus in a hot, potent deluge.

He thrust again and again, his orgasm never seeming to wane, until finally, blessedly, it was over. His pulse thundered. Perspiration drenched him, and he was hovered over her, his respiration labored, his thoughts in disarray.

Collapsing to the side, he buried his face in the pillows, his fingers on her breast.

How would she perceive his behavior? What would she say? He'd been too overcome to be gentle or passive, and he imagined it would always be so. Without trying, she goaded him to new heights of desire.

She wiggled away, her hand slithering down onto her abdomen. "Is this your seed?"

"Yes." He glanced at her as she dipped a finger into the

sweltering pile, and daubed it to her tongue, sampling its flavor.

"Will you spill yourself in my mouth sometime?"

Flabbergasted at her nonchalance, he rolled his eyes. "You'll be the death of me, woman."

"Do you think so?"

"I *know* so."

The air was heavy with the smell of fornication, humid from their sweat and toil, and he crawled off the bed and retrieved a towel and a wet cloth, then he returned to her and scrubbed clean the stain on her skin. Quiet, studious, she observed all until he'd completed his task.

"Was it wonderful for you?" she shyly probed.

"Oh, yes." Grinning, he tossed the towel away. "If it had been any more exhilarating, my heart might have quit beating."

"So I did it correctly?"

He was charmed by her maidenly doubts. "You couldn't have been better."

"Does that mean we can do it again?"

Shaking with mirth, he stretched out next to her, spinning her and spooning himself behind her. "Give me a few minutes, you little hussy. I need to catch my breath."

"I don't."

"Well, I'm not as spry as you."

"How long will you need?"

"As long as it takes." He swatted her on the rear. "We're going to rest."

"I'm not tired."

Rising up on an elbow, she glared at him over her shoulder, appearing rumpled, satisfied, her cheeks rosy, her lips sulking. She was so beautiful, so enticing and alluring. And she was all his. At least for now.

"I want to snuggle with you," he said.

The news mollified her. "I'd like that."

He settled her down, an arm under her head, the other across her waist. She cuddled nearer, pressing her delicious ass into his groin.

"I guess I *am* a tad exhausted." She emitted an unladylike yawn.

"Close your eyes."

"I daren't fall asleep."

"I'll watch the clock."

She yawned once more, her inhalations slowing, and shortly, she was slumbering peacefully.

Shutting his own eyes, he memorized every detail of the stunning encounter. He couldn't predict if she'd ever join him for a subsequent tryst, and he wanted to be sure that if this was the last one, he would never forget a single particular.

Riffling through her hair, brushing over her skin, he traced her arm, her waist, her hip, marking the nips and tucks, the ridges and valleys.

She fit against him just right, as though God had created her as Phillip's perfect mate.

What a cruel jest! The Good Lord must have a bizarre sense of humor.

Phillip had spent his entire life on the outside, looking in, yearning to belong, waiting for his legitimate place at the table, but he'd never garnered it. She was the epitome of all he'd ever wanted, all he could never attain, and the realization tore at him, killing him with how he hungered for so many things that could never be his.

"I love you, Livvie," he whispered, and he could feel her smile. Despite her deep sleep, she'd heard and understood.

With the ebbing of their ardor, the room had cooled,

so he tugged a blanket over them, wrapping them in a snug cocoon, and he stared at the clock so that he could wake her before the cock crowed with the approach of dawn.

CHAPTER TWELVE

Penelope stomped down the hall to her room. In a temper, she swept inside and slammed the door forcefully enough to rattle the paintings on the walls.

"How dare he!" she fumed.

Since that dreadful night in the gazebo, she'd seen Freddy Blaine on a trio of separate occasions, and all three times, he'd ignored her.

Another interminable meal had just concluded, with Freddy lounging across from her at the table, and despite how often she'd tried to garner his attention, he hadn't so much as glanced in her direction. After the repast, she'd strolled out on the verandah, at a moment when he could have trailed after her without being noticed, but she'd waited and waited, and he hadn't come out.

"Bastard," she grumbled, relishing the crude word.

He thought he was so bloody magnificent. Ooh, how she hated him! A pox on his despicable hide!

While she couldn't quit ruminating about what they'd done together, about how thrilling it had been when he'd held her down, when she'd fought him, it seemed to her that he hadn't been moved in the slightest. And the realization that she'd had no effect on him infuriated her.

Of all the boring, stupid fellows she'd met at Salisbury, she'd chosen him for a tryst, but he wasn't grateful. In the gazebo, he'd repeatedly insulted her, had touched her in terrible, exhilarating ways, and even though she'd ordered him to stop, he hadn't heeded her commands.

Then he'd had to gall to try and make her put her mouth on his ghastly, manly rod. When she refused, he'd taunted her, sending her away as if she'd misbehaved. His scorn continued to incense her. It was like a burr under her saddle, enraging her, aggravating her.

No one was ever rude to her. No one was ever condescending or belittling. Others knew who she was, who her father had been, and they exhibited the respect and deference that was her absolute due. Yet he felt as if he had the right to treat her like a common whore.

Who was he to deem himself so grand? According to her mother, he was naught but a poverty-stricken neighbor who came sniffing round at supper, just so he'd have something to eat.

How she longed to get even!

She yanked the pins from her chignon and let her hair swish down, preferring it free and loose, and it made her wild and reckless. She abhorred that Margaret insisted she keep it bound, that she use combs and caps to conceal it. When men espied her auburn tresses, they were mesmerized. They wanted to run their fingers through it, to smell and pet it.

If Blaine were to see her beautiful hair, he wouldn't regard her as a child. He wouldn't tell her her breasts were too small or that she was a tease. He'd desire her, as a man desires a woman. She'd humor him, would watch him become aroused, would feign a bit of passion, and when he was chafing and ready, she'd walk away.

She'd show him who was in control. She'd teach him the consequences of trifling with her.

The notion of how she'd humiliate him caused her to

grow very excited. She'd welcomed their scuffling, how he'd bared her breasts and pinched them so hard. He'd hurt her, and for some reason, she was delighted that he had. She'd liked being anxious and unable to escape, and though she'd tried to deduce why it had been so stimulating, why she was so eager to do it again, she couldn't figure it out.

She'd flirted with many, many boys, but none of them had acted comparably, so she had no means of comparison. However, she'd relived that amazing encounter over and over. She wanted to dally with him, to experience what he would do to her, but when she'd had enough of his groping and pawing, she'd change the ending.

She would insult him. *She* would offend and slander, by remarking on his poor amatory skills, his sissified character, then she would have him trotting off like a coddled baby who hadn't got his way.

The idea of putting him in his place had her gleeful. In a thrice, she conjured a dozen methods by which she could extract revenge.

She *would* retaliate, and he would be *so* sorry.

At the window, she loitered. It was a warm, cloudless night, the stars twinkling, the moon illuminating the grounds and rolling hills beyond. She looked down into the yard, and she could detect the outline of the gazebo, the white paint stark in the dark garden.

A light glowed on the steps. She narrowed her gaze, focusing in, and . . .

It was he! Freddy Blaine!

Bold as brass, he was slouched against the railing and smoking a cheroot. His horse was tied in the rear as it had been for their previous rendezvous.

Hah! He'd wanted her, after all. Oh, this would be so amusing. She'd settle the score between them and be back in her bedchamber with scarcely a minute wasted.

Marching to the wardrobe, she grabbed her cloak, then tiptoed to the corridor and peeked out. Everyone was downstairs socializing, and her mother believed she'd gone to bed with the woman's headache, so it was a simple matter to sneak out.

She crept into the hall, detouring through Olivia's room. Within seconds, she'd found her sister's portfolio of drawings, and she hefted it onto the bed and dragged out the sketches. There were many new ones, evidence of an increasingly torrid romance. The stablemaster was portrayed naked, his privates exposed, though for the life of her, she couldn't fathom how Olivia was managing to engage in such intimacies.

They went riding every afternoon, and twice Penny had tracked them as best she could, but all they did was talk. She hadn't come close enough to hear what was said, but she'd seen nothing they couldn't have done in front of Margaret. How was Olivia accomplishing it?

She pilfered three of the most indiscreet poses, in which the stablemaster's masculine staff was prominent and unmistakable, then she made for the servants' stairs and out the door.

When she revealed them to Freddy, he'd never call her *child* again!

Speeding across the grass, she slowed once she approached the gazebo. She wasn't about to let him know she'd rushed to be with him, and she dawdled, hiding behind a hedge so that her breathing could level off.

After calming, she ambled onto the pathway and sauntered over, but as she neared, he chuckled as if he'd been observing her through the entire journey.

"Well, well," he crooned, as he took a lengthy draught from a bottle of liquor, "if it isn't the spoiled little rich girl. What brings you out so late? Did you lose one of your dolls?"

Seething with fury, she strove to remain aloof and disdainful. "I don't play with dolls. I have many more interesting toys to occupy me."

"Really?" he scoffed. "Tea sets and samplers?"

Strutting past him, she seized the bottle and flounced onto a bench. She drank from the decanter, too, making sure he saw how she could swallow the vile stuff.

"No. I'm an artist," she lied, and she set the bottle on the floor and removed Olivia's illustrations from beneath her cloak.

As she'd calculated, he followed her like a fish on a line. "What have you there?"

"Some of my sketches."

Ignoring him, she tipped one drawing toward the moonlight. The individual Olivia had depicted was difficult to identify, but she could discern that it was a man and that he was nude.

"It's one of my lovers," she fibbed. "He was so pleased with me that he permitted me to draw him after we were finished."

"Did he enjoy fucking a child?"

"I'm *not* a child!" she repeated.

"You could have fooled me." He snatched the pictures away from her, leaning toward the railing so that he would have a better perspective. "This chap's hung like a racehorse," he declared. "Did he take you like a bitch in heat?"

"Of course," she claimed. "I let him do whatever he wanted."

"Do you know what I think?" he asked, bending down. "You didn't create these. You've never come within a hundred yards of a naked man."

"I have too," she maintained. "I'll prove it to you! I

would sketch you, right here, right now, but I'll wager you're too scared to disrobe."

"As if I'd strip down for the likes of you." He scrutinized the pages. "They're very good. Very sensual. Where'd you find them?"

"They're mine." The illustrations weren't having the effect she'd hoped. She stood and attempted to yank them away from him, but he dangled them just out of reach. "Give them to me."

"No." He lifted them higher, and she jumped in her efforts to retrieve them. "Is your mother aware that you have these? I wonder how she'd react if I told her?"

"Blackguard!"

"Tut, tut," he scolded. "Is that any way to speak to your elders?"

She started to struggle in earnest, kicking with her feet, and lashing out with her fists, but she couldn't land any blows. Tired of pestering her, he tossed the papers away, and he pinned her wrists behind her.

"Your mother has failed in raising you." His fingers slithered inside the bodice of her dress, and he tweaked her nipple. "You could benefit from firmer discipline. Perhaps a whipping would suit you."

"Let me go!" she hissed.

"Is that what you require? A spanking?" He was angling her onto the bench. "You are such an impossible brat. I'd be more than happy to administer one."

Suddenly, she was lying down, and he was on top of her, though he was too tall to fit completely. A knee was on the floor, the other draped across her legs.

He loosened his grip, and she endeavored to slap his arrogant face, but he easily prevented her. "If you don't behave, I'll tie you up. Now do as I say."

"I won't!"

She continued to battle him, but not vigorously. It

was so fascinating to be held down, to be incapable of moving, while guessing what he might do next.

He'd tugged at her dress so that her breasts were bared, her nipples visible, and he was twirling and squeezing them in a painful fashion that made her squirm and grow wet between her legs.

He began kissing her, and she turned her head back and forth, striving to avoid him, but he clutched her chin. He stuck his tongue into her mouth, and he tasted like an adult male, like brandy and tobacco.

She hadn't been kissed like this before, and she was titillated by the naughtiness of it, by how different it was from the tepid mauling of the boys in the stable, but she wasn't about to let him know. She bit him. Hard.

Lurching away, he retaliated by crushing her nipple so that she cried out in agony, but he smothered the sound with his large palm. He whispered, "You hellcat. Try that again, and I'll strangle you."

Dipping to her bosom, he rooted and gnawed on her nipples, and she battled him, feigning aversion. It seemed much more gratifying, much more depraved and dangerous, when they were wrestling.

The alcohol she'd gulped was disorienting her. Before coming outside, she'd filched plenty of sips in the house, and the total quantity, coupled with the glasses of wine she'd had at supper, had her dizzy, irrational.

He was being very rough, and in a tiny part of her mind, she recognized that this wasn't going as she'd planned, that he wasn't pleading or groveling. They'd traveled beyond any sensible limit, and she should call a halt, but she truly didn't wish to. She craved this, had yearned for it for a very long time. It was far and away the most revolting, shocking thing she could conceive of doing.

There was no adult present to dissuade her, or order

her to refrain. No one knew where she was, or what she was about. She was free of her mother's criticisms and complaints, unfettered, and on her own.

He was hoisting her skirt and petticoats, meandering up her calf, then her thigh. She wasn't wearing any drawers, and with no warning or delay, he slipped his fingers inside her, and crudely stroked them.

"You're dripping, you strumpet."

"I loathe you. I'm sickened by the sight of you."

"That's not what your body is telling me."

As he pushed her skirt up to her waist, she glanced down at her crotch. Most of his hand was impaled, and the vision was bizarre, absurd. She couldn't credit that she was lying there like a limp noodle and allowing him to fondle her.

He sundered her nether lips and inspected her.

"I don't like fornicating with a woman who has hair on her privates. Steal a strop and a razor, and shave it off before our next meeting."

"That's disgusting. I won't."

"You will," he decreed. "Shave under your arms, too, so I won't have to look at it. I want you smooth and soft, like a young girl."

He wanted her to seem younger than she was? How very peculiar. She'd been trying to act mature, so he would reckon her to be much older. There was something important and vital concealed in his ultimatum, but she was too inebriated to deduce what it was, and she giggled, deeming the circumstances to be hilarious.

Down below, he was fiddling with his pants, and promptly, he was propelling himself into her, but not with his fingers. Whatever he was using was enormous, blunt, and it was stretching her to an uncomfortable width.

She whimpered, even though she hadn't meant to,

and she grappled to press her legs together, but he was wedged between them and inching into her, and his purpose dawned on her. For an eternity, she'd been weary of her tiresome virginity, and she'd sought methods to be relieved of it, but she was questioning her decision, and not positive she should go through with it.

Especially not here. And most especially not with him. He was too elderly. Too assertive and domineering. Too diabolical.

"You're hurting me," she protested. "Desist! At once!"

"Not bloody likely." He clasped her arms to her sides. "Go ahead. Fight if you want. Your petty skirmishing is amusing to me."

"I don't like this."

"Too damned bad. You're about to get exactly what you've been pleading for me to give you."

"Well, I don't want it anymore!"

"How many lovers have you really had?" He flexed his hips, and with a single lunge, drove himself into her.

The pain wasn't nearly as intense as she'd imagined or had heard it could be, but it wasn't as exciting or romantic as she'd heard, either. It was actually quite foul, and she mentally detached from what was transpiring. Her state of intoxication made it seem unreal, as if it were happening to someone else.

They were both sweating, and there was a strange smell in the air created by the joining. He was thrusting into her, squashing her so that she could scarcely breathe. While he appeared to relish what he was doing, *she* didn't note any emotion except for a fervent desire that it would soon be over.

He spilled himself inside her, and even that was a disappointment. He groaned and shuddered, then he collapsed onto her, and she suffered a frantic instant when she wondered if he'd had an attack of the heart.

Good God, had the oaf died?

But as he exhaled, her fears were allayed. Pulling out of her, he stood and adjusted his pants. He was calm as you please, while she was partially naked, her bosom still exposed. She didn't want him seeing her so disheveled, and she sat up. At her center, she was sore, wet and sticky, and she dragged her skirt down and tucked her breasts into her bodice.

He was insolent, preening, and he glared down at her. "We've determined, without a doubt, how many lovers you've had, haven't we?"

"You may have more experience than me," she sneered, "but the extra practice hasn't helped. I've dallied with boys who are better than you. You don't even know how to kiss!"

"I don't have to waste time *kissing* to get what I want from a woman." Scooping up the brandy, he took a swig, then wiped his sleeve across his lips. He offered her the bottle, and when she refused, he grabbed her by the neck and forced her to imbibe.

"You must learn to do as I say."

"You'll never make me."

"Don't be too sure."

He compelled her to drink, and she tried to keep her mouth shut, but he would have gladly sloshed it down her front, so she complied, gulping several draughts that burned her throat and watered her eyes.

"You need a stern master," he announced, "and I'm just the man for the job."

"Hah! You're never going to see me again."

"Yes I am," he replied. "You're like a dog at a bone, sniffing around. You've had a small taste, and you'll be back for more."

"I won't!"

"Your soul's as black as mine. You won't be able to resist."

Did she have a black soul? Was he correct? She'd always been different from everyone else, bored with the morals and restrictions others placed on her. It was thrilling to lie and steal, to engage in stealth and secrecy. There was constantly the risk of being caught, and it spurred her to increased recklessness.

Trifling with him was the very worst thing she could have done, the farthest line she could have crossed, yet she felt no remorse. At the very least, the loss of her virginity warranted that Margaret couldn't auction her off like a prized cow to a pompous, fusty old man, as she was trying to do with Olivia.

Was she evil? Debauched?

She grinned. Corruption was a bloody sight more fun than being a bluenosed puritan. Snatching up the brandy, she partook of a lengthy swallow, and he smirked, clearly expecting nothing less.

"Be here tomorrow night," he said. "I'll bring more liquor. And some opium. Have you ever tried it?"

"No."

"It will tickle your fancy." He picked up Olivia's sketches and held them out. "Now, return to the manor before you're missed."

"So what?" she chided. "I don't care."

"I'm not ready to be discovered with you. Not yet, anyway."

She had no idea what he meant, and it didn't occur to her that she should ask. Too rapidly, she rose and reached for the drawings, but she was dizzy and muddled. He attempted to steady her, but she yanked away.

"I don't need your assistance."

"That's what you think."

"You're a pervert, a prig, a . . . a . . ." Her brain wasn't working as it should, and she couldn't muster the names she yearned to hurl at him.

"Yes, I am," he freely admitted. "Tomorrow at midnight."

"I won't come. I hate you."

"If you don't show up, I'll sneak into your bedchamber. I'll tie you up and whip you. Then, I'll make you do it to me with your mouth. Even if you beg me not to."

"You're despicable, repulsive."

"So are you. We're destined to be great friends."

He shoved her toward the stairs, and she stumbled, then straightened, and departed without giving him the satisfaction of glancing back. She started down the pathway, and had just rounded the curve, when she ran into Olivia who, apparently, was out for an evening stroll.

"Penny?" she queried. "What on earth? I thought you went to bed an hour ago."

"I needed some fresh air," she fibbed.

"You've been tippling."

"What if I have?"

The gazebo was a few yards away, so they could hear Freddy mounting his horse and trotting off. Olivia frowned and peered through the shadows, trying to identify who was quitting the property.

"Who was that?" she inquired. "What have you been doing?"

"None of your business." She endeavored to walk around her stepsister, but Olivia blocked her.

"Was that Mr. Blaine?"

Penny shrugged, neither confirming nor denying who it was.

"Oh, Penny," Olivia admonished, clucking her tongue in dismay. "Tell me you haven't been out here with him."

"What I do isn't any of your affair."

"Oh, but it is. Would you embarrass your mother? And me? At the earl's house? We're his guests. What's come over you?" She stared into the darkness, as though she could behold Freddy's retreating form, but he was long gone. "Promise me that you won't speak with him again."

Penny remained aggravatingly, doggedly silent.

"If you won't give me your word," Olivia threatened, "I'll go to your mother."

A wave of fury swept over Penny. Who was Olivia to be issuing orders and chastising? It was irritating enough to listen to Margaret's incessant harping. She wasn't about to tolerate it from her whiny, mewling sibling.

"No you won't."

"I will," Olivia insisted.

She and Olivia were the same height, the same weight. She advanced until they were pressed up together, their skirts tangled, and she captured Olivia's forearm and pinched as hard as she could, causing Olivia to lurch away.

"I know about you and the stablemaster," Penny informed her.

"What?"

"I have some of the pictures you drew." She retrieved them from under her cloak and brandished them. "If you tattle about Mr. Blaine, I'll show them to Margaret."

Olivia blanched, fading to a ghostly white. "Penny!"

"We'll see who's in the most trouble then, won't we?"

Visibly afraid, Olivia studied her. "You could never do anything so wicked to me."

"Couldn't I?" She moved nearer, and her timid sister flinched. She liked the power she wielded, enjoyed witnessing Olivia's fear. "I don't care about you. I've *never* cared about you."

Appalled, aghast, Olivia recoiled. "You're mad."

Penny laughed, a low, malevolent chuckle that boded ill for any person foolish enough to cross her, then she turned and sauntered to the mansion, leaving Olivia quaking out on the lawn.

Jane peeked around the large chamber where the girls gathered to do their sewing. There were only a few left who hadn't finished their allotment, and she was one of them. With her benefactor having cut off her stipend, she had to earn her keep, and she spent many hours every day completing the required pieces.

Frantically, she stitched, panicked over her fate and what awaited her on the streets of London when she was ousted at age thirteen.

If she didn't accomplish a sufficient quantity, that dreaded moment would arrive even sooner, and she was desperate not to let it happen. Among the orphans, there'd always been rumors as to the horrors on the outside, and Jane believed every story.

She simply did not know how she would survive once she was handed her small bag and told to go.

Without warning, tears flooded her eyes. Throughout her stay at the orphanage, she'd dreamed that her mother and father would come for her. Mrs. Graves contended that her parents were deceased, that she was truly an orphan, but Jane had never been persuaded. If she had no family, who had paid her board for twelve years? A grandfather? A compassionate uncle?

She'd developed many romantic notions about who that individual might have been, and what had transpired to stop his routine support. Mrs. Graves asserted that her benefactor hadn't been her kin, but had made payments as a charity, had been sustaining an indigent girl as his Christian duty.

Jane hadn't accepted that folderol, either.

In her heart, she had felt that her parents were out there, hoping and searching, that they'd lost her and had been trying to find her all this time. But as her thirteenth birthday approached, she was forced to conclude that she'd been wrong. There was no one to save her, no one who would rush to her rescue.

She was all alone in the world, and the realization was too sad to bear, so she shook off the doldrums that had swamped her.

With so much work to do, she couldn't waste a single second bemoaning her fate. Even with her patron's support, she'd had sewing to do, and she had more now, plus she'd acquired the burden of doing it for Helen, as well. She'd tried and tried to explain the chore to the girl, to teach her to focus on the needle and thread, but Helen couldn't concentrate.

Jane couldn't account for why she was so fond of Helen, but she couldn't let her blunder through the perils at the orphanage on her own. She was so defenseless, so pitiful, and Jane was terrified that she'd be expelled for some misdemeanor, or that she would be given to those men who were interested in very young children.

Whenever Jane was advised the peculiar fellows were on the premises, she concealed Helen in a wooden chest. Jane had described the bad men, and Helen seemed to understand the danger. Without a fuss, she would climb in, and Jane would sit on the lid as though it were her customary perch, for she never wanted any of them to see Helen's amazing white hair, or her big blue eyes.

They had a habit of picking the fairest ones, and Jane was certain that they would select Helen, despite her abnormality. She was too fetching to escape their notice.

Toiling on, Jane stitched far into the evening, until it was too dark to continue. Mrs. Graves wouldn't let them use valuable candles, so she had to quit. She'd missed the bell to supper, but the cook was a kindly woman, and she would have hidden some bread and cheese for Jane in the kitchen.

She packed up her supplies, then went to locate Helen so they could sneak down to eat. Mrs. Graves was already gone, but Mr. Sawyer would be lurking about. Usually, he was napping, or indulging in spirits in Mrs. Graves's office, so Jane didn't need to worry about being detected.

In the girls' common room, she'd anticipated that Helen would be on her bed, but she wasn't there. Jane had escorted her to breakfast, and had ushered her back, counseling her not to go anywhere. On all other days, Helen had obliged. She could dawdle forever, not talking or noting the activity around her.

Jane hunted for her, peeking under beds and behind dressers, but her alarm escalated.

Had one of the sinister men abducted her without Jane's being apprised? Had she wandered off? She was so quiet, she could slip out the door without anyone's being aware.

She hastened down the stairs, as another girl was climbing up. "Have you seen Helen?"

"Who's Helen?"

"Martha," Jane amended. "The mute."

"The imbecile?" The other girl snickered.

"Yes," Jane said, biting down a scathing retort. "She was with Mr. Sawyer."

"Where were they going?"

"How would I know?" The girl shrugged and kept on.

Jane's heart plummeted to her feet. Mr. Sawyer was a queer, skulking swine, the exact sort Jane avoided at all costs. Once, he'd tried to drag her into a closet. She wasn't sure what he'd meant to do to her, but she'd fought like a cat, scratching and clawing at him, until she'd managed to flee, and he'd left her in peace ever since.

But he'd done the same with other girls, who hadn't been fortunate enough to get away, and they whispered about what had occurred.

What if he'd maltreated Helen?

She never enmeshed herself in the affairs of others, particularly now that she had to pay her own way. Her situation was too precarious, and if she angered Mrs. Graves, she could be tossed out in the time it took to pack her meager belongings.

Yet, she felt as if God had placed Helen in her hands, that Jane had been chosen to watch over her and keep her safe. Helen couldn't fend for herself. Jane had to be responsible for her, and she couldn't fret over the consequences.

If she didn't protect Helen, who would?

She tiptoed down to the kitchen where she obtained a broom and a knife. She tucked the knife into the pocket of her pinafore, then walked toward the front of the building.

No child was allowed on the main floor this late, and if she was caught, she'd be in dire trouble.

At night, the hallways appeared more grim and dingy than usual. She peered into the main parlor, the cozy, pleasant salon, where Mrs. Graves met with visitors so they would have the impression that the remainder of the facility was equally cheery.

The room was empty.

Trudging on, she examined one room after the next, slowly moving toward the rear. As she converged upon

Mrs. Graves's office, the door was ajar, and the dim glow from a candle glimmered through the crack. She crept closer. Halted. Listened.

There was a long silence, then Mr. Sawyer's evil chuckle wafted out. "You're a pretty, pretty girl, Martha," he said, "and you'll be my special *friend*. We'll have such fun."

Jane stepped up and peeked in.

Sawyer was in the chair behind the desk. Helen was on his lap, her ivory hair shining like a halo as he stroked it. She was solemn and motionless, staring into space, not seeming to be cognizant of his touching her.

Jane was so furious, she thought she might explode with rage, and she gave herself no chance to calm or come to her senses. Bursting through the door, she pushed it so hard that it swung open all the way and slammed against the wall with a sharp clack.

Mr. Sawyer whipped around so rapidly that Helen fell onto the floor, and she whimpered in dismay as she landed on her knees.

"What the hell . . .?" he barked.

Before he could protect himself or react, Jane rushed over and hit him with the broom handle. She raised it to administer another blow, but he grabbed the end before she could smack it down.

"I'll kill you for that!" His cruel eyes narrowed as he jerked the broom away and flung it into the corner.

"I'm not afraid of you!" she declared, though she was shaking.

Helen glanced up.

"Run away, Helen!" Jane urged. "Run fast! Hide till I come for you!"

Helen responded to Jane's urgency and scampered off, her tiny feet retreating down the hall, and Jane stood blocking the threshold, a speechless bulwark of wrath, until she was positive the girl was away.

Mr. Sawyer advanced on her, a large, violent drunkard, but she bravely confronted him. When he lunged for her, she pulled out the knife and brandished it at him. From the astonishment and fear that swept across his harsh features, he didn't doubt she'd use it, and he leapt out of range.

"If you so much as look at her again," Jane warned, "I'll wait till you're down here, passed out. Then, when you least expect it, I'll murder you in your sleep."

"That's mighty ferocious talk for a spit of a girl."

"I'd be very careful if I were you." She inched away, intent on departing before he recovered his mettle and charged her.

"Catty little strumpet." His foul breath washed over her, making her want to retch. "You think you're so tough? So smart? I'm straight to Mrs. Graves, I am. You'll be out on the streets like that!" He snapped his fingers.

"She'll never believe you over me."

"I wouldn't be too sure if I was you."

"I'll tell her what you do to the girls."

"As if she'd do anything about it." He laughed, the sound of it sending a chill down her spine. "Maybe I'll convince her she ought to sell you to Mr. Aires, whether you agree or not. I'll persuade her to sell your idiot chum, too. We'll see who's *afraid* then."

"She never would."

"Hah! Miss Priss, aren't you the know-it-all? You deserve to be brought down a peg or two." He bolted toward her. "Threaten me, will ya? How's 'bout I give you a taste of what's in store for you at Mr. Aires's *house*."

Jane spun and fled, knowing she'd used up whatever advantage she'd gleaned through her surprise entrance.

She sped down the hall and up the stairs, to the shelter provided by the other orphans whose presence would prevent him from committing mayhem.

She didn't pause till she was at her bed, and she slumped down onto the lumpy mattress, where she struggled to compose herself. A few of the older girls studied her, but posed no questions as to her disheveled state, and she was glad for their distance.

Panicked, forlorn, she was awhirl with dreadful speculation.

Sawyer was correct in everything he'd uttered. The cards had been dealt, and she'd played her hand the only way she could. The consequences, however disastrous they might be, would begin to rain down very soon.

Terrified, devastated, she started searching for Helen.

CHAPTER THIRTEEN

Edward stood at the fence, his forearms braced on the top rail, observing his handsome, dynamic son out in the field with a mare and her colt. With the grass so green, the sky so blue, and the fluffy clouds floating by, it was like a placid scene out of a fairy tale.

Who could guess that so many undercurrents were rushing through the tranquil setting?

Since that dreadful afternoon they'd fought behind the barn, they hadn't spoken, and he felt terrible about the horrid comments Phillip had hurled. How he wished there was some way to bridge the gaps that divided them.

Would Phillip always loathe him? Would their relationship remain that of employer and employee—two men who had nothing to discuss but horses? Could he repair the damage he and his wife had wrought?

For a long while, he'd deemed they were progressing. When Phillip had returned from his stint in the army—half-starved, partially crippled, and looking like death warmed over—Edward had been so relieved that he'd taken one of the few brave steps in his life: he'd begged Phillip to move into the manor. Much to Edward's dismay, Phillip had declined, but as a compromise he came for supper every evening.

Then, stupidly, Edward had canceled their arrangement so as not to embarrass his current guests. At the time, the request had seemed prudent, but he'd made a huge mess of it, insulting Phillip and hurting him, when he'd never meant to. He'd merely wanted an easy solution to where Phillip belonged.

Edward could never quite decide, and therein lay the crux of the problem. Where did Phillip belong? What role should he assume? It was unfair to treat him like a member of the family when it was convenient, but to hide him when it was awkward.

He was ashamed of himself, and the result—which served him right—was that he needed Phillip's advice and wise counsel, but he wasn't entitled to receive it. An enormous quandary was plaguing him, the answer impossible to glean on his own, yet his demolishing of their cordial association ensured that he dared not seek Phillip's guidance.

Should he marry Olivia? *Could* he marry Olivia? The recent letter from his solicitor was filled with rumors about the Hopkinses' finances, so how could he refuse? Was he so callous that he could send the women home to fend for themselves?

He didn't think so.

A proposal would ameliorate their fiscal predicament, and his wretched pursuit of a bride and heir could be concluded.

Olivia was a sweet, amiable girl, and he presumed they could trudge through matrimony together. There were many worse choices.

As he thought about it, he shook his head. Why was he willing to settle for so little? Decades earlier, he'd made the sensible selection, had followed the proper course, in picking his first wife. Their union had been ordinary, conventional, all that he'd expected and nothing more.

He'd been bored to tears. Each and every day.

Perhaps it was advancing age that made him restless

and dissatisfied, but the notion of enduring another such humdrum partnership left him weary and annoyed. He didn't want monotonous and mundane; he craved fire and spice and excitement.

Vividly, he could picture Winnie, dancing in the rain in the yard, her robe plastered to her skin, her breasts outlined whenever lightning had flashed. He could feel her mouth on him, her damp, luxurious hair brushing his thighs. Why was he so attracted to her? They were barely acquainted, and he knew nothing of significance about her save that she'd lost her virginity to an old love, but just from his recalling their wild encounter, his pants were growing tight.

They'd rutted like a pair of animals. Gad, but in his passionate frenzy, he'd ripped off her nightgown, had actually torn it down the center and tossed it away! He still couldn't believe he'd acted so savagely. In all his previous sexual trysting, he'd never been spurred to such ardent agitation. The woman goaded him beyond reservation or restraint.

Meeting her, knowing her, fornicating with her, had altered something deep inside, had him pondering his beliefs and convictions.

Another staid, tepid match was pointless and unpalatable. He wanted what he'd shared with Winnie. Why couldn't he have it? He was like a petulant child, denied his favorite toy. What was the benefit of his fortune, his status and power, if he couldn't possess his heart's desire?

Ever since he'd arisen, alone in his bed, to find her gone, and the minx having tucked her ruined negligee under his pillow, he hadn't seen her, but that hadn't prevented him from obsessing over her. He couldn't get her out of his mind, and he kept flirting with the most dangerous question: What if?

What if he cast off precedent and tradition? What if he abandoned his search for an aristocratic bride, and married Winnie?

The thought was so outrageous and so reckless that it had been keeping him awake, causing him to pace in the dark of night. To throw off societal shackles and wed a female of her station was asinine, scandalous. It was like demanding he agree that the earth was square or the ocean yellow. Yet the idea had his pulse pounding, his hopes soaring.

Could he? What if?

It went against every tenet that had been drilled into him from birth. Bloodlines mattered above all else. Position and rank determined one's path. No other option was available.

He couldn't marry her, but he couldn't conceive of how to forge on with a marriage to Olivia, either. In light of the uncontrollable ardor he harbored for Winnie, he saw naught but an interminable string of miserable social situations, with Winnie seated at his table, the two of them disconcerted and unspeaking.

The alternative was to make Winnie his mistress, and he tried to envision them sneaking around behind Olivia's back, but he couldn't imagine it. Winnie was too honorable, and he, himself, couldn't bear the furor that would ensue if they were discovered.

Oh, he was a mess! Distraught. Confused. Frustrated by his pedigree, and where it deposited him in the dilemma.

If only he could chase the women away, invite Phillip to the house, and parley confidentially! Phillip had a keen insight into people and their conduct, and Edward would give anything to probe the boy's opinions, but after their latest upset, Phillip would probably never debase himself by dining with Edward again. Edward pined for a return to those pleasant, quiet meals. Phillip was bright, interesting, funny, sincere, trustworthy, the sort of fellow any man would be proud to call friend. Or son.

Edward couldn't understand why they let so many trivial factors affect their relationship. Why couldn't they just get along? Was the past destined to forever haunt them?

Phillip had finished with his task in the pasture and was stomping toward the spot where Edward waited. Shielding his trepidation, Edward watched him come. Their gazes locked, Phillip's blue eyes dazzling in the sunshine, and he looked so much like his mother. Like Edward, himself. He was so athletic. So vigorous and lithe. So fine.

Phillip approached, his demeanor reflecting his anger, his stance combative, and he stopped so that they were toe to toe, though a gate separated them.

"What do you want?" he snapped, resigned to a quarrel.

Edward had been groomed to be a haughty, imperious individual, and his initial reaction was to utter an inane remark.

Instead, he surprised them both by admitting, "I miss having supper with you every night."

"What?" Phillip was dumbfounded by the declaration, inferring he hadn't heard correctly.

"I miss you," he repeated, "and I hate it when we fight."

"Hmm . . ." Phillip mused, at a loss for words.

"Could we chat?"

Phillip was hesitant, unsure. "I suppose."

Edward opened the gate, not giving him a chance to demur, and he stepped through. There was a gauche moment as they frowned at each other, both wondering what to say.

There were so many issues between them that remained unaddressed and unresolved, and it suddenly seemed vital to Edward that he discuss what had been vexing him. He was suffering from the strangest impression that he might not have many more opportunities.

"I haven't been much of a father to you, and I apologize."

Shocked, Phillip's brows rose, and he grumbled, "You've been good enough."

"You don't have to lie," Edward said, chuckling, "or spare my feelings."

"Well . . ." Phillip shrugged and, for some reason, blushed.

"I was horrid. To your mother. To you and your sister." He gawked up at the sky, unable to abide his son's piercing regard. "I didn't mean to be. I just . . . just . . ."

How to explain and justify a lifetime of poor decisions and neglect? There was no adroit way. "I wish we could be friends."

"It's difficult," Phillip allowed.

"I know." He wandered toward the garden. There was an isolated footpath a few feet away, and he gestured toward it, anticipating it would be easier to talk to Phillip without staring at him. "Will you walk with me?"

"You're the boss."

"Don't be like that."

Edward placed his hand on Phillip's shoulder, urging him forward, and it occurred to him that it was the first occasion where he'd touched his son since Phillip had been a rambunctious toddler. Not even when he'd arrived home from Spain, bandaged and on crutches, had Edward touched him. On deducing that Phillip was hale and would recover, Edward had been weak with relief, but he hadn't possessed the temerity to march over and hug him.

The realization shamed and saddened him, inducing him to once again rue and regret.

Why did he insist on maintaining such distance? What purpose was served in keeping Phillip at arm's length?

"I never should have asked you to hide while my guests are here."

"I'll survive."

Edward glanced to the side, and Phillip was smiling. An auspicious beginning.

"Join us for supper tonight," he pronounced, without having fathomed he would express the suggestion, "so that I can introduce you."

"You might give them a collective fit of the vapors."

"Let them swoon."

Phillip scowled, studying him. "Are you going daft on me?"

"Is that what you think is happening? I've tipped off my rocker?"

"Yes." Phillip chuckled. "I'll forgo your invitation. I'm not ready to *dine* with the ladies Hopkins."

"Well then, after they're gone, we'll start eating together—as we did before. And I want you to reconsider moving into the manor."

"What if you marry?"

"What if I do?" he shot off.

"How would your wife deal with our living arrangement?"

"It's a bloody big house," he muttered. "She'd just have to adapt."

Phillip scrutinized him as if he'd lost his mind. Perhaps he had. They strolled, bound for nowhere in particular, when he inquired, "What's your sister like?"

"Kind, pretty, hardworking. Why?"

"What would she do if I traveled to Bath and knocked on her door?"

"Slam it in your face."

"She loathes me that much?"

Phillip halted, flushed. "Sorry. I didn't intend it to sound so harsh."

"It's quite all right," Edward maintained. "I've earned her disfavor. It hurts to hear of it, but it's warranted." A brilliant thought occurred to him. "Would you go with me? To Bath? You could be the conciliator and smooth over our reunion."

Phillip assessed him. "Are you ill?"

"I've never been better." Which wasn't true. With each passing day, he was more troubled by the past, more repentant over his actions, while fretting and stewing over the future and where he wanted to go. The portions that constituted the man he knew as himself seemed to have been jumbled, like puzzle pieces shaken in a box, until they didn't fit, or some of them were missing.

They rounded a corner, and the flash of a burgundy dress caught his attention. It was Winnie, ambling slowly. Her back was to them, so she didn't see him, and he was able to examine her without her being aware. His heart leapt with delight and something else, something potent and indefinable, that terrified him.

Was it love?

He scoffed at his whimsy. As if he, at age forty-five, would finally fall in love! Especially with a commoner, a spinster, who had a sordid history about which she refused to speak. He was an earl, a peer of the realm, a lauded, distinguished aristocrat. She was . . . was . . .

He couldn't describe what she *was,* but the notion that he might be in love with her was hilarious and ludicrous, and he discarded it.

Upon espying her, Phillip recognized her as a member of the Hopkins party, and nervously, he paused. His unease spurred Edward to new heights of folly.

"Winnie," he called softly, and he was instantly desperate to have her know his only boy.

She stopped in her tracks, her ear cocked as if baffled by his voice. Timid as a doe before the hunter's gun, she whirled around, and she was awash with frantic emotions: giddy joy, chagrin, fear, bewilderment.

He yearned to take her in his arms and console her. They had a connection that couldn't be denied, yet she was glowering at him as if he were Doom descending. Why had she avoided him since that glorious evening of erotic bliss? It had been spectacular, amazing, magnificent, and he would do it again in a thrice if she gave the smallest indication that she was interested.

"Winnie, I'm so glad you're here." He advanced on her. "There's someone I've been wanting you to meet."

Trapped, she gaped down the path as though gauging whether he could catch her if she ran, but her exemplary manners won out. She fell into a full curtsy that, in view of their intimate acquaintance, embarrassed him.

"Lord Salisbury." She was subservient, shoulders bowed, her focus glued to the ground.

"Get up, now," he chided, helping her to rise, but she wouldn't look at him, and that perplexed him. When she was balanced on her feet, and propriety demanded that he drop her hand, he kept it, tucking it into the crook of his arm as if they were bosom companions.

"Phillip, may I present Miss Winifred Stewart, Lady Olivia's cousin from London."

"How do you do, Miss Stewart," Phillip replied.

"Actually, I'm the countess's cousin," she corrected. "Olivia and I are no relation at all."

"Of course. My mistake," Edward said. "Winnie, Phillip is my son, and my stablemaster. He's a veritable genius with horses. I told you about him."

"Yes, you did." Positioned between the two of them,

she was a tiny thing, and she appraised Phillip as if he were an extraordinary painting of which she needed to glean every detail. Then she glanced at Edward, peeking out from under the rim of her bonnet, her splendid hazel eyes disturbed and wounded. "He's a marvelous boy, Edward. You're so very lucky to have him."

"Aren't I, though?" At the admission, he was tickled to note how Phillip started in astonishment. He smiled and squeezed her fingers, and a silence developed that was the most jarring he'd ever endured.

"It was very nice to meet you"—she hesitated—"is it Mr. Paxton?"

"Yes," Phillip said, "but you may call me Phillip if you like."

"I will. Good day, Phillip. Lord Salisbury." She nodded, then she tugged her hand free and flitted away so fast that it seemed as if she'd never been there.

He stared at the spot where she'd disappeared around the hedges, then he turned to Phillip. His shrewd son had detected the swirling undercurrents. He was curious, enthralled, a thousand questions perched on the tip of his tongue.

"What the hell was that about?" Phillip queried.

"I couldn't begin to explain," Edward remarked, sighing. "If I asked you about women," he posed, "could you enlighten me as to how they think?"

"No, absolutely not. I haven't the slightest idea what goes on in their heads."

"I was afraid you'd say that."

Phillip evaluated him. "Are you in love with that woman?"

"In love? With Miss Stewart? How preposterous." He laughed as if he hardly knew her, as if Phillip's intimation was absurd, and—he was positive—he'd damned himself to hell in the process. He sighed once more. "Would you excuse me?"

"Certainly."

"We'll talk later."

"Whenever you wish," Phillip acceded.

Edward strode off, but Phillip's inquisitive gaze cut into his back, and it was a relief when he slid around the corner and out of sight.

He couldn't see Winnie, but she'd been proceeding toward the house, so he went in the same direction. As he neared, he glimpsed her slipping through the door on the verandah, which would convey her to the main hall and up the stairs to her room.

He increased his speed, not sure of what he was doing, but with each stride, his resolve grew. He was angry with her, tired of her hiding, weary of her pretending that nothing had transpired between them. His feelings for her were the sole exceptional, intriguing thing that had happened to him in ages, and he wasn't about to tolerate further evasion.

The Hopkins family was scheduled to stay for another ten days, and by God, he would spend some of that time with Winnie—whether she liked it or no!

He fairly raced up the steps and into the manor. A few servants were scattered about, but his rapid pace guaranteed that none detained him. As he reached the staircase, he rushed to the upper floors where the bedchambers were located.

Hers was down the opposite hall from his, and for the briefest second, he halted outside her door to satisfy himself that no one was watching, then cocky as a rooster, middle of the morning, he sauntered in.

She was by the window, having just poured herself a stout glass of red wine, and she was grasping it with both hands to control their shaking. At his unannounced, inappropriate entrance, she paused in mid-sip.

"Go away!" she quietly ordered, woefully adding, "Please."

In response, he spun around and rotated the key in the lock, sealing them in. "No."

"I don't want this," she contended. "I don't want you."

"What you want, or don't, has ceased to matter to me."

In a fine temper, he stomped across the space separating them, grabbing her wine and partaking of a healthy swig. She stood her ground, furious herself, accusing, reproaching.

After setting the glass on the table, he embraced her, his mouth falling to hers, but she averted him, so he kissed her cheek, her neck, blazing a trail to her bosom, her cleavage. His fingers were busy in her lustrous hair, yanking at the pins so that it swooshed down.

"I'll have you now, Winnie Stewart. Now and again and again." He picked her up and carried her to her bed. "You can't deny me."

"I'll scream." She was lying. Neither of them dared draw attention to what he was about.

"Do . . . if you'll feel better."

"You're crazy," she asserted.

"Very likely."

"I'll request that the men from Bedlam come to fetch you."

"I'll go willingly, as soon as we're finished."

He felt as if a stranger inhabited his body, as if he were a conquering mercenary, bent on pillage and plunder.

Stretching out, he kissed her in earnest, mouth, teeth, tongue, toying with hers as he fumbled with her dress, with the laces on her corset.

Pushing down the bodice, he exposed her, the curvaceous mounds spilling into his hands. Caressing them, petting them, he pinched the nipples till she was squirming and writhing, then he suckled the lush tips, calming and soothing himself by nursing at her.

She arched up, offering more of herself, and he indulged, shifting from one breast to the other, dallying, trifling.

Below, he was lifting her skirt as he unbuttoned his pants and, resigned to what was about to occur, she didn't encourage or hinder his actions. He knew he should desist, or apologize, or clarify what was driving him, but he couldn't give voice to the insane urges she inspired.

His phallus was ready, eager, and he guided it to her wet, welcoming center, plunging into her like a randy boy, with no regard for her comfort or enjoyment. But she didn't seem to mind; she widened her thighs and pulled him close.

"You're crazy," she claimed again.

"Yes. Crazy for you."

"We'll be caught."

"I don't care," he declared. "I don't care about anything but this."

He started to take slow, measured strokes. She'd uncaged the beast inside him, a virile, menacing creature that was capable of any despicable deed, that would commit any outrageous exploit to achieve satiation.

He braced himself, his palms on either side of her, and she massaged his chest. Except for his cock protruding from his trousers, he was still fully clothed, for he hadn't the patience to dawdle, to woo or seduce.

"Are you going to marry Olivia?" she asked, a faint sheen of tears causing her eyes to glitter like diamonds.

"Hush. I don't want to speak of it now."

"Are you?" she demanded, and embarrassed, he looked away.

"Yes. No. I don't know."

"Promise me," she begged, "that if you do, you'll send me far away from here."

"Winnie—"

"To another part of the country, where it's too distant to visit. So I'll have valid explanations for why I can't come for Christmas, or for the christening of your first child."

"I couldn't agree to never seeing you."

She began to cry, the tears dripping down, and she hugged him, pressing her cheek to his. "If you marry her, I can't live here. It would kill me, little by little."

"We could buy you a house nearby," he suggested, devising the scenario as he went. It was insulting to conceive of her as his mistress, but he couldn't permit her to walk out of his life.

"In the neighborhood?" she facetiously posed. "Just down the lane?"

"We'll figure it out."

"No. Any association would be fraught with peril, and she can't ever find out what we've done, or how I've betrayed her."

She was making their rapturous link sound so terrible, when he wanted her to view it as rare and unique— as he did himself.

"We've *betrayed* no one." But even as he pronounced the sentiment, he felt guilty. Instead of trysting, he should have been downstairs, chatting with Olivia and Margaret.

By lusting after Winnie, he was being disloyal to so many. Yet how could such fervent yearning be wrong?

"Swear to me that you'll help me to move away."

"I never could."

"You must. Don't you understand? We can't continue like this."

"I don't *understand* anything. All I know is that you're here, and I can't stay away." He curled his hand around hers and kissed her fingers. "I can't predict what the future will bring. I can't see any farther than this moment."

"This is a disaster."

"No, it's not, Winnie. It's simple. It's you and me, alone." He sank into her, each thrust penetrating to her womb. "It's so right."

With a sob of anguish, she accepted what he was doing to her, joining in the rush to gratification. She wrapped her arms around his waist, her feet around his legs.

His tempo was no longer deliberate or purposeful. He'd leapt beyond restraint. There was only her, and his vital, compelling desire for her.

Reaching between them, he touched her with his thumb, and an orgasm swept over her. She moaned, and he captured her wail of ecstasy, letting it mingle with his own as he spilled himself inside her.

An alarm bell rang, but he couldn't heed its warning.

By spewing his seed, he'd transgressed in a fashion that was much more dangerous, and more immature, than the abuse he'd leveled on Phillip's mother. On this occasion, he couldn't use youthful naïveté or exuberance as an excuse.

He might have impregnated Winnie—as his potential bride was down in his parlor, sipping tea. There were a hundred reasons his behavior was callous and negligent, but he wasn't concerned. On the morrow, there would be plenty of opportunity to lament, but for now, he would rejoice, and wallow in the luxury of having had her in the only way that counted.

Immersed in her, Winnie's lavish torso enfolding him from head to toe, he couldn't remember ever feeling so happy. He was reeling, stunned, dazed by his burgeoning affection.

What if she were pregnant? Did he have a secret wish

for it to be so? If she were increasing, she couldn't trot off to the hinterlands, hoping to elude him. A babe would provide genuine justification for contact, for a persisting affiliation.

The possibility was electrifying, and it raised his pulse to such an elevated rate that he frightened himself.

Was he planning on fatherhood? On siring another illegitimate child? With an inappropriate, unknown woman, to whom his sole connection was strident sex? Had he learned nothing from his past mistakes?

Apparently not, for he coveted a family with her so badly that he could taste it. When he shut his eyes, he could envision perfect girls, with her brunette hair, dancing across the floor. Rowdy boys, who looked like Phillip, wrestling on the rug.

His need to make them a reality was primal, incomprehensible, and he declined to acknowledge them, forcing them to vanish.

"You shouldn't have done that," she whispered in his ear.

"I'm sure you're correct."

She sighed, the weight of the world on her shoulders. "What are we to do?"

"We'll make love till dusk," he said. "After that, I wouldn't hazard a guess."

She chuckled humorlessly. "I suppose there are worse ways to spend the day."

"I can't think of any better." He retrieved a blanket and dried the tears on her cheeks. "Don't fret, Winnie. It will work out for the best."

Agonized, she assessed him. "Don't hurt me in the end. My heart couldn't bear it."

"I never will," he vowed, even as he wondered if he could keep his pledge. How could any of this have a beneficial conclusion?

"If we're to dally"—she slid off him and commenced unbuttoning his shirt—"we might as well disrobe."

"A marvelous idea."

He grinned and rolled onto his back, letting her take the lead.

Penelope hovered inside Olivia's room, ready to sneak out. Olivia's portfolio was tucked under her arm.

After their encounter the previous night, she'd determined it would be advantageous to steal the satchel of pictures. It wouldn't do to have them disappear just when she needed to show them to Margaret.

She'd been positive that Olivia would have concealed the drawings in a new spot, so she'd been delighted to stumble across them still tucked under Olivia's pillows.

Olivia's main character flaw was that she was too trusting, too honest, and she naturally assumed that others were, too. For an adult, she was incredibly naïve. And stupid. In this instance, her idiocy would be her downfall.

While Penny had merely insinuated that she'd tattle to Margaret, she had no intention of waiting. If Olivia breathed a word, Penny would be sent to London, and she wasn't anywhere near finished with Freddy Blaine. He presented too many exhilarating prospects, and she meant to explore every one of them.

Others couldn't be allowed to spoil it for her. Least of all stuffy, proper Olivia.

Rubbing her thighs together, she relished the ache that remained from her wicked rendezvous with Freddy. While she wasn't certain how she'd ended up surrendering her virginity, she was thrilled to have it gone. The deed had been a tad less inspiring than she'd been led to believe, and definitely less romantic, but it was tolerable.

She would make her own choices, would do as she

pleased—with Freddy or anyone else who tickled her fancy—and she wasn't about to be dissuaded by a bit of pain or discomfort.

Smirking, she reflected on how furious her mother would be at this turn of events. Margaret had so many grandiose schemes, which included dukes and princes, but Penny had found a fellow who was much more to her liking, who knew what she wanted and needed, who went out of his way to obtain it for her.

And he was rich, too! Despite Margaret's grumbling about his finances, Penny had eavesdropped when the maids were gossiping, about his fine house and elegant carriage, his dapper clothes and toplofty friends. He'd be able to support her in the style to which she was accustomed.

There'd be no arranged marriage to some boring, tedious oaf like Edward Paxton. She craved excitement, action, the exact sort of existence she imagined Freddy would furnish on a daily basis.

She ran a hand down her stomach, to her privates, touching herself. Freddy had commanded that she shave, and just to annoy him, she was going to refuse, but the more she considered it, the more titillated she was by the depraved dictate. It would be decadent to walk around in polite company, knowing she'd removed the hair between her legs!

She'd snooped in an empty guest room and had located a razor, had taken it to her bedchamber and placed it in a drawer as if it belonged there. Now, she had to muster the courage to use it.

Peeking out, she checked to see if it was clear, when down the hall, another door opened, and Penny's eyes widened. She'd presumed she was the only one on the floor. If she'd deemed otherwise, she wouldn't have tarried.

To her amazement, Winnie poked her head out and scanned the corridor. Though it was late afternoon, her hair was down, and she was attired in a flimsy robe that was loosely tied at the waist, most of her naked torso exposed.

Espying no one, she stepped back, and the earl emerged! He bent down and bestowed a lingering kiss, then he strolled out and strutted to the stairs. At the landing, he stopped and gazed at her. They didn't speak, but the look he gave her was passionate, intense, riveting. He shrugged, flashed a rueful smile, and descended.

Winnie watched him go, then she slumped against the doorframe, her knees weak; she whimpered, and it sounded very much like despair. For a lengthy interval, she rested there, letting the wood brace her up, until she regrouped and closed the door. The key clicked in the lock.

"My, my," Penny murmured. Wasn't this intriguing?

The earl and Winnie were so greedy for each other that they'd risk philandering in broad daylight. Did the earl love Winnie? Might he be pondering marriage to her rather than Olivia?

Penny mulled the questions over and over.

This won't do at all, she resolved.

Olivia would wed Edward. Penny had already decided on it. Olivia loved the stablemaster, and she was likely contemplating how she could end up with him instead of the earl.

Wasn't she in for a rude awakening?

Nobody threatened Penny. Nobody told her what to do or how to act. By sticking her nose into Penny's business with Freddy, Olivia had made a grave error, and she would have many, many years to regret it throughout her protracted and monotonous marriage to Edward.

Winnie couldn't interfere in the impending outcome.

She had to leave the property, and Penny needed to determine how to effect her rapid departure. There were many details to be contrived, many feasible scenarios that could be set in motion. Which one was best?

She tiptoed into the hall and crept away, unheard and unseen, her thoughts awhirl with possibilities.

Chapter Fourteen

Olivia crept across the grounds, the waning moon lighting her way, but she needed no illumination to guide her. Her feet had a second sense that led her to her destination.

Up ahead, Phillip's cottage was outlined in the shadows, a candle burning in the window as he waited for her to arrive. She pulled up short, listening to the silence, staring at the cozy building, her heart pounding in her chest.

This was the last occasion she'd visit him. She would never again observe his house from this angle, would never have this wondrous feeling of anticipation, or suffer this exhilarating rush of joy.

The entire day, she'd been on pins and needles, braced for the shoe to drop, to be ordered to Margaret's room for the lambaste that would ensue, but it hadn't transpired. She'd been a nervous wreck, speculating and fretting over what the backlash would be.

By the time it had dawned on her that she should hide her portfolio, the pictures had vanished. She'd searched every nook and cranny of her bedchamber, praying that she'd somehow mislaid the satchel, that perhaps the maids had discovered it and moved it while tidying up.

She'd even dared to ask a servant if she'd seen the pouch, but the girl had denied any knowledge of its existence, and Olivia had believed her.

Where were the sketches? Did Penny have them?

Of course she does!

The glaring response rang through her mind. What else could have happened to them?

Oh, why had she drawn them? What was she hoping to achieve?

Yes, she was fascinated by nudity, by erotica and the novel impressions one experienced while perusing it, just as she was captivated by Phillip, by his shape, his masculinity. Her busy fingers had recorded every detail she could recall from their furtive assignations. There was no portion of him unexplored, no antic undepicted.

What would Margaret say? What would she do? Margaret was neither her mother, nor her guardian. Not even her friend, really. But Olivia showed her great respect out of deference to her deceased father. Margaret had never been the most agreeable person, but she and Olivia had shared the same home for years, and Olivia would never intentionally offend the older woman, for any slight would tarnish her father's memory.

She'd been such a selfish fool! Margaret had worked so hard to find a route out of their financial conundrum, but Olivia hadn't done her part. Through her impetuous actions, she'd ruined any chance she might have had to wed Edward. She'd let down her family, had forsaken her responsibilities to them. For what?

For her love of a man whom she could never marry.

From the first moment they'd met, she'd been bewitched, but she'd recognized, without a doubt, that they had no future. Yet she'd pursued him, had lured and cajoled and pleaded with him to dally. He had, but to what end?

Margaret would insist on proceeding to London, locating another suitor, aspiring to arrange another immediate marriage to stave off catastrophe. In the interim, what would become of Phillip? If Edward learned of the debacle, would Phillip lose his job, as well as his residence?

How had their immense affection brought them to this horrid juncture?

She shouldn't be going to him, but she couldn't stay away. She had to talk with him and confess her fears, had to be with him once more before the consequences began to rain down.

Suddenly desperate, she picked up her skirt and flitted across the remaining patch of lawn. As though fleeing from the devil, himself, she rounded a hedge and raced toward him. He was watching from the stoop, impatient and eager, and he whisked her inside, locking the door behind.

"I'd about given up on you." He plucked at her cloak, yanking it away and tossing it on the floor.

"Oh, Phillip . . ." Relieved, finally able to catch her breath, she felt her trepidation and apprehension lessen merely by being in his presence.

He hugged her, running his hands up and down her back. "What is it?" he queried. "What's wrong?"

"Everything," she murmured, "and nothing at all."

"You're trembling."

"From the cold," she lied. She was afraid and worried. After encountering Penny in what could be characterized as a deranged condition, Olivia couldn't predict what doom was pending. She only knew for certain that it was approaching, and it would be dreadful.

"Would you like me to start a fire?"

"No. Just hold me. Then I'll be fine."

"An easy request to honor, Lady O." Swooping her up, he carried her to his bed, laying her down and joining her. Warming her, he adjusted a blanket over them, then cuddled her to him.

As they snuggled, her breasts and tummy were pressed to his, legs tangled, and his superb scent soothed her. She could imagine no more spectacular spot to linger, and she wished she could nestle there in perpetuity. No problem could ever be too weighty to handle when she was in his arms.

"Tell me," he urged, after her shivering had abated.

She was glad she was burrowed tight, that she didn't have to look at him. "We can't rendezvous again."

He exhaled. "We knew we couldn't keep on forever. Are you returning to London?"

"Soon. You see, my sister, Penelope—"

"The red-haired hellion?"

"The very one." His description was extremely apt! "She found some of my pictures."

"Of what?"

"Of . . . of . . ." She'd never confided in him about her sketching. How mortifying to admit what she'd done!

"Spit it out," he coaxed when she couldn't finish. "It can't be that bad."

"I've been making portraits of you. And me." Her recounting was too coy, so she added, "We're . . . *together,* if you can understand."

He froze, shifted away so that he could gaze at her. "You've been drawing . . . erotica? Of us?"

He didn't need to kindle a fire. Her cheeks flushed such a hot pink that she was heating the room as efficiently as any brazier. She gulped. "Do you think I'll go to hell for it?"

"Livvie, you sexy minx!" He rolled onto his stomach, laughing merrily.

"This isn't funny."

"No, it's not," he agreed, but he continued to chortle, mirth sweeping him away, and his jollity irritated her.

"You're not being very helpful."

"I know, but this is too rich." He rotated onto his side, petting a comforting hand along her shoulder. "Am I displayed in the buff? Balls and all hanging out?"

"Yes, but more often, we're . . . we're . . ."

"So there's no question that it's me and you?"

"None. I'm not the most talented artist—"

"You're terrific."

"—but I can draft a distinguishable face."

"And a *distinguishable* body part?"

She punched him in the ribs. "Stop it."

"All right, all right." He ceased his teasing, shook his head, sighed. "What a tangle."

"Yes."

"How can you be positive she saw them?"

"She had several of them in her possession," Olivia explained. "I kept them in a portfolio under my pillow, and somehow, she discovered them. Now, the entire satchel is missing, and I'm sure she took it."

"Why?"

"Last night, when I was sneaking back to the manor, I caught her out in the yard. She'd been in the gazebo with your father's neighbor, Mr. Blaine."

"Freddy Blaine? What was *he* up to?"

"Mischief. Her hair was down, and her dress was askew. She was intoxicated."

"How old is she?"

"Sixteen."

"I'm surprised," he mused. "She's much more mature than he generally likes his partners to be."

"What do you mean?"

"Some men are titillated by . . . by . . ." It was his turn to blush and stammer.

"By what?"

"Let's drop it."

"No!"

"By . . . by . . . children."

"They're sexually aroused?"

"Yes."

"But that's perverted."

"It definitely is."

"Mr. Blaine is one of these people?"

He nodded.

"How do you know?"

"Livvie," he admonished, exasperated by her curiosity, but she couldn't desist.

What sort of insane reprobate would be stimulated by children? She shuddered at the notion, and he nestled her closer.

"Is this dangerous for her?"

"Probably."

"Oh, I can't decide what I should do."

"About what?"

"She threatened me."

He was startled, alarmed by the news. "She what?"

"She claimed that if I told anyone about her and Mr. Blaine, she'd give the sketches to Margaret."

"The girl's crazy."

"I concur. But her behavior is reckless and stupid. How can I be silent?"

"Would she follow through with her blackmail?"

"If you'd asked me that yesterday, I'd have said 'absolutely not.' But after seeing how out of control she was, I couldn't begin to guess what she might do."

"Would you like me to speak with her? I've had a few go-arounds with her when she's been lurking behind the stables. I seem to intimidate her. Perhaps I could scare her off."

"Lord, no." That was all she needed, for Phillip and Penny to have a quarrel. "She's very sly, Phillip."

"Yes, she is."

"If you talked to her, it would be obvious I'd rushed to you straightaway. She'd be certain of how attached we are. I'd rather have her wondering."

He mulled this over, his eyes searching hers. "If she shows them to your stepmother, will the countess insist that I marry you?" Tentatively, he smiled. "I would. In a heartbeat."

"Oh, Phillip . . ." His offer was so sweet, the idea of being his wife so thrilling, but it could never be, and she had to focus on that reality. She couldn't allow flights of fancy to take wing. "We've been through this before. A marriage to me has to include all of us."

"People have survived on less," he muttered, a tad bitterly, which made her angry.

Could he envision the five of them, living with him in the small cottage? Had he truly considered how ridiculous the concept was?

How would he afford their food? Their clothing? Penny had to make her debut, and they had dozens of retainers who required severance or pensions. That was for starters. There were so many expenses involved in selling the properties, in paying off the debts.

If she married him, the arrearages wouldn't evaporate. From where would the funds come to square the deficit?

It was unfair of him to chastise her, to act as though she were frivolously spurning him. He couldn't comprehend the pressure under which she labored, the strain she felt with regard to the females in her life. So much was riding on her shoulders, and he couldn't assume her load, or fix the dilemma for her.

Brutal as it sounded, money was the cure, the remedy she sought. He didn't have any, so he couldn't be the one. He was poor. The situation was no more elemental or complicated than that.

"Don't let's fight," she chided.

"We're not." He brushed a kiss across her lips.

"I've tried to figure out what Margaret will do." She shifted the conversation away from his finances—or lack of them. "I believe she'll have me go to London, to commence anew with another suitor. She won't want any scandal that might affect my reputation, and she wouldn't hazard having your father learn of our affair."

"So you'll be leaving soon."

"Maybe tomorrow." She rested her palm on his cheek. "Even if it's not tomorrow, I don't dare visit you again. It's too risky now."

They gazed at each other, and Olivia prayed he could read the sentiment she was concealing inside. She ached to confess how much felicity he'd brought to her, how much delight and gladness. He was like a ray of sunshine, and he had changed her, had furnished her with a fuller understanding of herself as a woman.

With every fiber of her being, she wanted to proclaim how much he meant to her, how much she loved him, but she kept quiet, hoping he could discern the secret for himself.

What good would it do to declare her emotions? Though he tried to hide it, he was chivalrous, had noble intentions. If she but asked, he would do anything for her. But it was grossly inequitable to request his assistance, or hint that she would embrace his aid, when she could never reimburse him for his loyalty and devotion with any long-term commitment.

If he realized how much she cared for him, he would feel compelled to obligate himself in whatever fashion she would permit, but their paths were on diverse trajectories, and they were shooting toward different universes. She wanted to spare him any repercussions caused by her rash conduct. She couldn't abide having him hurt or persecuted for what she'd wrought. He was valorous, and he might attempt to take the blame, to pretend their relationship had been at his instigation, which she could never countenance.

It was better to have him presume that he'd been a fleeting caprice. Let him suppose her esteem was heightened, genuine, but not overwhelming. It would be easier for both of them.

As for herself, she couldn't predict what would become of her. It was best that this folly be ended quickly and peacefully, for she couldn't wed Edward after having loved Phillip. But could she accept another suitor as her plight would demand? Could she marry another? Could she welcome him into her bed?

The answers to those questions were beyond her, too painful to contemplate, too depressing to ponder.

"I want to make love to you," he said.

"I'd like that."

"So you'll always remember what it was like."

As if she'd ever forget! Did he think she would? The blasted man.

This brief interlude had been the most exciting, exhilarating period of her life, and she would hold it to her heart, would never let it go. Should she be lucky enough to live to a ripe old age, she'd recall each and every detail with vivid clarity.

Such distinct, intense euphoria could never fade.

She pulled him into an ardent kiss, and with great relish, he reciprocated. He moved onto her, giving her his weight, and she hugged him close, cherishing the sensation of his large body pushing her down.

After her departure, he would have other women. But how many? Would they find such pleasure and bliss?

Oh, how the thought wounded her!

More terrible still, she imagined the day she would ascertain—in some unexpected way—that he'd wed. Maybe she'd see Edward in town, and he'd mention the estate. She'd hear Phillip's name in passing, that the newlyweds enjoyed a simple existence, that his bride had been elated to share his cottage, to birth him a gaggle of cheerful, boisterous children.

She shut her eyes and could visualize him laughing and content.

At that moment, she came nearer than she ever would to relenting, to forsaking her family. Was it so wrong to want this glorious man? To do whatever she could to make her dream come true?

Even as the greedy supposition presented itself, she shoved it away. She could never cast off the shackles that bound her. Selfishness had never been an aspect of her character, and her personal happiness would perpetually be secondary.

If she broke down and married, she wouldn't encounter this type of ecstasy, this negligent, burning passion that he inspired solely by looking at her. She wanted to experience every facet of his ardor, to saturate herself with the feel and smell of him, to bind herself so deeply and so completely that neither time, nor distance, nor altered circumstances could tear asunder the connection they'd forged.

He was fumbling with her dress, slipping the buttons through the holes, revealing her breasts. She went to work, too, opening his shirt, jerking down the sleeves.

Their upper torsos were uncovered, his chest hairs abrading her soft skin, inciting her to recklessness. She snuggled down, rooting to his nipple, and she took it in her mouth, licking and nibbling at the tiny nub, inducing his breath to hitch, his muscles to tense.

Previously, she hadn't been the aggressor, but had lain lazily, the recipient of the rapture he'd lavished on her. She'd been a novice, a pupil, anxious to master the techniques he taught, but tonight, she longed for more.

She yearned to tease and taunt him, to goad him beyond his limits. As he wanted her to recollect the stirring physicality that had blossomed, so too did she plan that—when their tryst was over—he would never forget, either.

He rotated them, so that she was on top, so that her breasts dangled over his enthusiastic mouth, and he nuzzled from one to the other, until she was wild for him.

"Talk to me about the sketches you drew of us," he coaxed. "Were we together like this?"

"Yes, yes," she moaned, scarcely capable of speech with the torment he was inflicting.

"Am I nursing at your breast?"

"Occasionally." Her stomach tightened in knots as he bit down on her nipple and rolled it between his teeth.

"Are the pictures arousing?"

"Very."

He was lifting her skirt, baring her calves, her thighs, his hands at the curve of her bottom, but maddeningly, he went no further.

Why didn't he proceed? She was a hot torrent of need, frantic for him to move those last, decisive inches, to alleviate some of her agony. He clutched her rear, and he was rubbing her privates into his.

"Would you like me to touch you?"

"Please." The word came out as a whimper.

"Where? Between your legs?"

"Yes. Now!"

"With my fingers? Or my tongue?"

"Either. Both. I don't care."

"Should I let you come? Or make you wait?"

The naughty banter thrilled her. Just as with the carnal illustrations, she hadn't understood that mere speech could provoke one to a frenzy.

"Let me—"

He wrapped his lips around her nipple, sucking hard, cutting off whatever she might have solicited. His fingers slithered up, up, but they never arrived where she needed them most. He massaged her thighs, her buttocks, her thighs again, and she was writhing, groaning, but to no avail. She couldn't find satiation.

Turning them, he tossed her onto her back, and with rapid, short bursts, he impaled her with his tongue. She panted and struggled toward the end, and a powerful wave coursed over her. Soaring to the heavens, she cried out his name, and he pinned her down, as the fervor peaked, as it began to wane. Yet when she'd regained her equilibrium, she wasn't sated, and she knew she could only be truly assuaged if he inserted his phallus into her.

He was kneeling before her, unfastening his trousers. There was a strange air about him. It was primal, feral, and he seemed to be perched on a precipice, teetering, uncertain. She wanted to set free whatever barbarian was trapped within. Dare she propel him over the edge?

"Take me, Phillip."

"No."

"I'm begging you to be the one."

"You *have* to marry, Livvie. Isn't that what you keep telling me?"

"Yes, but—"

"If I steal your virginity, you can never wed." He dipped into her with his fingers, fondled and spread her. "I won't make your predicament any worse than it is."

"I'll lie on my wedding night, I'll fake it, I'll . . . I'll . . ."

With what he was doing, it was difficult to concentrate.

Straining, she was impatient for the relief he could bestow. She didn't really wish to surrender her virginity, and in a foggy, confounded portion of her brain, she recognized that it was the most harmful thing she could possibly do, but lust had overwhelmed her better sense.

"Phillip!" she implored.

"Be still!"

Taut, agitated, sweat pooled on his brow and chest. His cock was out of his pants. It was turgid, erect, and he clutched his fist around it, stroking himself. Then he leaned in, aiming the blunt crown toward her.

He parted her nether lips, and she braced for the sharp pain that would ensue as he entered her, but to her dismay, he didn't progress. Draping her legs over his thighs, stretching her further, he peered down, studying and palpating her.

Flexing the slightest amount, he brushed the tip across her wet, swollen flesh.

"God, I could be inside you in an instant." Halting, he stared at the ceiling, as if praying for strength. "It would be so easy."

"Do it."

"Don't give me permission," he snapped. "I'm not a saint."

"Neither am I." She'd always considered herself to be moral and upright, but her bawdy disposition had routed every virtuous trait. "I can't visit you again. This is the only chance we have, and I want to discover what it's like. Don't make me learn of it from a husband for whom I have no tender feelings."

"Don't mention your future *husband* when you are in my bed."

"Then show me. I would have it occur now, with you, so that I will know joy and abandon. Not later, when it will be performed out of duty and obligation."

He scrutinized her, and she could almost see the battle that was raging inside him: He cared for her, and he couldn't bear to hurt her, or exacerbate her situation, but above all else, he desired her. Eventually, manly ardor won out over gallantry and wisdom.

"Lie back." Pushing her down, he tugged at his pants, exposing his hips, his flanks, then he kneed her thighs ever wider.

The beast within was loose.

CHAPTER FIFTEEN

Phillip braced himself over her.

Why not?

The question rang out.

Why not take her? What was impeding him?

Pride? Stupidity? Fear?

They were far past the point where common sense might kick in. As usual, passion had swept them away, though he couldn't explain why this occasion was more critical than the prior ones. Previously, he'd restrained his base instincts, had walked away from the ultimate act, but now he wondered why he should continue to deny himself.

By proceeding, he wouldn't be doing anything for which she hadn't pleaded. She wasn't some confused young lass. At twenty-three, she was a mature woman who knew her own mind. Why not give her what she craved?

Should he let misguided chivalry prevent him? Was it better to have her stepmother barter her to some aged noble sod? He could visualize an obese, malodorous gent sawing away between her pretty thighs, and his stomach roiled.

While another man might eventually call her wife, he couldn't move beyond the notion that she was *his* and always would be, despite where circumstances might convey her.

He was hungry to be her first. So that she couldn't

forget him. So that, in defiance of whoever claimed her through matrimony, Phillip would be the one she would see when she lay down in her marital bed and closed her eyes.

"Promise me something," he said.

"What?"

"Swear to me, that no matter what happens, or how situations evolve, you will never marry my father." It was a strange request to make, just before he ruined her, but her vow was vital to his sanity. "I couldn't bear it."

"I won't," she pledged. "I couldn't do that. To you. Or to him."

He nodded. "No regrets, Livvie. Never."

"No regrets," she replied.

Was he mad? Was he crazed to reach so high? To pine so tenaciously?

None of it signified. The only subject of import was her, and the exquisite joy he would find when he was inside her.

He started kissing her, his tongue darting into her mouth, then he dipped to her breasts, nursing, inciting, spurring her to the brink once more. Toying and playing, he dallied until she was tense, straining, then he stroked between them, fondling her, stretching her.

She was wet, relaxed from her initial orgasm, as ready as she could be in her virginal condition, and he centered himself at her opening. He spread her, prodding in, enabling her to become accustomed to his novel invasion, but it was all he could do to keep from plunging ahead. Jolted by the contact, he forced himself to moderate his pace, when every pore in his body was screaming for him to progress with all due haste.

Pushing in further, he was at her barrier, and he halted, desperate to finish it.

Anxious, she arched up, her hips writhing as she

struggled to escape his relentless entry. Though mentally she'd convinced herself she aspired to this, her chaste anatomy wasn't prepared. Her inexperience made her resist what she didn't know, and her alarm escalated.

"Phillip"—she was squirming, striving to get away— "I'm afraid. Slow down."

"No." He'd waited so long, all of his life it seemed, and he was too stimulated and couldn't indulge her maidenly apprehension. It had to be done, over. There could be no retreat. "I'll have you now."

"You're scaring me."

"It can't be helped."

"Phillip!" she repeated, begging.

"Hush!"

Gripping her hips, he pinned her in place, intending to allay some of the pain by holding her firmly. In a quick motion, he burst through her maidenhead, intruding to the hilt, the entire length of his cock implanted. She was hot, tight, her sheath clenching around him, her virginal blood a steamy, sweltering caldron that lured him to his doom.

His passage was brutal, and he recognized that he should delay, that he should allow her to acclimate, but he was too provoked to worry about her comfort.

He began to flex—he simply couldn't stop himself— propelling in all the way, then withdrawing to the tip. Again. Again. Glancing down, the sight of his swollen rod impaling her raised his lust to a frenzied level. His behavior was so wrong, and so outrageous, and the iniquity made it even more exciting.

Any hint of his gentlemanly qualities had fled. He showed her no mercy, riding her as a soldier would a whore after a vicious battle. He went deep, deeper.

She braved his foray, accepting what he inflicted on her, and he catapulted her across the bed, until she was banging into the headboard with each penetration. Grappling for purchase, her fingers tangled in the blankets and pillows as she fought to steady herself against the onslaught.

He wanted the joining to be so tumultuous, so raucous, that he would become part of her, that they wouldn't be two people, but one, that—when they were done—a piece of him would be left behind. Yet he couldn't delve into her far enough.

His fervor rose, peaked, his loins wrenching as his orgasm commenced. He endeavored to stave it off, to endure another few blissful seconds, but he couldn't contain the wave of pleasure.

He was rabid to spill himself inside her, to spray his seed into her womb. He yearned to mark her as his with his child. Formerly, he hadn't wanted a babe, hadn't dreamed of himself as a father, but suddenly, he wanted it more than anything. With Livvie as the mother. The urge was primal, savage, and he bit off a curse at the violent need that was driving him.

He couldn't impregnate her!

With a frantic effort, he yanked out of her, clutching her to his chest, her breasts flattened to his own, and he spewed himself onto her stomach, his semen disgorging in a fiery surge of gratification. He thrust over and over, the ecstasy never ebbing, the soft skin of her belly goading him onward.

The impetus abated, and he collapsed onto her, his weight pressing her into the covers. Very likely, he was smothering her, but he couldn't slide off.

He'd been a heedless cad, and with the ardor waning, he was too much of a coward to look at her. What would he see? Disgust? Horror? Resignation?

Though they'd talked about the deed, and had flirted around the edges of it, there was no method for clarifying what it was like. A virgin could only muddle through to the other side, hopefully without too much trauma attached to the episode.

With how he'd comported himself, she was probably torn and battered. Would she pardon him for being so rough? For using her so crudely?

The silence grew awkward, but he couldn't break it. Then, she kissed him on the nape, and he was amazed that she would. He dared to lean back, and she was watching him, her perplexity evident.

"I'm sorry." He brushed his lips to hers.

"For what?"

"I was so wild, so out of control."

"I hadn't expected you'd act any other way." She smiled. "I rather liked it."

"Are you hurt?"

"A little. I'll mend."

"I'd meant to be more deliberate, to be more reserved." He grinned. "You arouse me beyond my limits."

"I'm glad."

"Let me wash you."

Going to the dresser, he poured some water from a pitcher into a bowl and hauled it over to the nightstand. Cleansing away the traces of their sin, he wiped her abdomen, and dabbed at the blood smeared on her thighs. Then, as she studied him, he tugged off his trousers, and swabbed his privates.

When he returned to her, he was naked, and he crawled onto the bed.

"I'm constantly in such a rush with you," he said, "that I can't seem to shed my clothing before we start."

"I've noticed."

"I ought to at least *attempt* disrobing before I pounce on you."

She sighed. "I wish we had more time."

To what end? he almost inquired, but didn't.

"So do I." He wiggled his brows. "I can think of numerous wicked antics by which we could entertain ourselves."

"I'll bet you can." Chuckling, she stroked his chest, rubbing in circles over the spot where his pulse had lagged to a stable rhythm. "You pulled out at the end."

"Yes."

"Why?"

"We can't risk making a babe."

"Could we have? From doing it once?"

"Many people claim it's not possible, but I don't suppose we should take the chance."

"A wise precaution."

But oh, how he'd wanted to! Absurd as the notion was, he'd been eager, had coveted that outcome with such an ominous intensity that he couldn't say from where he'd mustered the fortitude to keep it from happening.

If there was a child, she couldn't walk away. She'd be in dire trouble, and their disparate stations couldn't separate them. She'd have to relent and wed him, despite their differences.

While he knew she was correct—that he couldn't provide for her large family—he was selfish enough to want to have the opportunity. He was a vain man, and it wounded him that his father was appropriate, merely due to birth and wealth, while he, himself, was not and could never be.

If she stayed with him, they would be poor—by her standards—but they would be happy. Why couldn't that be enough?

He should have been angry with her for making him feel unworthy, but he wasn't. The members of the Quality were indoctrinated to view themselves as exceptional and unique, and the somber fact was that she couldn't envision them succeeding. Societal prohibitions had been drilled into her, so she couldn't conceive of a contrary conclusion.

Her prejudices made him want to rail at her, but protesting couldn't change who she was, or alter her perspective of the world.

Saddened, despondent, he lamented over what could never be. Already, he could sense her slipping away. She appeared less distinct, as if her shape were fading, the contour lines wavering. Soon, she'd be but a distressing memory, the agony of which would dwindle until he'd wonder if he'd actually known her, if she'd been real.

What he needed was a token to remember her by, a tangible and unusual object that would reflect her character and disposition. What did she cherish? What did she have with which she could afford to part? What could he seek?

When the answer occurred to him, it was amusing, whimsical, but perfect. Considering that he'd just deflowered her, it was dratted timing to request it, but if events unfolded as he suspected they would, he wouldn't be able subsequently to solicit a gift.

"Would you do me a favor?"

"Of course."

"I want to have something of yours after you go. Something personal. Would you draw me a picture?"

"A picture? Now?"

"Yes."

"Of what?"

"Whatever you choose. You love art. I'll invariably recall that about you." He thought for a moment. "I have some rather heavy pieces of paper. And some sharpened pencils at my desk. Would you?"

She shrugged. "Why not?"

He hastened to the main room and brought her the

supplies. As he approached the bed, she was cross-legged, assessing him with heightened interest.

"Seat yourself against the headboard," she commanded.

"Me?"

Giggling, she nodded, an impish gleam in her eye. "You've asked for a sketch, and you said I could pick my subject. I've decided on you."

He hadn't calculated that he might be her model, and he wasn't sure he wanted to be. When he'd haggled for a sketch, he'd anticipated something a bit more mundane: a vase of flowers, his cottage. Hesitant, he blushed to the tips of his toes.

"Come on," she coaxed. "It'll be fun."

He couldn't tell her no, and grudgingly, he climbed onto the mattress, arranging the pillows, the carved wood cool on his heated back. She crawled to him, naked and sexy as a forest nymph, and the sight of her made his phallus stir and begin to grow.

"Down, boy." She patted the enlarging rod, causing him to bark with mirth.

"I've created a monster."

"I believe you have."

Arraying him, she lifted a knee, resting his elbow on it, a sheet concealing his lap.

"You're going to depict me in the buff?"

"That's how I fancy you."

"I won't be able to frame it and hang it on my wall."

"But it will remind you of this night. You insisted that you never wanted to forget."

"No, I don't."

"Later on, I'll duplicate the same pose for myself. So we'll both have a copy."

The idea made him smile, contemplating her in

London, in her elegant bedchamber, in her elaborate town house, a nude likeness of himself tucked into a secret hiding place.

The enterprise was curiously intimate, and as her pencil flew over the page, he observed her every move. It took only twenty minutes to complete the work, and shyly, she held it out, skeptical of her talent, and nervous about his opinion, just as he was apprehensive as to how she'd portray him.

The representation was uncanny, exactly like him, and anyone who saw it would know it was he. He was muscled, fit, his hair tousled, his beard darkening his cheeks, but his mouth was pursed in an arrogant smirk, and he seemed more cocky than he visualized himself to be, more self-assured and conceited.

It was a disturbing display, which hinted at carnality and masculinity, and he had a smugness about him that left no doubt he'd recently been satisfied in a sexual fashion.

"I look like a damned corsair."

"Do you recollect the erotic book in your father's library? You're the spitting image of the sheik, surrounded by his harem."

"You noticed, did you?"

"Yes, you bounder. The first time you sneaked up on me, and I glanced up, I assumed that you'd jumped to life out of my fantasies. You scared me witless."

He laughed as she snatched up the drawing and, with a grand flourish, signed the corner: "My pirate, my sultan. Love always, Livvie."

She stared at what she'd written, as if confused by how the inscription had sprung from her hand, and she flushed, quietly stating, "You're the sole person, besides my father, who's ever called me Livvie."

"It suits you."

He accepted the portrait from her, reading the salutation, tracing it with his finger.

"Love always," he murmured, liking the sound.

"Love always," she whispered in reply, embarrassed,
and gazing at the mattress.

"Thank you."

"You're welcome."

"I'll treasure it forever."

He put it on the table, then tugged her across the distance that divided them, stretching her out so that she
was pressed to his chest, her torso draped between his
legs.

There were so many things he longed to confide: how
much he cared for her, how much he appreciated having
met her, and how much he would miss her when she was
gone. The undeclared regret was so poignant and so
prevalent that he felt as if it were choking him.

He'd never deemed himself to be a coward, but he
was, because he couldn't give voice to any of his emotions.

What good would a profession of strong sentiment
do anyway?

She had a path to follow that didn't include him, and
a confession would make their parting more unbearable.
During this last assignation, he didn't want them to be
maudlin. He hoped they would reminisce about it as a
magical episode they'd stolen for themselves before
reality had intervened.

Dipping down, he found her mouth and kissed her,
tenderly, gently, wanting to demonstrate with his body
what he couldn't convey with words.

Eagerly, she joined in, as if she too needed to physically impart the affection she dared not reveal aloud.

He laid her on the pillows and came over her.

"May I love you again?"

"Yes, please."

"Are you too sore?"

"No." Smiling at him, her admiration and regard shone through.

I'll remember her just like this, he told himself. So beautiful, so fresh and vibrant. So rare and fine. And his. His till dawn.

He kissed her, once more, and let passion take them away.

CHAPTER SIXTEEN

Margaret sat at the table in her bedchamber. The portfolio of Olivia's drawings lay before her, though the flap was closed. There was no need to look at the foul, disgusting pictures again.

She couldn't identify the knave who was with Olivia. At first glance, she'd thought it was Edward, but there were too many differences, namely that the individual was much younger. The blackguard might be the stablemaster, though she hadn't paid enough attention to the servant to say for sure.

How pathetic that Olivia would succumb to such a common ruffian, that she would risk so much on someone who was so unworthy of her. Had the girl lost all her sense?

Penny had discovered Olivia's shame, and had tattled on her, just as she'd divulged Winnie's offensive lusting with the earl, but Margaret couldn't deduce why Penny would want to cause so much tribulation for the two women.

As far as Margaret was aware, Penny had never exchanged a harsh word with either female. Olivia and Winnie regularly placated Penny, when she often didn't deserve their kindnesses. They were consistently pleasant and cordial, despite Penny's antics, which could be quite horrid and try even a saint's patience.

Yet Penny was suffering from an excessive amount of malice, and Margaret couldn't begin to guess what they'd done to incur her wrath. With Penny, one could never be confident of the motives that were driving her, so it could have been any minor slight.

She'd had a perfectly good explanation for being in Olivia's room, for finding the lascivious artwork. So too she'd justified how she'd seen Winnie and Edward. Margaret had asked pointed questions about both incidents, but Penny's answers had seemed too pat, as if she'd rehearsed them for maximum effect.

Obviously, Penny wanted Margaret to be incensed, to take drastic action, and of course, the revelations guaranteed that Penny would get her wish. But why was she so bent on revenge?

Margaret had been pondering the puzzle for the better part of an hour, when it occurred to her that the reason scarcely mattered.

The pair needed to be brought to heel. It was essential that they comprehend—in no uncertain terms—how desperate Margaret was for Olivia to marry Edward. No other alternative was possible, no other option viable, and she would be ruthless in achieving her goal.

Winnie couldn't be allowed to loiter about the property, flaunting herself at Edward, and distracting him, so that he could avoid making a decision about Olivia.

Previously, Winnie had philandered with a nobleman, had led him to folly and ruin. Her outrageous conduct should have taught her a lesson, but it hadn't.

What was she hoping to gain by dallying with Edward? A few trinkets as a reward for her sexual favors? Or perhaps she was simply a bitch in heat, who savored the vulgar experience of a man sawing away between her thighs. Well, whatever her incentives, the liaison had to be ended before it could develop into something more dire.

Heaven forbid that Edward would opt to marry the unrestrained slattern! There was no way on God's green earth that Margaret would stand by and watch Winnie become Edward's countess. Winnie couldn't be permitted to sink her claws into Edward's fortune—the fortune that was going to come to Olivia, and thus, to Margaret.

Winnie was a nobody, a promiscuous, immoral whore, who had imposed on Margaret's charity and patience for over a decade. Margaret wasn't about to accept betrayal as her final reward.

She trekked to the fireplace, Olivia's satchel in hand. Even though it was the middle of summer, she'd had a maid light the fire, and it had grown to a cheery blaze. Pulling up a chair, she fed the pages into the flames. One by one, the lewd sketches dwindled to ash. She observed the process dispassionately, once in a while using a poker to stir the pile so that every hint of Olivia's diabolical behavior was devoured.

As the last fragment disappeared, she stood and went to her luggage, tossing the empty portfolio into it, satisfied that all evidence of the girl's stupidity had been erased.

Down the hall, footsteps sounded, and Margaret recognized that Winnie was winging in her direction. Within moments, she'd glided in, evincing the serene, vapid smile Margaret despised. With her curvaceous figure and lush hair, men found Winnie attractive, but considering the conversation that was about to ensue, Margaret was revolted at being reminded of Winnie's power to bewitch.

"You wanted to speak with me, Margaret?"

"Yes." Margaret's fury was leashed with a slender thread, and she was ready to explode. "Close the door."

Winnie complied, then moved to her side. "What is it?"

"I know about you and the earl," Margaret hissed. "How could you do this to me? To us?"

Before Winnie could think or reply, Margaret slapped

her across the face. She reeled, and crumpled to her knees, though Margaret suspected she fell from the shock of being struck, rather than the impetus of the blow.

Dazed, gripping her cheek, she didn't try to rise.

"Margaret . . . stop . . ." she whined.

"You harlot!" Margaret loomed over her and slapped her again, harder. "After all I've done for you! Who helped you, Winifred? All these years! Who?"

"You did, Margaret."

"Precisely." She was trembling with rage. "It was *I* who hid your sin so that you could continue to go about in polite society. It was *I* who concealed the disgrace of your illegitimate brat. You've dined at my table! Slept in my home! And this is how you repay me?"

"I'm sorry," she murmured. "So sorry."

"At least you don't deny it."

"No, I don't."

Winnie was distraught, sniveling, the tears flowing, and Margaret was tempted to inquire *why*, why she would hazard so much, but Margaret had no interest in Winnie's excuses.

She merely wanted the loathsome business terminated. Immediately.

"You're traveling to London today. I've made the arrangements."

"Thank you."

"I'm wasting my limited coin. To rescue you once more."

"I'm sorry," she repeated.

"You're the most ungrateful person I've ever known."

"I didn't mean for it to happen, Margaret. I swear . . . I—"

"Shut up!" Margaret was so agitated that she could barely constrain herself from lashing out a third time. "Until your departure, you will stay in this room. You'll not talk to the earl, you'll not try to see him, or slip him a note telling him where you've gone. Do you hear me?"

Defeated, she gazed at the floor. "Yes, I hear you."

"I've never been more serious, Winifred. You've perpetrated such damage, and we'll be lucky if I can rectify your sabotage. If I ascertain that you've endeavored to contact him, I'll put you out on the streets. With only the gown on your back."

"I understand."

"You suppose your life has been so terrible, so difficult? I've assured that you had a roof over your head, clothes to wear, and food to eat. Just picture how it will be if you have nothing." She made a slashing motion with her fingers. "Nothing! That's what you deserve."

She marched to the door, leaving Winnie huddled on the rug. "A gig is being readied, and I will drive you into the village myself, where you will catch the public coach later this afternoon. If we encounter anyone, if anyone asks, we're off on a short jaunt, to take the air."

"Whatever you wish."

"I'm off to check on the preparations. I suggest you use the solitude to reflect upon what you've done, and how you will atone to me and the rest of the family."

"I will."

Margaret stormed out, grabbing the key and locking her in, then, forcing calm into her demeanor, she traipsed downstairs.

She couldn't remember when she'd ever been so angry. Probably the occasion she'd walked into the stable, and Penny had been with that boy, her hair down, her dress loosened.

The foolhardy lad had quickly discovered how dangerous it was to cross Margaret. Her temper could be formidable, but she was rarely placed in a position where

she had to reveal it, and when she was, people were surprised at how much vengeance she was prone to wield.

Winnie was not going to ruin this opportunity, wasn't
going to demolish what Margaret had worked to effect.

The earl's stable was efficient, and a sporty carriage
was parked by the side door, equipped for their use, a
youngster patiently tending the horse. It was the ideal
vehicle for two ladies to enjoy a brisk ride.

She ascended to fetch Winnie, their bonnets and
cloaks, and she ushered them down a rear stairwell, meeting no one. In silence, they journeyed to the village, and
Margaret located the coaching inn where Winnie would
wait. Though Winnie had the audacity to beg for a few
precious coins so that she could hire a hackney in London,
Margaret refused, unconcerned whether Winnie made it
safely to the town house or not. Without so much as a
good-bye, she paid the fare for the coach, and left Winnie
to her own devices.

The entire excursion went off without a hitch, with
no witnesses. Winnie's exit had been inconspicuous,
nondescript. As Margaret had planned, no one could say
that she was no longer on the premises.

When Margaret arrived back at Salisbury, she deposited
the gig at the stable, not having to dicker with any of the
employees. Undetected, she sneaked to her bedchamber,
shed her outer garments, and freshened up. Then, she went
downstairs to survey several of the salons, assessing the
feasibility of each, and settling on the earl's library. She
knew his schedule, had marked his routine, so if he maintained his regular pattern, he would be there in the next
hour to review his morning post.

She seated herself behind his desk, and she utilized
his writing supplies to pen a fake letter. After completing it, she dawdled, steeling herself for the pending discussion. Edward Paxton's future was rushing toward

him like a runaway carriage, and unfortunately for him, he wouldn't be able to halt the steady, unrelenting onset of his destiny.

Presently, he approached, and she feigned deep concentration and worry, focusing on the false missive she clutched in her hand. He entered, and was nearly at the desk before he noticed her.

"Margaret? I didn't see you."

She blinked, as though disoriented. "Edward?"

He studied her. "Is something amiss?"

"Oh . . ." she responded, pretending great despair.

"What it is?"

She stroked her brow, as if weary and confused. "May I confide in you?"

"Yes."

"You wouldn't hold it against Olivia, would you?"

"Olivia? Why, no. Why would you presume so?"

"She's an innocent in all this."

"Of course she is."

Pondering, fretting, she made a small moue with her lips. "I'm at my wits' end," she murmured. "I don't know where to turn."

"Tell me." He lugged over a chair, leaning forward, his elbows on his knees, eager to listen.

She offered him the faux letter she'd concocted. "I received it this morning, from London, and I've been heartsick ever since."

She watched as he read the lies she'd composed, and she was thrilled at how his eyes widened in horror when he saw Winnie's name, though he squelched any indication of recognition.

"Winifred," he mused as if he weren't acquainted with her. "Is the author referring to your cousin?"

"Yes. Oh, this is so humiliating."

"Do go on."

Margaret sighed. "She has an appalling problem."

"With what?"

"With immorality. She's drawn to men, and she can't control herself. I've prayed for her and struggled to assist her in modifying her behavior, but after this outrage, I have to conclude that it's impossible for her to change." She simulated a credible sob. "Oh, I shouldn't be mentioning this to you. What must you think?"

His cheeks were bright red. "It's quite all right. Continue."

"She promises, and weeps, and vows she won't do it again. Then, when she's caught, she begs for forgiveness. Now, to learn that she's wreaked havoc on another family . . . that she may have destroyed another marriage . . ."

Shuddering, she let the implication trail off, letting him assume the worst.

He swallowed, could scarcely speak. "She's in the habit of illicit fornication?"

"With married men!" Margaret nodded, fueling his astonishment, and she bent in and whispered, "Why, years ago, she birthed a child out of wedlock! You can't imagine the steps my late husband had to take to fend off a scandal."

"Gads," he muttered, seeming ill. "How awful for you."

"What would you advise, Edward?" She rested her hand on his wrist. "I'm sending her to London tomorrow. She shouldn't stay here around the girls—not with this newest turpitude brewing."

"No, no. She's not fit company for them."

"But what should I do with her once we're home? In the past, I took pity on her, because I'm her only living relative—she has no one else—but how can I persist in housing her with my daughters? I can't risk that her vices might rub off on them. Especially Penelope, when she's at such an impressionable age."

"Let me ruminate on it, will you? Maybe I could use my influence to intervene with the man's father. To keep it quiet."

"I couldn't impose on you." She massaged her temples. "I have the most dreadful headache. Would you pardon me if I spent the evening in my room?"

"By all means."

Retrieving the letter, she trudged out, striving to appear fragile and weak, and she could feel his stunned gaze following her.

Stupid as any male ever born! she grumbled to herself. Passion transformed them into blithering idiots. How easily he'd been duped! If she could just get the remainder of her scheme to progress as effortlessly!

She proceeded to Olivia's bedchamber, and Olivia was meekly perched on the edge of the mattress. When Margaret entered, Olivia stared at her so directly that there was no doubt she comprehended why Margaret had come.

Margaret shut the door and advanced. Olivia stood, braced, and they were toe to toe, eye to eye.

"I have one question." Margaret impaled her with a furious glare, letting the silence play out, and when she started to fidget, Margaret sneered. "Are you still a virgin?"

"Margaret!"

Shame burning her cheeks, she glanced down, and Margaret clasped her by the back of the neck, squeezing tight, her nails digging in. "Have the decency to look at me."

"You're hurting me."

"I don't care."

She squeezed harder. Never previously had she physically abused Olivia, but she was so enraged that she deemed herself capable of any despicable act, and it required every ounce of fortitude she possessed to refrain from slapping her as she had Winnie.

"I repeat: Are you a virgin?"

"No."

Margaret shoved her away, and she stumbled and grappled for purchase on the bedpost.

"I'm glad your father is deceased, so he isn't here to witness this hideous moment." Her scorn and disdain evident, she evaluated Olivia. "I didn't raise you to be a whore. Is this your true nature? Are you a slattern by temperament? Will you copulate with any common partner, like your dissolute brother?"

"I . . . I love him," she tediously claimed.

"Love, bah!" Margaret scoffed. "Will *love* put food in your belly? Buy your coal in the winter? Love doesn't signify in the slightest."

"It matters to me!" she spouted, clutching a fist to her breast, exhibiting some spunk.

"Well, not to me. I've just talked with the earl." The falsehoods were rolling off her tongue, each one simpler to voice. "He's decided to ask for your hand."

"No!"

"You can anticipate a proposal in the morning. You *shall* accept it."

"I won't!" She was trembling. "You can't make me."

"Oh, but I can."

"I want to return to London," she protested. "We'll commence with a new search. I'll wed whomever you select. I swear it! But not Edward Paxton. Don't demand it of me. I can't do it for you."

"Do you suppose suitors grow on trees? That I can

conjure another out of my hat—like a magician at a fair?"

"You're so clever, Margaret," she cajoled. "You can find someone else."

"There's the rub, Olivia. I don't wish to expend the time or energy."

"Please!"

"No."

"I'll refuse his suit. I will! It will embarrass all of us. Don't put me in that position."

Margaret closed the distance between them. "I don't believe you understand me, so let me be more clear: Before we left London, I arranged to have Helen admitted to a hospital."

She gasped. "What?"

"I didn't want the staff to be burdened with her while we were away."

"She's no *burden*."

Margaret ignored the asinine comment; the imbecile was a constant drain. "She's safe. For now. But if you reject the earl, I'll move her to an orphanage, and I will never tell you where she is. I'll go to my grave with my secret."

"That's barbaric!"

"Even if you managed to locate her and bring her home, London is such a dangerous city. Why . . . a moron such as her could trip down the stairs, or be trampled by a horse." She mused, "Who can predict what tragedies might befall her?"

"You would . . . would . . . kill her?"

Margaret taunted, "The girl should have been abandoned as soon as her abnormalities were discovered."

"But she's our niece!"

"Not mine. Not mine at all."

"Why would you do such a thing to me? To Helen?"

"I would have our financial situation rectified, our future stabilized. You have no idea how determined I am to have this successfully resolved."

"There has to be another way."

"There is no other *way*. You will wed Edward Paxton. By next Friday."

"I won't," she insisted again, and her petulance was beginning to grate.

"That is certainly your prerogative, but you might reflect before your decision becomes irreversible, for *I* am deadly serious."

Olivia sank down onto the mattress and gawked at the floor. Margaret could almost see the wheels spinning in her mind as she wrestled with this new reality.

She groused, "Even if he offers for me, how can I agree? He'll expect a virginal bride."

Margaret smirked at the remark, perceiving a capitulation. "There are many methods by which to fool a husband. You won't be the first bride to pretend to maidenhood." She shrugged. "A bit of theatrics, a display of nerves, a hidden vial of red dye . . ."

"You make it sound so calculated."

"I am willing to do whatever it takes to bring about this union. You underestimate me at your peril."

Olivia studied her. "I've always wondered where Penny comes by her viciousness. Now I know."

"Yes, you do."

"You're being too cruel."

Margaret's stance hardened. "If I've offended your delicate sensibilities, I care not. *You* are the harlot. Not me."

"But to punish Helen—"

"Cease your whining!" she barked. "I won't listen to your complaints. You've made your bed. The consequences are pending. How horrid or gentle will they be, Olivia? The choice is yours."

"I don't know what to do."

"Then I'll leave you to your introspection, but it shan't be accomplished here."

"What do you mean?"

"You'll not meet with your lover to seek his assistance."

"I hadn't intended to."

"A likely, and convenient, story," she jeered. "Winnie has gone to London."

"Why?"

"It's none of your affair."

"But she didn't say good-bye."

"There wasn't an opportunity. She was desperate to go and had been fussing about it for days. I grew weary of her harangue and assented." Margaret would divulge no more on the subject. "You will occupy her bedchamber. As it's directly across from mine, and I am a light sleeper, you'll not be able to sneak out. Plus, I have the benefit of a key. You'll be locked in. Until the wedding."

"You can't keep me prisoner!"

What a child she was! She was frantic not to be watched. Obviously, she'd hoped for a final tryst, a fond adieu with her lover, but she couldn't be allowed to make matters worse than they already were.

"How will you stop me? Will you run to the earl and humiliate yourself by confessing what a trollop you are? Will you blab to one of the servants about how unjustly you're being treated?" She started toward the door and held it open. "Let's retire to Winnie's room, shall we?"

A staring match ensued, and an eternity passed. When Olivia's acquiescence came, she was furious, mutinous, her thoughts awhirl, plotting how she could escape.

What a dolt she was. Couldn't she grasp the facts?

Her fate was sealed. She couldn't flee from it, despite how much she detested the notion of wedding Edward.

Why was she complaining, anyway? There were many far more ghastly scenarios that could have been foisted upon her.

Margaret gestured into the hall, and Olivia preceded her, marching down the corridor like a felon to the gallows. Margaret followed her into Winnie's bedchamber.

Olivia glanced around. "Winnie's belongings are still here. You said she left."

"I'm sending her things tomorrow. On the public coach."

Olivia looked as though she might raise more questions, argue, or further plead her case, but Margaret was having none of it. She retreated to the door. "I'll deliver a tray for your supper. Until then, I suggest you make yourself comfortable. From now on, you'll not go anywhere without my escort."

"Margaret, please!" She tried to reason one last time.

"Perhaps you should spend your leisure hours pondering Helen."

She slammed the door and spun the key.

For a moment, she tarried, considering the absurdity of it all. The two women who, for years, had made up her family had simultaneously gone mad.

Strumpets both. She wasn't surprised by Winnie's plunge from grace. But Olivia's? It was too strange to be true.

What a bizarre spiral of events!

Shaking her head, she descended to the lower floors in search of Penny, where she advised her of the plan. Initially, Penny was rebellious, disobedient, but as Margaret explained the necessities, Penny recognized that Margaret's scheme was for the best, and she conceded that her aid would be imperative.

Satisfied that the details were set in motion so that circumstances would unfold appropriately, she instructed the housekeeper to prepare supper trays, as well as to provide excuses to the earl for the evening absence of all of them. Then, she went to her room, where she would await the night and a successful outcome.

CHAPTER SEVENTEEN

Edward walked up the stairs of the grand mansion. It was very late, everyone abed, and he tiptoed through the quiet halls.

After his hideous conversation with Margaret, he'd fled the property, although he didn't imagine he'd slighted anybody. Margaret hadn't chosen to sup or socialize, either.

With such horrid tidings unveiled, he couldn't have tarried at the dining table, prattling through an unending meal.

How had he been duped so easily?

Winnie was a whore. A beautiful, licentious, lusty harlot, who seduced men for sexual pleasure.

He didn't want to believe it—he couldn't believe it!—but he'd seen the shameful accusations with his own two eyes. He'd listened to Margaret's stammering, abashed admission as to Winnie's disrepute, and he yearned to deny Margaret's veracity, to repudiate every word she'd uttered, but the story had to be true. Who would admit to such a disgraceful family secret if it wasn't?

Feeling betrayed, violated, he was more furious than he'd been in a very, very long while, though he wasn't sure why. Just then, if Winnie had been standing in front of him, he'd likely have shaken her until her teeth rattled.

How dare you! he ached to shout at her. How dare she be dissolute, promiscuous, loose with her favors?

He patted the pocket inside his jacket, heard the crinkle of the letter he'd stuffed there. It had been slipped under his door before he'd left the house. Like a talisman with magic powers, it had drawn him in, though he struggled to resist its appeal. He'd read it over and over until he'd had it memorized.

"My dearest Edward," the tidy script began.

"I know what Margaret told you about me. It's not true. I swear it! Please let me explain. I can't bear it that you're angry. Come to me. I'll be waiting . . ."

She hadn't signed her name, only the initial *W*.

Throughout the evening, questions had taunted him: What was her game? What was she attempting?

Did she hope to beguile him into philandering with her? To what end? What did she really want? Money? An illegitimate child he would be obligated to support? Or was it simpler, more elemental? Did she merely desire him physically?

She loves you; she's hurting.

The thought kept blasting through his head with the impetus of a battering ram, so potent and authentic that he throbbed with the revelation.

He was a good judge of character. He was! And during the blissful times they'd passed together, he'd never presumed that she'd had dubious motives. She'd entertained a deep affinity for him; he was convinced of it.

Yet he'd seen the appalling indictment posted to Margaret, had viewed the censure printed in it. Why would Margaret invent such a terrible slander?

At the landing, he dawdled, trapped in his agonizing introspection. In one direction was the lengthy corridor that led to his suite. In the other, the elegant wing filled with slumbering guests. She was so close, and he was anxious to rush to her, to barge in, to denounce her for her sins and command an accounting.

He vacillated, ruminated, vacillated some more, and his decision crystalized.

He had to learn the facts, so he had to ask Winnie. If he looked her in the eye, if he talked to her face to face, there was no way she could prevaricate. She had such an expressive demeanor that she couldn't conceal the truth.

If he ascertained that Margaret was correct, that Winnie was a woman of base virtue, so be it, but he couldn't allow her to depart for London without having the situation resolved. His need for reassurance was asinine and imprudent, but he couldn't put it aside. He'd liked her too much, and couldn't stand that she might have deceived him.

Prowling into the hall, he slinked toward her and the answers he was determined to receive. Quiet as a mouse, he opened her door and sneaked in. It was warm, and the bed curtains were tied off, a fresh breeze wafting in through the window.

He could discern her form snuggled under the covers, and he suffered a pang of irritation that she wasn't awake and impatient for his arrival, although he couldn't have guessed when she'd conveyed the note to him. Very likely, she'd been anticipating him for hours and had given up.

Not wanting to scare her, he crept to the bed and eased himself down. Her back was to him, and he leaned over her, more eager than he should have been for the instant she would discover it was he.

"Winnie," he murmured, but she was sleeping so soundly that she didn't stir. He whispered again. "Winnie. It's me. I'm here."

She mumbled, rolled over, blinked and blinked. "Lord Salisbury?"

His heart skipped several beats. It wasn't Winnie!

He was glowering at Olivia, and while he recognized that he'd made a horrendous error, he couldn't process the enormity of what had just occurred. For many tormenting, protracted seconds, he scrutinized her, his mind unwilling to grapple with the magnitude of his blunder.

He gawked around the shadowed chamber. Had he ventured into the wrong room? Had he been plunged into some grotesque, mutated dimension?

This couldn't have happened!

"Lady Olivia?" he stupidly inquired.

"Yes." She was becoming conscious of her surroundings. "What is it? Is something amiss?"

Without warning, she sat up, and because he was so near to her, their lips were inches apart. Her blue eyes were alert and inquisitive, and she appeared rumpled, adorable. She was clad in a thin, summery nightgown, with tiny straps. Her shoulders were bare, her blond hair unbraided, and it rippled in a golden wave.

The pose was sexy, provocative, for both of them. Their torsos were almost touching, the covers at her waist, and she lurched to grab them, shielding her bosom.

"Pardon me. I . . . I . . ." A sensation of peril swirled over him, and he started to disentangle himself, but it was too late.

Behind him, the door was opening, and he knew his fate was sealed. Propriety required that he vault off the bed, but there seemed no point to denials or disavowals.

Like the biggest fool, he'd walked into a carnal trap. Had Margaret set it to snare him into matrimony? If so, she was much more shrewd and insidious than he could ever have surmised, and though he was sick over what would come next, he had to congratulate her.

If she'd ambushed him, she was a master at cunning. If she hadn't, she'd still managed to bumble into the most opportune, fortuitous conclusion of which any family could have dreamed.

It was all Winnie's doing. She'd enchanted and captivated him beyond his limits, had enticed him as no female ever had. Like one of the Sirens of old, she'd seduced him to ruin, and a ripple of fury swept through him that she had gulled him into the predicament.

He wanted to lash out, to yell and rail at the injustice that was about to be leveled upon him—all because of her—yet he swallowed down his outrage. He declined to let Margaret Hopkins perceive how duped he felt, how powerless to save himself from a destiny he couldn't abide. The result couldn't be changed or altered. The only task that remained was to pick up the pieces and manipulate the debacle so there would be minimal scandal.

Was Lady Olivia an innocent or an accomplice? Was she playing her role in the scheme? Doing her best to paint herself the ravished maiden? Or was her agitation genuine?

Narrowing his focus, he evaluated her, and from what he could distinguish, he didn't assume she was culpable. She seemed downright terrified, and he didn't suppose anyone could feign that amount of alarm.

She was faultless, little more than a girl, and he couldn't let her character be soiled or besmirched because he'd acted the imbecile. For what was impending, he had no one to blame but himself.

Margaret traipsed in, clutching a lit candle. She was accoutered in a nightgown and billowy robe, a mobcap over her hair, floppy slippers on her feet. Lady Penelope trailed after her, also garbed in her nightclothes.

He winced. If Margaret had been the lone witness, he might have wheedled his way out of the fiasco, but with the younger sister observing all, the outcome was carved in stone.

"Olivia," Margaret said, "we heard a noise. We decided to check on you and—" She halted, her brows flying up in astonishment. "Edward Paxton! My lands!"

"Hello, Margaret," he replied, resigned.

"Mother," Lady Penelope piped up from the threshold, "is that Lord Salisbury with Olivia? Why is he in Olivia's bed? She's not dressed."

Margaret used her body to block the aperture so that Penelope couldn't enter, and Penelope was straining on tiptoe, trying to peek over her mother's shoulder.

"Penny," Margaret barked, "go to my bedchamber, and wait for me. I'll be with you shortly."

"But what's going on? Tell me!"

"Penny!" Margaret whipped around and stepped into the corridor, pushing Penny so that she was prevented from viewing the ignominious sight.

They had a torturous, lengthy conversation, with a great deal of hissing and exclamation, and Penelope stomped off in a huff. Then Margaret joined him and Olivia.

Edward had clambered off the bed and was perched next to it. Olivia was under the blankets, trembling, but she hadn't budged.

Margaret's umbrage was scarcely controlled. "I'll not ask what you're doing in here."

"Calm yourself," Olivia counseled. "This isn't what it looks like."

"Really?" Margaret jeered. "It *looks* like Edward has just visited you in your bed."

"I'm positive he has a perfectly valid explanation." Olivia glanced at him, imploring him to salvage the mess. "Don't you?"

He saw no reason to quibble and make the dreadful

incident worse. What was he to utilize as a defense? *I came to tryst with Winnie, but stumbled on Olivia by mistake?*

It was a pathetic justification, and he wouldn't embarrass himself by raising it. Nor would he drag Winnie into it.

"I have no comment."

"No, no," Olivia frantically interjected, "I'm sure you don't mean that."

"Shut up, Olivia!" Margaret snapped, concentrating her attention on him. "Edward, I never would have expected such behavior from you. I'm shocked!"

"My apologies."

She approached, the flicker of the candle accentuating the stark lines of her face, causing her to appear pitiless, grim, relentless. "Is there something you'd like to say to Olivia?"

"Certainly." He turned to Olivia, ready to speak, when she interrupted.

"Margaret, please. Don't force him into this. I'm begging you."

"Be silent," Margaret ordered.

"Margaret!" she tried again.

"Your sister beheld this spectacle, Olivia. Should we leave her with the impression that such licentious conduct is permissible?" Margaret glared at Edward, her wrath evident, giving no hint that she might have ambushed him. "Let's put this hideous episode behind us. Get on with it!"

"Lady Olivia," he formally pronounced, spitting out the bitter words, "would you do me the honor of becoming my wife?"

Olivia was horrified, tears glittering in her eyes. A portentous, unvoiced argument flashed between her and Margaret, filled with hidden significance he couldn't begin to decipher. For one, insane moment, he thought she would humiliate him by refusing. Her lips were pursed, mutinous, and she was loath to respond.

The encounter grew awkward, and Margaret snarled, "Olivia! Do you truly wish to spurn Lord Salisbury? Should we go back to London without your marrying him, just think of the *consequences* that could ensue."

Margaret assessed Olivia, another secret communication passing between them. It was as though they were parleying in a clandestine code, for which he did not have the key. Whatever the covert interpretation, Olivia understood the implications to which her stepmother alluded.

Worry and panic surged through her, and he presumed she was being reminded of their financial quandary, about which he wasn't to have been apprised. She was in no position to reject his proposal.

Gazing at her lap, she plucked at the blanket.

"Well, Olivia?" Margaret goaded. "What's it to be?"

"Yes, Edward. I'll marry you."

Margaret heaved a sigh of satisfaction. "Fine, fine." Beaming, she clapped her hands, making the candle wobble. "Considering the circumstances, I suggest a hasty, small ceremony, here at the manor. How about this Friday?" She didn't delay for his opinion. Apparently, it wasn't necessary. "I'll send out the notices tomorrow morning. I trust you can arrange the special license?"

Five days, he mused, calculating the time. Five days to come to terms with the indemnification Margaret had had every right to demand. Five days to persuade himself that Olivia would be a wonderful wife. Five days to adjust to the notion that he was about to commit himself to another loveless marriage.

After meeting Winnie, he'd hoped for so much more.

"I'll dispatch a messenger directly to the archbishop," he said. "It can be achieved by Friday without any problem."

"Marvelous," Margaret crooned.

He frowned at Olivia. She was ashen, shivering, pale with trepidation and repugnance, and he was so annoyed. What did the damned girl want? She'd traveled to Salisbury, seeking a husband, and his head had been served to her on a platter. Any female in England would have sacrificed an arm and a leg to be in her shoes.

What was the matter with her? She should be jumping for joy, not slumped in a heap, ready to sob.

Chomping down on his aggravation, he recollected her age, her overt astonishment at the stunning debacle they'd fallen into through his negligence. He patted her shoulder.

"Don't fret, Livvie," he consoled, intending to be friendly and supportive, but on hearing the pet nickname, she lurched as if he'd struck her.

"Don't *ever* call me Livvie," she asserted, much too sharply.

"As you wish." He nodded. "It will work out. Don't trouble yourself."

"I won't," she groused.

"Now then, Edward," Margaret said, "if you'll excuse us?" Exuding authority, and dismissing him, she gestured for him to exit.

"Of course. I'll confer with you in the morning to finalize the plans."

"I look forward to it."

Staring at Olivia, he was daring her—practically pleading with her—to acknowledge him, but she was coolly, maddeningly removed, reluctant to display any courtesy.

What was vexing her? Hadn't she wanted the union? Had Margaret coerced her into it? Well, it was too bloody late to quibble. Their path was set, and there could be no retreat.

His pride dented, he spun on his heel and stalked out, much more angry than he should have been, and he pulled the door closed with a determined click.

Across the hall was Margaret's bedroom, and Penelope was standing on the threshold, gawking at him. In the dark, her eyes seemed to glow, a weird green, like a feral cat's. Her auburn hair gleamed, too, as though it were afire.

She was grinning, her teeth white and straight, but it was a peculiar, insidious smile, as though she'd gotten just what she wanted and was eager to let him know it.

Did you have a role in this charade? he nearly roared. And, *Where the hell is Winnie?*

Was she secluded with Penelope? A participant? A prisoner? He was too furious to care.

Penelope continued to watch him, so eerie that she resembled a witch, or perhaps a witch's familiar, and his skin crawled.

Tamping down a shudder, he strolled away without remarking or glancing back, but he could sense her studying his every step. The corridor was a gauntlet that went on forever, and as the distance between them expanded, she came into the hall so that she could spy on him the rest of the way.

If she'd started to cackle, or spout incantations, he wouldn't have been surprised, and when he strode into his suite and slammed the door, he sagged with relief.

The girl terrified him, and bizarre as it sounded, he grabbed the key and rotated it in the lock, sealing himself in—and her out!

Betrothed, how galling, he thought. To be wed in five days. To a woman he didn't even especially like. Feeling ill, he stumbled to the bed and lay down. Blindly, he pondered a chink in the ceiling, the long, arduous night stretching ahead.

CHAPTER EIGHTEEN

Olivia strolled the estate grounds, arm in arm with Edward. Attractive, stylishly dressed, poised and assured, they were a handsome couple. People stared as they walked past.

A straw bonnet, with an extra wide brim, shielded her face, and she was glad for the protection it offered. She'd hardly slept a wink, and she was wan and pale, exhausted and achy. The sun shone down, making her eyes throb and water, and her knees wobbled so badly that she could barely take the next step.

Word of their betrothal had spread rapidly and far— Margaret had seen to it—so that by the time she'd dared to show herself downstairs at noon, her engagement wasn't news to anyone. Her destiny was winging toward her, and she was too paralyzed to jump out of the way.

When she'd been merely Edward's bridal candidate, the servants had been polite and helpful, but now, they were in awe of her new status. They studied her keenly, eager to please.

Soon, she would be their countess, and they all sought her favor. Wherever she went, employees stopped to congratulate her, with respectful bows and curtsies, exclaiming their joy over the pending nuptials. Edward took it in stride, cordially and generously thanking everyone for their felicitations, but she was terribly uncomfortable.

She felt like an impostor, that she'd earned the coming distinction through default.

Her mind was spinning over what had happened. How was it that, in a few short hours, she'd gone from incarceration in Winnie's room to being plighted to Edward?

Margaret had orchestrated the debacle—Olivia was certain of it—but how she'd accomplished the deed, and with so little fuss, was a mystery that had Olivia perplexed.

How had Margaret done it?

The bedchamber door had been locked. She knew because, over the interminable evening, she'd repeatedly tried the knob, hoping against hope that Margaret would make a mistake, that she would be able to sneak out.

She'd been desperate to send a letter to their housekeeper in London, inquiring as to Helen's whereabouts. Margaret had sworn that she'd dispatched Helen to an institution. Was it true? Or was it a lie Margaret had concocted to coerce Olivia into submitting to her scheme?

Was Helen safe at home? Or was she abandoned in some godforsaken place?

The grim prospects tormented her.

She'd wanted to speak with Phillip, to tell him about Margaret's threats, to seek his advice and assistance. In a crisis, he was the logical one to consult. He'd have traveled to the city if she'd asked him, and she'd intended to, needing proof as to Helen's location, but whenever she'd checked the door, she'd been imprisoned.

Fatigue had finally forced her to bed, and she'd dropped into oblivion, so that when Edward had entered, she hadn't had any idea. After he'd awakened her, several seconds had elapsed before she'd realized it was he.

How had Margaret lured Edward to her? How had she arranged it so that he'd appeared just when the door had been unlocked?

The questions were like an annoying sliver she couldn't extricate. They jabbed and poked at her, giving her no relief. Yet, what did it signify if she unscrambled the puzzle?

She couldn't change what had transpired. Couldn't roll back the clock so that Edward hadn't intruded, or that Margaret and Penny hadn't followed him in. Nor could she alter the conclusion Margaret had executed. She could only trudge forward, trusting that she could survive her wedding day—and night!—without embarrassing herself.

Oh, Margaret, she wailed silently, *how could you have done this to me?*

Margaret had always been a cold, reserved individual, with a temperament that didn't lend itself to spontaneity or whimsy, but Olivia had never understood how ruthless, how calculating and crafty, she was.

To the point of obsession, they'd haggled over their financial affairs, and Margaret had lamented their grave circumstances, as well as how serious she was about resolving their dilemma. But in a thousand years, Olivia couldn't have imagined that Margaret would go to such lengths to garner the resolution she desired.

Olivia felt as if she were a goose that had been cooked and served up as the main course in Margaret's machinations. She was bitter, furious, grieving, fearful, but she had to keep her agitation bottled up inside. By all accounts, Edward was a marvelous catch. There was no reason for her to be disconsolate, and she couldn't let him know she was distressed. He'd been naught but kind and courteous, and he definitely didn't warrant her rancor or disappointment.

She was dying to ask him why he'd been in her bedchamber. She had no clue, and curiosity was eating her alive. He hadn't been bent on ravishment, so for what other purpose could he have come?

If he'd wanted to propose—which, from his despondent, perfunctory attitude, he clearly hadn't—he could have done so any afternoon they'd socialized. Had he been looking for Winnie? It was her room. But he was scarcely acquainted with Winnie, so why would he have trespassed?

She remembered him whispering a remark to her, but she'd been slumbering so deeply that she couldn't recall what it was. She recollected opening her eyes and being shocked, but before she'd made sense of his arrival, Margaret had barged in.

How could she interrogate the man she was about to marry as to why he had deposited them in this predicament?

He wasn't any happier than she was. His reticence and melancholy were palpable, but he was too much of a gentleman to insult her by implying that he was less than ecstatic, and he was doing his best to hide his feelings.

She needed to confide in someone, to unburden her conscience, and voice her astonishment and incredulity. The world had suddenly speeded up, and it was whirling so quickly that events were evolving faster than she could track them. At the same time, she was moving in a type of dream state, where her conduct was slow and leaden. She was so confused and overwhelmed!

Phillip was the sole person to whom she could vent her woes, but she was praying she wouldn't run into him.

Ever since Edward had stormed out of her bedchamber, she'd been trying to deduce a method of contacting and warning him. But Margaret had confined her the entire night, and after she'd been released in the morning, she hadn't had any privacy. Either Margaret or Edward had been with her, so there'd been no opportunity to slip away, or pen a hasty message.

During their last, poignant, exceptional tryst, she'd sworn to him that she would never marry his father. She'd promised! Yet, not twenty-four hours later, she and Edward were engaged.

Had Phillip been notified?

She and Edward had been parading about the property, and Edward had maneuvered them away from the stables, as though he too was fretting over Phillip's reaction.

With every corner they'd turned, every row of bushes they'd skirted, every bench where they had tarried, she'd been afraid Phillip would pop up, that he would be waiting for them, grim and determined to hash it out, but he was conspicuously absent.

He was a proud man, with a temper, and his relationship with Edward had never been steady. When he was apprised of the situation, he'd be irate, indignant, he'd demand explanations and answers.

If he confronted them, how should she behave?

She wasn't supposed to know who he was, so she couldn't give the slightest hint of recognition. Yet, chances were great that she would never again be alone with him, so she wouldn't be able to relate how the betrothal had resulted. There would be no way of calming him, or having him grasp how inevitable it had all been.

Phillip was going to be hurt. Badly. He would never forgive her—or Edward—for what they were about to do to him. Edward would never comprehend why, but the tentative bond he'd been working to establish with Phillip would be shattered.

As for herself, till her dying day, she would rue and regret the role she'd played in breaking Phillip's heart and ruining his connection with Edward.

Edward had ushered them to the verandah. A romantic repast had been laid out for the two of them, and he escorted her to the table, held the chair while she seated herself.

This was the most difficult moment she'd endured so far. Up until now, they'd been walking, greeting the staff, so there'd been others to act as a buffer. Though there was a footman ready to serve the food, he was posted at a distance, furnishing them with a solitude she didn't want.

Nervously, she fussed with the silver, the napkin. The footman poured her a glass of wine, and she gripped the stem of the goblet, eager to do something normal, tangible.

Edward joined her, sipping morosely, staring off across the grounds and lost in thought.

"This is so awkward," he murmured.

"Yes," she replied, relieved that he'd acknowledged it.

"It will get easier."

"No doubt," she agreed.

"Where is your cousin, Miss Stewart?" he oddly queried. "I haven't seen her in ages. Will she be attending the wedding?"

"Winnie?"

"Yes."

"I wouldn't think so. She went back to London."

As though poked with a sharp stick, he stiffened. "When?"

"Yesterday."

"What time?"

"I don't know. Early."

"Did she say why?"

"I didn't speak with her. Margaret handled the details. But she's been very dejected."

"Margaret . . . hmm . . ."

She studied him, and it occurred to her that she had to disclose their fiscal quandary, Helen, and so much more.

A spark of optimism ignited. Perhaps, upon learning of her family's deceit, he would cry off.

If he tossed her over, it would be humiliating, and she would be compromised beyond repair, but it would be an escape.

In London, when she'd allowed Margaret to persuade her of the viability of their crazed conspiracy, the plan had seemed so prudent and rational, but now, it had been reduced to a disgraceful confession. She took a breath.

"There's something I need to tell you."

"What is it?"

"I hope you won't be angry."

"I'll try to control myself."

He flashed a wry smile so much like Phillip's that she flinched. Was this how the rest of her life was to proceed? Would she spend each and every minute gazing at her husband, but searching for signs of her beloved?

"Our financial status might not be exactly as we've led you to believe."

"I'm conscious of that fact," he said, surprising her. "Margaret advised me this morning, but I was cognizant of your plight."

"But . . . how?"

"My solicitors had been investigating."

"You knew all along?"

"Yes."

She blushed, wondering how he had tolerated being so civil to them. "I apologize."

"Accepted."

She suffered from a contemptible need to defend her duplicity. "We were so desperate."

"I realize that."

"So it doesn't make any difference?"

"How can it? After last night, it's quite irrelevant."

Resigned and dolorous, she nodded. "Although I'm

sure I don't merit any benevolence, I have a favor to ask."

"Whatever I am capable of granting you, I will."

Did he have to be so kind? It made her ashamed. "I have a niece. Her name is Helen. I want her to come and live with us."

"A niece?" This was news, a hidden tidbit his lawyers hadn't exposed. "I wasn't aware that your brother had any children when he died."

"She is . . . well . . . a . . ."

The term *bastard* was too risqué for her to utter, nor could she discuss her brother's licentious tendencies, so she was saved when he reached out and patted her hand. "I understand."

"She's a tad peculiar."

"How so?"

"She's very quiet, and she doesn't talk or play like other children." Emboldened by her admission, but not wanting him to envision the worst, she hurried on. "But don't worry. She's very precious, and I'll be responsible for her. You'll never know she's around."

"I won't mind having her here, Olivia"—his generosity had her feeling even more ungrateful—"and it will be pleasant, having a child about. Anything else?"

How calmly he'd received the information! When preparing for their trip to Salisbury, Olivia had been tormented by Margaret's tales of how Edward would view Helen's abnormalities. Olivia had accepted every horror story Margaret had spewed. Why?

Why had she let Margaret have such dominion over her? When had she become such a dunce? A fool?

Considering all that had ensued, she was terrified of Margaret and what she might do to Helen. So too she was troubled by Penny and the mischief she might wreak on Olivia's marriage. Edward was amenable to her wishes, and she wouldn't bypass an opportunity to be shed of the two women.

"I should like it if Margaret and Penny did not reside with us."

"On this matter, we are in complete accord." He chuckled, but without humor, harboring his own aversion to the pair. Was he speculating as to their complicity, as was she?

"Their separate maintenance will be an additional expense."

"Don't concern yourself over it."

"But I also need to request that you assist Winnie. I want her free of my stepmother. Could she stay at Salisbury, too?"

Edward assessed her, and it seemed there was a vital and urgent comment on the tip of his tongue, but after a protracted contemplation, he chose not to reveal it. "No, but I will provide for her."

"Thank you."

What more could she possibly seek? Her family was secure, her fiscal mire settled, an advantageous marriage about to transpire. He was being sympathetic and altruistic when there was no reason for him to be. Yet she was so miserable!

How could she be so unappreciative? So dissatisfied? What an ill-mannered wretch she'd grown up to be.

Embarrassed, disconcerted, it was her turn to stare off across the yard, and what she saw panicked her.

Phillip was marching toward them, his lengthy strides covering the grass, though he was limping, and she imagined his war wound was plaguing him. From his demeanor, there was no doubt as to his destination.

He looked fierce, imposing, assertive, and so very handsome. Magnificently dressed, he wore a tailored blue coat and crisp white shirt, tan breeches, shiny black riding boots that came to just below his knee. With his fashionable attire, his noble bearing, his arrogant disposition, he was a sight to behold.

Edward noticed his approach, but by then, there was little either of them could do. He was almost upon them.

Olivia's pulse thudded in her chest, so loudly her ears were ringing.

What did he intend? Would he tell Edward about their affair? Was he about to declare himself? What would Edward say? What would he do?

Scared out her wits, she was dizzy with apprehension.

With the smooth grace of a leopard, he hustled up the stairs to the verandah, strutting over to them.

Edward stood, uneasy, anxious, and as fretful as she about Phillip's purpose. On this, the day of their betrothal, he simply couldn't introduce Phillip to her.

Oh, the lies! The sophistry!

She wanted to jump up and shout that she knew his name, that she knew all about him. She yearned to claim him as her friend, to affirm a prior association, but she was a craven coward. For though he meant the world to her, she dawdled in her chair, like a lump of clay, pretending no recognition.

"Phillip, how nice to see you," Edward began.

"Edward." His regard was cold, his fury barely contained.

"I'm glad you stopped by. I'd been going to come down and advise you myself"—an outright fabrication, she was sure!—"that I announced my engagement this morning."

"I heard."

"Yes . . . well . . ." Edward cleared his throat. "May I present Lady Olivia Hopkins, soon to be the next Countess of Salisbury."

Edward offered her his hand, inclined to support her

as she rose, and she frowned, knowing Phillip analyzed their every move. Yet she couldn't snub Edward by refusing to take it.

Time ground to a halt, the three of them frozen in place.

She wanted to die! For the earth to open and swallow her up. To vanish into thin air.

Do it! an inner voice screamed, and she affixed a bland smile, and linked their fingers. Once she was up, he tucked her arm in his, as he had when they'd strolled in the garden, so that it appeared as if they were sweethearts.

Phillip smirked, and she wanted to yank away, to push Edward off, or step back so that she could create space between them, but she did nothing. She said nothing.

To her eternal shame, she confronted him indifferently, as if he were a total stranger.

"Olivia, this is Phillip, my . . . my . . ."

Edward couldn't finish the sentence, and Olivia wanted to weep with frustration. It was the most horrid, painful experience of her life.

Phillip was no help, standing like a defiant prince, daring his father to blurt it out.

"I'm your what?" he taunted.

"My . . . my . . . stablemaster," Edward said, taking the coward's route, just as she had done, and she winced at the feeble disavowal.

Oh, how they'd wounded him! The result was instantaneous, as he seemed to deflate, as if Edward's renunciation had stabbed a hole in his being, and all the substance was leaking out. His cheeks flushed bright red, and his eyes were shiny, clogged with tears of ire or disappointment.

"Not anymore," he stated.

"What?" Edward queried, confused, while Olivia comprehended what they'd wrought.

"I'm not your stablemaster any longer."

"Of course you are. You always will be."

"No. I quit." From inside his jacket, he whipped out a letter of resignation and tendered it to Edward. "Effective immediately."

Edward scanned it, then tore it to shreds, the pieces fluttering to the ground. "Well, I don't accept it."

"I don't care."

He spun on his heel, ready to stomp away, but Edward touched his arm, and the contact checked him. He glared over his shoulder.

"You're not leaving . . . ?"

"At once."

"This is so sudden. What has happened to upset you?"

"Nothing of import ever *happened* here," he caustically alleged, cutting her to the quick.

"Is there anything I can do?"

"No."

Not having any success at swaying Phillip, Edward endeavored to exert pressure through his station. Imperiously, he contended, "You can't go. I won't allow it."

"You can't stop me."

Phillip's lack of deference had Edward stammering. "But I . . . I thought you were happy here."

"Here?" Phillip questioned scathingly, and his attention drifted to her, his rage and sense of betrayal sinking in, before it gravitated back to Edward. "There's nothing *here* that matters to me in the least."

Edward was stunned, bewildered. "I don't understand you."

"You never have."

There were so many undercurrents swirling, and she couldn't abide any further upheaval. She'd observed the conversation as Edward's silent, feckless conspirator, and she was hampering the two men in their argument. They needed privacy for a final farewell that couldn't be vented in front of her.

"Edward," she interjected, "perhaps I should go inside so you can consider this more fully."

"Don't bother, milady," Phillip chided, before Edward could respond. "The earl and I have naught to talk about. We never did."

With that, he walked away, maneuvering down the stairs and striding across the yard. She and Edward watched him, lost in their own misery, but incapable of reacting. Her stomach churning, her heart aching, she felt physically ill.

Go after him! her conscience shouted, but like a marble statue, she tarried, anchored to the crook of Edward's elbow. As Phillip traveled farther and farther away, he grew smaller in size, so that he was a tiny speck, the only object she could perceive.

Was this to be the end between them? After the joy they had shared, were these pernicious, hateful comments to be the last they ever spoke to one another? Would she never see him again?

She couldn't fathom how it would occur. In some far-off future, she tried to imagine him, merciful as to her sins, returning to the estate, older, wiser, maybe married, with a family of his own.

The vision was so excruciating that she suspected she might swoon. Her chair was behind her, and she eased down into it, needing to balance her weight against the cushion so that she could hide her distress from her fiancé.

As it was, he was so distraught himself that he scarcely noted her condition. He persisted in gazing across the lawn to where Phillip had disappeared into the stables.

"Would you excuse me?" he requested.

"Certainly."

"I think I should probably . . . I should . . ."

Following after Phillip, he was mumbling, but she couldn't decipher his ramblings. He proceeded to the stable door, and as he neared, Phillip rode out on a beautiful, roan-colored mount, a portmanteau tethered behind the saddle.

He was really going! Although she'd heard him say he would, and she was witnessing every detail as the scene played out, she couldn't credit what she was viewing.

Edward called to him—he pronounced *Phillip* very sharply—and Phillip reined in. Edward went to the horse, and laid a comforting hand on Phillip's calf, though it had no effect. They had a heated argument, with Edward gesturing to the numerous paddocks, asking Phillip how he could abandon his cherished animals. Phillip shrugged, and seemed to mention London, but it might have been any word. She was simply so desperate to know where he would be, so that she could picture him in some safe, distant location.

Already, she was visualizing him in the city. Where would he live? What would he do to earn a wage?

She suffered a ludicrous flight of fancy, of someday running into him in London, of meandering down Bond Street, rounding a corner and . . . there he'd be, smiling and merry and having forgiven her after the passage of so many years.

They'd chat and reminisce. Old chums reunited.

The exchange between father and son concluded, and though it was evident Edward was still trying to convince Phillip to stay, Phillip shook his head. He trotted away, down the tree-lined lane where they'd taken so many rides together.

The shadows swallowed him up, and presently, it was as if he'd never been there at all.

I'm sorry, she mourned, *so sorry.*

Edward waited until he'd vanished, then he started toward the verandah. She shifted about, needing to flee so she could compose herself, but as she began to rise, Margaret pulled up the chair next to her.

"Was that the stablemaster?" she casually broached. "Penny told me she'd seen him strapping a bag onto his horse. Rumor has it that he's quit his job."

After the dreadful encounter Olivia had just endured, the sly innuendo was too much. "I'm unwell. I believe I could use a nap. If you'd make my apologies to the earl?"

"Don't be silly, Olivia." Margaret grabbed her wrist. To a passer-by, the move would have seemed innocent, but Margaret was squeezing so tightly, it was all Olivia could do to keep from squirming. "We've a wedding to arrange, and not much time to do it."

"I'm not in the mood right now."

"Nonsense. Every woman's in the *mood* to plan her wedding." As Edward approached the table, she compelled Olivia to seat herself. "And here's Edward. We'll want his opinion."

"Hello, Margaret," Edward said, smiling, though a tad frostily.

"Was that your stablemaster departing?"

"Yes."

"Gone for good, I suppose. I swear, the lower classes have so little loyalty." She motioned dismissively. "Ah, too bad for you. Competent employees are *so* difficult to find." He had no retort, so she added, "Olivia and I were just discussing the wedding."

"How nice," he murmured.

"Let me tell you what I've accomplished so far."

Olivia pretended to listen, and Margaret's litany washed over her, smothering her with its false pleasantness.

She'd been seduced to folly and ruin by a combination of Margaret's avarice and her own stupidity. Through her idiocy, she'd destroyed any number of lives. Her own. Phillip's. Edward's. Very likely, she'd wreaked even more havoc—of which she was, as yet, unaware. She hadn't intended any disasters, so how could she have perpetrated so much harm on so many?

Weary, she closed her eyes, as Margaret droned on and on, so calm and unflappable that Olivia could barely refrain from screaming.

She was trapped, and there was no way out.

CHAPTER NINETEEN

Jane stood at attention, stiff and unmoving as a soldier. Helen was beside her, her tiny hand clutched in Jane's much larger one.

For days, she'd been anticipating this moment of reckoning. Mr. Sawyer hadn't tattled right away, and she couldn't figure out why. Every morning, she'd arisen, expecting to be ordered into Mrs. Graves's office. Each hour had passed with agonizing slowness, each approaching footfall causing her pulse to pound, as she was positive it would be the message commanding her to report downstairs.

Now that judgment was upon her, it was almost a disappointment. Her fears and dread had sprouted into a tempest of fret and worry that had left her amazingly detached. There was nothing Mrs. Graves could do, no punishment she could impose, that would have much of an effect.

She didn't regret her actions, and she had no feelings over the possible sentence. She was benumbed, though she was distracted by Helen's presence in the room.

Was Helen to suffer the same fate as her? How could she have brought such a result onto the child?

"Jane, I'm very surprised at you." Mrs. Graves tossed a file onto the desk, and it smacked against the wood. "With any of the other orphans, I could have predicted mischief like this. But you!" She tsked, making an irritating clucking sound. "You've been with us so long, and have such a stellar record."

Jane knew this was the point where she was supposed to apologize, and plead for mercy, but she'd bite off her tongue before she would.

Mr. Sawyer loafed in a chair in the corner, tipping it so that it was balanced on the rear legs. A piece of straw dangled from his mouth, as he chewed on it and silently surveyed the proceedings.

"As to *her*"—Mrs. Graves indicated Helen—"what's her name?"

She searched her documents, trying to deduce whether she'd listed Helen as *Martha* or *Mary,* but Jane offered no hint, mutely, furiously declining to speak.

"Yes, Martha," Mrs. Graves continued. "Considering her lunacy, I had reservations about admitting her, but to learn that she can turn so violent. My, my . . ." She tsked again. "Such a little mite, too."

Jane scowled. Helen hadn't done anything during the altercation except run. "*Violent* how?" she demanded.

"Don't pretend to innocence, Jane. It doesn't become you." She gestured to Mr. Sawyer. "You know how hard she bit him. Why, Mr. Sawyer had to have it sewn."

Jane glanced at the despicable swine, and saw that he had a bandage across three of his fingers. The wrap was dirty and colored brown with dried blood that had seeped through. The wound looked genuine, but he hadn't obtained it from Helen.

"How convenient," she sneered, and he straightened and flopped the chair down on all four legs as if he might lunge for her.

"Jane!" Mrs. Graves barked. "Cease your belligerence!" Refusing to be cowed, Jane met the woman's angry glare. Mrs. Graves was unaccustomed to such insolence, especially from a ward as meek and helpful as Jane had always been, and she shifted uncomfortably. "Due to your exemplary disciplinary history, I will allow you the courtesy of a defense. What do you have to say for yourself?"

Suspicious, Jane studied her. Any explanation was useless. The consequences would be the same, no matter what she did or didn't do. Still, Sawyer was such an evil man.

"He brings girls down here." The words rushed out before Mrs. Graves could thwart her. "In the evening. He touches them under their clothes. The really young ones, who can't fight back."

"Honestly, Jane!" Mrs. Graves scoffed.

"It's true," she declared. "I don't care what lies he's told you. And *Martha* never bit him. He had her on his lap, and he was—"

"Desist!" Mrs. Graves snapped. "Your prevarication just makes this worse." She stared at Jane, then sighed. "You leave me no choice. You'll have to be put out. Martha, too. She's far too demented to be in the company of the other children."

Jane swallowed. "As you wish."

Mrs. Graves nodded. "Go upstairs and pack your possessions. There's no need to stop here for a goodbye, but Mr. Sawyer will be waiting to check that you haven't taken anything that doesn't belong to you."

With that tepid farewell, Mrs. Graves enmeshed herself in paperwork, ignoring them.

Jane's heart plummeted to her feet. While she'd realized this crossroad was drawing nigh—with her thirteenth birthday for a certainty—she hadn't believed it would ever arrive. The speculation and the reality were very different, and with her recent apathy, she'd thought she was beyond fear, but apparently not.

She'd been excused, but she couldn't force her feet to move. This was the only home she'd ever known, Mrs. Graves the sole adult with whom she'd been friendly for years. She wanted to cry.

The orphanage was her last connection to her parents, the final link to her past. What if they came for her after she'd gone? Would anyone remember that she'd been there? How would they find her?

And what about Helen and her rich family? Where were they? What if they changed their minds and wanted her back?

Jane recalled the fine clothes Helen had been dressed in when she'd been dropped off. She was kin to somebody. Somebody wealthy and important. She wasn't some ragamuffin to be pitched out into the streets.

Their penalty was too cruel to be borne. It would be difficult enough to support herself, but having the weight of Helen's custody foisted on her, as well, seemed too high a hurdle to vault over.

Was life ever fair? Would justice ever prevail? What had she done to deserve any of this? She'd been obedient, obliging, kind, and where had it landed her?

She yearned to kneel before Mrs. Graves, to hug her and beg her pardon, to weep and describe how frightened she was, to ask for some compassion, some understanding.

Mrs. Graves glanced up. Her eyes were cold, dismissive. "Was there something else?"

"No," Jane murmured.

"Be off with you, then. And Godspeed."

"Come, Helen." Jane squeezed Helen's hand and led her into the hall.

Behind her, the door closed, as Mr. Sawyer's malevolent, victorious chuckle wafted out.

• • •

Olivia walked down the regal staircase, destined for the receiving parlor and the dining room beyond. As per Margaret's instructions, she wasn't alone. A few steps ahead, Penny strutted down, too.

Tension between them was so intense that Olivia felt she was suffocating. An antipathy and temper she'd never previously experienced had overtaken her. She was ready to throttle the wicked shrew, to simply wrestle her to the floor and beat her black and blue.

Though Penny was full of aspersions and wily smirking, they hadn't talked about what had happened, or the role Penny had played in Olivia's downfall. Margaret had been a buffer between them, so Olivia hadn't had a chance to state her opinion, but she was eager to let loose.

Given the slightest opportunity, Penny would receive a blistering castigation she'd never forget.

Supper would be tedious. Surrounded by Margaret and Penny, Mr. Blaine and Edward's other neighbors, she would have to smile and chat, to feign delight over her pending nuptials. All the while, she'd be burning inside, a caldron of animosity and anguish.

She couldn't erase the vision of Phillip riding out of the yard, his satchel tied to his saddle. The argument he'd had with Edward rang in her ears, until she longed to clasp her hands over them to drown out the sound.

How could she have betrayed him? Would he ever forgive her? Would she ever forgive herself?

She was trying to be pragmatic, to accept the shattering outcome of her rash conduct with a stoic acquiescence. Every boon she'd hoped to gain through marriage to Edward would be achieved. Time would heal the damage she'd inflicted on Phillip. They would all carry on.

Edward was humane and generous—not the inflexible

ogre Margaret had painted him to be—and Olivia imagined they would find common ground, once they adapted to each other's routines and habits.

Her loss of Phillip cut like the prick of a sharp blade, but her affection for him would fade. In the subsequent months and years, she would recollect less and less of their affair, until very likely, it would seem that she'd never known him at all.

Eventually, he would be naught but a fond, distant memory.

If she could just get through the remainder of the week! If she could just endure the wedding fete and folderol! She was strong, and she could persevere to the end! Despite how terrible she felt, she was positive that no one had ever expired from excessive sorrow.

"Three more days," she grumbled. Soon, it would be over, the house would quiet down, and she would have plenty of opportunity to rue and regret her decisions.

For now, she had to put one foot in front of the other, had to smile and nod and be cheerful.

Penny had reached the foyer, and she halted and looked up. "What did you say, Olivia?"

"Nothing." Olivia refused to converse, for she was afraid that any discussion would deteriorate into a shouting match.

"You said *something*," Penny goaded. "Surely you're not lamenting your marriage. What would the earl think if he was advised that you are?"

Olivia advanced to the bottom of the stairs, and she and Penny were toe to toe.

Evaluating her, Olivia speculated as to what was going on inside her devious head. Was she trolling for a reaction? Or was she bent on causing trouble with Edward? With her, it was so hard to discern her motives, which were invariably suspect.

Without planning to, she blurted out, "Are you happy?"

"Whatever do you mean?" Penny queried.

"You were intent on having me wed to Edward, but why is it so vital to you?"

"You can't guess?"

"No."

Hatefully, Penny chuckled. "I heard that the stable-master has left the estate."

"Yes."

"Pity," she replied.

Olivia could barely refrain from slapping her. She took a deep breath, held it, let it out, urging her anger to evaporate. "So you've brought about my wedding . . ." She pretended scant interest, declining to give Penny any satisfaction. "Are you content with what you've wrought?"

"Very."

"Perhaps I should reciprocate by telling Margaret about you and Mr. Blaine."

"Do it. I dare you." She nodded up the stairs, to where Margaret would be following along shortly. "Let's see who she believes, you or me."

Olivia exhibited an equal amount of nonchalance. "You're bound and determined to ruin yourself, though I can't comprehend why. If you're caught, you'll end up wed to him. You realize that, don't you?"

"Maybe, maybe not," she retorted.

Olivia flashed a brilliant smile. "I can't conceive of a more grand event than your wedding to Mr. Blaine."

Penny was instantly dubious. "What are you implying?"

"You and Mr. Blaine were made for each other. I'll sit in the front pew at the church."

"You're jealous."

"Absolutely," Olivia gushed.

"At least Mr. Blaine is still here," she caustically

remarked. "*And* he's welcome at the earl's table. Where's your precious stablemaster, hmm?"

Where, indeed? Olivia pondered. It was a question that would haunt her forever.

"Hurry, Olivia," Penny mocked, "your fiancé awaits."

She flounced down the decorated hall, and into the parlor. Olivia watched her go, her bottom swaying, the ringlets on either side of her chignon bobbing with each step.

What would become of Penny? What would become of all of them?

Sadly, slowly, she trailed after her, steeling herself to confront the bevy of cordial, exuberant visitors who had traveled to Salisbury to celebrate her engagement. The moment she strolled into the salon, she would have to smile, exuding the sort of bubbly exhilaration that any recently betrothed woman should be feeling.

Without warning, someone grabbed her from behind. A hand was clasped over her mouth, and she was dragged into one of the unoccupied chambers lining the corridor. The door was shut, and she whipped around, terrified of who she'd encounter.

"Phillip!" she whispered, her heart leaping with joy, her emotions roaring with despair.

"Shh . . ." He hauled her over to an open window, which he'd used to enter the house.

"What are you doing?"

"I couldn't leave you here." He gripped her shoulders, his fingers digging in to the soft part of her upper back. "I rode toward London all afternoon, but then I turned around. I couldn't desert you."

Oh, God! Oh, God!

Her mind was reeling. Her panic rising. He still wanted her? After all she'd done? She glanced to the door. What if they were discovered? What calamity would ensue?

Too much had happened! She couldn't take it all in! Her pulse was beating so furiously that her chest hurt with the tension, and she couldn't form any words to untangle the myriad sentiments shooting through her.

"I'm going to speak with Edward," he was asserting, "and I'll inform him we're in love. That we wish to marry. That he can't have you, because you're mine."

"You'd do that for me?"

"Yes."

She could picture the dreadful scene. There would be harsh condemnations, accusations of betrayal and treachery. All true. All well founded.

After the fight Edward and Phillip had had over his resignation, she couldn't fathom how their relationship could survive another. While she'd naïvely and optimistically hoped that, in the future, the two men would reconcile, it wouldn't occur if the facts underlying their quarrel ever came to light. Should Edward learn how duplicitous she and Phillip had been, there would be no way to allay his justified ire.

Could she inflict such discord?

No!

The loud answer reverberated through her, and she wanted to rail and rage, to moan and weep, over the unfair options available to her. She had acted so impetuously, had allowed herself to be inundated by ardor and passion, and she'd courted catastrophe with a reckless abandon. In every direction, damage had been accomplished through her imprudence.

Would the ramifications of her selfishness never cease?

"We can't confess, Phillip. He'd be devastated. He'd never forgive you."

"I don't care."

"Yes you do."

Phillip chewed on his lip, digesting her statement, and accepting it. Then he grasped both her hands, squeezing tight, making her feel as though he were a tether, securing her to the earth.

"Then come with me. Right now," he declared. "We'll elope to Scotland. My horse is behind the stables. We'll take another one for you. We'll simply ride away from all this." He moved toward the window, tugging her with him. "Let's do it! We'll send a note later, explaining where we've gone and why."

The window loomed like a yawning hole in the universe, ready to suck her through into the unknown. She was an unmitigated coward. She couldn't propel her feet toward it, couldn't step through.

Could she lope off with only the clothes she was wearing? Was he mad? Was she?

Phillip had no job, no income, no home to which they could return after a hasty trip to the north. Though Edward was a compassionate man, he had his limits. He'd never permit them onto the estate after they'd humiliated him.

So what would they do? Where would they go? How would they support themselves? What about Winnie? And Helen?

She understood the lengths to which Margaret would go to ensure the success of her machinations, and she was alarmed as to Helen's fate. If she trotted off with Phillip, what might Margaret do to Helen in revenge?

Edward had offered to provide for the people Olivia loved, the only ones to whom she had any connection in the entire world. Dared she cast them to the vagaries of circumstance? Could she forsake them to Margaret's plotting and intrigue?

Without a doubt, Margaret's retribution would be swift and horrible. She would never pardon Olivia for spoiling her scheme, but Olivia would be safe in Scotland, while

Winnie and Helen would be in London, unprotected and subject to Margaret's retaliation.

Her head was spinning with uncertainty. She yearned to escape with Phillip, to let him take her away from her predicament, but her rapaciousness had already caused significant adversity.

Was there no end to her arrogant behavior? How much, precisely, was she willing to relinquish in order to gain her heart's desire? Could she renounce Helen and Winnie? Could she make an enemy of Edward when he'd been naught but kind to her?

"I can't decide what's best, Phillip," she wailed. "There's so much you don't know, and so much I need to tell you. What you're asking is so difficult."

"It's not *difficult*," he contended. "It's easy, and it will work out. I love you and you love me, and that's what matters. The rest will fall into place."

He was so confident, so upbeat, while she was dying inside, overwhelmed by choices for which she wasn't prepared.

He stopped their steady progress toward the window, shifted away, and scrutinized her. "Unless I was wrong," he said. "Perhaps this love is a tad one-sided?"

"I love you, too," she affirmed. "I do, but . . ."

There was a dangerous pause. "But what?"

"This is so sudden, so unexpected. There are so many people counting on me. I need to reflect on what you're requesting." At a loss, she held her hands out, palms up, pleading for understanding. "You're demanding that I make instant, life-altering decisions in a thrice, but whatever I do, will affect many more people than myself. Helen has been—"

"I don't give a bloody damn about Helen or anyone else," he claimed, cutting her off. "Just you and me."

Footsteps sounded in the hall, and they froze. Someone rapped on the door.

"Olivia, are you in there?" Margaret summoned.

She rattled and spun the knob, when thankfully, a person down the corridor distracted her. Hesitating, she conversed, furnishing them with a few more valuable seconds.

Olivia's trepidation was spiraling out of control. She hadn't had the chance to apprise him of Margaret's threats to Helen, so he didn't comprehend her anguish. He was angry, thinking her flighty, fickle. After so many repeated upheavals, her nerves were raw, her strength depleted, her spirit crushed. She truly, truly could not abide one more tribulation.

"It's now or never, Livvie," he murmured, escalating the pressure to an unbearable degree. "What say you?"

He extended his hand, beseeching her to seize it. It hovered there, in the air between them, a lifeline, a reprieve, a salvation.

Take it! her braver self shrieked. *Grab hold! Don't let go!*

But she was paralyzed, unable to respond or react.

"Don't do this to me. Please," he begged. "Don't marry my father. Don't break my heart."

"Olivia," Margaret called, once more.

Frantically, Olivia peered back and forth, between the door and the spot where Phillip tarried, imploring her.

She needed more time! More space! More options!

But though she was silent, Phillip heard her with a stunning clarity.

"So be it," he spat out. "I hope you'll be very *happy*." Whirling away, he climbed out the window. In a flash, he'd disappeared.

On the inside, she screamed and cried out his name, and she imagined him acknowledging her shout, that he was reaching for her, smiling and glad at her boldness. She saw herself as courageous and assured and running with him across the yard. Laughing and joyous, she felt him lift her onto her mount, felt the wind in her hair as they dashed away through the darkness.

"There you are," Margaret snapped from behind her, irritated at having had to search. "Your guests have arrived, and the earl is waiting for you to attend him."

Olivia shut her eyes, letting it sink in, that blissful vision of what might have been. Then she shuddered, wrestling with a despair that was killing her.

Almost in a stupor, she turned and followed Margaret into the hall.

CHAPTER TWENTY

Phillip strode down the London street, cursing under his breath every step of the way. He hated the crowds and the noise and the smells, but this was where any employment opportunity would be located.

He wasn't sure what type of position he wanted. Of course, it would never hold the prestige of managing Edward's stables, but he was confident he could find something palatable.

With valorous military service to his credit, and work experience for a respected lord as his reference, there had to be somebody who would hire him. But whatever the post, he prayed it would be out of the city. If he wound up having to labor in the middle of town, he wouldn't last long before the swarm of the metropolis drove him mad.

His first stop had been to parley with his old commander, Stephen Chamberlin, whose father was the Earl of Bristol, but he'd been disappointed to learn that Chamberlin was still convalescing at the familial estate. Spain had been a bloody, messy rout, and the battle had rendered many of his colleagues crippled and maimed, with the ill-fated ones left behind, buried on foreign soil, without a marker to denote the spot. At least Stephen was alive and had the chance to recover.

Well, there were other fellows about; he was convinced of it. His regiment had been full of the third and fourth sons of the aristocracy. Those who'd been fortuitous enough to come home had incomes and horses, and he intended to prevail on the friendship of every one of them.

There had to be a man who could use his skills and assistance.

Luckily, he had sufficient money to tide him over through his search. Edward had paid him a decent salary, and when he'd resided at Salisbury, there'd been no need to spend any of it. The cash guaranteed that he could rent a room, bide his time, and pick his situation, without having to hurry.

If worse came to worst, he could always pack it in and travel to his sister Anne's house in Bath. Much as she'd grumble, she'd welcome him.

Anne operated a women's health emporium and bathing spa, and he grinned, attempting to picture himself hauling mineral water and filling tubs for the rich, obese patrons who frequented her business, but the image wouldn't gel.

A group of boys ran toward him, and he pressed his coat to his chest, ensuring that their nimble fingers couldn't lift his wallet as they flitted by.

How he abhorred seeing so many homeless waifs! Though he'd been raised by his mother, with no support from Edward, they'd had a roof over their heads and food in their bellies.

Who birthed these urchins? Who abandoned them so that they wandered like wild animals?

At the corner, he dawdled, assessing his direction, when a girl approached and held out an orange.

"Would you like one, sir?"

With a fair complexion and auburn hair, she must have once been fetching, but she was skinny as a rail, appearing half-starved, and so grubby that he was loath to touch the piece of fruit. A very tiny girl stood at her side, silent and detached. With white-blond hair, and the biggest blue eyes, she looked like a little doll, and his heart went out to her.

Who could have forsaken such a precious lass?

"Is she ill?" he asked the older child, gesturing toward the other.

"No. She doesn't like to talk." She offered him the fruit, again. It was wilted and inedible. "The orange, sir?"

Just then, the young one peered up, her gaze piercing into him so sharply that he felt it probing and jabbing inside him. The sensation was eerie, and he shuddered, wanting only to be away. The pair made him terribly uncomfortable.

"Keep your orange," he said to the older one, and her enthusiasm faltered. "Sell it to another."

Overwhelmed by guilt, he slipped several pound notes into her hand. It was a fortune for someone as downtrodden as she, and if any of the other street scavengers espied what he'd given her, she'd be robbed.

The girl gaped at the money.

"This is too much." An honest soul, she tendered the wad of bills, trying to decline the boon.

He wrapped her fingers around it, shielding it from passers-by. "I have plenty more," he affirmed. "I'm happy to share."

She studied him. "Thank you."

"Hide it, and guard it carefully."

"I will."

He started off, when the mute stared at him once more. Her keen regard had unsettled him, and he was inordinately affected by their plight. She had him pondering Olivia's niece, who was also mute, but safely lodged in the Hopkinses' grand town house in Mayfair.

Even with the trappings of the nobility, Helen had a difficult future. What would it be like to have less, to be unable to converse, but as a poverty-stricken vagrant?

The depth of his worry emphasized that his final quarrel with Olivia had rendered him overly emotional.

He never should have gone back for her!

From the moment he'd heard about her engagement to Edward, he'd been angry and hurt, and his initial impulse had been to depart and never return. His temper had invariably been his most unruly trait, and it had regularly landed him in trouble. Once again, he'd let it guide his actions, and he'd ended up alone and tormented.

After the horrid scene with his father, followed by the miles of riding through the quiet countryside, he'd calmed and begun to reflect rationally upon what had occurred.

With an abiding certainty, he'd concluded that a dreadful calamity had transpired at the manor, that Olivia had been dragged into the betrothal against her will. During their last tryst, she had sworn to him that she would never marry Edward, and he'd trusted her.

Only a catastrophe could have forced her to break her vow.

He'd traveled back to Salisbury, prepared to rescue her, merely to discover that she was in no predicament. That she didn't need saving. She was content with events, and ready to proceed to matrimony.

When he visualized the two of them—his father and his beloved—strolling arm in arm around the estate grounds, accepting the congratulations of the servants, he gnashed his teeth. When he envisioned them chatting and enjoying a romantic meal on the verandah, he yearned to smash something.

Though he'd wanted it to be otherwise, Olivia's composed capitulation wasn't feigned, and the actuality hadn't hit home until he'd embarrassed himself by begging her to elope.

He couldn't say what had him more chagrined: the fact that she'd refused him, or the fact that he'd made such a complete and total fool of himself. Whenever he recalled his asinine profession of undying devotion, he blushed with shame.

What had he been thinking? It was obvious she didn't love him! Despite her tepid claim.

How had he convinced himself that she could harbor an affinity for a common bastard? The sole explanation he could devise was that his feelings for her were authentic and true, potent and unwavering, so he'd blindly discounted the realities of their stations.

She was the daughter of an earl, born and bred to the Quality, and her trifling with him had been naught but a fling. While it had been easy for her to pretend affection while they were together, when push came to shove, she'd gravitated to her own kind.

He sighed. He should have expected nothing less, but lust had rendered him oblivious.

Up ahead, he detected the notorious Stevens brothers' gambling hall for which he'd been searching. Previously, he'd amused himself there, sowing his wild oats before hieing off to the madness in Portugal and Spain. The establishment was popular with the aristocracy, and he hoped some of his old chums would be drinking and wagering inside.

He entered the lavish foyer just as another person was exiting, but he'd been so fixed on his destination that he wasn't paying attention, and they collided. Glancing up, he was surprised to note that he'd bumped into a female.

As she was wearing a hat, with a veil that shielded her face, she wasn't eager to be recognized.

"Pardon me," she said, stepping away so he could move past, then she gasped. "Phillip Paxton? Is it really you?"

"Yes." Narrowing his focus, he strove to peek through

the weave of the veil. "Winnie Stewart? I thought you were still in the country."

A grim smile flitted across her lips. "I came back a bit early."

He remembered that peculiar afternoon, when he and Edward were in the garden, and they'd encountered her. She and Edward had been so awkward, making it clear that they had a relationship of which others were unaware.

Had Edward sent her away? Or had she fled when she'd been apprised that he was to marry Olivia?

He felt a kinship with this woman whom Edward hadn't wanted. He, himself, had endured a lifetime of Edward's fickleness as to who was worthy of an association and who wasn't, and he'd never tolerated Edward's mercurial rejections with much grace.

It had to be awful for her, to ascertain how inconstant Edward's fondness could be, and he wanted—in some small way—to alleviate her anguish.

"Was it because of the wedding?" he broached.

"The wedding?" Aghast, she clutched a fist to her chest as though her heart were aching.

"You didn't know?"

"No." She was shaking. "Margaret maintained he would propose, but I never believed her."

"It was announced Monday."

"The day after I left," she murmured. "When is the ceremony?"

"Friday."

"Tomorrow . . ."

On hearing the news, the air seemed to rush out of her, and, afraid she might collapse, he gripped her elbow, steadying her. An alert footman was hovering nearby, and he also approached.

"The lady's had an upset," Phillip advised the man.

"Might we have a private room, while she collects herself?"

"Yes."

The servant escorted them to an adjacent salon, and as Phillip guided her to a sofa and eased her down, the footman poured her a brandy, extended it to Phillip, then slipped out, shutting the door behind him.

Phillip pulled up a chair and offered her the glass. She stared at it, then lifted the veil on her hat, grabbed the beverage, and drank it down in a long swallow. The large quantity of alcohol had an immediate effect. Her trembling abated, and she set the glass aside.

"You loved him," he suggested.

"If I did or didn't, it hardly matters now, does it?"

"I guess not." A becoming blush colored her cheeks, and he realized how pretty she was, how wise and mature. He wished Edward wasn't such a snob, that he'd had the good sense to marry her instead of Olivia. She would have been an admirable partner for him.

"Would it soften the blow," he volunteered, "if I confessed that I was madly in love with Olivia?"

"Really?" She chuckled, but without humor.

"Yes. I actually tried to persuade her to cry off, to elope with me."

"She never would have, Phillip," she gently stated. "She wouldn't shirk her responsibilities to the family."

"I understand that." He grinned. "If it's any consolation, I've been wondering whether Edward intended to propose. With the speed that the wedding's looming, maybe some misadventure coerced him into it."

"Ahh . . ." she mused. "Margaret must have concocted some ploy to snag him."

"That could very well be."

"She was bound and determined to have them wed. At any cost."

The assessment was sound, though it didn't make Phillip feel any better.

They were silent, reflective, when Miss Stewart ruefully said, "We're a pitiful pair, aren't we?"

"Yes, I'm definitely licking my wounds."

"They heal," she counseled, "as I've learned from prior experience." She exhaled a heavy sigh. "I didn't need this on top of everything else. I can't tackle another disaster."

"What's happened?"

"Nothing with which you need concern yourself."

"Tell me, Miss Stewart."

"Winnie, please," she urged.

"Perhaps I can help, Winnie." He scrutinized the elegant decor, but it was a club for males, where women weren't allowed—and with valid reason. There was a nude painting hanging on the wall behind her. What could have induced her to enter such a disreputable place?

"May I inquire as to why you're here? It was quite a shock to stumble upon you."

"Yes, I suppose it was." She studied him, to evaluate if he could be trusted, and ultimately decided he could be. "I'd come looking for a friend about a problem that developed while I was at Salisbury."

"But he wasn't here?"

"No."

"What is it?"

"Olivia has a niece—" she started.

"Helen, yes. Olivia told me all about her."

Winnie raised a brow, as if his possession of this information elevated him in her esteem. If Olivia had confided in him about Helen, then they had truly been close. "She disappeared while we were away. I've tried to get a straight story from our servants, but they have differing tales about when and how she went missing."

Helen lost? He couldn't process it. Such appalling events never befell the offspring of the rich. This was the sort of debacle that occurred in the life of the poor.

"Have you notified Olivia?"

"I hadn't a penny to post a letter, but our housekeeper claims that Margaret was advised, and that she retained a gentleman"—she rummaged in her bag, found a scrap of paper with a name scribbled on it—"a Mr. Lassiter, who has been hunting for her."

"Have you spoken to him?"

"He wouldn't meet with me, so I was hoping to prevail upon my male acquaintance to conduct an interview for me. I presume that a *man* might have more success in dealing with him."

"Do you know where his office is located?"

"Yes."

He rose and held out his hand. "Let's go."

"You'll assist me?"

She gawked at him, as though she couldn't credit his overture, and he scowled. What was it about the women in this family? Why did they automatically infer he was a laggard?

Tough nuts to crack, he thought, amused and aggravated by her reticence.

"Of course I will. Now, let's be off. Time's a-wasting."

Within minutes, they were clopping down the street in a hired hack, then halting at the brick building where Mr. Lassiter's business was lodged. It was a prosperous structure, near the courts, and packed with solicitors, accountants, and other men of commerce.

He left Winnie in the coach, with strict instructions to stay put, then he went inside, examined the directory, and barreled up to the second floor. As he burst into Lassiter's office, the man's secretary jumped to his feet.

"I'd like an appointment with Mr. Lassiter."

The thin, snippy employee frowned over the rim of his spectacles. "And you are . . . ?"

"Viscount Salisbury," Phillip lied. And why not? He was dressed to the nines, and strutting in as if he owned the accursed place. For extra import, he added, "Son and heir to Edward Paxton, Earl of Salisbury."

The titles had the fellow snapping to attention. Income was about to be generated! "I'll see if he's available."

"You do that. And be quick about it."

He slithered into the inner office, and after some extensive whispering, peered out. "Mr. Lassiter *is* available."

Phillip marched by the secretary without giving him another glance. Lassiter stood behind his desk, an obese, weaselly character, with balding pate, rotund stomach, and seedy disposition. He was the type who would cheat and rob you while smiling, so that you wouldn't notice when he was stabbing you in the back.

Phillip detested him on sight.

"Lord Salisbury," he greeted him fawningly. "What an honor. What can I do for you?"

"Where is Helen Hopkins?"

Lassiter faltered, but swiftly regrouped. "Helen Hopkins . . ." he brooded, tapping a finger against his lip. "Helen Hopkins . . . hmm . . . I've never heard of her."

"Let me refresh your memory." Phillip rounded the desk. He was much taller than Lassiter so he towered over the smaller man, severely and effortlessly unnerving him. "She vanished while the countess and Lady Olivia were in the country. Where is she?"

"I have no idea—"

Phillip grabbed him by the lapels of his jacket and yanked him off the floor, the shoulder seams popping. "Where is she?"

"I don't . . . she's . . . you're . . ."

Gulping, stammering, he was terrified of Phillip and what Phillip might do, and Lassiter was wise to be afraid. After the humiliations Phillip had recently suffered, he felt capable of any dastardly deed. He'd be thrilled to vent some of his frustration on a despicable villain who clearly deserved it.

With Lassiter balanced off the ground, his toes dangling, Phillip gripped him by the throat, squeezing and cutting off his air, and he plucked at Phillip's fingers.

"You're not being very forthcoming, Mr. Lassiter."

Lassiter gestured toward a cabinet, and Phillip tossed him away like a rag doll. With a loud thud, he flew and banged into the wall, then he slid to the floor. Moaning, he curled into a ball.

The secretary scurried in. "What the devil . . . ?"

"Shut up, and get out." Phillip shot the underling such a malevolent glare that he hurried off, running for the stairs and shouting for help, though Phillip couldn't imagine who might rush to his aid. A gaggle of clerks?

He tugged at a cabinet drawer, pleased to note that Lassiter was tidy in his affairs, his records neatly cataloged and arranged. With no difficulty, he identified the Hopkins file, whipped it open and scanned the contents.

"An orphanage?" he muttered, tucking the folder into his jacket. "What the bloody hell?"

Stomping to the rear of the room, he saw Lassiter was still huddled in a heap. "I won't listen to your excuses as to why you'd engage in such an iniquity, particularly for money, but you'd better pray she's alive and healthy when I find her."

He kicked Lassiter in the ribs, the toe of his boot making excellent contact, then he swept down the hall and the stairs. Frightened bookkeepers and scribes peeked out, eager to deduce the cause of the commotion. As he raced by, they slammed their doors, and he knew he must look like a madman.

The driver of the hackney was familiar with the orphanage, and Phillip learned that it was situated in a gruesome neighborhood. He climbed into the carriage, worried about breaking the news to Winnie.

"Did you have any trouble?" Winnie asked as he clambered in.

"None at all," he fibbed.

The coach lurched away as he dropped into the opposite seat. There was no easy way to say it. "The countess had Lassiter kidnap Helen and deliver her to an orphanage."

She gasped. "What? That's craziness."

"I don't understand it, either."

"She *paid* him to do this?"

"Yes. And to keep quiet about it, if anybody raised a stink."

He gave her the folder, letting her read the details. Lassiter had been explicit, probably to cover his sorry behind in case the scheme went awry, and he'd meticulously described his numerous dealings with Margaret Hopkins. Winnie perused the pages more slowly than he, delving more deeply into factors of which he hadn't wanted to be apprised.

Suddenly, she froze, growing white as a ghost, all color draining from her face. The file skidded off her lap.

"What is it?" he queried, alarmed by her pallor.

"Oh, my Lord . . ." As if she might be ill, she pressed her fingers to her mouth. "Oh, my Lord . . ."

She leaned into the squab, tears dripping down her cheeks.

"Winnie! What is it?"

"Lassiter had a prior transaction with her," she managed to blurt out.

"Another?" Retrieving the page she was holding, he skimmed the information Lassiter had jotted down. "When was this? Twelve years ago?"

"Almost thirteen."

She was so stricken that he hated to pry. "You knew this girl?"

"Oh, my Lord . . ." she repeated over and over.

"Tell me!"

Finally, she said, "When I was younger, I did a terrible thing."

He couldn't picture her doing anything more horrid than using the wrong fork at a fancy supper. "What?"

"I fell in love, and I had a baby."

Aah . . . Perception dawned. "Out of wedlock?"

She nodded, the tears flowing. "I had nowhere to turn, so I came to London. To Margaret. She didn't want to be bothered, but her husband—a very kind man, Olivia's father—insisted she foster me. So she had to, though she loathed the notion."

"This other girl . . . she's your daughter?"

"She has to be. The dates match perfectly." She pulled at the curtain and stared out the window. "Margaret told me she'd negotiated an adoption, to a lonely couple on a farm in rural Yorkshire. All this time, I've envisioned her there, but instead, she's been in that institution. Oh, I just want to die!"

Phillip posed no more questions. He'd heard enough, and his temper was flaring.

Ever since Olivia had become affianced to his father, he'd wanted to make someone pay, and Margaret Hopkins seemed a fine choice. Nothing would satisfy him more than to extract a bit of revenge from the nasty old crone. She could benefit from a meal of just desserts, and he would happily shove every bitter bite down her craw.

The carriage rumbled to a halt, and Phillip peered out at an imposing edifice that towered over the street. From the outside, it wasn't too shabby, but the interior would be another story.

"We've arrived, Winnie," he cautioned. "Can you bear to go inside with me? Or would you rather wait?"

"I must accompany you."

"Then compose yourself."

"Am I a mess?"

"Yes." That brought a wan smile, and he removed a kerchief from his jacket, so that she could dab at her eyes, though it didn't do much good.

"There's no hope for me. I'm beyond repair."

"It doesn't matter. This is our sole visit, so who cares?" He smiled, too, and offered his hand. "Let's get this over with."

They exited the hack, and presently, they were in a drab but tidy foyer, and a servant showed them into the matron's office. A Mrs. Graves introduced herself as the administrator.

The woman was no dunce, and she scrutinized their clothes and demeanor, assessing their financial status. Phillip deemed her to be shrewd and pragmatic, impressed by wealth, subservient to authority, likely corrupt, and presumably amenable to a bribe.

"I am Viscount Salisbury," he lied again, and Mrs. Graves straightened. "And this is my cousin, Lady Winifred Stewart."

Imperious and arrogant, Winnie played her part, slipping her arm into his, evincing a joint sense of connection and affront.

"What may I do for you, Lord Salisbury?"

"We've come to collect two of our relatives who were mistakenly left here."

"We have no such exalted wards. We're very prudent in our admissions."

"I'm sure you are." His sarcasm oozed through, and she shifted uneasily. "Helen Hopkins, age three, and—" He glanced at Winnie.

"Rebecca Stewart, age twelve," she supplied.

"We have no such girls here," Mrs. Graves contended.

"Why don't you review your records?" Phillip cajoled. "To be positive."

"There's no need. I'm personally acquainted with all my charges."

Phillip studied the matron, trying to decide what would scare her the most. Various threats would suffice. "Perhaps we should call the orphans down"—he hesitated, letting her assume the worst—"so that we can talk to them and see for ourselves."

"Helen Hopkins," she abruptly mused, "and Rebecca Stewart. We had two girls by those names. But they've been discharged."

"What do you mean?"

"There was a disciplinary disturbance, and they were judged to be a danger to the staff and—"

"The bloody child was mute and demented!"

"And three years old!" Winnie injected. "What could she possibly have done?"

"It was the older one," Mrs. Graves declared. "She had a vicious row with a caretaker."

"I'll just bet she did," Phillip seethed. "So you tossed them out onto the streets? To fend for themselves?"

"Well . . ."

He was so irate, he wanted to wring her neck. "When were they put out?"

"Four or five days ago."

Four days? They'd missed them by *four* days? Where was the justice in that?

"Bring everyone downstairs," he ordered, "and line them up. I wish to interrogate them."

Mrs. Graves huffed. "They're already gone!"

"Pardon me, madam, but I don't believe you." She dawdled, considering refusal, and he flashed her his most haughty frown. His unflappable attitude had garnered him success in the army, where he'd been able to outlast any subordinate. "You have five minutes, Mrs. Graves, to have them assembled, or you shall quickly discover how much power my family wields in England."

He bent nearer. "Have you ever been to Australia?"

No fool she, Mrs. Graves grasped his reference to the penal colonies, and she lurched around him. A flurry of noise and activity sounded in the hall.

With no delay, they resolved that what Mrs. Graves claimed was indeed true: The pair had had a quarrel with the night watchman, and had been ousted because of it.

Pondering what the purported *quarrel* might have entailed, he shuddered. By all accounts, Rebecca had resided peacefully at the orphanage her entire life, when all at once, her behavior had become violent. It didn't take a genius to read between the lines. Rebecca had been protecting Helen, and Phillip loved her for it, loved her spunk, and her style, and her bravery.

Discouraged, they departed, but not before receiving Mrs. Graves's assurance that the custodian involved with Rebecca would be fired—a promise Phillip would check upon to guarantee the termination was carried out. He also issued several dire warnings to Mrs. Graves as to her future job security.

Let her stew! Phillip thought, as he lingered on the stoop, a grim, dauntless Winnie clutching his arm. If nothing else came of the wretched experience, he would request that his father have the ownership of the orphanage examined so that managerial changes could be implemented.

"What shall we do now?" Winnie queried.

"We'll find them."

"How?"

"I have absolutely no idea," he said. "But we will."

He stood, scowling at their hack, the driver waiting for them to make a decision.

There were so many abandoned, lost children in the city. They could be anywhere—if they were still alive. How could he locate them in such a mass of humanity? Where on earth were they to begin?

"What do they look like?" He was distracted, desperate to formulate a plan.

"I'm not certain about Rebecca. If I had to guess, I'd say she resembles me, with auburn or brunette hair and hazel eyes."

"And Helen?"

"She's so beautiful. Like a porcelain doll. With very white hair—so white it glows like a halo—and big, mesmerizing blue eyes that seem to probe inside you when she stares."

He stopped in his tracks, his heart skipping a beat. It couldn't be. It simply couldn't be. What were the chances?

Marveling, he gazed up at the sky.

How strange the world could be. How bizarre the unseen maneuverings of fate. Was this the hand of the Lord intervening? Was the reunion predestined? Meant to be?

"I know where they are," he told her. "Come. Let's go fetch them home."

. . .

Winnie was awhirl with fury, determination, and hope.

She'd supposed that nothing could have been more dreadful than her posthaste exodus from Salisbury.

Her life once again in shambles, she'd returned to London, only to walk into a household uproar, the servants fighting about Helen. They were fearful of being blamed or charged with her disappearance, while the housekeeper had been suspiciously unperturbed. She'd alleged that Margaret had been informed, that she'd instituted an investigation through Mr. Lassiter, but Winnie had deduced that the elusive Mr. Lassiter wasn't toiling at it very thoroughly or very hard.

The hunt for Helen had given her a focus, something to concentrate on besides Edward.

She'd been tormented: Would he miss her? Would he be furious that she'd sneaked off without a good-bye? Or would he, more likely, be relieved she was gone?

The questions had haunted her, exacerbating her misery, but with the shameful news Phillip had uncovered, her agony and suffering had metamorphosed into hot, potent anger.

How dare Margaret! How dare she banish Rebecca to an orphanage! How dare she lie to Winnie about what she'd done! All these years!

Winnie had perpetually fantasized about her daughter, about her placid existence in the country. How could she have been so trusting? So stupid? Why hadn't she demanded proof of Rebecca's situation through letters or reports?

Winnie was aware of how brutal and relentless Margaret could be, yet she'd chosen not to be apprised. Accurate facts would have been too painful, much worse than the tepid, sentimental daydreams in which she'd engaged, so perhaps she hadn't wanted a genuine inventory of her daughter's condition. Perhaps she'd wanted to pretend that everything had worked out for the best.

Margaret will pay for this!

Then and there, Winnie vowed to retaliate, so that Margaret would forever rue her wicked deed. If it took every last bit of Winnie's fortitude and energy, if it took till her dying breath, this betrayal would be avenged.

They were deposited at a busy corner, and Phillip helped her out.

"I saw them here, not three hours ago," he explained. "They were selling oranges."

There were people milling everywhere, going into shops, entering and alighting from carriages. They strolled through the throng, analyzing, exploring, back and forth, back and forth, up and down the surrounding blocks and alleys.

She spun around and, as if by magic, the crowd parted, and there they were. Standing side by side, they were holding hands, watching a delivery wagon pass so that they could cross the street. They were ragged, dirty, their pinafores muddy and torn, their faces unwashed. Helen's ivory locks had been chopped off, and she had a frightful scrape on her knee that hadn't been tended.

"Phillip, look!"

As if sensing their presence, Rebecca glanced toward them, and Winnie felt as if she'd been punched in the stomach. She was staring at an exact copy of herself at the same age. Rebecca was tall, thin, with short brown hair and kindly green eyes. And she was pretty. So very, very pretty.

Her rage at Margaret surged anew. How could her cousin have perpetrated such a hateful crime against this exquisite angel?

"Helen," she called, but as she'd expected, Helen gave no sign of a response. Rebecca stiffened, though, and tightened her grip on Helen's hand. From their earlier encounter, she recognized Phillip, and she stepped in front of Helen, shielding her with her body.

Phillip assumed the lead, and Winnie was glad. Her emotions were in turmoil and she couldn't talk, could barely move.

"Do you remember me?" Phillip asked Rebecca.

"Yes, sir."

"We've been searching for Helen. When I ran into you before, I didn't realize that it was she."

Rebecca was extremely dubious. "You've been *searching* for Helen? Why?"

"She was sent to the orphanage without our knowledge. We just found out where she was and came to get her."

"Helen and I belong together," Rebecca asserted. "You can't have her."

So courageous! So protective! So loyal!

"We're her cousins," Phillip fibbed, obviously deciding to temporarily avoid a deeper clarification.

"So *now* you want her?"

At the notion that they might abscond with Helen, Rebecca seemed defeated and forlorn. Evidently, she thought they would leave her behind and alone, without even Helen for companionship.

Winnie couldn't bear it, and she proclaimed, "We haven't been searching *only* for Helen. We've been hunting for you, too."

"For me?"

"What's your name, darling?" Phillip inquired.

"Jane."

"No. No, it isn't," Winnie corrected. "Your name is Rebecca. Rebecca Stewart."

"Rebecca . . ." her daughter murmured, as if tasting it on her tongue. "Why do you say so?"

Winnie couldn't resist. She reached out to touch Rebecca's shoulder, desperate to be assured that she was real and not an illusion, but Rebecca flinched, refusing to allow the contact.

"Because I am your mother," Winnie said, biting down on her hurt. "And I've come to take you home."

Incredulous, Rebecca gawked, inspecting every detail of Winnie's fine clothes, her fashionable shawl and shoes. "*You* are my mother?"

"Yes, I am. When you were born, I believed that I'd given you up for adoption. I didn't know that you'd been placed in that orphanage. Until today."

Rebecca frowned at Phillip, beseeching him. "Is this true?"

"Aye, lass," he affirmed. "Every word. I swear it."

Rebecca's eyes rolled back in her head, and she fainted dead way.

Chapter Twenty-One

Olivia stood at the mirror, as a servant made final adjustments to her hair.

"You look lovely, milady," the maid murmured as she finished.

Did she?

Olivia studied herself, trying to assess her appearance impartially.

With so little time, there'd been no opportunity to have a gown made for the wedding, so she'd had to wear clothes from her traveling trunk. For the occasion, she'd selected a light blue summer dress. It had a scooped neckline and puffed sleeves, a high waist and flowing skirt. Her hair was braided and coiled on her head, a wreath of bright flowers circling like a halo. The colors should have accentuated the blue in her eyes, the creaminess of her skin, but they didn't. She was dreadfully pale.

An ice queen, she brooded, poised, distant, and collected, with a glacial gaze and a wintry complexion.

She was cold, so cold that she felt her innards had frozen. Her hands were trembling, and she couldn't bend her frigid fingers. She yearned to warm up, to swathe herself in a woolen shawl, and snuggle down before a blazing fire, with a cup of heated chocolate.

"I could use a hint of pink on my cheeks."

"Of course," the maid agreed. She rummaged through

a box of supplies, and with several deft strokes she'd added a blushing hue, so that Olivia didn't appear quite so numb, so pallid.

"Better?" the woman queried.

"Yes, thank you."

Though she hated the idea of being alone, she couldn't think of any other tasks for which she required the servant's assistance, so Olivia excused her. As she tiptoed out, Olivia glanced at the clock.

"Ten fifty-three," she noted. Seven minutes to the ceremony. Walking to the window, she peered out across the garden, wondering where Phillip was, where Winnie was.

She'd never been more isolated.

As an adolescent, she hadn't dreamed much about her wedding day, but had she, it would have been far removed from this debacle.

She'd have pictured the huge cathedral in town, the organ blaring, her father proudly escorting her down the aisle, her brother grinning from the front pew. Surrounded by friends and relatives, she'd have been ecstatic and joyous.

Instead, she was marrying a man she hardly knew, who was no more enthused about their union than she, and her sole companions at the festivities would be Penny and Margaret. The pair had generated such animosity and bad feelings that Olivia wished she'd had the fortitude to forbid them from attending.

To make it through the next few hours, she had to mentally detach herself, so that she was aloof and indifferent to what was transpiring around her.

She had to persevere, to be cordial and sociable, so that others would be lulled into believing she was a cheerful bride. Most of all, she needed to buck up for the wedding night when Edward would join her in her bed.

The very thought of lying down with him, of partici-
pating in the physical acts Phillip had shown her, made
her stomach roil with nausea.

How could she go through with it? How could she
not?

A knock sounded, and Margaret peeked in.

"Have you seen Penny?" she inquired. "I can't find
her anywhere."

"Perhaps you should ask Mr. Blaine."

"Freddy Blaine? What on earth would *he* know about
Penny?"

"I can't imagine," Olivia replied, feigning ignorance.

"The earl is downstairs." Margaret changed the subject, content to disregard Olivia's blatant innuendo.
"Are you ready?"

Olivia glared at her, so many scathing retorts on the
tip of her tongue that she couldn't utter a word, lest she
let loose with a stream of invectives that would have had
others rushing in to determine the cause.

As she was about to promenade down to greet her
groom, she dared not initiate a quarrel that would have
her fuming and furious. What good would it do?

Margaret had pushed and shoved until Olivia had had
no other option. At this late juncture, how could she
recant? The female retainers were lining the stairs,
equipped to throw rose petals as she promenaded down.
The guests were seated in the parlor. If she refused to
proceed, she would heap shame on her father's memory,
would embarrass herself, and humiliate Edward.

Edward, of all people, didn't deserve to suffer disgrace and scandal simply because she'd been so stupid.

The lone choice was to trudge forward, a step at a
time, until she arrived at the end. She wasn't the first
woman in history to be miserable on her wedding day,
and she wouldn't be the last. She could get through this!

She had the strength to survive. It was merely a day, a single day, out of all the other lengthy days in her life.

When she didn't respond to Margaret's question, Margaret entered and stomped toward her as Olivia watched.

The older woman had manipulated all of them. She would achieve exactly what she'd wanted. How sad that, when events were concluded, she was the only person who would be happy.

"Well?" Margaret snapped.

"Yes, I'm ready."

Olivia pulled up to her full height, meeting Margaret's calculating expression, and she was pleased to detect that Margaret blanched and shifted away.

Within the hour, Olivia would be a countess, too, and she needed to remember that fact. Margaret might be more mature and have more experience, but Olivia would be her equal, and she would be sure never to underestimate her stepmother again.

"I'm glad you're being sensible," Margaret reproached. "It wouldn't do to exhibit any imprudent histrionics."

"Shut up, Margaret. I'm so weary of you."

Shoulders straight, she circled around her stepmother, hoping against hope that this would be the final occasion they'd be obliged to interact. Edward had sworn that Margaret and Penny would live elsewhere, and Olivia had decided that a request for them to visit would never be issued.

High society might titter and gossip as to whether there was a rift between them, but she cared not.

As she went by, Margaret clutched her wrist, and Olivia threatened, "Don't presume that you have the right to touch me." Glowering at the point of contact, she flashed such a malevolent scowl that Margaret dropped her hand.

"I brought you this." Margaret held up a vial, containing a dark red liquid. "For tonight."

Olivia speculated as to whether it was wine, or some poor animal's blood, but she didn't want to know, and she didn't accept it.

"You can't have him discover that you're not a virgin," Margaret insisted.

"Or what? Will he publicly cry foul? Toss me over? Seek an annulment?"

Margaret was aghast, assuming that Olivia might skew the deal, and Olivia chuckled inwardly. It was amusing to terrify her.

"You think this is a game?" Margaret countered. "That you can confide the truth and be forgiven? You suppose he'd *understand* your sexual promiscuity? Go ahead. Try it." She gestured toward the door. "March down and tell him. March down and tell them all."

Because he'd been kind to her, and because he was Phillip's father, Olivia would never be so cruel. She and Phillip had done enough, and she would never make it worse.

Jerking the vial away from Margaret, she slipped it into a drawer in the dresser next to the bed.

"Wise girl," Margaret chided.

"Get out of here."

"We're going down together. After guarding you so vigilantly, I'll not have you stealing out the second you're by yourself."

"I won't permit you to accompany me." Sauntering over to the window seat, she perched on the cushion. "Hell will freeze over first."

They engaged in a silent staring match, and a minute ticked by, then another, and another. Soon, it was ten past the hour. The earl, Vicar Summers, and the guests were awaiting her. They'd be checking the time to see how tardy she was.

Margaret's malice and frustration were visible, and she yearned to grasp Olivia by the arm and haul her into the hall like a recalcitrant child, but Olivia wouldn't budge. Ultimately, Margaret yielded, worried about rumors if they persisted in dawdling.

Whipping around, she stalked off. "You'd better be directly behind me," she hissed. "Don't forget: I'm the only one who knows where Helen is."

Olivia loitered a bit longer, just to vex Margaret as much as she could, then she fixed a serene smile on her face and started down the hall.

At the landing, someone waved a signal, and a pair of violins began to play, the soothing music drifting up toward her.

She took a deep breath and descended, stretching the moment on forever. Her measured strides looked like a bridal procession, but in reality, she couldn't bear to reach the foyer.

The serving girls, many of them shedding buoyant tears, scattered their roses, whispering their congratulations as she passed. At the bottom, the male footmen stood at attention, forming a double row that led to the parlor. They too grinned and extended their felicitations.

Incapable of further delay, she advanced to the salon, where she paused at the threshold, assessing the details.

There were two dozen people present to witness her nuptials, mostly Edward's neighbors—thankfully, not Mr. Blaine—as well as members of the upper staff.

Edward stood beside the hearth, which had been filled to the brim with blooming bouquets and potted plants. Vicar Summers was with him, his prayerbook at the ready.

Sensing her trepidation, Edward held out his hand, and it gave her the courage to continue. Floating toward him, she focused on that hand and nothing else, and when she approached him, she grabbed onto it, capitulating, sealing her fate.

He tucked her arm in his and linked their fingers. The violin duo ceased. The vicar opened his book and commenced reading.

" 'Dearly beloved'," he intoned, " 'we are gathered here in the sight of God to join this man and this woman in holy matrimony . . . ' "

The remainder was a white blur, a buzzing in her ears, and later in life, she would be able to recall none of it.

Penny struggled against the ropes that Freddy had used to tie her to the bedposts.

When she'd agreed to the exploit, he'd promised he wouldn't bind her too tightly, but as usual, he'd lied, which meant that—once again—she'd progressed much farther than she'd intended.

She wasn't certain how she'd come to be naked and sprawled on her bed, the ropes cutting into her, but he had an ability to cajole her into wickedness that she couldn't resist. An acquaintance had furnished him with an opium pipe from India, and he'd let her experiment with it. She liked the lethargy it induced, liked the smell and the haze, the secrecy and stealth.

Though she hated to admit to such personal weakness, she'd discovered that he could spur her to many acts she'd ordinarily decline to perform, if he tempted her with the potent drug.

It was an elixir that mesmerized, that seduced her into wanting more and more. He would allow her a tiny sampling, and within minutes, she would be afire and craving another application.

She felt woozy, dizzy, her perception disoriented, but though she was lazed and comfortable, she comprehended that she had to get moving.

The clock was across the room on the mantel, but Freddy had the drapes drawn, so it was difficult to distinguish where the hands were pointing. They seemed to indicate eleven-thirty, which couldn't be, because if that was accurate, the wedding would be nearly over.

After the mischief she'd instigated to ensure that Olivia wed Edward, she wasn't about to skip the illustrious event. She planned to appear front and center, beaming at Olivia. Then she'd spend the day hovering at Olivia's side, the ecstatic, rapt younger sibling.

She would annoyingly flaunt her success—until something more amusing came along.

To aggravate Margaret, she had sneaked off well before the ceremony. Margaret would have searched everywhere, and would have been incredibly harried when Penny couldn't be found. She'd met Freddy in the woods, on a deserted path that led from his property to the estate. He'd plied her with brandy and the pipe, and before she knew it, she'd lost track of where she ought to be and when.

With no trouble, he'd lured her to the mansion, and up the back stairs to her bedchamber, and she still couldn't figure out how he'd managed it.

"What time is it?" she asked him.

He lounged beside her, as naked as she, his cock a limp, satisfied noodle. "Who bloody cares?"

"I can't miss the wedding."

"You should have thought of that before you failed to secure me an invitation."

He'd been royally peevish, his excessive pride

damaged, that the earl had snubbed him, and she'd sworn she'd fix the situation, but she hadn't.

Though she'd never tell him so, she'd made no plea on his behalf, for any entreaty would have been suspicious and garnered more notice than she was prepared to endure.

Freddy hadn't proposed yet, and until he did, she couldn't give Margaret any hints as to her escapades, because Margaret would spoil everything.

Penny wasn't about to return to London, to their stuffy town house, filled with Margaret's insipid rules and regulations, to her mother's frilly parties and suffocating soirees, to the vapid, pimply faced boys she insisted on introducing to Penny as potential husbands. The very idea of shackling herself to one of those oafish idiots made her skin crawl.

Penny had big dreams, and they didn't coincide with Margaret's.

"Bring me the pipe," she decreed, but he chuckled and didn't obey.

"You know you have to earn my permission to use it."

"Bastard!"

After she was married to him, and residing in his home, she'd find his hiding spots and enjoy the accursed thing whenever she wanted. He wouldn't be able to dole it out, to tantalize and tease her with its succulent allure.

She would show him who was in charge!

Why, she might buy her own pipe! She'd determine who supplied the illicit potion to him, and purchase it herself! Once she was his wife, she would have plenty of pin money to do whatever she wished, and he would soon ascertain that he couldn't order her about or control her habits.

"Let me go," she commanded, fighting against the restraints.

"No."

"I have to be downstairs!"

"Sorry, but you're not going to make it."

"Prig, beast, brute, churl . . ." She couldn't devise enough names to call him.

"My, my," he jeered, "such foul language."

"I'll give you foul language, you swine."

She tried to lift her legs, to knee him in the groin, but her ankles were bound as firmly as her wrists. The bondage hurt, but thrilled her, too, and she didn't understand why she permitted him such liberties.

The sole explanation that seemed logical was that she relished the naughtiness so much she didn't want to quit. Her behavior, when she was with him, went against everything she'd been taught, everything that was suitable or befitting. It was the most horrid, offensive, dastardly conduct of which she could conceive, the maximum leap she could take from being the prim, proper girl her mother exhorted her to be.

He rolled onto her, and his John Thomas was erect once more. Down below, he fingered her, toying with her bared genitalia. To titillate him, she'd shaved herself, but he'd never evinced the slightest sign that he realized she had, and she was furious that she'd expended such effort without so much as a compliment being uttered.

He pushed his rod inside her. Luckily, after their previous indiscretions throughout the morning, it glided in.

"I loathe you," she asserted.

"Believe me, my dear, the sentiment is mutual." He started to thrust as vigorously as he could.

Early on, she'd discerned that he could be particularly huffy over insults to his masculine size and prowess, and she loved taunting him. "You think you're such a manly man. Why, your cock's so small, I can scarcely feel it."

"If you don't shut up," he snapped, "I'll stick it in your mouth, so I don't have to listen to you."

Pressing his palm over her lips, he stifled any further remarks, which also cut off her air. Instantly, she calmed. She didn't like it when she couldn't breathe. It was the only way he could scare her.

He plunged into her over and over, but as so often happened, his cockstand began to wane. She wasn't sure why this occurred, and she pondered whether it was normal, but once prior, she'd made the mistake of commenting, and he'd whipped her with a strap, so she kept quiet.

"I'm already bored with you." Groaning in disgust, he jerked away and flopped onto his back. "That didn't take long."

The statement frightened her. She couldn't have him changing his mind or getting cold feet. He had the income to rescue her from her current circumstance, and he couldn't discard her. She wouldn't tolerate any rejection.

"You can't be *bored*," she contended. "I've done what you've demanded of me. Every time!"

"With too much sass, for my money."

"Well, if you weren't such an absolute boor, I wouldn't have to keep reminding you of it."

"What a spoiled, arrogant little shrew you are." He came up on his elbow and studied her, then sighed. "Oh, well, I can put up with a lot to obtain what I want."

"What is it that you *want*?"

He didn't answer, but climbed off the bed and walked across the room.

"What are you doing?"

"Unlocking the door."

"Why?"

"Our moment of *discovery* has arrived."

Her pulse pounded with excitement. "Then we'll have to marry."

"Yes."

"We won't have any choice."

"No, and we've fornicated sufficiently that I can insist you're pregnant."

Glancing down at her flat stomach, she envisioned it swollen and bloated. She'd never considered that they could create a babe, hadn't fathomed that it was a possibility. "I could have a baby?"

He was ignoring her. "If you're increasing, the old bat can't refuse the match. I'll bet we can have it accomplished in the next two or three days." He brushed his hands together in anticipation.

Suddenly worried, she barked, "I might have a . . . a . . . child?"

"Of course. That's the plan." She was so aghast that he added, "You can't presume I've philandered because I'm *fond* of you."

"But I can't have a baby! I hate children!"

"So we'll hire a few nannies. It isn't as if we won't be able to afford them." He shrugged and clambered onto the bed to stretch out beside her, nude and anxious for someone to stroll in unexpectedly. He untied her feet, then toiled at the bindings on her wrists.

"How many trust funds do you have?" he inquired. "What are the terms? Have you been apprised of how much cash we'll be allotted immediately after the wedding?"

"My trust funds?"

"Does any property come with your inheritances? I hope there's an acceptable house in London, so that we won't have to be bothered with buying one."

"A house? In London?" She sounded like a dolt, repeating his questions, but the word *baby* kept screaming through her head, and she could focus on no other topic.

"Ah, London," he mused. "How I'm eager to go."

"But I don't want to live in London," she protested. "My mother is in London. I want to stay here in Salisbury."

"As if I'd remain in this godforsaken place. Especially after your fortune is ceded to me." Gleeful, he lay on the pillows and laced his fingers behind his neck, staring at the ceiling. "My exile is about to end! Oh, how I'll rub my brother's nose in it!"

"Rub his *nose* in what? What are you blathering about?"

"So how much do you imagine will be distributed straightaway as a lump sum? How are the dispersals scheduled? Monthly? Quarterly? Annually?"

"What dispersals?"

"Your trusts! Your trusts! The assets in your dowry! How much will we receive?"

"I don't have a dowry."

"Yes you do. Your da was a damned earl."

"My father was destitute. He had nothing."

Shocked, he froze. "What did you say?"

"He died penniless."

"You're claiming he didn't leave you a farthing?"

"No."

"What about Lady Olivia's father? Your stepfather? He must have left you *something*."

"He was beggared, too. That's why we're here. My mother is praying that Lord Salisbury will bail us out of our penury."

Looking frantic, he lurched away. There was a peculiar air about him that had her squirming.

"Tell me that you're joking. Please!"

"As if I'd lie about my finances. I'm so glad we're to be wed, so that I can be with you and do what I want."

Appalled, gaping in astonishment, he frowned, then he leapt to the floor.

"Oh, Jesus!" he wailed. "Oh, Jesus Christ Almighty! Where the hell are my clothes?"

He was fumbling around, stumbling, and muttering curses. Her wrist was still cinched to the bed, and she struggled to her knees and fussed with the knot. Eventually, she was free, but as she was inebriated, she snuggled onto the mattress rather than stand up.

"Do be silent!" she snarled, as he located his pants. "I can't abide your whining."

"Damn . . . damn . . . double damn . . ."

He wasn't paying attention to his pipe, so she took it and sneaked a bit of pleasure while he was distracted. "Why are you so upset? Everything will work out fine."

"Not bloody likely."

"What do you mean?"

"I *mean* that I don't have a penny to my name. I thought *you* did."

"No." Giggling, she fell onto her back. "I'm poor as a church mouse."

"Gad! I'm a fool! I have to get out of here! What if I'm caught with you? Aah!"

She tried to grasp the significance of his panic, but she was confused, intoxicated, and thus mentally muddled. If he was broke, and she was, too, how could they marry? He couldn't be indigent!

He was landed gentry, with a fancy residence, a jaunty carriage, and a dapper wardrobe. Whenever they met, he plied her with brandy, opium, and other delicious treasures. He had scads of money, she was convinced of it; yet he was complaining. Who was he to gripe?

She was the one who'd been ruined, and she was ready for what would come next, prepared to wed him so that she could escape her tedious existence in town.

She wanted her independence, as well as the depravity and vice with which he tempted her, and she wasn't about to have him renege, not when her affairs were arranged, not when she'd taken herself to a condition of no return, to where Margaret would have to accede to whatever stipulations Penny leveled upon her.

"Listen, you!" She sat up and kicked the covers away, her breasts bared to the cool room. Freddy was beside the bed, naked but for a foot stuck in his trouser leg, his shirt clutched to his groin and shielding his privates.

Hah! As if she hadn't seen it before! As if he could hide that shriveled worm from her!

Harried footsteps reverberated in the hall, winging in their direction. Bracing, they both halted. Would the person stop or pass by?

Whoever was there tarried, then the knob was spun. The door began to open. Wide. Wider.

Freddy was stiff with fear and alarm, while she chortled and reposed, arraying her body so that she would be decadently sprawled for the pitiful sod about to enter.

Cunningly, she smiled. Her destiny had arrived. Just in the nick of time.

CHAPTER TWENTY-TWO

Like a convict at the gallows, Edward faced the vicar. He hadn't heeded the words droning out of the minister's mouth, but the ritual had to be nearing the end.

How many more ways could a man say *I do* and *I will*?

For Olivia's sake, he was trying to be glad. This was her wedding day, and she was very young, and he wanted it to be special for her. Even though he'd rather find himself shackled and tortured in a medieval castle than where he was, he'd resolved not to let her know how he was dreading the ordeal.

He wasn't such a cad that he'd spoil it for her. Despite how much he abhorred the marital trap into which he'd fallen, he wouldn't have his displeasure showing.

There were two dozen guests, and he could feel their curious eyes cutting into his back. After the festivities, many of them would dash to London, so that they could parley over the details.

The sole story he wanted circulating about town was that Olivia had been a beautiful bride, himself a doting husband, and the wedding a huge success.

Throughout the ceremony, she'd been clutching his arm, and he persisted in holding her hand. Her skin was icy cold, and she was trembling. She looked fragile, delicate, but brittle, too, as if the slightest sound or movement might cause her to shatter into a thousand pieces, and he truly felt that if he released her, she might crumple to the floor.

His tight grip was the only thing keeping her vertical.

She wasn't any happier about their nuptials than he was, and she was also hiding any negative reaction, and he cherished her for it. He loathed scandal and gossip and would hate to have their union start off mired in them. They would have sufficient difficulties, without having to weather the innuendo and slander of high society.

Hoping to impart his support, he squeezed her fingers.

They would survive the horrid day. Just as they would survive the coming weeks and months, and he sighed. What a wretched statement about the remainder of his life! His marriage yawned like a black vault of doom, ready to suck him into an abyss of tedium and despair.

Out in the hall, activity erupted. Brisk footsteps were hastening toward the decorated salon where they stood. Employees lined the corridor and, as the strides converged on them, a fierce buzzing commenced.

He couldn't fathom who would disrupt the affair, and he kept his attention fixed on the vicar.

"Father, stop!" a man pleaded from the rear of the room. "We need to talk before you proceed any further."

Scowling, he froze, flustered by the interruption. Was he imagining this? Had the chain of catastrophes left him daft? Was he so off balance that he couldn't distinguish reality from dreams?

The voice had to be Phillip's. It couldn't have been another's. Phillip had referred to him as *father*. Out loud. In front of the assembled company. Yet Phillip was in the city, searching for employment, having abandoned Edward to his lonely fate.

The voice came again. "Father!"

Olivia stiffened. Vicar Summers ceased his prattle.

Others had heard the commotion, too. Someone—
Phillip?—was behind him and calling out. He wasn't
hallucinating, and at having been publicly claimed by
his son, he suffered an amazing wave of exhilaration.

He and Olivia twirled around together, hands still
joined. She blanched, growing so pale that he was afraid
she might faint, and he clasped her even more firmly.

"Phillip?" Though he could observe his son perfectly
well, he couldn't process the sight. "What are you doing
here? I thought you were in London."

Phillip approached, strutting between the chairs that
had been arranged by Margaret. No one had missed his
use of the title *father*, and guests were bending and
straining to view every aspect of the lurid encounter.

So much for quelling any gossip!

Edward's heart swelled. Phillip appeared so dashing,
so handsome. Confident and poised, he was dressed for
traveling, in tan breeches and a brown jacket, and once
they were toe to toe, there could be no doubt as to the
relationship between them.

Among the Quality, rumors had abounded that he'd
sired a bastard child or two, but he'd never acknowledged or denied the scuttlebutt.

Well, the guessing was certainly over!

"My most humble apologies, Lady Olivia," Phillip
said. "I'm sorry to intrude."

Olivia stared at the floor. "It's quite all right," she
mumbled. "I'm sure you have a very good reason."

"Father," he repeated, "may we speak privately?"

The vicar cleared his throat. "Lord Salisbury . . .
umm . . . should I continue?"

"Put your book away," Edward ordered. "For now."

The command stirred the audience to a frenzy of
whispering, and it expanded when Winnie entered, a

child on either side of her. Both of them were girls, and they were dirty, unkempt, and wearing clothes that were little more than rags.

"Helen!" Olivia breathed. "What on earth . . . ?"

Her anguished gaze locked with Phillip's, in a heated exchange that Edward didn't understand, then, shocking everyone, she fled the makeshift altar and rushed to her niece. Kneeling down, hugging her, she mourned over Helen's chopped hair, and she massaged Helen's arms and legs, as if checking for injuries.

In a sort of reverie, he beheld the touching tableau, wondering what was occurring. Events seemed to be happening in slow motion, as if they were swimming through water. He studied Winnie, who looked determined and furious, and assessed him in return.

"Winnie . . ." he couldn't help murmuring, and his longing was pathetically apparent.

He'd planned that if he ever saw her again, he would be too angry to be civil, but he'd been fooling himself. At knowing she was safe, and in his home, where he thought she belonged, he felt a surge of joy sweep through him.

"Edward," she greeted, imploring him, "listen to what Phillip has to say."

"What is the meaning of this outrage?" Margaret leapt to her feet and gestured to the butler who was leaned against the back wall and gawking along with the rest of the crowd. "We're in the middle of a wedding. See to your duties! Evict these interlopers!"

The butler straightened, and tugged on his coat, torn by what should be the appropriate behavior, but Edward forestalled him with a brisk shake of his head. He scanned the gathering, which now included a gaggle of curious servants peeking in from the hall.

"Would all of you excuse us?"

The housekeeper was experienced with handling any

social situation, and she jumped into action, going to a door that led out to the verandah. In anticipation of the conclusion of the ceremony, the food had been laid out.

The woman had deduced the obvious—that there would be no *conclusion*—and that the guests might as well dig in to the repast. She began guiding people outside.

The butler opened the opposite door, to another parlor, and Edward herded the involved family members into it. Winnie gave the two girls to a housemaid, with instructions to feed them while the grown-ups consulted.

Momentarily, he was sequestered with Margaret, Phillip, Olivia, and Winnie, and the instant they were alone, Margaret whirled on Winnie, seizing the offensive.

"How dare you come here!" Margaret growled. "How dare you interfere—after all I've done for you!"

A dangerous calm permeated Winnie. "How dare I?" She took a step toward Margaret, then another. "How dare I?"

Stunning him to his very core, she lunged at Margaret, as if she intended to physically attack her.

Edward vaulted between them and captured Winnie, wrapping his arms around her so that she couldn't land any blows.

"Winnie! My goodness!" He struggled to restrain her.

"Let me go, Edward," she begged. "Let me at her."

Containing her was like trying to hold on to snow. She was in a frenetic state, charging and jabbing at Margaret. If he loosened his grip for even a second, she'd pummel Margaret into a bloody pulp.

What an interesting wedding day it had turned out to be!

He peeked at Phillip, who was watching, not upset in the least by Winnie's raving. If the decision had been up to Phillip, he'd have stood aside so that Winnie could assault her cousin.

"What's this about?" he asked his son.

"It's Winnie's secret to divulge," Phillip maintained.

"Harlot," Margaret seethed.

"Desist, Margaret!" Edward admonished. "I won't tolerate that kind of crudity. Do you hear me?"

"Yes, I hear you," she groused, and she glared at Winnie with such malice that Edward was confounded by the savagery of her dislike.

"Winnie?" He shook her. "Tell me."

Winnie said nothing. She glowered at Margaret with an equal amount of venom, and Olivia intervened in their stalemate, placing a comforting hand on Winnie's shoulder.

"What is it, Winnie? You can confide in us."

Olivia's soothing manner had a beneficial effect. Winnie's eyes brimmed with tears, and she gulped for air. "Years ago, I had a child."

So . . . the tale Margaret spun was true. Edward flinched at the tidings, and abruptly regretted it. Winnie felt his recoil, and pushed away from him.

"I won't apologize for it. Not ever again," she hotly proclaimed, and he was extremely disconcerted.

Was he so stuffy, so snobbish and superior, that he would condemn her for the same mistake he'd made himself? Wasn't he a better man? A more compassionate man?

Winnie spoke to Olivia. "Your father forced Margaret to assist me, though she didn't want to. She lied and pretended she'd had Rebecca adopted. By a family in Yorkshire."

After an awkward pause, Olivia prodded, "But she wasn't?"

"Margaret dumped her at an orphanage, as if she

were a piece of rubbish that could be discarded. She's been there, waiting for me. All this time."

"Margaret!" Olivia chided. "Shame on you!"

Margaret wouldn't be chastised. "As if any respectable couple would have sheltered your bastard! I did the best I could. By her, and by you."

"How did you learn of this?" Olivia inquired of Winnie.

"When I arrived home, Helen was missing. Margaret had had her kidnapped and sent to the same orphanage."

Olivia gasped, and frowned at Margaret, her censure manifest. "You told me she was in a hospital."

"When Phillip and I located them," Winnie went on, "there had been an incident at the orphanage. A caretaker had tried to hurt Helen, and Rebecca came to her aid, which was against the rules. They'd been evicted by the matron and were living on the streets."

"On the streets?" Olivia echoed, disbelieving.

Accusingly, both women scrutinized Margaret, and she pulled up to her full height. "You should have left them there, to fend for themselves. Look at the damage they've already wrought."

"How could you?" Olivia was horrified and bewildered. "Helen is a child! A tiny, defenseless child!"

"She's demented!" Margaret insisted. "She's deranged, she's—"

"That's enough!" Phillip roared at Margaret. "Get out of here, you old witch, before I tear you in half."

"Curb your tongue!" Margaret imperiously responded. "I will not be ordered about by a servant."

"Margaret," Edward interjected, "Phillip is my son." He was irked by her pomposity, dazed by her duplicity and deception. "I expect you to treat him accordingly."

"Your son, bah!" As if dispersing a foul odor, she fluttered an arm in the air. "With his illicit ancestry, who knows what rock he slithered out from under? Besides, you've only his common mother's word for it that he's yours." The insult was so coldly delivered, and so reprehensibly thrust, that he couldn't form an answer, and she kept on before he could regroup. "We've delayed too long, and we're courting scandal. We must get back to the parlor and complete the vows."

She moved toward the door, but no one went with her.

Edward stared her down, but she was a stern character and couldn't be cowed.

Did she suppose that they could go on as if nothing had transpired? Did she imagine they would stroll into the main salon, invite the guests to reseat themselves, and conclude what they'd started?

She was amazing. Brash. Overbearing. Rude. Curt. And she had more audacity than anyone he'd ever encountered. No doubt remained that she'd lured him into Olivia's bedchamber to coerce this farce.

"We're not going to finish it," he said. "Not now, anyway."

"Of course we are," she declared. "You'll not dishonor Olivia in front of the entire world. Our family will be a laughingstock, and I won't stand for it."

Edward glanced at Olivia. Her cheeks were a bright pink, heated by anger. "How would you like to proceed, Olivia?"

"I can't continue right away. Too much has happened."

"My feelings exactly," he concurred.

"Don't be an idiot!" Margaret scolded her stepdaughter. "Would you renounce this opportunity? Think! When news of this fiasco leaks out, you'll never have another chance at marriage. There isn't a man in the kingdom who will have you. What will become of your precious Helen then?"

"Actually"—Phillip interrupted her tirade—"there is

one man who would have her." He gazed at Olivia. "If she'd agree."

Olivia and Phillip?

Edward assessed the two of them, and when he did, their affection was so obvious. It explained so much: Phillip's outbursts of temper, his departure from the estate; Olivia's tepid and waning interest in matrimony, even though she'd traveled to Salisbury for the specific purpose of snagging a husband.

They'd met. How? Without his suspecting it, they'd fallen in love. Why hadn't either of them admitted it? Why had they permitted this travesty to progress? Did they find him to be such an ogre that they couldn't have confessed?

They were perfect for each other, and a huge wave of relief billowed over him. He'd never wanted to be with Olivia, and this information furnished him with the ideal pretext to cry off without offending her.

Phillip could have her—with Edward's blessing— and Edward would escape the marital noose.

The sense of liberty sweeping over him was so refreshing that he was giddy, and he had to stifle a giggle of glee. He was released, unencumbered, and he yearned to shout the tidings to the heavens, yet he couldn't embarrass Olivia by exhibiting his joy.

He queried, "Phillip, is there something you need to tell me?"

Before Phillip could reply, Olivia pleaded, "Please, Phillip. This is not the time."

"I should say not!" Margaret huffed. "And it will never be *the time*, so I advise that you consider your modest station and position before you speak out of turn and humiliate both yourself and the earl."

How fascinating! Margaret knew about their affair. Was he the sole person who'd had no clue?

"Olivia is twenty-three, Countess," Phillip pointed out. "You have no authority over her."

"She will *do* as I bid her."

"No I won't." Olivia asserted herself. "You've always led me about, but after these . . . these . . . affronts to Helen and Winnie, there's no opinion you could offer that I would deem to be valid." She regarded him, her smile a tad tremulous. "I'm sorry, Edward, but I can't marry you. I never should have accepted your proposal. Somehow, she tricked us into this, and when it was occurring that night in my bedchamber, I hadn't the courage to refuse you. So I'm doing it now. I'm sure it will save us decades of grief."

"You can't do this, Olivia!" Margaret yelled. "You absolutely cannot!"

"It's not up to you," Olivia said. She was wearing the gold band he'd slipped onto her finger during the abbreviated ceremony, and she removed it and gave it to him.

Upon witnessing what she'd done, Margaret wailed, "I wash my hands of you! I simply wash my hands of you!"

She stormed out, and in stunned silence, they watched her go.

Edward dropped the ring into the pocket of his vest, even as he wondered if they'd stopped soon enough. Were they already wed? How far did one have to advance through the vows before the union was established?

For months, perhaps years, he foresaw wrangling with the church and the law to have it straightened out, but he was unconcerned.

He was free! Free to do whatever he wanted. Free to marry or not. Free to choose another bride. Free to . . . to . . . pick Winnie, whom he should have selected from the very beginning, titles and blueblood and the peerage be damned!

Evaluating her, he recalled how outraged she'd been

for Rebecca, how she'd fought to get at Margaret, how he'd had to restrain her. She was a wildcat, a tigress, an Amazon, and she could be his if he was brave enough to reach out and grab for her.

As a commoner, she was the antithesis of everything he'd thought he'd wanted. She'd committed the inconceivable; she'd birthed a child out of wedlock. Did any of it matter?

The question surged through him, and the thunderous answer was so clear that he was chagrined he'd felt the need to ponder it. They had both made mistakes, had both sinned and erred, and by tying the knot with her, he could right so many wrongs.

He could love her and cherish her, could provide a stable home for her abused daughter, could give her many more children of her own, who would have the benefits of his wealth and status.

What a merry life they were destined to have!

"Let's have a round of brandies," he suggested. "I believe we could all use one, and there are a few things I'd like to get off my chest." He glared at Phillip. "And there are a few things you need to divulge, as well."

A sullen crew, his companions loitered, milling about, and it took several minutes to locate the butler, to have the libation poured and served. Just as he tipped the rim of the glass to his lips, a haunting, keening lament could be heard, wafting down from the upper floors.

Listening, then scowling, Olivia mentioned, "That sounds like Margaret."

Exasperated, Phillip said, "I'd better check it out."

He raced off, Olivia and Winnie hot on his heels.

Margaret sneaked to the rear stairwell. Thankfully, the staff had herded the guests outside, so she hadn't run into a single soul who would have mortified her by asking either what was being discussed behind closed doors, or when the ceremony would resume.

Had anyone dared interrogate her, she was too furious to respond.

Winnie! The strumpet! To have brought her disgraceful urchin to Salisbury! What was the woman thinking? Had she no pride? No shame?

Likely, she assumed the earl would support her, and her waif, too.

Margaret harumphed. She knew the way a man like Edward Paxton would *support* Winnie. She would have to earn her keep, flat on her back, with her legs spread.

Was that the existence she envisioned for herself? To be naught more than Edward's concubine until he tired of her? What then? Where would she go? What would she do?

Ultimately, he'd toss her over. She'd be alone and destitute, and Margaret would be damned if she'd aid the pitiful Jezebel again.

It was marvelous to be shed of her! She didn't have to feign friendship. Winnie would have to grow up and walk her path without Margaret's assistance.

As would Olivia.

"Stupid, stupid girl!" she muttered as she left the stairs and stomped toward the sleeping chambers.

Olivia was about to learn a cruel lesson: A female had no power, and no protection, but what she could garner for herself. While parents lied to girls and told them that matrimony and a spouse would seal their futures, the reality was that a woman couldn't rely on luck, fate, or a husband. No one would coddle you. You had to fend for yourself.

Two worthless, impoverished husbands had taught her that painful fact.

Life hadn't slapped Olivia in the face yet, but it would. Olivia was young, a dreamer who presumed that everything would always be resolved for the best.

Well, she'd find out the value of casting her lot with some indigent, illegitimate workingman. He'd had the audacity to claim he was the earl's son! Of all the nerve!

Olivia could have her coarse scoundrel. She could birth him a gaggle of yapping brats, and reside with him in humble squalor, where there was never enough cash to buy food for their hungry bellies.

When she'd had her fill of poverty and strife, she'd crawl to London, appealing to Margaret for help, but she'd discover how imprudent she'd been.

Olivia could beg on street corners, could starve, become a vagrant. Margaret cared not.

It was time to focus on Penelope.

Praise be, she had a daughter who understood the importance of money and security. Penny might fuss and stew, but she had inherited Margaret's shrewdness and bold manner of carrying on.

With a bit of pressure, she'd come around to Margaret's point of view.

Previously, she'd deemed Penny too immature and headstrong to be a wife, but there was no alternative. Olivia had betrayed them, so they needed to change course.

They would journey to London at once, so that they could commence their quest for a spousal candidate. There had to be an available rich gentleman who would sustain them, and Margaret intended to ferret him out. Very, very soon.

Where was Penelope? What was she up to?

During the morning's nuptial preparations, Margaret had been busy, so she couldn't be bothered with Penelope. What with berating the sloppy servants, and battling

Olivia to ensure she attended, Margaret, herself, had entered the matrimonial salon almost fifteen minutes late. Penny hadn't been present, and by then, Margaret couldn't search for her.

She peeked inside her bedchamber, hoping to espy Penny, but she wasn't there, and Margaret's temper flared. Within the hour, she wanted to vacate the premises, and she wasn't about to waste a second hunting for her recalcitrant, wayward daughter.

A maid strolled by, and Margaret ordered her to pack their bags, then she strode to Penny's room. Just as she reached it, a door opened farther down. In dismay, she saw Vicar Summers and his wife exiting a bedchamber, and she could barely smother a groan. They were the very last people Margaret wanted to encounter.

Mrs. Summers was sickly, and the housekeeper had arranged for a room where she could rest if she was fatigued, and it galled Margaret that Edward would allow such fraternization.

What was the world coming to when such ordinary folk shared space with their betters?

"Countess!" the vicar called, waving. "Oh, Countess!"

Margaret yearned to pretend she hadn't seen him, but there was no way she could. "Yes, Vicar Summers, what is it?"

"Have you spoken with the earl? What's to be done?"

"I have no idea. You'll have to ask him."

The couple approached until they were next to her.

"Quite the peculiar ceremony, eh?" The vicar was eager to dawdle and gossip, but Margaret would have bitten off her tongue before uttering a word.

"Yes, quite," she said glacially. "I'm in a hurry. If you'll excuse me?"

"Certainly, Countess. Pardon us."

Desperate for privacy, Margaret turned the knob on the door and, with more force than was warranted, shoved at it, and it flew back.

Margaret blinked and blinked. Though her perception was unimpeded, she couldn't process the spectacle before her.

Penny and Mr. Blaine? Naked? Together? Just before noon?

"Sweet Jesu!" the vicar exclaimed. "Stand aside, Mrs. Summers! Shield your eyes!" He jostled his wife away from the threshold, sparing her the gruesome sight.

Empty liquor bottles were strewn about, and a pungent smoke was in the air that created a haze and gave the area an illusory ambiance. Penny was on the bed, the blankets tangled around her legs, while Mr. Blaine loafed with his shirt wadded up to conceal his privy parts.

There could be no dispute as to what they'd been doing. From their guilty looks, it wasn't their initial tryst, either.

A terrible ringing began to clang through her head. Her vision clouded with a strange reddish hue.

This was where Penny had been? This was whom she'd chosen?

A dangerous, shrill madness tore through her, and suddenly, she couldn't predict what might happen.

"Mr. Blaine!" the vicar barked. "What have you done?"

"I can explain," the hapless nude oaf contended.

"I don't suppose any *explanation* is necessary," the vicar countered. "The situation speaks loudly for itself."

"Mother," Penny chimed in, sitting up straighter and pushing her hair over her shoulder, exposing her breasts, her nipples. "Guess what? Mr. Blaine and I are to be married."

"The sooner the better, I'd say," the vicar agreed.

"No, no, really," Blaine attempted to interject, "not marriage. We hadn't contemplated mar—"

"Mr. Blaine!" the vicar scolded. "Don't make the debacle any worse than it already is."

The roar in Margaret's head grew deafening, so excruciating that it felt as if her skull might split in two. She started to scream and scream and scream, a high, piercing wail that had people covering their ears, and servants and guests rushing in to discern the cause.

Rabid, delirious, she sped across to the fireplace, seized an iron poker, and ran to Freddy Blaine. She let loose, attacking him with the ample strength of her fury, beating him about the face and genitalia, until he was a bloody, crumpled heap on the floor.

It took the stablemaster, along with three burly footmen, to pull her off and wrestle her to the ground.

Rebecca snuggled into the bed that had been provided to her. The mattress was stuffed, plush, and she sank down, the softness surrounding her. The sheets were clean and smooth, and they smelled so fresh. She couldn't stop sniffing them.

Someone had found her a nightgown. It was a little large, but the fabric was white, and very silky, with pink flowers stitched along the neckline and cuffs, and a matching pink ribbon in the front that tied in a pretty bow. She couldn't ever remember touching a garment so precious, and she'd been surprised that they'd permitted her to wear it.

She'd had a bath! In a tub, with hot water and rose-scented soap! Winnie had helped her, had even scrubbed her hair, then they'd lounged by the fire, with Winnie brushing out the snarled strands and talking in that dear, gentle way she had.

Rebecca hadn't worked up the courage to refer to Winnie as *Mother*. The notion was too intimidating, a beloved symbol that could be snatched away. She couldn't embrace the concept of a parent, for she couldn't bear the possibility that her mother might somehow be lost to her.

Too much had been given, too much promised, in too limited a period. She was wary of trust, frightened to hope. Winnie was splendid, composed and refined, and everything that Rebecca had fantasized her mother might be like. So she would be cautious, brave, but prepared for any eventuality.

Tears flooded her eyes, and she lay, gazing up at the canopy, the four posts at the corners. It was the type of bed a princess might sleep in, and below the blankets, she pinched herself, welcoming the pain, needing to affirm that she wasn't dreaming. She was worried that, at any moment, she would awaken to find that none of it was real.

Beside her, Helen lay, quiet and motionless as usual, though Rebecca could sense the rapid flow of thoughts cascading through her mind. Many images and ideas flitted by, but they were so disorganized and fleeting that Rebecca couldn't decipher them.

Helen was confused, as appalled by their adventures as Rebecca was herself, but now that she was with Olivia once again, she was calming and beginning to feel safe.

Rebecca didn't know if she felt *safe,* yet. It would take constant reassurance and convincing, but she was anxious to believe.

Winnie and Olivia had tucked them in, had chattered about plans that needed to be made. The two women had been short on specifics, but had vowed—over and over—that all would be well in the end.

Rebecca didn't understand what had occurred, though her unexpected appearance had wreaked upheaval for many. Olivia's wedding to the earl had been postponed. Winnie's cousin, Margaret, had gone mad, plunged into a state of insanity that had everyone in a dither.

There were so many secrets swirling about, that she couldn't keep track of them. Servants were clucking their tongues and repeating astonishing tales, house-guests were packing and departing with odd haste.

She'd given up trying to figure it out. She merely wanted tranquillity to prevail, so that the adults could move beyond the bizarre day and achieve some peace. Then maybe they would have the opportunity to decide if they were glad she'd arrived.

Her belly was full, her body relaxed, and for the first time in a long time, she wasn't scared. She shut her eyes, and offered up a prayer, imploring that the earl let them stay at the estate. That they be allowed to remain forever.

She rolled to her side, and Helen did, too, so that they were facing each other. Under the covers, they clasped hands.

"I like it here," she said, but Helen didn't respond. She simply stared, absorbing Rebecca's every word. "Everyone is very kind. My mother is pretty and nice, and she seems to want me. This is a good place for us. I'm sure of it."

The tears that had threatened started to fall, and on witnessing them, Helen frowned, perplexed by what they meant.

"I was so afraid," Rebecca confessed. "When we had to leave the orphanage, I didn't know what would become of us, or how I would care for you."

The recent trauma overwhelmed her, and she cried in earnest, so many tears dripping down that she had to use the sheet to wipe them away.

She could picture that busy street corner, how the crowd had parted, and she'd turned to see her mother and Phillip walking toward her.

Miracles did happen. Dreams did come true.

Squeezing Helen's fingers, she gulped down the swell of emotion that made it difficult to speak or breathe. She now had the chance to be a normal girl, who could grow up to be a fine young lady, who had a family that loved her, that would cherish and treasure her.

It was what she'd always craved, more than she'd ever conceived she would have, and her wonderful, terrifying future dangled before her. She was determined to reach for it, to hold it close and make it her own.

"My mother has arranged for me to have some new dresses," she whispered. "The seamstress is visiting tomorrow, to measure me. I can pick any colors I want." The prospect was so delicious, and she was so fearful it would never result, that she voiced the desire aloud, hoping that by doing so, she could force it to transpire. "Master Phillip says he intends to buy me a horse, and teach me to ride." She smiled. "And . . . he's going to get you a pony!"

Helen smiled, too.

CHAPTER TWENTY-THREE

Winnie stood by the window, staring out at the darkened lawn of the estate. A cool evening breeze rustled the curtains, and she relished how it swept across her heated skin.

From the moment in London, when Phillip had passed her the folder that detailed Rebecca's whereabouts, she'd been feverish. Naught could calm the tumultuous beating of her heart, or the frantic swirling of her thoughts. The incidents of the trying day here at Salisbury certainly hadn't extinguished the fire burning within. She was weary, distraught, and still furious.

When she recalled the duplicity Margaret had practiced, and Rebecca's lost childhood, she felt ill.

She'd always fancied herself a rather smart individual, so how had she been so stupid? Why had she been so ready to believe Margaret's stories about Rebecca?

Had she wanted to know the truth? Or was she a coward? Out of fear and shame, had she abandoned Rebecca to her fate?

The questions were eating at her.

A sound emanated from the adjoining room. The door between the chambers was open, and Helen and Rebecca snuggled together in the big bed. She went to check on them, as she'd been doing incessantly since she'd tucked them in.

They were nestled under the covers, looking like two little angels, and though they were fine, Winnie fussed with the blankets, adjusting and tugging on them so that she would have an excuse to linger.

Not surprisingly, Rebecca was wide awake and following Winnie's every move.

"Are you having trouble sleeping, darling?" Winnie asked.

"Yes."

"So am I." Winnie rounded the bed and eased onto the mattress. "There's been too much excitement. I can't relax."

"It's very nice here. Almost like a fairy tale."

Winnie smiled. Weeks earlier, when she'd first arrived, she'd pictured it much the same. "Yes, it is."

"Do you think the earl will let us stay?"

"I don't know, Rebecca, but don't fret over it." Smoothing the hair off Rebecca's brow, she loved that she had the chance to perform such a simple, maternal chore. "If we don't remain here, we'll find somewhere just as wonderful. I promise you."

She couldn't fathom how she'd make good on her vow, but she was resolved to bring it to fruition. From this juncture onward, Rebecca would have security, a roof over her head, food in her belly.

"We won't have to live with your cousin Margaret, will we?"

"No," she answered. She had no doubt about that particular. Regardless of where they ended up, it wouldn't be with Margaret and Penelope.

"I'm glad," Rebecca said. "Helen is afraid of her."

"Really?" Winnie glanced over at Helen, fascinated anew by the pair's ability to communicate. Helen's brain was a mystery, and Winnie couldn't deduce how it worked. If the girl could talk, what tales she might impart! "Did she say why?"

"When they were alone, the countess would whisper

terrible things, about how wicked Helen was, about how the countess could make her disappear. And Penelope used to pinch and hit her, very hard. Once, she pushed Helen down the stairs."

"She told you all this?"

"Yes," Rebecca replied, as though her discussions with the mute lass were normal.

Winnie fumed. How much abuse had Helen suffered, of which Winnie and Olivia had been unaware? What secret torments had Margaret and Penelope inflicted on Helen, without others being cognizant of their tortures?

In a way, Winnie was delighted by how events had transpired. If Margaret hadn't initiated the shenanigans that had led to her downfall, they might never have unearthed the depths to which she was willing to descend. Helen would have endured a lifetime of anguish and wretchedness of which she was unable to speak.

Ooh, how Winnie yearned to wrap her fingers around Margaret's pitiful neck! If only Edward hadn't intervened and prevented her from physically venting her wrath!

She and Margaret had the same blood running through their veins, and she wished she could slit an artery and let the amount that linked them flow out onto the ground.

Sighing, she was outraged and amazed by how circumstances had evolved.

There would be a wedding in the house, the next day in fact, but it wasn't Edward's and Olivia's. Penelope was marrying Freddy Blaine. Winnie had never met a more loathsome, disreputable individual, yet Penny was thrilled. Penny hadn't grasped the error in judgment she'd made, though she'd figure it out soon enough.

With Mr. Blaine as her husband, Winnie couldn't imagine what would become of Penelope. By all accounts, Mr. Blaine survived through the charity of his older brother, and had no income. He didn't own his residence, pay his servants, or his bills. Rumor had it that his family had banished him from London, due to a heinous scandal. Plus, he wasn't too keen on the notion of marrying Penny, and he'd been trying to insist that a dreadful mistake had been made, though no one would listen to him.

Any marriage could be difficult, but with a bride-groom who was adamantly opposed to the nuptials, it would be awful.

Why had Penny pursued such a rash path? Had it been immaturity? Her typical recklessness? Or was it due to her quintessential obstinacy? She'd been fixated on doing what she wanted and couldn't be dissuaded from delinquency.

Well, her stubbornness had caught up with her, and over the pending months and years, she'd learn some harsh lessons. Whatever befell her would most likely be deserved, and Winnie wouldn't concern herself over it.

No, Winnie would be occupied in deciding what to do with Margaret. The older woman's discovery of Penny's antics had been too much for her. Her mind had snapped, causing her to attack Mr. Blaine, but after the initial commotion had been contained, and Phillip had subdued her, it was obvious that there had been a significant shift in her mental functioning.

She was down the hall, solidly sedated with laudanum, and tied to a bed, lest she wander and assault someone else.

Aside from juvenile Penny, Winnie was Margaret's sole living relative, and thus she had a responsibility to supervise her treatment and recovery. Hopefully, Margaret would regain her sanity, but what if she didn't? What should be done with her?

The tables had been deftly turned, and for a change, Margaret would have to rely on Winnie. Though it was a diabolical aspiration, she wanted Margaret to have occasional episodes of lucidness, just so she would realize that she was beholden to Winnie for everything. It was a petty retribution, but gratifying nonetheless.

In her prevailing mood, Winnie would be tickled to condemn her cousin to an insane asylum, so that Margaret could personally experience the indignity and horror. But Winnie never would. She might be Margaret's kin, but she possessed none of the woman's malice or evil.

"Don't worry about Margaret or Penelope," she soothed Rebecca. "And be sure to tell Helen that she needn't worry about them, either."

"I will."

"She won't have to see them again."

"She'll be relieved."

"Now, it's very late. Try to close your eyes."

"I can't seem to doze off. Too much has happened."

"You're right about that."

Rebecca stared and stared, as though cataloging her features. "Will you be here in the morning?"

"Of course I will. I'm never leaving." Winnie took Rebecca's hand and squeezed it. It would probably be ages before Rebecca trusted her. "Would you feel better if I sat with you?"

"Would you?"

"Roll over onto your tummy."

Rebecca hesitated, then did as Winnie had requested, and Winnie patted her back as if she were a tiny babe. Within minutes, she was slumbering soundly, her breathing languorous and steady. Winnie tarried, imprinting every aspect of the precious contact into her growing store of memories.

Slipping off the bed, she pulled up a chair, observing, pondering everything she'd missed. How long would it take to make it up to the poor girl? How many acts of contrition would she have to accomplish before Rebecca could forgive her? Would there be a sufficient number of years to atone?

She felt Edward's presence before she saw or heard him. He was in the doorway that connected the two bed-chambers. Silent, patient, he was watching her, waiting for her to acknowledge him. She had been expecting him for hours, though she was torn about meeting with him.

After her providential interruption of the wedding, they'd chatted briefly. He'd been kind, asking about her adventures with Phillip in London, and he'd offered her lodgings at Salisbury until her affairs were settled. She'd thanked him, then had surrounded herself with the children so they wouldn't have another opportunity to converse. He'd been busy, tackling the wild messes created by the failed ceremony, Margaret's hysterics, and Mr. Blaine's depravity, so she'd been able to avoid a confrontation, and she wished she could put it off forever.

She wasn't sure what she wanted to say to him. Many angry remarks were fermenting inside her that shouldn't be voiced aloud. Upon her declaration that she'd birthed a child out of wedlock, he'd been shocked. Whether his reaction had been induced by disgust at her immorality, or her shady history, she cared not. She wouldn't apologize for having had Rebecca.

In light of his past, who was he to point a condemnatory finger anyway? At least she'd loved Rebecca, had pined away, heart and soul, while he scarcely evinced interest in his own two offspring, the only ones he might ever have. Who was he to throw stones?

She rotated in her chair, and they studied each other, separated by an unbridgeable expanse. He was dressed in his trousers, his feet bare. A robe covered his torso, but it was open at the front, revealing his handsome chest, his broad shoulders.

They were the sort of shoulders a woman could lean on when her burdens were heavy, when she was alone and scared and at a loss as to what she should do next, but she refused to be affected by the sight of them.

Because she'd been afraid of dishonor, she'd tossed away the most important thing in her life. She'd relied on others, praying they would rescue her from her many follies, but she never would again. She would fend for herself. Whatever path fate chose to contrive, she would persevere and hope for the best.

After an interminable pause, he extended his hand, beseeching her to cross the floor and take it. She gaped at him but didn't move.

He murmured to her, anxious to coax and cajole her into going to him. Concerned about waking the girls, she motioned for quiet, then stood and walked by him into her room. He shut the door.

His eyes searched hers, but the shadows kept him from reading what was written there. Reaching out, he grazed her cheek, then bent down, attempting to kiss her on the mouth, but she turned away, and his lips brushed her hair instead.

Imposing distance, she went to the window, away from him.

He muddled her, making her brood and chafe over what she wanted and how she should proceed. When he touched her, she became confused, couldn't be strong, accurately appraise events, or hold on to what she recognized was proper for her.

"You shouldn't have come," she said, though she'd never doubted he would. She hadn't bothered to bar her door, for a lock wouldn't have dissuaded him.

"You knew I would."

"Yes, so please say whatever it is you're determined

to say. Get the whole bloody harangue off your chest, then depart. I can't abide any more emotional upheaval."

She was being petulant, far beyond the bounds of civility or courtesy, but she couldn't desist. She wanted to lash out, at everyone and everything, and she couldn't find the mercy or compassion she usually harbored for others.

Very likely, he was hurting, too; after all, he'd had a few bad days. But she was beyond empathy, beyond agonizing over what he might need, or how she could comfort him.

He gazed at her so poignantly that she wondered if he would ever speak. Or perhaps he couldn't verbalize his comments. He looked pained, as though the words were stuck in his throat.

Ultimately, he announced, "I'm sorry."

He was sorry? Why? What had he done but be himself? He'd been attracted to her, and he'd acted on his attraction. Out of loneliness and discontentment, she'd succumbed.

"You're *sorry?* Whatever for?"

"For judging you. For believing you weren't good enough for me."

There was nothing quite so brutal as a bit of candor. Nothing like being apprised—to your face!—of precisely why you were unsuitable. "Apology accepted. Pardon granted. We're finished. You may go."

Scrutinizing her, his attention roved over her curvaceous form, which was concealed solely by her flimsy summer nightwear.

"It's not *over*."

"Yes it is."

He took a step toward her, then another. Gradually, he approached, and panic flickered in her mind. What did he intend? He couldn't suppose she'd be willing to rekindle their liaison.

She had too many new burdens and couldn't complicate matters with another fling. Her physical desire had fled, and she couldn't conceive of how it would reappear. Her base instincts had caused her enormous trouble, and she wouldn't yield to any of them again. Despite how much she'd treasured Edward's company, she was an adult who could and would control herself.

From now on, she planned to carry on like a celibate saint.

He advanced on her. "I never told you how much you mean to me." Another step. Another. "Or how much joy you brought me."

The admission startled her. "Well, you don't need to confess at this late date."

"Yes I do. I absolutely do."

He neared until they were toe to toe, and astoundingly, he fell to his knees and clasped her hand. "Winifred Stewart, I love you. Will you marry me?"

He *loved* her? He wanted to . . . to . . . *marry* her? This couldn't be! Of all the scenarios she'd imagined, a proposal hadn't been in the realm of the most preposterously fanciful potentialities. Her ears had to be playing tricks.

She started to tremble, her legs barely supporting her.

"Don't be absurd. No, I will not marry you." Tugging on his wrist, she tried to drag him to his feet, but he wouldn't budge. "Stand up. You're embarrassing me."

"I haven't begun to *embarrass* you." He wrapped his arms around her waist, his fingers on her buttocks, his nose buried in her cleavage.

Her body reacted, her breasts swelling, her nipples throbbing, and she longed to quell the response, but indifference was impossible. The man affected her as no other ever had; he titillated and aroused and thrilled, and she couldn't feign apathy, although she didn't have to make a fool of herself, either.

Her enchantment might still be potent, but she didn't have to submit to it.

"All I ask," she said, as calmly as she could, "is that you let us stay until I can chart another course. You've already agreed, so we have nothing further to discuss."

"Oh, we have a few more items to consider than that."

"I can't fathom a single one."

"You can remain at Salisbury, but on my terms."

She stiffened. "Which are?"

"Marriage. To me. As soon as the details can be arranged." His hands left her bum and slithered down, dipping under her nightgown, then commencing a leisurely journey up the backs of her thighs.

"You're mad."

"I'm sure you're correct." Chuckling, he located her bottom once more, but this time with no fabric as a barrier. He rubbed in enticing circles, and she tightened her leg muscles, forcing restraint.

"I'm completely inappropriate," she felt obliged to point out. "I have a scarlet past."

"Yes, you do."

"I'm an indigent commoner."

"Yes, you are."

"I haven't a drop of the precious blue blood you're so determined to mix with your own."

"No, you don't."

"Lunacy runs in my family," she mentioned, referring to Margaret's mental breakdown.

"And it's a vicious strain."

"God, stop being so flippant!" She shoved him away and stomped off, but he rose and came up behind her.

"Let me take care of you, Winnie. For the rest of your

days." He nestled her to him, her back spooned to his front, his tone low and tempting. "Let me be a father to Rebecca, and a husband to you. Let me give you more children, an entire houseful, whom we will love and raise together."

He sounded so sincere! Why would he offer her so much—she who deserved nothing at all? "You're not serious."

"I am!" He nibbled at her nape, sending shivers down her spine. "I want to be happy, Winnie. That's all I've ever wanted. *You* make me happy."

Her pulse was racing. He was eager to lavish her with everything she craved, everything for which she'd dreamed. Why, then, was it so difficult to furnish him with an affirmative answer?

Didn't he realize how far down he would be stooping? His peers would never forgive him, and she was desperate to save him from himself.

"You couldn't show your face in London."

"Oh, woe is me!" he mocked.

"You couldn't socialize or visit your clubs."

"Any man who would snub me because I'm wed to you isn't a friend, so his opinion wouldn't signify."

"You maintain as much now—"

"As I will tomorrow, and the next day, and the next after that."

"This morning, you were set to marry Olivia."

"A grand mistake, I admit."

"You can't have switched from one woman to another in the blink of an eye."

"Yes I can. I'm an earl. I can do whatever I please." With scant pressure, he spun her to him and gave her a light shake. "Marry me. Say *yes*."

He was so insistent, burning with ardor and conviction, that a tiny spark flared deep inside her. What if she accepted? She had naught to lose and everything to gain. *He* would suffer through marriage to her, but if he wasn't concerned over ostracism or exclusion, why should she be?

Could this work?

She remembered the night of the thunderstorm, when she dashed inside, wet and drenched, and he'd been waiting for her. She'd felt as though he were her destiny, that he was the one and only man the Good Lord had created just for her. Her spirit had soared, her soul had eased.

Surely, their connection had a purpose. In the greater scheme of the universe, wouldn't it be wrong to shun such an affinity?

She gazed at him. He'd claimed that he wanted to be happy, that it was all he'd ever wanted. Happiness was what she wanted, too, and there was no more marvelous gift she could bestow—on him or herself.

He would provide her with a home of her own, a family, babies to cherish, a husband to adore. It was so much more than she'd assumed she would find, more than she could have guessed she'd attain. A blessing. A stroke of luck. A boon beyond imagining.

"Swear to me that you mean it. That you'll never regret asking."

"Oh, Winnie! As if I ever could *regret* loving you."

She opened her arms, and he leapt into them, hugging her with all his might.

"Yes . . . yes . . . yes . . ." she murmured, and his kisses rained down upon her.

CHAPTER TWENTY-FOUR

Phillip stopped at the door to the cottage that had been his home for many years. Edward had again asked him to move into the manor, and he might, when the furor had died down. For now, the Hopkins women hadn't resolved their troubles, so he couldn't avail himself of Edward's invitation.

After contending with so much drama, he needed solitude and privacy, and his small house behind the stables seemed the best place to find it. Though it was after midnight, the mansion was abuzz, the last of the guests awake and conferring, the staff rushing around to finish their chores.

Edward hadn't been able to manage the aftermath of his failed wedding. He'd been as distraught as everyone else, so Phillip had dealt with the servants, fielded the questions, and given the orders.

Phillip had soothed Vicar Summers, had arranged for the immediate marriage of Mr. Blaine and Lady Penelope, which would occur as soon as a messenger could ride to London and return with a special license. He'd locked the disgraced, ruined girl in her bedchamber so that she couldn't instigate more mischief, and he'd escorted a bruised and battered Freddy Blaine off the premises. He'd even intervened with that old bat, Margaret Hopkins, had supervised her subjugation and restraint, and he'd received an incredible amount of pleasure from seeing her brought low.

After the misery she'd caused to so many, it had been a delight to witness her downfall.

The one person he hadn't run into all day was Olivia, though he didn't know why he'd supposed he would. In his mind, he'd irrationally conjectured that, by racing to the country with Winnie and the girls, he had been riding to her rescue. By escorting Helen to safety, he'd been showing Olivia how much he loved her, how much she could trust and rely on him.

He'd presumed that his actions would work a miracle, that he would paint a different image of himself. He'd deemed that she would view him in a new light, as a fighter, a champion, an ally upon whom she could depend, and that his conduct would confer the impetus she needed to overlook their disparate stations.

Sadly, his behavior had had no effect, and he had to accept the fact that he could do nothing to alter her opinion. Standards and principles had been drilled into her—by Margaret and others just like her—that people of diverse antecedents couldn't be together.

He couldn't count the number of proposals she'd rejected. Four? Five? He'd begged her to marry, to elope, to favor him instead of another, but to no avail. How many times did he need to hear her say no?

A vain man, he wasn't about to suffer through any further rebuff. She was the type who would debase herself in a brief fling, but that was as far as she could go. No matter how fervently he wished it weren't so, or how rigorously he sought to orchestrate another ending, it wasn't meant to be.

Sighing, he stared across the groomed lawn of the estate, studying the windows of the manor. Some of them had candlelight gleaming through.

Many exhilarating nights, he had waited for her in this exact spot, watching as she'd sneaked across the grass, and he caught himself wondering where she was, what she was doing, which bedchamber was hers.

Disgusted, he whirled away. Would he never learn?

He had to stop ruminating over her!

If he'd had any doubts about their affair's being over, he needed only think back to the dreadful family scene where Margaret had hurled so many insults.

In front of his father and the assembled company, he'd tried to profess his feelings for her, but Olivia had cut off any declaration, claiming his timing was poor. Which it was.

With Edward and Olivia draped in their matrimonial finery, and the guests mingling on the verandah, it hadn't been the most opportune moment to shout out his undying devotion. But there had been no chance for him to announce anything later, either.

With Margaret having gone mad as a hatter, he'd been detained for hours. As he'd carried out his various tasks, he'd kept glancing over his shoulder, anticipating that she would be there, but she'd been markedly absent.

She'd been too busy to so much as utter a *thank you* for his recovery of Helen.

The ingrate!

Ignoring him, she had sequestered herself upstairs with Helen in her private quarters, concealing herself from all but the most senior servants. He could scarcely condemn her for fretting over Helen's condition, or wanting to be with her, but he was irked that she'd picked Helen over himself.

How pathetic! He was jealous of a three-year-old child!

The inevitable conclusion was that perhaps, despite her protestations to the contrary, she loved Edward, or at least liked and respected him, and had truly wanted him for her husband. Their nuptials might proceed, and

Phillip had to acknowledge that reality if he was to have a continuing relationship with Edward.

As they'd flitted from one disaster to the next throughout the arduous day, he and Edward had had several scattered conversations about the future. Edward's sincere desire was to have Freddy and Penelope relocated as far from Salisbury as possible. After their egress, he intended to purchase Freddy's property from Freddy's brother.

With its lush meadows and bubbling streams, Edward thought it would make a splendid horse farm, a decision with which Phillip enthusiastically concurred. Edward had inquired if Phillip would be interested in directing such an enterprise, and he'd hinted that it could become a wedding gift should Phillip ever decide to settle down.

Phillip wasn't certain what the sly old dog was intimating, but he wasn't about to repudiate the stake he'd dreamed of acquiring.

Pride be damned! Some things were too rich to pass up.

He'd invest his unflagging energy in the idea and the endeavor, and if in the interim, Olivia married Edward, he'd grit his teeth and be a cordial neighbor. Difficult as it would be to feign apathy, he could do it. For his father. For Olivia. And for himself.

What a foolish, wayward heart he had! He hadn't realized that he had such a penchant for ardor and romance, that he was so desperate for affection. At having been tossed over by her, he was so despairing that he felt he might break down and cry like a baby.

Spinning the knob, he went inside. He hadn't been gone long enough for Edward to have removed his possessions, or to have offered the house to another, so his belongings were still in place. The familiarity provided a solace that, considering his disordered, ragged emotional state, was greatly appreciated.

He'd expected the air to be stuffy, for the rooms to have a deserted ambiance, but someone had been in to tidy up. The windows were open, a cool breeze blowing in, the curtains rustling. To welcome him home, a lamp had been lit, and there were fresh flowers in a vase.

Setting his portmanteau on the table, he shucked off his coat and loosened his cravat, freeing the buttons on his shirt and rolling up the cuffs of the sleeves. He lifted the flap on the traveling bag, and much to his chagrin, the first item he encountered was the drawing Olivia had made of him during their final assignation. He wasn't sure why he'd kept it, or why he'd taken it to London, when he should have pitched it into the fireplace.

It was embarrassing to peruse it now, to observe himself naked and vulnerable. His yearning for her was accurately captured in his expression and his posture.

In the corner, he saw where she'd signed her name, and the salutation she'd written.

" 'Love always,' " he read aloud, and he shook his head. "Well, that lasted about fifteen minutes."

Casting the sketch aside, he vowed to dispose of it in the morning, though why he didn't rip it to shreds that very second was a mystery he declined to ponder.

A noise sounded behind him, and he froze, listening. He peered around. The door to his bedroom was ajar, a lamp lit there, too. There was someone inside. Who?

The sole person he could conceive of was the maid who'd cleaned before his arrival, but she'd have come quite a bit earlier.

He walked to the door, pushed at it. It swung back and . . .

There was Olivia, stretched out on his bed. Scantily attired, she looked like a blasted harem concubine. With her blond hair down, the lengthy ends were curled across his pillows. Her upper torso was naked, her breasts exposed, her pouty nipples pointed and alluring, and it appeared as if she'd reddened them with a cosmetic to accentuate their shape and size.

The lower half of her face was masked with a flimsy pink scarf, her crimson lips visible beneath the fabric, and the veil emphasized her magnificent blue eyes. They were large and round, and she was gazing at him with stunning force.

Her legs were sheathed by a peculiar pair of pants, fashioned out of the same material as the kerchief on her face. The trousers fell to her knees, and outlined the curve of her ass, the slope of her thighs.

His cock swelled and tented the front of his trousers and, appalled by his reaction, he was frantic to hide it from her.

What was she trying to accomplish? What did she plan?

She couldn't assume they would tryst. Could she be that daft? That insensitive?

How dare she visit! How dare she infer that he would want to philander with her!

After his recent trials and tribulations, he couldn't abide another nasty scene. It killed him to have her flaunting herself, teasing him with what he wanted but could never have.

He'd let her go, had bid her farewell, had allowed her to humiliate him over and over, had let her stab in the knife and twist it. He couldn't endure more anguish!

Have mercy on me! he longed to wail. *Please! Have mercy!*

Anger overtook him. At her. At all that she was and all that she represented. He was prepared to relinquish her, to deny that they'd rollicked with such abandon, yet she showed up anyway, taunting and tormenting him.

"What are you doing here?" he snapped.

"Waiting for you."

Like a lazy cat, she arched her back, thrusting her breasts up and out, just in case he hadn't noticed them. As if he hadn't! The vixen!

Next to her lay the accursed book of erotic illustrations, *A Feast for the Senses,* that had originally brought them together. Obviously, she'd retrieved it from the library and lugged it to the cottage, though he couldn't fathom why she would.

Rotating onto her side, she rested her hand on a page, seductively rubbing her fingers across a depiction of seminude women who were dressed very much as she was, with nude bosoms and skimpily clad bottoms. It was the Arabian illustration, with the sheik in the middle who resembled himself.

He glared at her, brooding over her character. While he'd thought she was an individual of high morals and integrity, apparently he knew very little about her.

With scarcely any reflection, she'd surrendered her virginity to him, then she'd discarded him and become engaged to his father. Very likely, she still was. Not once had he heard anyone pronounce that the wedding was permanently called off.

So what was she up to? Was she here to practice more of her perfidy on Edward? Well, he wasn't about to join in her scheme.

She'd made her choice, and it was his father. He didn't like it, but so what? He was resolved to get over it, to tolerate Edward's marriage to her. If he had to suffer so terribly, he wasn't about to sugarcoat matters, or delude himself into believing they shared an affinity. They didn't, and she needed to be in the main house, in her own bed, and out of his.

"I adore this picture," she claimed. "It's very naughty.

It makes me want to do all sorts of things I oughtn't."
She wet her lips. "Why do you suppose that is?"

"I haven't the foggiest," he lied. The likenesses were
meant to beguile and provoke; that's why the artist had
created them. She was aware of it as well as he, and he
wasn't about to indulge her whim. "A whore might
enjoy them," he crudely stated, wanting to hurt her, to
goad her into departing, "but why they'd affect you, I
haven't a clue."

"Yes, you're correct. A disreputable female would be
stimulated. So what does that say about me?" She
grinned, a conniving, tempting grin that had him contemplating things he shouldn't. "My disposition is much
more debauched than I ever imagined. Wouldn't you
agree?"

"Absolutely," he concurred. "You have the unmitigated soul of a harlot."

The wench laughed! A sultry sound that tickled his
nerve endings. "I never used to be this way. I'm blaming
it all on you."

"On *me?*"

"Yes. I was such an ethical, incorruptible girl before I
met you." Commencing at her shoulder, she ran her fingers down her anatomy, and they slithered across her
breast, her tummy, her hip and flank. "And now look at
me."

His eyes couldn't help but follow the risqué trail of
her hand, and he felt like a rutting beast, primed for
mating.

Despite her deceptions and disloyalty, he was ready
and eager to copulate. He was so weak! So lacking in
principle and honor!

"Get out of here, Olivia."

"No. I want to frolic. Let's pretend I'm a concubine

from this drawing—and you're my sheik." She wiggled her brows. "Won't that be fun?"

"I can't think of anything more unpleasant."

"Really? That's not what your body seems to imply." Her torrid attention crept down, meandering across his chest, his stomach, his groin. She analyzed his erection, and under her blatant assessment, his phallus expanded further.

He fought the strongest urge to cross his arms over his crotch, but concealing his situation was pointless. She excited him beyond his limits, and nothing had changed about their physical attraction. Nothing ever would. The horrid truth was that, after all the distress she'd caused, he still wanted her.

"I'm not immune to titillation," he told her. "Any lewd conduct arouses me. Even yours."

"Is your cockstand painful?" she queried. "Would you like me to tend it for you?"

"No."

"You'll feel better. Why don't I?"

Rising up, she slinked off the bed, advancing on him, her appealing hips swaying as she walked, then she knelt down. Rigid as a marble statue, he stood, watching her, wondering how far she'd go, how willing she was to debase herself.

She tugged the hem of his shirt from the waistband of his trousers and pushed the lapels aside, stroking her palms up his chest. She removed her scarf, and brushed it across his belly, inducing his abdominal muscles to clench, his balls to wrench with lust, then she threw it away, and it fluttered to the rug.

She went to the placard of his pants, the buttons dropping away, and he did nothing to dissuade her, keeping his emotions shielded.

His trousers were loosened, and as she reached inside,

his mounting temper and increasing desire warred with each other. He was hard, aching, his body demanding satiation, and as she licked the oozing tip, as she sucked at him, he couldn't tamp down a hiss of breath.

Other than that minor lapse, he was able to block any response, for he wouldn't let her discern how unsettled he was.

Her mouth was hot, slippery, and within seconds, he was at the edge. It would serve her right if he proceeded, if he spilled himself in her throat. If she was determined to act the whore, why not treat her like one?

He thrust. Thrust again, but he was too close to climax, and he grabbed her by the neck, viciously pitching her away. With a soft cry of alarm, she toppled over.

Stomping off, his back to her, he straightened his clothes, himself. For an agonized minute, he stared at the wall, calming his passion, his fury, then he whipped around. "What do you want from me?"

She was on her knees, and massaging a wrist that had smacked the floor when he'd shoved her, but he wouldn't feel any sympathy. After what she'd put him through, whatever happened to her was justified.

She tottered to her feet. "Can't you guess?"

"No. I haven't any bloody idea."

"I want *you*."

"Oh, stop it," he scoffed. "You're humiliating yourself."

"I do want you," she protested, appearing hurt and confused. Beseeching him, she held out her hand, took a step toward him, then another. "You're all I've ever wanted."

"You have an intriguing way of showing it." His fingers shaky, he refastened his shirt, fumbling with the buttons. "What do you intend? A romp for old time's sake? Another pathetic cuckolding of my father? Well, I'm sorry, but I can't oblige you."

"Whyever not? There's no one to say what we can or cannot do."

Was she purposely taunting him? Playing dumb? Why would she? Didn't she grasp that her very presence was torture? "Shouldn't you be up at the manor, getting your beauty rest so that you're prepared for the resumption of your wedding ceremony?"

"Oh, didn't anyone tell you?"

"Tell me what?"

Coyly, she went to his bed and started to climb onto the mattress.

On seeing what she was about, his ire spiraled, and he rushed to her and yanked her away. He did not want her on his bed ever again!

"Tell me what?" he shouted, clutching her by the shoulders and whirling her around.

"I'm not marrying Edward."

He didn't want to ask why; he didn't want to *know* the reason. He didn't care about her. Yet before he could prevent it, the question flew out. "Why not?"

"Because I've decided to marry someone else."

Disgusted, wounded anew, he scathingly evaluated her. "Aren't you amazing?" Sickened, he lurched away, wondering how he could have thought he knew or understood her. "What kind of person are you? You take me as your lover, then you agree to marry Edward—when you swore to me you wouldn't."

Resigned, she sighed. "Yes, well, it turns out I can't wed Edward."

"Has he tossed your over?"

"Actually, yes. He's advised me that he's in love with another."

"Who?" As if he had no inkling! In the two stressful days he'd spent with Winnie, locating the children and delivering the three of them to Salisbury, he'd come to treasure her. How lucky his father was!

"Winnie," she confirmed. "I assume he's proposing to her even as we speak."

"So you dashed out here to fornicate, the moment he rejected you?"

"Yes. And I can't figure out why you won't participate." Boldly, she examined his crotch. "It's not as if you don't *want* to."

"You can't comprehend why I'd spurn you? How about the fact that, in a smattering of weeks, you plowed through me and my father, and now you're off to someone else. What is wrong with you? Do you have so many men falling at your feet that you can't pick a favorite? Or are you simply fickle beyond imagining?"

"He's a rather fine gentleman." She was strutting about, comfortable with her nudity, with the situation. "Handsome, intelligent, compassionate, dynamic, brave, loyal, and true. He possesses all the traits a woman craves in a man, *and* he's about to be endowed with property that will earn him an excellent income. I couldn't pass up the opportunity."

What a mercenary leech! Astounded and aghast, he hadn't realized she harbored such ruthless tendencies!

Facetiously, he countered, "No, you definitely shouldn't miss out on such a remarkable fellow! Felicitations, Lady O, on your shrewd maneuvering. I hope your rich catch garners you all the happiness you deserve."

She laughed again! Had she no shame? No regard for his feelings? He would have done anything for her, would have given her the world, made any sacrifice, scaled any hurdle, sustained any hardship, and this was how she repaid him!

"Please leave," he pleaded. But she didn't budge, so he snarled, "At once!"

"Oh, you silly oaf," she gently chided. "I'm teasing you."

"About what?"

"It's you, you fool! I'm going to marry *you!*"

"Well, isn't that grand, Lady Olivia, but I haven't asked you to marry me." Not today, anyway. He'd offered in the past, but he was no longer interested. He couldn't abide the whirlwind she put him through.

He was anxious to reclaim his sedate life—the one he'd enjoyed before she'd burst into it, where he'd been surrounded by his cottage, and his horses, and his stablemates. He'd thrived on routine and habit, on the spasmodic relationship with his father.

He yearned for peace and quiet. No discord. No upheaval. No sorrow or adversity. He wanted to be left alone.

"Go ahead, then," she needled. "I'll accept."

She was batting her lashes, positive he'd relent, that he'd leap at the chance to demean himself. He wouldn't! He couldn't! He couldn't put himself at risk.

She was grinning, waiting, but he said nothing, and her smile began to falter, then faded entirely. It was as if the lamp had been extinguished, or the sun had flitted behind a dark cloud.

Bucking up, he declined to pity her, or pay any heed to how he'd dashed her excitement.

"Unless you don't really want me," she murmured, and it was a grotesque reenactment of the evening he'd begged her to elope, only in reverse. "Unless you never meant it."

"Oh, I meant it, all right. Every damned time. I just grew tired of being told no."

"I won't say no."

"How convenient. I've met many women of the *ton,* but I do believe you're the most inconstant of them all." He gestured around the small, unpretentious room. "This is who I am, what I have. My father is dangling a potentiality before me—which may or may not come to fruition—and suddenly you're dying to wed me. What if it never transpires? What if he never follows through, and you're stuck with this tiny cottage?" Leaning nearer, he sneered, "What if you meet someone tomorrow who can provide you with more?"

"Is that what you suppose this is about? That you might inherit a bit of land so now I'm eager?"

"That's what I'm sure it's about." He pointed to the door, wanting the hideous quarrel to end. "Go!"

She studied him, and he could see her irritation escalating. Her cheeks flushed with color, her pulse pounded. "Do you have any notion of what the last few days have been like for me?" She marched over to him—naked breasts and all—and jabbed an irate finger at his chest. "Do you?"

"Well . . . I . . . I . . ." Having concluded that she was delighted at snagging her earl, he hadn't pondered what she'd been through. It hadn't occurred to him that she might have been miserable, that she might have been laboring under dire stress, herself.

His resolve started to melt. He'd erected a wall around his heart, and though he struggled to keep it in place, it commenced collapsing, brick by brick.

"Penny tattled to Margaret about our affair. Remember? I informed you that she would."

"Yes, I remember."

"Margaret confronted me, and I insisted I couldn't marry Edward, that I loved you. So she threatened me.

She said that she had put Helen in a hospital. If I didn't proceed, she would never bring Helen home, or reveal where she was."

"I didn't know that," he grumbled.

"No, you didn't." She continued to jab her finger at him, emphasizing each important word. "Then, somehow, she lured Edward into my bedchamber in the middle of the night. Margaret conveniently walked in on us, with Penny as a witness, so Edward had to propose to avoid a scandal."

So that's how it had happened. He'd been curious. "It must have been difficult for you."

"Difficult!" She was the one shouting now. "Let me explain the meaning of *difficult!* When I stumbled downstairs the next morning, the staff was making wedding preparations. The invitations had been penned and sent to the neighbors. I felt as if I'd been trampled by a wild stallion, and there was nothing I could do." She shoved him and stalked away. "Don't stand there with your sad eyes, chastising and berating me, and complaining about how you've been abused. For I declare to you that whatever indignity you suffered couldn't possibly compare with what I've been through, and I've had all of the nonsense and drama I can handle!"

He chuckled, infuriating her even more. "You have, have you?"

"Yes, and I'm at my wit's end. So ask me! And be quick about it, before I lose my temper!"

She was a sight, her golden hair streaming down, her blue eyes glowing with wrath. Garbed solely in her diaphanous pants, she was trembling with rage, her chin defiantly stuck out, and she looked like an ancient goddess, an Amazon warrior. If a lightning bolt had crackled forth to smite him, he wouldn't have been surprised.

"Well?" she demanded.

Impatient, she tapped her toe and crossed her arms over her bosom, tantalizing him with glimpses of her nipples. Half-dressed and giving him what-for, she had him utterly flustered.

He didn't want to be angry. He didn't want to fight. It disturbed him to learn how upset she'd been, to hear details of what she'd endured. She'd been in anguish, had been frightened and troubled, but she hadn't sought him out.

Did she think he wouldn't have helped her?

"Why didn't you tell me?" he queried.

"Because she said she'd kill Helen. And I couldn't let her. Helen is all I have left of my parents and my brother."

He had no doubt that Margaret had coerced her, or that she would have progressed to murder if thwarted. In his opinion, Margaret was insane, capable of any nefarious act, and if it had been up to him, she'd already be in a coach, and on her way to Bedlam. Luckily for her, it was Winnie's choice, and not his own.

She began to cry. "I don't care if we live in a hovel. I don't care if we wear rags. I don't care if we eat offal to survive. I just need to be with you."

"Oh, Livvie."

"My world has been turned upside down. I've lost almost everything that mattered to me. Don't force me to go on alone. I can't."

He couldn't remain detached, couldn't judge or condemn her, couldn't castigate her for carrying on as best she could. His animosity vanished like leaves in the wind.

"As if I could stay away."

He opened his arms, and she rushed into them, and he hugged her with all his might, thrilled—as always—to discover how perfectly she fit. He kissed her hair, her cheeks.

"I know what you need," she said.

"And what is that?"

"You need a home of your own. A family. Children to love." She pulled away and assessed him. "Let me give them to you. Let me make you happy."

Gazing down at her, he massaged her warm skin, inhaled her dear scent. He felt whole, complete. For the very first time. Every dream he'd ever had seemed as if it could come true.

Visions danced in his head, of a successful horse farm, with some of England's finest animals. Of a cozy house, filled with boisterous, giggling children. Edward and Winnie would be doting grandparents, with a family of their own besides. Helen and Rebecca would be merry, vivacious cousins to both of their increasing broods.

And Livvie. Forever Livvie, welcoming him home after a long, hard day. To what more could a man aspire? What more did a man need?

Smiling, he felt as though he might burst with joy. "Yes, please," he answered her. "Marry me. Make me happy."